"I don't need your help. I don't need anything from you."

"I know. You made that perfectly clear enough seven years ago when you chose this house over me."

The memory of it echoed inside Farlan like a bomb blast. Nia took a step closer, close enough that he could see her heart beating beneath the fabric of her top.

"That's not how it was."

"I was there, remember? We were both there, only at some point you started reading from a different script."

Nia blinked. "We weren't in a movie, Farlan. You can't just write the ending you want."

"You did."

There was a beat of silence and then she shook her head slowly.

"No. I didn't. I did what I thought was right for both of us. But it wasn't what I wanted."

"What did you want?" He'd meant to sound scornful, but instead his voice was shaky, urgent.

Her eyes found his. "I wanted you. I've only ever wanted you."

Dear Reader,

When it comes to romantic novelists, there is Jane Austen and then there is everyone else.

The godmother of romance wrote six fabulous, witty novels, and in my opinion none is more romantic than *Persuasion*.

Imagine Lizzy and Darcy don't get together, that her prejudice and his pride keep them apart, only for fate to toss them back into one another's orbit seven years later.

That is where *Persuasion* begins, with the regrets and recriminations of the past not yet resolved. It has a self-made hero with charisma and charm: Captain Wentworth. An imperfect heroine: Anne Elliot. And the most swooningly romantic love letter in literature.

"You pierce my soul. I am half agony, half hope."

It was these words, Wentworth's desperate confession of his enduring love for Anne, that inspired me to write *The Man She Should Have Married*.

Set against the beautiful backdrop of the Scottish Highlands, it is my take on Jane Austen's classic novel of second-chance romance, and I hope you enjoy reading about Nia and Farlan's story as much as I loved writing it.

Louise x

Louise Fuller

THE MAN SHE SHOULD HAVE MARRIED

HARLEQUIN
PRESENTS

HARLEQUIN®
PRESENTS®

Recycling programs for this product may not exist in your area.

ISBN-13: 978-1-335-40389-6

The Man She Should Have Married

Harlequin Enterprises ULC
22 Adelaide St. West, 40th Floor
Toronto, Ontario M5H 4E3, Canada
www.Harlequin.com

Printed in U.S.A.

Louise Fuller was a tomboy who hated pink and always wanted to be the prince—not the princess! Now she enjoys creating heroines who aren't pretty pushovers but are strong, believable women. Before writing for Harlequin, she studied literature and philosophy at university, then worked as a reporter on her local newspaper. She lives in Royal Tunbridge Wells with her impossibly handsome husband, Patrick, and their six children.

Books by Louise Fuller

Harlequin Presents

Craving His Forbidden Innocent
The Rules of His Baby Bargain

Secret Heirs of Billionaires

Kidnapped for the Tycoon's Baby
Demanding His Secret Son
Proof of Their One-Night Passion

Passion in Paradise

Consequences of a Hot Havana Night

The Sicilian Marriage Pact

The Terms of the Sicilian's Marriage

Visit the Author Profile page
at Harlequin.com for more titles.

To Lori. I miss you x

CHAPTER ONE

SMOOTHING HER LONG, dark blond hair away from her face, Nia Elgin took a deep breath and followed Stephen, the butler, through the wood-panelled hallway of her family home, Lamington Hall.

Except the beautiful Georgian manor house wasn't her home right now.

For the next year at least, she would be living in the gardener's cottage along the drive.

And Lamington was being rented out to Tom and Diane Drummond, an American couple who were taking a sabbatical in Scotland to research Tom's ancestral roots.

This evening was her first visit to the house since the Drummonds had moved in a week ago, and it felt strange walking past the family portraits and suits of armour as a visitor.

But that wasn't the reason her heart was in her mouth.

As Stephen's fingers rested on the door handle, she took another breath, forcing herself to stay calm, trying to prepare for what lay on the other side of the door.

Not what, but who.

Her heart lurched.

Farlan Wilder.

Even now, she could still picture the first time they'd met.

He had been twenty-two, three years older than her, with eyes the exact same green as summer bracken and a smile that had made Morse code messages of excitement beat through her body.

It had been love at first sight, at first touch, at first everything—swift and as certain as a swallow returning home from its wintering grounds in spring.

And he had loved her right back, just like the heroes in her favourite books.

That year, the summer of their love, time had slowed, days had lengthened and the warm, lazy heat had spilled through September, nudging into the first few days of October.

Six months and two days after they'd met Farlan had proposed. She'd accepted, but they'd decided to go travelling first.

Her breath burned her chest.

And then, just as swiftly, it had been over.

Ended by her.

And, just like the swallows, he had upped and left the cool, inhospitable shores of Scotland for a new life in another country.

She shivered.

The fact that he was back in Scotland at all made her want to reach past Stephen and clutch the door handle for balance.

But the fact that he was here, at Lamington, was the cruellest cut of all.

Her stomach dipped with a desperate, panicky

plunge, just as it had been doing ever since Tom and Diane had invited her to join them for Burns Night supper and she had stupidly agreed to join them.

Would she mind awfully if there was one extra for dinner? Tom had asked, and of course she had said no without thinking.

'It's a big deal for us, him coming. He wasn't even supposed to be getting here until next week,' Tom said slowly. 'You see, he hates Burns Night.'

She hadn't known who 'he' was then, and—incredibly—she hadn't cared.

Tom had shaken his head, as though not able to believe what he was saying. 'Something to do with a woman, I think. But I told him, you can't hate Burns Night, my boy, not if you're a Scotsman.'

The look of outrage on his face had made her burst out laughing. 'So why did he change his mind?' she'd asked.

He'd grinned. 'I played my trump card.'

'And what was that?'

'*You.*' Tom had grinned again. 'Changed his mind real quick when I told him Lady Antonia Elgin was going to be here. Apparently, you and he crossed paths once a few years ago. Must have made quite an impression on him.' He'd winked. 'I've gotta say I was surprised. I've never known anything or anyone change Farlan's mind before, and that's a fact.'

He had carried on talking, but she hadn't been able to hear what he was saying. Her heartbeat had swallowed up his words.

Inside her head, her thoughts had started to unravel. *It must be a coincidence.*

It couldn't be Farlan—not *her* Farlan.

But apparently it was.

She glanced at Stephen's back.

Her stomach knotted. If only she could just turn and run away, hide in the bothy on the estate, where she had always gone as a child to escape her parents' incessant demands.

Or, better still, if she could just rewind, smile apologetically to the Drummonds and say, *How kind, but unfortunately I have other plans.*

But she could neither change her character nor turn back time, so she was just going to have to get through it.

Stephen opened the door, and as she followed him through her heart stopped and for a few agonising half-seconds she scanned the room.

But it was only Tom and Diane, turning to her and smiling.

She forced herself to walk forward as Tom held out his arms in welcome.

'Good evening, Lady Antonia—or should I say *fàilte*?'

She smiled. Whatever her feelings about seeing Farlan again, Tom and Diane must not be made aware of them. Not when they clearly knew nothing about their past relationship.

But what about Farlan?

How was he going to react?

It was a question that had been playing on a loop inside her head. And she was still no closer to answering it.

'Farlan will be down in a minute,' Diane said, her

face softening. 'He only arrived in Scotland at lunchtime.'

'Got his own private jet.' Tom grinned. 'And then he flew himself down in a helicopter. Landed right out back.'

She kept smiling somehow. 'Really? That's amazing.'

Tom handed her a glass of champagne. 'To a Burns Night to remember. *Slàinte mhath*.'

She raised her glass mechanically, then took a deep drink.

Part of her couldn't believe this was happening. She'd have sworn this house was the last place on earth Farlan would ever want to visit again. And she knew that because he'd told her.

Her heart felt like a crushing weight in her chest as she remembered that last terrible stilted telephone conversation.

Except the term 'conversation' implied an exchange of ideas and views, and she had been the only one doing the talking, trying to apologise, to explain, pleading with him to understand.

He hadn't spoken until right at the end, when he'd told her that she was a fraud, a coward and a snob, and that she was less than nothing to him now.

His silent anger had hurt; the ice in his voice had hurt more.

But not as much as the one-note, accusatory disconnection tone when he'd hung up on her.

With an effort, she dragged her mind back into the present. *'Slàinte mhath,'* she repeated.

Tom grinned. 'I can't tell you how happy it makes

me, Lady Antonia, to finally say those words in the land of my forefathers and in your beautiful home.'

'It's *your* beautiful home tonight,' Nia protested. 'And please call me Nia. Being called Lady Antonia makes me feel like I'm about to open a fête.'

He roared with laughter. 'Nia it is, then.' He glanced at her glass. 'Now, let me top you up—we've got some celebrating to do.'

Panic was prickling beneath her ribs.

She didn't feel like celebrating.

But she was a guest, and she could almost hear her mother's smooth, polished voice telling her that a guest should always be 'pleasant and accommodating.' Tilting her glass, she let Tom refill it with champagne, his undisguised happiness making her smile properly.

'Tom, you look magnificent. You know, being an Elgin, I shouldn't really admit this, but the Drummond tartan has always been one of my favourites.'

It was true. The red and green weave was so gutsy and vibrant, so defiantly and unapologetically proud of its clan roots.

In contrast, the Elgin tartan of brown and cream seemed inhibited—timid, almost.

But perhaps, like dogs and their owners, a tartan reflected the character of the person wearing it. Farlan would certainly think so, she thought dully.

Obviously pleased, Tom gave a mock bow. 'It is a fine tartan, and it looks particularly attractive on my beautiful wife.'

Tom pulled Diane closer, planting a kiss on her lips as he did so.

Such easy, open displays of affection were rare in

this house. In fact, Nia couldn't remember the last time anyone had held her close or kissed her.

She felt her face start to tingle.

That was a lie.

She could remember exactly when she had been held, and how she had been kissed. More importantly, she could remember who had been doing the holding and the kissing.

Only she couldn't think about that now.

It would hurt too much to have the past and the present in the same headspace, and so, pushing the memory back into the darkest, most remote corner of her brain, she said quickly, 'I agree. You look amazing, Diane.'

Diane laughed. 'I do feel rather regal.' Her face softened. 'But you, my dear, are quite, quite lovely.'

Glancing down at her sleek one-shouldered black dress, Nia felt a blush creep up over her skin.

Compliments were also in scarce supply in her daily life.

She knew that she was a good boss, and her staff liked her, but it was her job to offer praise and encouragement, not theirs.

And although her parents loved her, they both had that tendency common in the spoiled and wealthy to expect perfection and focus on the tiniest of flaws.

Without any siblings to divert their focus, being Lady Antonia Elgin was both a privilege and a burden. It had been lovely growing up surrounded by Old Masters, and being able to ride across the estate on her pony, but there were so many expectations and responsibilities to shoulder.

She felt her throat tighten. It was only after she'd met

Farlan that it had involved making sacrifices too. He was the one person who had made her feel she was special, and she had let him go. Actually, she had pushed him away.

The glass felt suddenly slippery in her hand, and she tightened her grip. 'Thank you, I haven't got dressed up in a while so it's a real treat.'

Basically, her social life consisted of an occasional lunch with girlfriends and those events in the social calendar that were absolutely unavoidable.

'Well, it was worth the wait,' Diane said gently. 'And what a beautiful brooch.' She stared admiringly at the striking thistle-shaped diamond and amethyst brooch that was holding Nia's sash in place. 'Is it a family heirloom?'

Nia nodded. It was one of the few pieces she hadn't been forced to sell.

'It was my great-grandmother's. My mother gave it to me on my eighteenth birthday.'

Once upon a time her beauty had pleased her mother. Now, though, her delicate features and soft brown eyes seemed mostly to remind the Countess of Brechin of her daughter's failure to find a suitable husband.

Diane sighed. 'It's perfect. You're perfect—' She glanced over Nia's shoulder, her eyes lighting up. 'Don't you think so, Farlan?'

Nia felt her whole body turn to stone. The familiar details of the drawing room spun around her as if she were on a fairground ride.

Earlier she had wanted the evening to be over as quickly as possible. Now she wanted the floor to open and swallow her whole.

Frozen to the spot, she watched Farlan Wilder walk across the room, her pulse slamming in her throat.

It was seven years since he had left Scotland. Seven years of doubt and loneliness. And regret.

She had never expected to see him again.

But now he was back, and how things had changed.

When they'd met, outside a pub at the Edinburgh Festival, she had been out with friends, enjoying a gap year before taking up a place at Oxford to study history.

Seeing him that first time had made her shake inside. He'd been cool, cocky, outrageously flirty and heart-stoppingly beautiful. An art school dropout and wannabe filmmaker with nothing to his name. No money, no family and no belongings. Just raw, untried talent, an unshakable self-belief and plans and promises aplenty.

Her throat tightened. Plans that had worked out just as he had promised.

Not only was he a *bona fide* film director now, he had already won multiple awards, and his latest movie had been *the* blockbuster of last summer.

And it showed, she thought, in the casual confidence of his walk.

The cockiness of youth had shifted into an unmistakable authority that came along with crossing an ocean in economy class and returning on a private jet.

She watched, her smile pasted to her face, as he grabbed a tulip-shaped glass of champagne and kissed Diane on the cheek.

'She certainly is quite something,' he said coolly.

He shifted his weight and, expecting him to lean forward and kiss her too, she braced herself. But instead he held out his hand, the dull metal of his expensive Swiss watch glinting in the firelight.

At the touch of his fingers his eyes met hers and a burst of quicksilver darted through her veins.

She had thought about this moment so many times—dreamed about it, conjured up almost this exact same scenario.

She would turn to face him, and he would be angry, but not with the ice-cold fury of that last conversation.

In her imagination, his anger was hot and spilling over with the passion of so many wasted years apart so that within seconds they were both crying and he was pulling her close and she was kissing him—

As she stared at him, for a few half-seconds she actually thought she might still be asleep and it was all just a dream.

But then he lifted his chin and, gazing into his narrowed green eyes, she knew with breath-crushing certainty both that she was awake and that nothing had changed.

Farlan hated her.

Nia couldn't move. Her body, her limbs, seemed to have stopped working, and her ribs seemed suddenly to have shrunk.

She had thought herself prepared for this.

But too late she realised that nothing could have prepared her for this tumultuous rush of feelings, none of which she could reveal as her eyes met his.

He might have become a big shot in Hollywood, but he hadn't changed much physically—or if he had it was for the better.

Seven years ago he had been a beautiful boy, with

a scruffy mohawk and a heart-splitting smile. Now he was a wildly attractive man.

Yes, he was, she thought, her stomach clenching in a sharp, unbidden response.

He wasn't wearing a kilt, or even a hint of tartan. Instead he had chosen to wear a snow-white shirt and dark grey trousers, and yet his conventional clothing only seemed to emphasise his extraordinary bewitching beauty.

The leanness of youth had matured into broad shoulders, and the dark mohawk had been replaced by a buzzcut and a shadow of stubble that showed off the perfectly contoured planes of his cheekbones and jaw.

But he was no longer smiling.

Or at least not for her, she thought, her heart contracting as he withdrew his hand and switched his gaze to Diane, his mouth curving upwards.

'Sorry I'm late, Dee. My head's still back in LA. With my razor.'

He ran his hand over his stubbled jawline, smiling crookedly, and for a moment Nia couldn't breathe, couldn't think. All she wanted to do was reach out and touch his face, stroke it like she'd used to.

He had been like a cat that way, lying on the sofa with his head in her lap, hitching his chin to push up against her hand.

Her head was spinning, her heart crumbling, but if Diane sensed the flickering undercurrent of hostility in the room she gave no sign of it.

'Thank you for coming, darling boy.' She smiled up at him. 'I know this isn't your favourite night of the year so I really appreciate it, and Tom does too.'

'It's the least I can do.' Farlan smiled back at her. 'You were there for me when I needed you. I was pretty hard work back then, but you never pushed me away.'

Nia felt her whole body tense as his eyes locked with hers.

'Most people don't have your heart, Dee. They don't have the courage to trust their own judgement.'

His face was blank of expression, his voice too, but his eyes were the same dark forbidding green as the pine forests that edged the estate.

'Well, you've been there for us too.' She glanced at Nia. 'It's thanks to Farlan we're standing here right now—isn't it, Tom?'

Clapping his hand on Farlan's shoulder, Tom nodded. 'We've been talking about it for years, but something always got in the way. Would have been the same this time only he got mad. Told us we needed to make a decision and stick to it. That's how he got himself all those awards. It's not just about having a vision. My boy doesn't falter.' He winked at Nia. 'I bet you knew he was going to go all the way to the top.'

Farlan's gaze scraped against her skin like sandpaper.

'Yes, I mean... I didn't—' she began, but Farlan interrupted her.

'I'm not sure I made that big an impact on Lady Antonia. I was just a farm boy—a stupid, naive kid. Of course I've grown up a lot since then.'

His pointed use of her title made swallowing difficult. 'I remember you perfectly,' she said quietly.

It was like drowning. She could see every single moment of her life with him playing out on fast forward in front of her eyes.

'When we met. How we met. You were making a film about the Fringe,' she said.

He smiled at her now, but it was a smile that stopped at his mouth. There was no corresponding warmth in his eyes. It was just a consequence of muscles moving beneath the skin.

'Not about the shows. It was the performers that interested me.'

His eyes met hers, the green irises steady and implacable.

'All the sacrifices they made. I wanted to document that commitment. Show people what they could achieve if they believed in themselves and others.'

I did believe in you, she wanted to say.

But before she had a chance to open her mouth, Diane tapped Tom on the arm.

'We need to call Isla and Jack.' She turned to Nia. 'We usually have a Burns Night supper with our Scottish friends back home, and we said we'd call them and show them how it's done in the old country.'

Still flustered from her showdown with Farlan, Nia stared at her blankly. 'Show them...?'

Pulling herself together, she realised what Diane was asking.

'You might have to go to the kitchen to make a video call. The internet never really works in this part of the house—'

'The kitchen?' Diane hesitated. 'Oh, we don't want to leave you two—'

'Just go, Dee.'

Farlan was smiling, but there could be no mistaking the authority in his voice. Nia could almost picture him behind the camera on set, his all-seeing gaze directing every line, every glance.

'You don't need to worry.'

She tensed as his gaze flicked towards her face, his green eyes hardening.

'I'll take care of Lady Antonia.'

As the door closed behind them there was a beat of silence. Glancing at Nia's face, Farlan thought she'd flinched. Then again, it might just have been the flicker of the candlelight, but a part of him would have liked to know that she was feeling even just a fraction of his pain. A pain that seeing her had resurrected with a speed and sharpness that alarmed him.

He tried to calm his mind. Only that was hard to do when she was so close. Close enough to see the flecks of gold in her light brown eyes and the pulse pushing frantically against the smooth, pale skin of her throat.

Maybe he'd be doing better with it if it hadn't been so sudden. Not the ancestry stuff—Tom and Diane had been talking about that for ever—but coming here, to this particular house.

When Tom had first told him that they had rented Lamington Hall he had actually thought he'd misheard. That there was another Lamington Hall, a different one, that had nothing to do with the Elgin family.

Or more specifically with Nia.

Of course when finally he'd accepted that it was *that* Lamington, it had felt like a bad and not especially funny joke, and he had cursed himself for having not paid more attention to the Drummonds' whole house-hunting business.

His breathing stalled in his throat, and suddenly he had that too-big feeling in his chest—the one that made him sometimes wake up with his nails biting into the palms of his hands.

Only what difference would knowing have made really?

Even without the memory of what had happened with Nia, Scotland was still such a raw wound.

Tom and Diane had helped open doors for him in the States, even as they'd opened their hearts to him, but he had held back so much from them about his life, his past.

Even now, after all these years, the thought of telling them everything made his stomach tense.

They had met by chance. Their car had broken down and he'd stopped to help. Of course Tom had noticed his Scottish accent right away and instantly invited him over for a drink.

Drinks had turned into dinner, and soon he had been dropping round all the time.

And then Diane had offered him a room.

Even though he'd turned her down, then spent months avoiding them, they had never faltered in their friendship. It was only after spending yet another night on their sofa he'd realised that he'd already crossed the line.

But there were still so many locked rooms inside his head. So many doors that needed to remain closed.

Including the one at Lamington.

His shoulders tensed. It had simply never occurred to him that Nia would leave her home, much less rent it out to strangers. Clearly her father's need for a warmer climate had forced her hand, made some unwanted but necessary changes.

He glanced over at her set, pale face. Nia hadn't changed, though. She was still the most beautiful woman he had ever seen.

Nothing—no amount of time—could change the delicate bone structure beneath the smooth, flawless skin or thin that full, soft pink mouth.

His eyes snagged on the curve of her lower lip, his body tightening without warning as he remembered the feel of her mouth on his, the way she had moved against him—

Blanking his mind to the Nia of seven years ago, he forced himself to look at the woman standing in front of him.

He was wrong. She had changed; she'd lost weight. A little too much, in fact, he thought critically, wanting, needing, to have that small victory. And it wasn't just her weight. Her light brown eyes had lost their sparkle.

Aged nineteen, with her long dark blond hair falling in front of her face and that pale peach-soft skin, she had looked like a goddess or a princess in a fairy tale.

Sounded like one too.

It had been one of their shared jokes that he had been born in London but had a broad Aberdonian accent, whereas Nia—thanks to her expensive boarding school in Berkshire—spoke with a kind of smooth drawl that held no trace of her Scottish upbringing.

The chill in his stomach began seeping through his body.

Her voice wasn't the only misleading thing about her.

He had thought she loved him without reservation. She had told him that she did.

And yet when it had come down to choosing between him and a bunch of bricks and beams she had left him sitting at the train station like an unwanted suitcase.

'So what happened?'

She glanced up at him. A flush of colour crept over her cheeks and her eyes widened with shock, or maybe confusion. 'What do you mean?'

'This…' he gazed slowly round the room '…was once so very important to you.'

It was why she had broken up with him. And the other side of that statement, the unspoken truth, was that he hadn't been important enough for her to walk away, to leave Lamington behind.

'So what changed?' he asked. 'Why are you playing house down the drive?'

This time there was no mistaking the swift, startled flinch in her eyes, and a part of him hated it that he had caused that flicker of pain. But another part—the part that had never fully forgotten or forgiven the pain she'd caused him—felt nothing.

She shook her head. 'I'm not playing at anything.'

His chest felt suddenly too tight. She sounded as shaken as he felt. And he knew it wasn't just his accusation. He knew she was feeling the shock of this encounter just as much as he was.

'You played me.' His voice cut through the air like a blade. 'You made me think it was real.' She had made him care and hope and believe. 'So what was I? A gap year adventure? A way to shake up your family a little?'

'No, that's not true.'

'Really?' He rolled his eyes. 'You know, I might have believed that. *Once upon a time*.' The tension in his voice was making his accent more pronounced. He could hear the influx of glottal stops, the rolled 'R's. 'But guess what, Lady Antonia? I don't believe in fairy tales any more.'

'It's not a fairy tale.' Her voice was fraying. 'It's the truth.'

'Is that what you tell yourself?' He shook his head.

She had gone to talk to her parents. Left him standing in the kitchen like some delivery boy.

His heart twisted. He should have known then how it was going to go.

But he had loved her, trusted her—

Even at that distance it had stung, hearing her father say that she would lose her inheritance if she went ahead and married him. But not as much as when she had broken up with him the following day over the phone.

The unrelenting misery of those hours swept over him, the shock of her betrayal as raw and intense as it had been on the day.

'You used me, Lady Antonia, and then you dumped me.'

Lead was filling his lungs. That first year away from her had nearly broken him. And the worst of it was, he had been there before. A different time, a different kitchen, but the same old story. And yet even though he had heard the thin, shrill whistle of the missile and known what it meant, he still hadn't seen it coming.

He'd thought Nia was different—special. And he'd been so smitten with her that he'd ignored both the obvious and the lessons of the past.

Idiot that he was, he had actually believed that he was special to her.

'Your parents thought you might follow your heart. They needn't have worried. You don't have a heart, do you, Lady Antonia? Plenty of pride, but no heart.'

'Just saying things doesn't make them true.'

Her voice was still shaking, but maybe with anger now, and that was good. Anger was easier to fight. It made it easier for him not to care about the way she was bracing her shoulders.

'Oh, I know that—thanks to you. How about "I love you, Farlan. I want to be with you." Or maybe, "Wait for me at the station." Yeah, you're good at saying things that aren't true.'

'I was nineteen.'

Her cheeks were flushed, but the rest of her face was paler than the marble statues in the garden outside.

His breath caught.

It had been close to freezing that night at the station. He had sat there for three hours. He had called her maybe thirty times.

When, finally, she had called back, he had known even before she'd started talking that it was over.

The Scottish were supposed to have over a hundred words for different kinds of rain. He knew from experience that there were almost as many kinds of silence.

There was the silence of wonder.

The silence of fear.

And the silence just before that moment when the woman you love tells you she doesn't want to be with you any more.

He could still hear it now, inside his head, whenever he was with a beautiful woman—that flutter of hesitation. It would start small, but it always ended up swallowing him whole, and he was sick and tired of it.

Life was good—most of his life anyway. He had friends, more money than he could spend, a career he loved. And Tom and Diane.

Even now their generosity and faith both astonished and scared him. He had been so angry, so wary when they'd first met, but they had persisted.

And that, in part, was why he was here. To try and repay them for giving him what his own flesh and blood had failed to.

A home.

Not grudgingly, or reluctantly, or as some kind of temporary fix, but a real home.

They had done so much for him, and he had told them what he could bear to share. But nothing about Nia. Not even her name. It hurt too much—and, besides, they couldn't fix everything.

He couldn't either, apparently, judging by his complete lack of any love life.

Sex, yes. But love…

Tom and Diane were right.

He was ready. He wanted what they had. Only the memory of that last conversation with Nia still haunted him.

It was certainly the reason he avoided Burns Night. But then Tom had told him on the phone that Lady Antonia Elgin was joining them for supper and he'd felt that fate was giving him a chance to put the past to rest.

It was why he'd flown five thousand miles.

Only he wasn't going to share that fact with Nia.

He shrugged. 'And now you're twenty-six.' His eyes locked with hers. 'How are you finding living in the gardener's cottage?'

She opened her mouth to reply, but as she started to speak, the door opened.

'I am so sorry.' Diane hurried in. 'I didn't mean for that to take so long but they were so excited to see everything. Anyway—' She broke off, her eyes shining with excitement, as from somewhere in the house a distant melancholy wailing swelled up. 'I think we're ready to eat.'

CHAPTER TWO

AS THE PIPER marched slowly into the room, his fingers moving deftly over the chanter of the bagpipes, Nia managed to keep smiling. But inside, she was reeling at Farlan's words.

Given how it had ended between them, she had expected him to be distant with her. But the fact that he had been willing to see her at all had given her hope that time might have diminished his hostility.

She'd been wrong.

His attack had been so swift, so bitter, so unfair, it had left her breathless.

Tom held out his arm. 'Would you do me the honour, Nia?'

She nodded mechanically. 'Of course.'

Diane and Farlan followed them, and she was so conscious that he was there, behind her, that she forgot where they were going.

They stood behind their chairs and she felt a buzzing in her ears as she saw that she was seated opposite him. Feeling slightly sick, she waited as the piper finished playing, and then joined in the applause round the table.

'Great job.' Tom was grinning like a small boy. Turning round, he shook hands with the piper. 'You think maybe you could give me a couple of lessons?'

Nia barely heard the reply. She was too busy trying to make sure that her face was giving away none of the feelings that were turning her inside out.

It should be easy—she had lived most of her life hiding her thoughts from her parents—but Farlan had been the first person to bother looking beneath the surface. He had made it easy for her to talk, for her to be herself. And that was why having to close herself off to him had been so hard, and hurt so much.

Tom solemnly read the Selkirk Grace, and then it was time to eat.

The meal started with a traditional cock-a-leekie soup.

'That is the best darn soup I've ever eaten,' Tom said, laying down his spoon.

Nia nodded. 'I don't know anyone else who can turn a chicken and some vegetables into something so sublime. Molly calls herself a cook, but I actually think she's an alchemist.'

Farlan leaned back in his chair, his green eyes glittering in the candlelight.

'That probably says more about you than her,' he said softly.

'What do you mean?' Her face felt warm and she knew that her cheeks were flushed.

'Look at all of this.' He gestured towards the gleaming cutlery. 'Everything you own is gilded, Lady Antonia. Why should the food you eat be any different?'

His eyes locked onto hers and she felt ice tiptoe down her spine.

'You more than anyone should know that there's no place for base metals at Lamington,' he added.

He was smiling, so that it looked and sounded as if he was teasing her, but she could hear the edge in the voice.

Her mouth was bone-dry. 'I just meant that in my opinion Molly is modest about her talents.'

'In your opinion?' He held her gaze. 'It's good to know you have one.'

She swallowed past the lump in her throat as he turned towards Diane and began asking about the house.

After that he avoided speaking to her directly. Not that he made it obvious. In fact, he was so subtle about it she was pretty sure Tom and Diane hadn't actually noticed.

Somehow when he spoke he made it seem as though he was including all of them in his stories and jokes, expertly directing the flow of conversation so that she was simply required to nod and smile.

It might feel organic to everyone else, but she knew he was pulling the strings, that he had already planned this scene in his mind, and now it was just playing out under his critical green gaze.

Probably that was why he was such a successful director.

As if on cue, the piper returned to a roar of approval from Tom, and this time he was followed by Molly, carrying the haggis on a silver-gilt platter.

As the host, it was Tom's duty to address the haggis, and his chest was swelling with such obvious pride and emotion that Nia felt tears well in her eyes.

Soon it would be over.

And afterwards there would be no risk of them ever

having to meet again, she told herself. Farlan would make sure of that.

The meal was excellent. Crisp *pan haggerty*, creamy *neeps* and *skirlie*.

The nutty, toasty stuffing wasn't traditionally served on Burns Night, but Molly knew it was Nia's favourite. Only tonight it might as well have been sawdust.

'I'm guessing this is a big night for your family, Nia,' Diane said, pouring some whisky cream sauce over the haggis. 'You must have a whole bunch of traditions.'

Did having your heart broken count as a tradition?

Nia couldn't look at Farlan. Instead, she smiled across the table at Diane, hoping the misery in her heart wasn't visible on her face.

'Before I went to boarding school it was like having a second Christmas. It was so exciting. All the staff used to come to Lamington in the afternoon, and then my parents had a big party in the evening for their friends.'

But for the last seven years there had been nothing exciting about Burns Night. Instead, everything from the first champagne cork popping to the final chord on the bagpipes was just a tortuous reminder of all the what-might-have-beens in her life.

It was the one day in the year she wanted to be anywhere but Lamington. Only not being there was impossible, for it would mean having to explain to her parents, and she couldn't face having that conversation.

To her mother and father the whole affair with Farlan had been an unfortunate, imprudent aberration to be quickly forgotten.

And she *had* forgotten.

Months, days, goodness knows how many hours of

her life had passed since, and she couldn't remember how she had spent any of them. And yet she could still remember Farlan's exact words, and the intensity in his green eyes as he'd pulled her against him on that snowy afternoon.

They'd been sledging in Holyrood Park in Edinburgh. It had been a cold day, but with Farlan's body pressed close to hers she hadn't noticed. As they'd tumbled into the snow he had held her tight and kissed her fiercely.

'I want this to last for ever, Nia.'

The heat of his mouth had burned her lips and stolen the air from her lungs, so that she had thought she might faint. And then he'd slid the ring onto her finger and she had known a happiness like no other.

'Let's go away—just the two of us. Let's not get caught. Let's keep going.'

She had wanted to go with him so badly it had made her whole body ache, and in those sweet, shimmering moments of unrestrained happiness she'd even thought she might go through with it—

But of course people like her, the sensible, reliable ones who never broke the rules, always got caught.

Glancing up, her eyes rested on his flawless profile.

And she was still being punished for it now.

Raising the glass of Laphroaig to his mouth, Farlan tried to remember why he had decided this was a good idea.

They were sitting in the drawing room now, drinking coffee and whisky. He had purposely taken an armchair—there was no way he was going to end up sitting on some sofa with Nia—only that meant uninterrupted views of the room.

Success in Hollywood had given him an entrée into some of the most beautiful homes in the world. But the grandeur and scale of Lamington still jolted him more than he was willing to acknowledge.

The first time he had come here he'd barely noticed anything other than the shift in air temperature as they had sneaked into the house through the back door.

The memory snatched at his breath.

The warm, peppery smell of gingerbread cooking, the gleam of copper pans and Nia's fingers tightly wrapped around his like mistletoe around the branches of an oak tree.

He had stayed in the kitchen, but he doubted he would have noticed anything that day even if she had given him a guided tour. He had been too cocooned by the immense certainty of what he was feeling, what she was feeling—

Or rather what he'd thought she was feeling...

His gaze snagged on the Turner watercolour on the wall opposite and he felt suddenly blazingly angry.

Somehow it made it worse, finally seeing it again in person, knowing that Nia had quietly and calmly weighed him up against all of this.

Back in LA he'd been stunned, and then almost blinded with fury to learn that Tom and Diane would be staying here. But after he'd cooled off coming back to Lamington had seemed to make perfect sense. There would be a certain satisfaction in knowing that he was staying there, in *her* house.

His spine stiffened.

Much as he didn't like to admit it, his reaction had confirmed what he already knew but had ignored.

Nia was still in his head.

In his head, in his dreams, and sometimes he would even see her in the street or a restaurant or climbing into a cab.

Of course, it was never her, and he knew that.

But it always stopped him in his tracks just the same—left his whole body trembling with a longing and a loneliness that made it hard to stand up, to sleep, to eat, to think.

He'd hoped that seeing Nia again would flip some kind of switch inside him, and at first, in the drawing room, it had felt as if it had.

Now, though, he wasn't so sure.

Confronting her had felt good, satisfying. He hadn't wanted or needed to hear her excuses or explanations. But throughout the meal he'd kept feeling his gaze drawn to her beautiful pale face at too frequent intervals. Not so he could feel some kind of triumph, but because he hadn't been able to look away.

Not liking the implication of that particular thought, he lowered his glass and tugged at Diane's hand. 'So, Mrs Drummond, when are you and the big man here meeting the genealogist?'

'On Friday. And then next week we're going to take a field trip up to Braemar. That's where Tom's family originally came from,' she said to Nia.

Keeping his gaze fixed on Diane's face, he felt rather than saw Nia nod.

'It's very beautiful round there,' she said, 'and the castle is quite significant historically.'

'Is it?' he asked softly. 'I thought it was just a hunting lodge for the Earls of Mar. But I suppose I've been spoiled. I mean, Craithie is a piece of Scottish history.'

So much for not talking to her.

Her eyes jerked up to meet his. 'What's Craithie Castle got to do with anything?'

'Oh, didn't Diane and Tom tell you?' He let his gaze drift lazily over her face. 'I'm thinking of buying it. Partly as an investment, partly as a retreat. These last few years have been hoachin', and I want somewhere I can kick back and relax. Do some creative thinking.'

A flush of colour was spreading over her cheeks. She looked stunned—probably because she knew the asking price.

Tom grunted. 'Make sure some of that creative thinking is about more than just work. I'm not saying it doesn't matter,' he said, picking up his wife's hand and pressing it against his mouth, 'but other things matter more. Like finding Mrs Wilder.'

Mrs Wilder.

The words spun in front of his eyes, glittering like the snowflakes that had fallen on Nia's face that day in Holyrood Park when he'd proposed.

Did she even remember it? Or know what it had taken for him to say those words? Even now it made his heartbeat slide sideways like a car on black ice.

He held up his hands in surrender. 'Then I know you'll both be pleased to hear that I'm ready to make a fool of myself over a woman again. Any number of women, in fact.'

That wasn't quite true.

He knew he would never let any woman get close

enough to do that and, glancing over at Diane, he felt a spasm of guilt. She cared about him. Tom did too. They were the parents he'd never had. Kind, loving, warm. And, like any child lucky enough to have that kind of parent, he knew they only wanted the best for him.

Always had, even when he'd been at his worst.

His jaw tightened.

And his worst had been pretty appalling.

But they had stayed calm and firm, somehow sensing— although he'd never done more than hint at his past—that he needed proof they would stay the course. And they had given him that proof.

They had shown him love—shown him how to love, and why love mattered. Passion mattered too, but mostly they wanted him to have the kind of love they shared.

And theoretically he wanted that too.

Only that kind of love required a trust that wasn't in him to give.

Thanks to the woman sitting opposite him.

He let his eyes rest on her face until finally she looked up at him.

'You know the type,' he went on. 'Beautiful, beguiling and believable. But then a poor farm boy like me shouldn't expect anything else. Wouldn't you agree, Lady Antonia?'

'Oh, take no notice of him, Nia,' Diane said, shaking her head. 'He's not poor, and he wouldn't know a tractor if one ran him over. And you—' She turned to Farlan. 'If you really are serious about finding the love of a good woman, my boy, you need to think seriously about what you want.'

For a moment his reply stalled in his throat. That was

the point. He had been very serious—once. His feelings for Nia had been sacred almost. For him, she was the mythical 'one.'

There had been others over the years, but in truth he'd only ever wanted one woman. Nobody else had come even close to matching Nia.

'You're right, Dee. I have thought about it, and the one thing I really want in a woman is that she has to know her own mind.'

He glanced over at Nia. The edges of her face seemed blurred, almost like the brushstrokes of the watercolour behind her head.

'That's what matters to me,' he reiterated.

'Well, we'll have to see what we can do. I'm sure they'll be no shortage of takers.' Tom grinned at him. 'Now, how about another drop of whisky? And then I might see if I can have a little try of those pipes. Nia, another glass?'

'Oh, no, thank you, I really should be going. I have such a lot on tomorrow. But thank you so much for a wonderful evening—'

Something in her voice pinched him inside.

He knew he had been cruel, and purposely so, but then he remembered how she had made him feel.

Getting to his feet, he watched as Diane and then Tom hugged her, steeling himself for the inevitable moment when he would have to embrace her.

'Now, Farlan will see you home. Farlan—?'

His pulse jerked as Diane turned to him expectantly.

'Yes, of course,' he said finally, filling the small, awkward pause. 'Let me get your coat.'

* * *

It seemed to take for ever to get out of the house, and for Nia, every second was agonising.

Now her pulse beat in time to the crunch of Farlan's footsteps as he strode down the drive.

She could easily have walked home alone, so why hadn't she said so? Why did she always choose the path of least resistance?

Her gaze lifted irresistibly to Farlan's face.

She might have lost his love, but she still had her pride.

As soon as she was certain they were out of sight of the house, she stopped and turned to him.

'I'll be fine from here. It's not even a half a mile.'

She made to step past him, but he blocked her path.

'I know where it is.'

His eyes found hers. In the darkness they seemed more black than green, but the hostility in them was still unmistakable.

'Good. Then you'll understand.' Her voice sounded odd, as if someone was squeezing her ribs, but she didn't care. She just wanted to get away. Not just from Farlan, but from the whole damned mess of her life.

'It's pitch-black.'

'I know the way.' Before he could respond, she moved past him, darting forward into the darkness.

It was starting to rain, and a brisk breeze was blowing thick dark clouds across the sky, playing peek-a-boo with the moon. But even if it had been a dry, clear night she knew he wouldn't have followed her.

Why would he when she had given him a ready-made excuse not to bother?

It's finished, she told herself. *You did it. You saw him; you talked to him. The worst is over.*

Why, then, did she feel not relieved but miserable?

She had barely started to answer that question when she heard him moving swiftly through the darkness, his long strides easily catching up with her.

'Hey, slow down—'

Catching her sleeve, he spun her round, staring down at her as if she was a disobedient dog who had slipped its collar.

'Look, I get it, okay? You'd rather break your own neck than let me walk you home. Well, guess what, Lady Antonia? I don't want to walk you home either.'

She stared at him, mute with emotions she didn't want to feel.

Back at Lamington, with his expensive watch reflecting the flames from the fire, he had seemed both familiar and yet unnervingly different. Like the large Flemish tapestry in the drawing room after it had been taken away for refurbishing and returned with its previous faded tones restored to lush colour.

But out here, with his coat hunched around his shoulders and his rain-splashed face tipped up accusingly, he looked exactly like the beautiful wild boy she had fallen in love with at first sight.

Only he no longer loved her. Instead, she was just a woman he had agreed to walk home for a friend.

It was too much to bear.

The misery inside her twisted sharply, flared into an unfamiliar anger. 'So don't do it, then. Just turn around and go back the way you came.'

His face hardened. 'If it was up to me I would. But

unfortunately Diane asked me to walk you home and I said I would.'

Even through the thick wool of her coat, the disdain on his face made her skin sting.

'And, unlike some people, I keep my word.'

She tugged herself free. 'Fine—but let go of me.'

'With pleasure.'

They stepped apart, squaring up to one another like two squalling cats, and then he handed her the umbrella Diane had insisted he take.

'Here, have this.'

She was about to refuse, but he had already turned and was walking away.

The moon peeped out from behind the shadow of a cloud and then instantly retreated. *Lucky moon*, she thought, feeling bubbles of anger and misery bobbing inside her chest as he silently kept pace with her.

The worst is over.

The words replayed inside her head and she breathed out shakily. How arrogant, how naive, how frankly ridiculous that sounded.

The worst wasn't over—it was just beginning.

She might have finally seen Farlan again, but they hadn't so much met as *un*met.

Her heart beat unsteadily in the darkness.

Seven years ago they would have found it impossible to be so close and yet not touch or talk. Despite coming from such different backgrounds, they'd had more in common than any two people she had ever known. Their tastes so similar, their feelings so in tune.

Now, though, they were walking at arm's length in silence, and it felt as if they were strangers.

Except that strangers at least had the chance to get to know one another better.

She and Farlan wouldn't even be able to do that.

Up ahead, she could see the porchlight of the gardener's cottage. Relief flooded her body, and she sped up so that two minutes later she was standing on the doorstep.

She closed the umbrella and half turning, not wanting to see his face, said stiffly, 'Okay—I'm home now, so you've kept your word. Thank you and goodnight.'

She pushed down on the handle and opened the door.

'Are you kidding me?'

The snap in his voice made her hand jerk backwards. She turned towards him, her eyes wide. He was staring at her as if she had grown horns.

'Please tell me you didn't leave the house unlocked.'

He was outside the circle of the porchlight, his face in shadow, but she could see the tilt of his jaw, hear the tension in his voice.

'I never lock it. Well, I would if I was going away. But I was only down the road—'

Farlan was already moving past her into the cottage.

Heart pounding, Nia stumbled through the door after him, smoothing her damp hair away from her face. 'You don't need to—'

She blinked. He had found the light switch and she watched dazedly as he stalked from one room to the other, then up the stairs.

She heard his footsteps reach her bedroom and suddenly she was undoing her coat, making her way to the kitchen. Finding a glass, she filled it from the tap and gulped greedily, the chill of the water burning her throat.

'You need to be more careful.'

She turned to where he stood, his shoulders grazing either side of the doorway.

'The back door doesn't even lock.'

His voice was rough, raw-sounding, and she stared up at him, wanting to believe that there was concern beneath the anger, but also not wanting to add to the tangle of feelings at being alone with Farlan.

'It does. You just have to jerk it a little—'

He was staring at her in disbelief.

'Just get a new lock.' His lip curled. 'Oh, sorry, I forgot. You need to run everything past a third party before you make up your mind.'

Her anger flared again at this sudden, unexpected, unasked-for confrontation.

'That's not fair, Farlan.'

'Fair? *Fair!*' He stared at her disbelievingly. 'That's rich, coming from you.'

She took a breath, the bitterness in his voice making her head swim. Stepping back, she gripped the kitchen counter. 'Look, I get that you want to punish me for what happened between us, but my door locks have got nothing to do with you. In fact I don't even know why you're here.'

He took a step closer, so close that she could feel the tension radiating from his skin.

'I'm here because I wasn't going to make it awkward for Diane and Tom.'

'If you didn't want them to feel awkward then maybe you shouldn't have come in the first place.' She knew he was angry with her, but it was unjust of him to blame her for this. 'You knew I was going to be there. If you didn't like it you could have just stayed away.'

His jaw tightened.

'Why should I stay away? They're my friends and, in case you hadn't noticed, you don't live there any more, Lady Antonia.'

Her eyes were suddenly blurry with tears. She hadn't wanted to leave Lamington, or to rent out her home. But she'd had no choice. The alternative would have been to sell it, and that had just not been an option.

It shouldn't have come to this. For years now she had tried talking to her parents, explaining their finances over and over, showing them how their outgoings always outstripped their income.

But the Earl and Countess of Brechin had both been raised to pursue their every whim, and it had been impossible to make them understand the severity of the situation.

Her mother had reacted with outrage; her father had simply refused to discuss it. It was not possible for him to spend less, and that was that.

Persuading them that it was a matter of urgency had been an exhausting and thankless task, but she hadn't cared.

What mattered was keeping Lamington safe.

Now more than ever.

Her fingers pinched the kitchen counter.

She'd always loved her home, but for the last seven years it had been the focus of her energies—her whole life, really.

It wasn't the first time she had acknowledged that fact. But it was the first time she'd done so standing next to Farlan, and it hurt in the same way as seeing him walk into the drawing room, with a sting of regret travelling a beat behind her pulse.

Feeling his gaze on her face, she looked up into his eyes, saw the pride smouldering there.

'But I suppose the Elgins have been kicking people off their property for four hundred years. I guess old habits die hard.'

Her head was spinning, his accusation jamming up against the memory of telling her parents about Farlan.

She closed her eyes briefly. 'My father shouldn't have said what he did.'

'Actually, it was what you *didn't* say that mattered more to me,' he said coldly.

She stared at him in silence, wanting to say it now. Only it was too late. Too much time had passed…too many things had happened.

'So staying at Lamington is your way of getting back at me,' she said hoarsely. 'For what I didn't say.'

His eyes glittered, the green vivid against his dark brows. 'I hadn't thought about you in years, but when Diane invited me I guess I was curious.'

He was so close she could see the muscles clenched in his jaw.

'I wanted to see whether Lamington was worth it.'

She felt his eyes rest on her bare shoulder, and then his gaze tracked slowly round the small living room, seeing what she could see and had tried to ignore—that it wasn't just her home that had shrunk, but her hopes, her dreams, her life itself.

'And was it, Nia? Do you still think keeping your title

and your ancestral home and your wealth was more important than me? Than us? Than our love?'

It was the first time he had called her Nia and her heart clenched as she wondered if it would be the last time too.

'I didn't think that,' she whispered.

'I know.' His smile made her heart twist. 'You let yourself be persuaded into thinking it.'

It was true—her parents *had* persuaded her that marrying Farlan would be a mistake. Telling them that he was brilliant and talented and special had done nothing to dent their opposition. And yet if it had been just her parents' objection she would have resisted them.

She could feel the words building, backing up in her throat. *Let me explain.* She almost said it out loud but what was the point? Farlan didn't want explanations. That wasn't why he had come back to Scotland or why he had wanted to see her again.

Like he said, he was just curious.

'I should probably go—'

'Yes.' She managed to nod.

Good manners dictated that she should show him out, but her body wouldn't respond. And he didn't move either. Instead, he stood staring down at her, and then her breath stalled in her throat as he reached out and touched her thistle-shaped brooch.

'Do you remember that day?'

She nodded slowly, her pulse skipping like a stone across her skin.

They had gone to the seaside. It had been the hottest day of the year—so hot that the sun had looked like a scoop of melting ice cream.

'*Taps aff*,' he'd yelled, dragging her across the dunes.

They had walked and talked, picking up the shells and wave-tumbled pieces of smooth glass that were scattered at the shoreline. After weeks cooped up in Farlan's tiny, airless flat, the air had been so fresh and clean they'd been almost high on ozone.

But it had been more than that.

Walking along the seafront, they had understood that this was it for both of them. There would be no one else. It didn't matter what anyone said or did, they had known.

It wasn't young love. It was a love that would span a lifetime, cross oceans, scale peaks.

And so they'd decided to get tattoos.

Her breath echoed in her ears, short and uneven.

It had been a dare at first, and then a test of how much they trusted one another.

Farlan would choose hers, and she'd choose his.

The catch: they wouldn't get to see them until after they were finished.

But of course they had chosen the exact same tattoo of a thistle.

'Every moment,' she said quietly.

His eyes found hers and she felt her pulse start to hammer, softly at first, and then more heavily, so that it felt like an undertow, pulling her down and back through time to those frantic, endless moments in his small flat.

Mesmerised, she watched his fingers trace the outline of the brooch—and just like that she remembered the warm caress of his hand, the way she had burned so feverishly at his touch.

A current of heat rippled through her body, wrapping itself around her heart. It had been there right from the moment she had seen him walk into the room, simmering beneath the surface, only now he was too close for her to pretend it wasn't happening. So close she could see the colour streaking his cheekbones, feel his warm breath mingling with hers.

'Farlan…' she whispered.

Their lips were barely an inch apart.

His eyes widened, and every part of her tightened in anticipation. She wanted to kiss him so badly she didn't even realise she was leaning into him until the sharp, ragged screech of a vixen punctured the quivering silence.

Abruptly his face was shuttered and he withdrew his hand. 'Get some sleep. You look tired.'

Completely unable to speak, and sure that her face was showing everything, she watched as he walked swiftly to the door.

As it closed, she moved across the room on autopilot, locking it this time.

It's over, she told herself.

Only this time she wasn't talking about the ordeal of seeing him—she was talking about the tiny, involuntary hope that maybe, possibly, there might be a second chance for the two of them. That somehow she might manage to persuade him to try again.

Whatever had just passed between them had made it clear that it was too late. There was no hope. There would be no reprieve.

And she was going to have to live with that for the rest of her life.

CHAPTER THREE

PUTTING HIS FOOT down on the accelerator, Farlan eased the big car forward, his eyes tracking the low pale sun in the blue sky above the Cairngorms.

Having got used to the warm, sun-filled days of life in Los Angeles, he'd almost forgotten the fickle Scottish weather.

Four seasons in a day, his grandmother used to say.

And it was true. Right now the white clouds scudding above the heather-covered hills looked positively jaunty, but when he'd set off this morning it had been drizzly and dreary and grey—*dreich*, in other words.

Dreich.

Now, that was a word he hadn't used in a long time.

No need for it, living in Los Angeles. Not that anyone would have known what he was saying anyway.

His mouth twisted up at the corner. When he'd first arrived in California it had been so difficult to get people to understand what he was saying. It hadn't just been his accent, although that hadn't helped. It had been all the words he'd used without thinking—like *dreich* and *scunnered* and *clarty*.

They had mostly slipped from his speech through

lack of use, and his accent had softened over time. But other things had stayed as solid and immutable as the granite tors that reared up across the moorlands.

He felt his lungs tighten, so that he had to force himself to breathe.

Eyes narrowing, he slowed down and scooted past a racing cyclist in a glaringly luminous green jersey, then accelerated. He felt a childish but undeniable rush of satisfaction: the seven hundred and ten horsepower, four-litre twin turbo engine was explosively fast.

He wasn't really fussed about the money he was making now. It was nice not to have to worry about it any more, and he liked being able to look after people. Mostly, though, he just liked the 'convenience' of being rich.

Doors really did open if you had a lot of money. Everything was faster, slicker, less stressful. There was never any waiting around for a table in a restaurant. When you wanted to leave a limo was always on hand to whisk you away. And you didn't have to bother with shopping. People just sent you stuff. Clothes. Sunglasses. Smartphones.

He glanced at his wrist.

Watches.

Maybe that was why he hadn't been tempted to go on a spending spree.

That could be about to change, though.

He glanced admiringly at the smooth leather and carbon fibre interior of the supercar that had been delivered to him this morning. Another perk of being Farlan Wilder, film director.

He had met the racing team last year, when he'd

flown to Austin for the United States Grand Prix. As a VIP, he'd been invited into the paddock and told to get in touch if he ever wanted to test drive anything.

He'd just been waiting for the right moment.

And where better to put this incredible machine through its paces than these endless empty roads with their backdrop of stunningly beautiful scenery?

Thankfully, LA's bumper-to-bumper gridlock didn't seem to have impaired his driving skills.

He shifted in his seat. For him, being in a car had always been a means to escape reality, to suspend real life. His mother used to put on some music, and for however long it had taken to get where they were going all of them—he and his parents and his older brother, Cam—would act like a normal family.

Briefly, the rows had stopped.

He stared at the horizon.

They'd stopped permanently when his mother had left. It had been all right for a while, and then his dad had basically moved in with his new girlfriend, Cathy, and he and Cam had been left to raise themselves.

In those years before his brother had left too, he and Cam had gone on 'road trips.' Of course, that had been just something Cam had called them, to make it sound cool.

They hadn't gone anywhere special—just far enough away to make it feel as though they had left themselves behind.

But he knew better now. He knew that it didn't matter how fast you drove, how many miles you put between yourself and the person you blamed for the dark cloud spreading inside your chest, you never left your-self behind.

As what had happened in the cottage with Nia had so gut-wrenchingly proved.

He thought back to that moment when he had stepped towards her.

Or had she leaned into him? He couldn't remember. Memory required a functioning brain, and his had melted into his heartbeats the moment he had looked into her eyes and seen—

Seen what?

He swore softly.

Seen what he'd wanted to see. Or, more precisely, seen what his body had wanted to see. Nia's eyes…those beautiful soft brown eyes…misty with desire.

But it had been a mirage. An illusion. A teasing, flickering slideshow made up of memories and wish fulfilment.

Gritting his teeth, he pushed up the revs.

He understood wish fulfilment better than most of the population. As a film director he produced movies that were designed to satisfy people's conscious and unconscious desires.

His mouth twisted.

Clearly, though, he should have been concentrating on satisfying his own—then maybe he wouldn't have found himself standing inches apart from his ex with what could only be described as a hard-on.

He still couldn't quite believe it. Walking back to Lamington afterwards he had felt as if his body had betrayed him. Nia had broken his heart. It made no sense for him to feel anything for her but hostility and resentment.

Okay, she was still a beautiful woman, and they'd been alone, and they had a history, but surely her crime should have stifled his desire. Why, then, had his body reacted in that way?

But he knew why.

It had been an instinctive response. Like reaching for something when you saw it fall. Automatic, unthinking. *Foolish.*

He had come so close to kissing her...so close to pulling her body against his and giving in to the sharp pull of desire.

The fact that he hadn't done so was less to do with will power and more to do with a chance encounter between a fox and a vixen.

A soft, expensively restrained ringtone filled the car's cabin and gratefully he pulled his mind away from Nia's soft lips.

'Answer phone,' he said curtly.

'Farlan.'

It was Steve, his producer. He had noticed a missed call from him yesterday, and had been meaning to get back to him.

'Steve—sorry, man. I was going to call you—'

He glanced at the clock on the dash. It was barely six a.m. in Los Angeles, but it didn't surprise him that Steve was already up and making business calls. Most people he'd met in the movie industry seemed to work all hours of the day and night, and he was no exception, only today it had slipped his mind.

His hands tightened around the steering wheel.

Or perhaps it might be more accurate to say that it had been squeezed out by thoughts of Nia.

'No worries. I just wanted to let you know the good news.' Even from five thousand miles away the elation in his voice was unmistakable. 'Travis Kemp loved the pitch. So it's on, baby.'

The road dipped but that wasn't what made Farlan's stomach plummet.

The pitch.

How had he forgotten? That should have been first on his agenda, and normally it would have been, but thanks to Nia his mind had lost its usual razor-sharp focus.

With an effort, he kept the confusion and irritation out of his voice.

'That's great news, Steve. Really great news. Thanks for letting me know and thank you for making it happen. I know you put in a whole lot of effort on this one.'

'It was an easy sell. They loved it, and they love you. In fact, Travis is having a gathering this weekend and you're on the guest list. Check your in-box. You'll need the zip code to find it. It's in the middle of nowhere.'

Farlan gazed blindly at the view through the windscreen.

The weather had changed again. Dark swollen clouds were rolling low over the hills, swallowing up the light, turning the landscape bruise-coloured and carelessly flinging raindrops at the car like a commuter chucking coins in a busker's hat.

Travis Kemp was a 'name.' He didn't just greenlight films—he made legends. Even to be invited to one of his 'gatherings' was a coup.

He felt a hum in his chest…could feel it spreading out, fluttering down his arms.

Tom and Diane would understand. Particularly Tom. He was close enough to the movie industry to know what a connection to Travis Kemp could mean.

There was every reason to go back to California, and only one to stay here in Scotland—and it had nothing to do with Nia.

The reopening of the Gight Street Picture Palace was his project, and he'd always planned on visiting it while he was over here. But in the run-up to his leaving LA the trust that managed it had invited him to the reopening ceremony, and he'd agreed.

He could cancel. Only he could still remember his own disappointment when he was at the beginning of his career and people had blown him out.

And then there was Nia.

Her face, her soft brown eyes wide and drowsy with desire, slid into his head.

The memory of her rejection had haunted him for seven years. Seeing her was supposed to have changed things. Put the past back in its box. And yet it wasn't her rejection that was playing on a loop, but those few, febrile unfulfilled seconds when he had unleashed a different part of their past.

A part that was nothing to do with rejection and everything to do with attraction.

In the distance, the sun was pushing back at the clouds. Suddenly everything was brilliantly illuminated in colour, the hillsides a jigsaw of sapphire and rust and gold like a stained-glass window.

If he went back now she would always be there in his head.

This was his one chance to erase her for ever and have a chance at finding the happiness that Tom and Diane so wanted for him.

That he wanted for himself.

'I can't make it, Steve. You know I was heading back to Scotland for a couple of weeks? Well, I decided to go a little earlier.'

'You did? Are you there for the shooting? Or just catching up with "auld acquaintances"?' Steve made a poor attempt at a Scottish accent.

'Nice try, mate, but I'm from Scotland—not Ireland.'

Just as he'd intended, Steve laughed.

But Farlan didn't join in with the laughter. Instead, staring coolly at his own narrowed green gaze in the rear-view mirror, he slowed the car and, using the passing place, turned it around.

Just one 'auld acquaintance'—and he was going to do whatever it took to make sure that this time he would forget her.

'Oh, my dear, you made it. I am so pleased.'

Nia smiled as Diane hurried towards her and kissed her on both cheeks. She held up a pile of books. 'I thought I'd pop these back in the library. I borrowed them before I moved out.'

'Well, we're all in the library right now, just this moment stopping for tea. It's going very well.' Diane's eyes were shining with excitement. 'How was your trip to London?'

'It was fine,' Nia lied. 'But I'm always happy to come back to the Highlands.'

Sometimes she met a friend for lunch or shopping, but after her meeting with the family accountant she hadn't been in the mood for either small-talk or tapas.

Douglas McKenzie had known her grandfather. He was nearing retirement now, but he was still sharp and straight-talking.

'Your parents' personal expenses are not just ridiculous—frankly, they're jeopardising everything you are trying so hard to prevent,' he'd said, with typical bluntness. 'If this carries on, you're going to have to seriously consider letting out Lamington for longer. Two, maybe three years.'

It had been like a sharp slap. 'Surely that can't be the only option, Douglas?' *Two, maybe three years* was too long to live in limbo.

Catching sight of her face, his expression had softened. 'I'm sorry, Nia. I don't want or need to scare you. You know what's at stake. It's your parents who simply refuse to deal with the reality of their finances.' He'd hesitated. Then, 'I know it's none of my business, and I'm sure you had your reasons for turning down Lord Airlie, but he's a good man and I think if he had the slightest encouragement from you...'

Breathing out slowly, Nia blinked as the library came back into focus. Through the long windows at the end of the room, she could see the distant heather-covered hills.

The Most Honourable the Marquess of Airlie—or Andrew, as she called him—lived just over those hills, in a castle that made Lamington look like a dolls' house.

He was one of the wealthiest men in Scotland, a handsome blue-eyed Highlander, and a kind and generous man.

When he'd proposed to her a year ago she had known that he would be a kind and generous husband. But she could no more marry him than she could marry Douglas McKenzie.

She felt a shiver run over her skin.

Her parents had been apoplectic with fury when she had turned him down. They had raged, threatened, pleaded with her, but she had been firm.

This time she had been firm.

Her mouth compressed.

After what had so nearly happened at the cottage with Farlan she had sworn to stay away from Lamington. He was only staying for a fortnight. She could easily avoid having to see him again.

Then, just as she'd been boarding the plane back, Diane had called and invited her to tea, and to meet Finn McGarry, the genealogist who was researching Tom's Scottish roots.

The hope and warmth in her voice would normally have made Nia accept immediately. But even the thought of seeing Farlan again had made panic swamp her and, stammering slightly, she had started to make her excuses.

It was very kind of her, but they already had a guest staying, and Farlan was only over for such a short time—

Diane had laughed. Not so short, she'd said, that he couldn't take himself off on a round trip to Inverness.

Nia had felt relief wash over her.

Apparently Farlan had arranged for some amazing supercar to be delivered to the house and would be heading off after lunch.

But just to make sure... 'So did Farlan get off all right?' she asked now, casually.

Or at least she had been aiming for casual.

Even just saying his name out loud made her skin heat, just as it had in the cottage when he'd reached out to her. She could still feel it now—the way the air had changed around them, how it had seemed to turn liquid.

Or maybe that was just her...

Her cheeks felt as though they were burning. It had been instant and un-tempered, and for a few glorious half-seconds she had forgotten the past as a dizzying rush of hunger had risen up, drowning out logic and the unchangeable fact that it didn't matter how badly she wanted to reach out and stroke his face, or press her lips against his beautiful mouth, she had forfeited her right ever to do so again.

'He did.' Diane turned to her and shook her head. 'But then he changed his mind. He got back about a quarter of an hour ago.' She lowered her voice. 'I don't know what's up with that boy. He's been like a cat on a hot tin roof since he got here. Can't seem to sit still for more than five minutes. Tom... Farlan,' she called out as they walked into the library, 'look who's here!'

It was only good manners and some kind of residual momentum that kept Nia walking forward.

Farlan was sprawled across a sofa, the sleeves of his dark jumper rolled up.

She tried so hard not to look at him that she almost tripped over the edge of one of the rugs, and her cheeks flared anew as she imagined him remarking on her clumsiness.

But when she stole a quick glance in his direction, he wasn't even looking at her. He was looking at Finn McGarry.

She took a breath, forcing air in and out of her lungs. Had she given it any thought, she would probably have expected the genealogist to be an elderly man in a shabby, tweed suit.

But Finn was apparently short for Finola—and Finola McGarry was young and slim, with huge blue eyes and a dark pixie haircut.

She was also very pretty.

Farlan certainly seemed to think so, she thought, a slippery unease balling in her stomach as Diane handed her a cup of tea.

She watched as he gave Finn one of his slow, teasing smiles.

'All these questions, Ms McGarry…you're making me feel nervous.'

'Please call me Finn—and I doubt much makes you nervous, Mr Wilder.'

'It's Farlan. And a beautiful woman cross-examining me makes me very nervous.' His green eyes glittered. 'Unless, of course, you're a fan.'

'I am. I did an internet quiz on you the other day. Got every answer right except one.'

'Which was…?'

'Your middle name.'

Nia froze, her fingers tightening around the handle of her teacup, chanting the answer inside her head.

I know his middle name, she wanted to shout. *Jude.*

It's Jude. And I know that he always falls asleep with his arm under the pillow, and I know that Plein Soleil *is his favourite film. I know him as well as I know myself, maybe more.*

Farlan's chin jerked up, his eyes locking with hers, and for a horrible moment she thought she had spoken out loud.

But then he looked away, almost as if he hadn't seen her. 'It's Jude.'

'Like the song?' asked Finn.

Farlan shook his head. 'The saint, actually,' he explained.

Nia was starting to feel sick. It had been painful enough accepting that Farlan could not forgive her, and that there would be no second chance for the two of them. But imagining him in a relationship with another woman was a whole new level of agony.

She leant forward to put her cup down, letting her hair fall in front of her face so that she could no longer see Farlan and Finn.

Farlan and Finola Wilder. Even their names sounded good together.

'Could I have some milk?'

The cup in her hand jerked as she realised Farlan was standing beside her. 'I didn't think you liked it in tea—'

'My taste has changed,' he said flatly.

His gaze rested on her face and she felt her heart contract with shock at how much it hurt to look up at him and no longer find love in his eyes.

As she drank her tea, she managed to keep up a flow of polite conversation with Diane, but her ears kept tuning in to the couple talking on the other sofa.

'Unusual job for someone your age,' Farlan was saying, leaning back against the sofa cushions and stretching out his long legs. 'Was it always the plan?'

'Yes.' Finn nodded, then frowned. 'Actually, that's not strictly true. It was *my* plan. My parents wanted me to be a lawyer, and I did do a term at Edinburgh, but it wasn't what I wanted.'

Nia felt rather than saw Farlan lean forward.

'So...what? You dropped out?'

'Yeah, my parents went ballistic. They're all lawyers in my family, and they tried every which way to talk me out of it, but...' She shrugged. 'I wasn't going to change my mind.'

Farlan's eyes were fixed on her face. *'"I have dared to do strange things—bold things, and have asked no advice from any."'*

The sudden intensity in his voice made Nia spill a little tea in her saucer.

Diane looked up and sighed. 'That is so beautiful. Is it Robert Frost?'

'Emily Dickinson.'

Nia and Farlan both spoke at the same time.

His eyes locked onto hers, and for a few pulsing seconds it was as though they were alone in the vast book-lined room.

'Oh, I almost forgot.' Diane put her cup down with a clatter. 'Finn, we have a book of photographs we want to show you. The packers put it in the wrong crate, but you must see it. Farlan, could you help Tom get it down for me?'

Nia watched as everyone left the library.

She took a shivery breath, feeling the gap in the room where Farlan had been.

Nobody had asked her to go too. And nobody would notice that she hadn't followed them.

Picking up the pile of books she'd brought back, she made her way to the spiral staircase that led up to the galleried second floor of the library.

She felt adrift.

Her body felt as though it had short-circuited.

She couldn't do this—couldn't just sit by silently and watch Farlan fall in love with someone else.

Her heart twisted.

How could he not fall for Finola McGarry?

She was beautiful, and passionate, and she knew her own mind. Finn had followed her heart, and Nia knew that to Farlan that made her irresistible.

Slowly, she made her way along the shelves, sliding the books carefully back where they belonged. Typically, the last one, the biggest and heaviest of all of them, came from a higher shelf.

Glancing down at her high-heeled court shoes, she frowned.

She could just squeeze it in anywhere—only then finding it again would just be down to luck. Picturing her mother's face, she sighed and, gripping the ladder with one hand and clutching the book in the other, she began climbing.

Annoyingly, it was still a little out of reach, but if she just leaned over—

'Nia!'

She jerked round, her foot slipping sideways, and

suddenly the book was sliding from her fingers and she was grabbing for the ladder.

Strong hands grasped her waist and she felt her body connect with a hard chest.

'What are you doing?'

Those same hands spun her round and lowered her to the floor. Looking up, she almost forgot to breathe. Farlan was standing next to her, his green eyes narrowed in disbelief.

'I was just trying to put a book back.'

'In *those*?'

Farlan looked down at her shoes and then immediately wished he hadn't as he felt a stealthy stirring of lust at the sight of her long, slender legs in what were quite conceivably stockings.

Watching her eyes widen at the harshness of his voice, he felt like a jerk. But Nia wasn't the only one who had been caught off balance.

Imagining what would have happened if he hadn't been there to catch her made him feel sick.

But it was his body's swift, treacherous reaction to how good it felt to have her pressed against him that had shaken him more.

In the car, everything had seemed so clear. Deep down he'd known he was avoiding her, and that was why he had turned around and driven back to Lamington. To prove to himself that what had happened in the cottage had been either a fluke or just a final twitch of muscle memory—that there would be no next time.

And he'd been doing just fine.

Until Nia had sashayed into the library with her hair

falling in front of her face, looking like a cross between Jessica Rabbit and a Hitchcock heroine in a pencil skirt and shiny high heels.

Who the hell wore heels like that when they were popping over for tea?

Realising he'd lost his train of thought while he'd been staring at her legs, he gritted his teeth. 'Why are you even up a ladder anyway? Don't you have staff to put your books back for you?'

Her hair had fallen back from her face and, gazing down at her, he felt his heartbeat accelerate. She looked stunned, and furious, and for a moment he thought she might slap him or stalk off, but instead she just shook her head.

'No, I don't. Now, do you mind?'

He felt a tic of anger and something else pulse through his chest as she pushed his hands away from her body and edged backwards, as if he'd been trying to mug her rather than save her from breaking her neck.

Her neck...

His eyes were a beat behind the words, but as they dropped to the smooth, creamy skin of her throat he felt the hum in his head slither down his veins.

Had those pearls she was wearing been a gift? And, if so, who had given them to her?

The most likely answer to the question sharpened his anger to a point. 'Yeah, I do mind, actually,' he said curtly. 'I mean, do you have any idea what would have happened if I hadn't been here?'

A flush of colour spread over her cheeks. 'Nothing would have happened.'

'So no need to thank me, then?' he said sarcastically.

She frowned. 'Thank you? For what? Haranguing me?'

Containing his temper with an effort, he shook his head. 'If I hadn't come along when I did it would have been like a game of *Cluedo* in here. Lady Antonia, in the library, with a ladder.'

'Why are you making this such a big deal? My foot slipped—that's all.'

He stared at her in frustration, maddened by both her lack of gratitude and the smooth Englishness of her voice.

'I was fine. In fact, if you hadn't scared me I probably wouldn't have lost my balance.'

So what was she saying? That this was his fault?

He stared at her in silence, her words and her light floral scent tangling with the emotions in his chest.

Reaching down, she picked up the book she'd dropped.

He plucked it from her fingers. 'I'll do it.'

She snatched it away again. 'I don't need your help. I don't need anything from you.'

'I know. You made that perfectly clear seven years ago when you chose this house over me.'

The memory of it echoed inside him like a bomb blast.

She took a step closer, close enough that he could almost see her heart beating beneath the fabric of her top.

'That's not how it was,' she said.

'That's exactly how it was.'

Bitterness was rolling through him like a juggernaut. She had never needed him. Wanted him, yes, but not for ever—not like she'd promised.

'I was there, remember? We were both there. Only at some point you started reading from a different script.'

The script her parents had written.

She blinked. 'We weren't in a movie, Farlan. You can't just write the ending you want.'

'You did.'

There was a beat of silence and then she shook her head slowly. 'No. I didn't. I did what I thought was right for both of us. But it wasn't what I wanted.'

'What *did* you want?' He'd meant to sound scornful, but instead his voice was shaky, urgent.

Her eyes found his. 'I wanted you. I've only ever wanted you.'

He stood, frozen. For a few seconds they just stared at one another, and then she took a step closer, and his heart jerked as she brushed her lips against his.

It was a light, tentative, tantalising not-quite kiss. She had kissed him like that once before, that very first time. Before all of this had happened, when there had been nothing but hope and hunger and heat between them.

Heat was filling his lungs. He had come back to Lamington to put the past behind him. Only not this piece of the past.

Pulse stuttering, his hands moved automatically to her waist and he kissed her back.

He heard the book fall to the floor, and then her fingers began moving down his body, roaming clumsily over his shoulders and chest, pushing up his sweater, pulling his T-shirt aside.

He breathed in sharply as her hands slid over his bare skin, feeling his body harden. Pressing her closer, he tugged at the buttons on her cardigan until she was open to him. His fingers splayed over her stomach... his heartbeat melted into her skin.

She moaned softly as he cupped her breasts and then, lowering his face, he sucked a swollen nipple into his mouth. His blood pumped faster as she arched against him, and then his hand was pushing under the hem of her skirt, finding more warm, irresistible skin and the tops of her stockings.

Breathing raggedly, he found her mouth again and, walking her backwards, slid his hand through her hair, cradling her head so that he could deepen the kiss.

There was a muffled thump as they collided with the shelves, and then more thumps as books began falling to the floor, but he didn't care. All he cared about was the fierce, hot pressure in his groin.

'Farlan—'

His eyes fluttered open. She was staring at him, her hair mussed, her lips swollen. From somewhere inside the house he heard Tom's booming laugh.

What the hell were they doing? What the hell was he doing?

Drawing back, he watched her grab the front of her cardigan. Clearly Nia was thinking the same thing.

'I'm sorry,' she said shakily.

Her eyes dropped to the books on the floor and, crouching down, she started to pick them up.

'Leave it.' He pulled her to her feet. 'I'll sort it out.'

'You can't just put them back anywhere.'

Her eyes were too bright, but her words gave him an excuse to vent his panic and confusion.

'It's just a few books, Nia.' He shook his head. 'What

is it with you and this damn house? Always wanting everything to be perfect.' And obviously that excluded some nameless nobody like him.

Her face stilled. 'It's not just a house. It's my home.'

Something in her answer, in her voice, made his chest tighten. 'Nia, I—'

But she stepped past him, moving so swiftly that she was already halfway down the spiral staircase by the time his brain had caught up with his breathing.

He stood for a moment, heard her words echoing around the still, silent room, and then, bending down, he picked up the books and began slowly and carefully putting them back exactly where they belonged.

CHAPTER FOUR

GAZING OUT OF her bedroom room, Nia felt her heart swell. No matter how many times it happened, it was still magical.

It had snowed overnight, transforming the drab, muddy fields and spiky hedges of the Scottish countryside into an endless white wonderland.

There must be six inches, at least. Enough to cover the lawn in a thick blanket and make the philadelphus and camellia bushes buckle.

Not enough to make the world stop turning.

Her throat tightened.

No, only Farlan Wilder had the power to do that.

She glanced across the fields to where Lamington rose, pale and splendid, beneath a pewter-coloured sky. It felt strange, knowing he was there, that he was sleeping in the guest room just yards from where they would have shared a bed *together* if she hadn't broken up with him.

Although, judging by yesterday's performance in the library, they didn't actually need a bed.

She felt her face heat.

Even now the memory of that kiss stunned her.

It had been such a stupid thing to do, and it should have felt wrong on so many levels.

They had parted on such bad terms, and he didn't even like her. Yesterday, after the way he had acted, the way he had spoken to her, she hadn't liked him very much either.

But when her lips had touched his she had more than liked him. She had wanted him with every fibre of her being.

And he had wanted her too. She had felt it in the urgency of his mouth, the press of his fingers against her skin.

She stared blindly through the glass at the glittering white landscape.

Time was like snow. It covered everything so that after a few weeks—days, even—you forgot what lay beneath.

But all it took was a few moments of intense heat and things started to reveal themselves.

Or, in this case, feelings. Feelings she had buried… feelings she'd thought had faded to manageable proportions.

But here, in this small, neat bedroom, with its chintz curtains and low beams, she could admit that even after all this time a part of her still wanted Farlan.

Was that really so surprising?

It was hardly unusual for ex-lovers to feel desire long after affection had faded.

Farlan being back had obviously stirred up all kinds of feelings.

Add in to that already potent mix the fact that he was

staying at Lamington, and it would have been incredible if there hadn't been any repercussions—

But was that enough to explain how she had acted?

Could desire really overrule everything? Not just the past, but all the anger and confusion that still simmered between them?

Her heart began banging against her ribs.

It wasn't just desire.

Remembering Finola McGarry's wide-eyed beauty, she clenched her hands, her nails digging in deep.

The years had softened the ache of Farlan's absence. But seeing him with Finn had been a new, fresh pain, even though it shouldn't have been that much of a shock.

After all, he'd made it clear just a couple of days ago that he was looking to 'make a fool of himself with any number of women.'

Yet she hadn't been prepared for exactly how much it would hurt. How every time his eyes had skimmed past her to settle on Finn's face it had felt as though the air was being ripped out of her lungs.

But he wanted me as much as I wanted him.

It was so tempting to listen to that tiny, treacherous voice in the back of her head…to think about the tantalising possibility that they might get back together.

Only what would be the point?

There could be any number of reasons why he had kissed her like that. Habit…curiosity. Or perhaps, like her, he had just lost control and given in, momentarily, to the pull of the past.

It didn't much matter either way, and it certainly wasn't going to happen again.

She and Farlan had split up for multiple reasons.

Maybe those reasons had been misguided, and maybe she had spent the last seven years regretting her actions and resigning herself to never meeting a man like him again. But no matter how passionate the kiss, it didn't change the facts.

Whatever it was she and Farlan had shared, it hadn't been solid or strong enough to survive real life.

The thought of deliberately drawing a line under their relationship made her shiver on the inside. But she knew what it had taken for her to get over him the first time. She couldn't relive that. The time for what-might-have-beens was over.

And if she needed further proof of that she should remember how he'd looked at her when she had tried to pick up the books. There had been nothing lover-like about him then. He'd been just as angry and resentful as he had been all those years ago.

On the table beside her bed, her phone pinged.

Glancing down at the screen, she frowned. It was a text from Johnny, the head ghillie at Lamington, asking if she still wanted to meet and would she like a lift.

Of course—how could she have forgotten?

Tom and Diane might be living at the big house, but she was still overseeing the running of the estate, and she had earmarked today for catching up with the outdoor staff. The ghillies, stalkers and gamekeepers who knew the hills and the winds and the waters of Lamington best.

It would be a long, tiring morning, spent trundling round the estate in a car without a fully functioning heater. But on the plus side she would be too busy to give any more thought to the enigma that was Farlan Wilder.

Having texted back yes to the first question and no to the second, she showered and dressed and ten minutes later was bumping over the snow-covered road in her battered Land Rover.

When she arrived at Johnny's house, a trio of khaki-green ATVs were already waiting for her. Leaning against them, a cluster of men all dressed identically, in boots, thick trousers, quilted jackets and beanies, were talking and drinking what she knew would be hot, sweet tea from Thermoses.

As she slid out of the car, the men all turned to face her. 'Good morning, Lady Antonia.'

'Good morning, everyone. I know you're all dying to have some fun with all this lovely snow, and hopefully there'll be some time later for that, but first—'

'Sounds great.'

Looking up, she felt her stomach jolt even before she recognised his voice.

Shifting against the bonnet of the nearest ATV, Farlan downed his tea and screwed the top back on his Thermos as though this was all completely normal to him.

'Are we talking snowballs or sledging?'

She stared at him in silence. 'I didn't know you were joining us, Mr Wilder?' she managed finally.

'I wasn't.' He gazed at her, his green eyes clear and steady. 'But Johnny dropped round to the house to pick up the key for this.' He patted the bonnet. 'So we got talking, and he told me you were all meeting up, and—'

And what? she wanted to scream.

His smile could have melted a polar ice-cap. 'I don't have much on today, except a call to my producer. So I thought I'd tag along. Have a tour of the estate.'

Tag along?

She felt blindsided, just as if he'd scooped up a ball of snow and thrown it at her head. Surely he wasn't planning on spending the whole morning with them?

As if he could read her thoughts, his eyes met hers. 'But only if that's okay with you, Lady Antonia?'

No, it's not. It's actually extremely inconvenient, she thought, biting back a strong desire to tell him so. *And unfair.*

It felt as if the whole world was weighted against her, tipping her ever more into his orbit just when she had come to terms with their last encounter.

'It's really not very exciting,' she said.

'Good,' he said softly. 'I've had quite enough excitement in the last twenty-four hours.'

His eyes rested on her face, and for a second she couldn't breathe as his words wound around her skin.

'Well, I don't have any objections,' she lied. 'So, shall we get on? Or does anyone have anything they want to discuss before we leave? Any questions?'

There was a general shuffling of feet and then Johnny raised his hand. 'Just the one. Is Mr Wilder going to be using Lamington as a location for one of his films? Only Allan, here, got his drama badge in Scouts…'

Everyone roared with laughter.

Farlan grinned. 'That's my leading man sorted, then.'

Watching him, Nia felt dizzy. Most of the men who worked on the estate were reserved with strangers, and yet here they were, chatting to Farlan as if they'd known him their whole lives. As if he was one of them.

But Farlan had a knack of engaging with people... making them see the world differently, act differently. It was what made him such a successful film director, she thought. With him, everything seemed possible.

Unlike her family, he made everything feel as simple and certain as the heather-covered hills.

She had felt more sure of herself when she was with him. He had seen qualities in her that others had ignored...seen beneath the poise and reserve and made it clear how much he liked what he saw.

For those six months they'd been together she had never been happier. It had been an actual tingling feeling, like sherbet exploding on her tongue. And in that state of unending, incomparable happiness she had thought that she could have it all. Farlan and Lamington.

Only life didn't work like that. You could never have it all. Sacrifices had to be made.

But she hadn't wanted him to have to make them.

He'd had so much passion and talent and determination. He'd wanted to travel, to see the world and seize his place in it, and she hadn't been able to bear the idea of tethering him to her.

But without him her world had shrunk...grown small and domestic. The days had slipped by unmarked. Outside of Lamington's thick walls the seasons had changed, but she had stayed in hibernation, neither asleep nor awake.

Until yesterday.

'I'll drive.'

Her chin jerked up. He was beside her, and somehow the air no longer felt cold, but warm.

'Or do you not mind driving in the snow these days?'

It was a deliberate hook to their past, but if the last few days had taught her anything it was that returning to the past was a bad idea.

She glanced pointedly over his shoulder. 'I'm sure you'll have a lot more fun in one of the ATVs.'

'You didn't answer my question.'

'That's because the answer is irrelevant. I'm not spending all morning sitting in a car with you, Farlan.'

'Why not?'

'You know why,' she whispered, glancing over his shoulder again. Johnny and Allan were looking over at them curiously.

'You mean because you're worried you won't be able to keep your hands off me?' he murmured.

'I am *not*.'

'So what's the problem?'

You—you are the problem.

Biting her tongue, she stared at him in mute frustration. She didn't do confrontation very well. As an only child she'd never had to fight her corner, and by nature she was shy and moderate.

Now, though, she wished she could just get into her car and drive off, like a character in a film. But if she did that it would be all over the estate by noon, and then Tom and Diane might hear something, and—

'There is no problem,' she said crisply. 'But if you change your mind you'll have to walk back. This is a working estate, and some of us are still working.'

With twin bright spots of colour burning her cheeks, she got into the driver's seat and slammed the door.

As they slithered along the road he leaned back, stretching out his legs. 'It's pulling a little to the left— you might want to check the brakes.'

Staring stonily ahead, she followed the ATVs up over the snow-covered hills. Her heart had begun to thump loudly.

Last time they'd parted he had been tense and sparring for a fight, the heat from their kiss still flooding his veins. But his mood seemed lighter this morning. Probably because he was back in the director's seat. Or rather the passenger seat of her car.

'So where are we going?' he asked.

'Up to Inverside. It's at the far edge of the estate. We'll go there first and work our way back. The radio doesn't work so well around here, but if you want to listen to music there's a couple of CDs knocking around.'

At least that way she could just concentrate on driving and try and forget he was even there…

'Actually, I thought we could talk.'

Her spine tightened so swiftly she thought it might snap. 'Talk?'

'About what happened.'

She jerked round, her eyes widening with shock. When the car followed the direction of her gaze he reached across and gently straightened the steering wheel.

'You know… In the library.'

Her breath was trapped in her throat, the memory of that moment echoing through her like the bells of the local church.

This was one of the many differences between them. His directness.

Most of the people she knew—herself included— fudged things, and in the past she'd always admired Farlan's ability to go straight to the point.

Not right now, though.

'There's nothing to talk about,' she said.

She felt his gaze on her face.

'Really? So that's an everyday occurrence for you, is it?'

An everyday occurrence? Hardly.

Even now the memory of his lips on hers made her feel as if her skin was on fire. The last time she had kissed a man had been over a year ago, and it had borne no resemblance to what had happened with Farlan in the library.

She felt a prickle of guilt.

Andrew was quiet, and a little old-fashioned, but he was also sweet and generous. And sensitive. They could have had sex. She was on the pill to help manage her hormone-related migraines, and part of her had wanted to sleep with him—the same part that had wished she could fall in love with him.

But it hadn't felt right.

So she had told Andrew she wasn't ready and he had said he was happy to wait. Not once had he put pressure on her or badgered her for an explanation.

She frowned. What would she have said if he had?

Seven years was a long time *not* to get over someone.

Most people—her parents, for example—would think it was melodramatic and self-indulgent to hold on to pain for that long, to let the absence of something—

someone—put a grey filter over the rest of your life. But that was what it felt like to have loved and lost Farlan.

Not that she was about to tell *him* that.

Ignoring his question, she bumped over a snow-covered cattle grid.

'It shouldn't have happened.'

'And yet it did,' he pressed. 'You kissed me, and I kissed you back. In the library at Lamington Hall. What would the Earl and Countess of Brechin say?'

On the surface his tone was mild, as if he were just enjoying a pleasant conversation. But she heard the taunt in his voice, and the hurt pride.

'Where are they, by the way?' he asked.

'They're staying with my aunt and uncle in Dubai. My father needs a warmer climate for his chest.'

She parroted the 'official' explanation for her parents' decision to leave their home. The one that would allow them to hold their heads up high.

'Why didn't you go with them?'

'Lamington isn't just where I live,' she said quickly. 'I run the estate.'

That wasn't the only reason. Seeing her aunt and uncle would have been just too painful. But she couldn't explain why to Farlan—*especially* not to Farlan.

'Couldn't you get in a temporary manager?'

'That would just mean even more disruption for everyone.' She stared through the windscreen, over-concentrating on the road. 'Besides, I don't like the heat.'

'I wouldn't say that was true…'

Her mouth was suddenly dry, and she felt her belly

clench. She wanted him, but she was fighting the attraction.

'We're not doing this, Farlan,' she said slowly. 'I get that you're still angry with me for what I did. And I'm sorry I hurt you. If it makes you feel any better, I hurt myself too.'

In front of her, the ATVs were slowing. She watched distractedly as they stopped and parked in a line. Breathing out unsteadily, she stopped the car behind them, her fingers curling around the door handle.

'But we don't need to discuss what happened in the library. It was meaningless for both of us, I'm sure.' His eyes flickered but she ploughed on. 'It was a mistake. I wasn't thinking. But it won't happen again.'

She was already halfway out of the car. 'Now, if you don't mind, I need to get back to work.'

She was wrong, Farlan thought as he followed her across the snow. That kiss hadn't been meaningless for either of them. It had been too raw, too desperate, too spontaneous to be anything other than sheer compulsion.

Something she had confirmed in her next breath.

'It was a mistake. I wasn't thinking...'

His pulse dipped.

He was pretty sure that, like most people, Nia had chosen those particular words to distance herself from her actions, to make it sound as though there was some cosmic force in play over which she had no control.

Ironically, in claiming that, she'd made their kiss more, not less, meaningful.

Nia hadn't been thinking because lust didn't require thought.

Kissing her back hadn't required any input from *his* brain either.

Lust was an inarticulate craving, a wordless hunger that overrode logic and self-preservation.

The difference was he could admit that—privately anyway.

His chest tightened. For him, too, it had been involuntary. He hadn't wanted his body to respond to hers, and he was angry with her and himself.

She had lied to him seven years ago, deemed him unworthy, and he couldn't understand how he was still so drawn to her.

After what had so nearly happened in the cottage, he'd been sure he would call a halt. That he hadn't— or rather *couldn't*—had been the reason he'd been so brusque with her afterwards.

But, like hers, his mind and body had been playing push-me-pull-me with the past.

It was inevitable—and entirely predictable. Of *course* he wanted to taste her again.

Only now he wanted more than just a taste…

The rest of the morning was spent crossing the vast estate, checking the herds of deer and cattle and inspecting gates and fences.

Nia was a good boss, he thought, watching her with Johnny and the other men. Maybe that shouldn't have surprised him, but when he'd found out from Tom and Diane that she 'oversaw' the running of the estate, he'd been more than a little sceptical.

At nineteen, she'd been the smartest, most cultured person he'd ever met. And the sweetest. Picturing the shy, quiet girl of seven years ago, he'd found the idea of her running anything improbable, and had assumed that it was a vanity job for the daughter of the house.

But Nia clearly knew what she was doing. And it was clear that her staff liked and respected her. Probably because she listened and valued their opinions.

'How big is the estate?' he asked.

She turned. It would be natural to think that her cheeks were flushed from the cool air, but the slight tension around her jawline told a different story.

'It's just under twenty-eight thousand acres.'

He stared at her. Her hair had come loose and was framing her face, and he wondered why he'd thought she had lost her sparkle. There was a luminosity to her skin that rivalled the glittering snow, and the delicate curve of her jaw and high cheekbones made the faces of those around her look smudged and unfinished.

'And you manage it all?' Gazing across the white hills with their craggy outcrops, he couldn't help but be impressed.

'With help,' she said quickly. 'I couldn't possibly do it on my own. I don't have the expertise or the experience.'

'So what? I couldn't make a film on my own, but I'm still the director.'

She frowned, her forehead furrowing as a patch of sunlight bowled across her face. 'Exactly—you make it all happen,' she said.

'With help,' he echoed. He saw her eyes drop to his mouth and he smiled. 'I mean, I know how to work most of the equipment, but I'm no expert—and I certainly can't act. Although I have tried.'

He felt his heart start punching against his ribcage as her mouth fluttered at the corners.

'I thought that memory might be seared on your brain.' He screwed up his face. 'Probably trying a cockney accent was a little ambitious...'

She bit her lip. 'The high heels were a nice touch, though.'

His eyes held hers. 'Fortunately for me, you're my only witness.'

'True. But, unfortunately for you, I didn't sign an NDA.'

He knew he was staring at her again, but it was impossible to look away from her soft brown eyes and even softer pink lips.

'Oh, I can think of more enjoyable ways to stop you talking,' he said slowly, his eyes holding hers, letting her know what he wanted.

The silence shivered between them.

Watching her irises darken, he felt his body harden, and then her eyes jerked away from his as they heard someone shout.

It was lunchtime.

'Let me drive.'

Farlan held out his hand and this time Nia handed him the keys with some relief.

The Land Rover was a solid workhorse, but the brake pads were a little worn and sometimes it felt as if the wheels were slipping away from her.

And Farlan liked driving. He had that combination of focus and control that made it look effortless.

Suddenly she realised he had peeled off from the

line of ATVs heading down to the lake. 'Where are you going?'

'You did say there'd be time for a little fun later.'

'And you said that you had a call with your producer—'

'I'll speak to him tomorrow. Right now, you and I have a date with a hill and a sledge.'

A date.

The air thumped out of her lungs, his words spinning inside her head, glittering and fragile, like a flurry of snowflakes.

'I don't have a sledge with me,' she said quickly.

'Actually, you do.' He grinned. 'I borrowed Allan's. It's in the back.'

He slowed the car. 'Come on, Nia. It's just a bit of fun. For old times' sake.' His mouth tugged at the corners.

She felt her heart hurtle as if it was on a sledge already. He was so hard to resist, and she could feel herself responding, her body unfurling as if it was reawakening after long years of hibernation.

After what had happened in the library she knew it was too risky. Only refusing would make him more determined to persuade her. He was single-minded, driven in a way she had never understood and couldn't hope to emulate.

And his eyes were so soft and intent…

'We did have fun, didn't we? It wasn't all bad,' he murmured.

Her stomach flipped over.

It had been glorious. A daisy chain of perfect hours. He had made her laugh and dream and *live*.

'It was never bad,' she said quietly.

Not until the end.

Now, more than anything, she wished she could change that.

Maybe this would make that wish come true?

'Your choice, Nia.'

She glanced down at the disappearing ATVs and then moments later, the car crested the slope.

Beneath them, the estate stretched out towards the Cairngorms in the distance. Even after all these years it still took her breath away, and always when she came up here she felt humbled.

It was epically beautiful.

But that wasn't why her heart was knocking against her ribs. After everything she'd promised herself this morning, she'd almost lost her head again a moment ago when they were talking, but now his eyes on hers were clear and determined.

'I'll get the sledge,' he said softly.

Tiny shavings of snow fluttered past her eyes. It would be too risky, too easy to lose track of time. They should come back tomorrow, or another day.

But she couldn't say the words out loud—didn't want to risk losing the sweetness of this renewed intimacy.

And yet... 'The forecast is for more snow—'

'Come on, Nia,' he urged. 'When was the last time you had some fun?'

That was easy. She knew the day...the date. She could probably tell him the exact time too. It had been a day just like this—a day of pure white snow and happiness and wonder.

How could she resist that? *Him?*

Five minutes later she was standing at the top of the hill, gazing down the slope.

'Ready?' he asked.

She nodded.

Farlan was beside her, his green eyes glittering. Taking her hand, he pulled her onto the sledge, slotting her in between his legs. His arm curved around her waist, anchoring her close to him.

She had missed this.

She had missed *him* so much.

And it felt so right—as if their bodies recognised each other.

He brought his face close to hers and she felt his stubble graze her cheek.

'Hold tight,' he instructed.

Time rewound. She was back in Holyrood Park and Farlan was in love with her. He was seconds away from asking her to marry him.

She was trying to stay strong, detached. But his nearness suffocated her resolve…her senses reacted dizzily to the snatch of his breath and the smooth muscles of his thighs on either side of hers.

Leaning back against him, she closed her eyes, her fingers gripping his arms as the sledge skimmed over the snow.

The hard heat of his body melted the minutes away. When she glanced up at the sky next, it was bleached of colour, and had that clarity that preceded a blizzard.

As the wind began whipping up the snow, she felt a prickle of warning. 'We should probably go back now. It's getting late and it's quite a way.'

They could go off-road, but it would be risky. Drifts

could make it impossible to gauge how deep the snow was, and there were hidden obstacles—ditches, rocks that could take a tyre out...

'Just one more time?'

He phrased it as a question, but she knew it was a formality. He'd already made up his mind.

As if to prove her point, he smiled at her—that smile no one could resist.

She hesitated. There was just a fingernail of sun left in the sky. 'I'm not sure that would be a good idea.'

The temperature was already dropping, and she knew from experience that in this kind of environment minutes mattered.

'I really think—' she began.

But it was too late. He was already pulling her against the heat of his body.

As they ploughed into the snow at the bottom of the hill she glanced back over her shoulder.

The sky was quivering.

Pulling out her phone, she felt a sudden panic as she saw that she had no signal.

'Farlan, we need to leave before it starts snowing.'

It already was. As she spoke, fat, shaggy flakes began to drift and spin down from the sky.

Inside the car, he began fiddling with the heater.

'It doesn't work,' she said quietly.

She should have said something earlier. Farlan hadn't been in Scotland for so long he'd probably forgotten how swiftly the weather could deteriorate.

'Which way?' he asked.

'Head towards the lake.' She glanced up at the putty-coloured clouds. Hopefully they would get back to the road before the snow got any heavier.

They didn't.

She watched, with a sense of dread building in her chest, as the windscreen wipers began to grind against the snow.

He turned to her.

'Is there somewhere we could go? A barn, maybe?' His voice was calm, but she could see the tension in his shoulders. 'Some kind of shelter?'

She shook her head. 'There's nothing close…' Her stomach clenched with a rush of hope. 'No—that's not true. There's the bothy. It shouldn't be locked, but—'

Her eyes found his and, reaching out, he gently touched her cheek. 'Only one way to find out.'

It was difficult to see now. Outside the car everything was a tumbling mass of white, as if a feather duvet had burst.

'I think that's it,' she said hoarsely.

Up ahead, there was a dark, angular shape. The Land Rover crunched over the snow towards it with agonising slowness, the wind blotting out the whine of the transmission. As it juddered to a standstill, Farlan yanked up the handbrake.

'Wait in the car.'

He was gone before she could speak. Left alone, she tried to stay calm. What if they couldn't get in?

She checked her phone: still no signal.

The door opened. He was back, snowflakes glittering at the ends of his long, dark lashes.

'It's open. And there's a place where we can put the

car. I just need to clear away some snow. Do you think you could drive? I might have to push if it gets stuck.'

As she nodded, he reached past her and grabbed a shovel.

'Give me five minutes.'

She clambered into the driver's seat and then slowly began inching the car forward. Even though she was shivering with cold, she could feel perspiration trickling down her back.

The windscreen wipers were too clogged to move now, and she drove blind until suddenly the noise of the wind faded. With relief, she stopped the car.

'Are you okay?' Farlan slid in beside her.

She started to nod, but he was frowning.

'You're shivering. Here.'

He yanked off his jacket and wrapped it around her. The lining of his jacket still held the heat of his body. How was he so warm? she thought.

'I'm sorry,' she said. 'This is my fault.'

'How?' His forehead creased. 'You tried to tell me and I wouldn't listen. But it'll be okay.'

He pulled out his phone and glanced at the screen.

'The signal's pretty weak, but I'll text Tom. Hopefully it'll get through at some point.'

With an effort, she kept her voice steady. 'It's probably safer to stay here overnight. Unless you want someone to come and get us?'

There was a silence. Gazing into his eyes, she felt her brain jam. As he leaned forward and brushed a strand of hair away from her face she shivered again, but not from cold.

The car felt suddenly small. Every breath, every

heartbeat, was separate and audible. She could feel the leather beneath her legs and his fingers warm against her cheek.

'I don't want that,' he said softly.

The air rushed out of her body. She could feel his gaze but she couldn't look at him—knew that if she did he would see everything: her regret, her need, her hope.

'What do you want, Farlan?' she asked finally.

He didn't answer, and as the silence stretched she wondered if her words had got lost in her heartbeat.

Then, reaching over, he gently turned her face to his.

Everything blurred. She thought she was gripping the steering wheel to stop the car sliding sideways, only to realise that it wasn't moving.

'Let me show you.'

Her pulse jolted and then he lowered his mouth to hers and kissed her.

CHAPTER FIVE

NIA FELT HERSELF catch fire. His thumbs captured her face. She felt his mouth brush over hers, gentle at first and then harder, his tongue parting her lips. His hands were sliding over her body, pulling her across the car so that she was straddling him.

The space was so small that her shoulder scraped against the window.

He was very hard. She could feel him through the layers of their clothing, feel the rawness of his desire.

Heat was flooding her limbs.

She kissed him back clumsily, her mouth seeking his, her hands winding around his neck.

He drew her closer, fumbling with the front of her jacket, tugging her arms free.

She felt his hands slide under her jumper, his fingers warm and decisive against her bare skin, gasping out loud as he caressed her stomach.

Heat rippled across her body as his hands splayed against her back to find the clasp of her bra, and then his palms were cupping her breasts, the thumbs finding her nipples.

Hunger reared up inside her.

She moaned, wanting more of his touch, more of his mouth, and as though he could follow her thoughts he tipped her head, baring her throat to his lips and then, lowering his face, taking one nipple into the heat of his mouth.

Breath shuddering, she shifted against him, pushing down against the hard press of his erection, wanting, needing, to appease the pulsing ache between her thighs. And then she was pulling at his belt, her fingers yanking at the leather, releasing him—

'Nia—Nia, I don't have any condoms.'

Condoms.

Her eyes fluttered open as the word echoed inside her head.

'I mean, I wasn't expecting to—'

His face was taut with concentration and she could tell from the tremor in his voice that he was holding himself in check, expecting, waiting for her to call a halt. All it would take was one word.

'I'm on the pill.' She hesitated. 'Are you…? I mean—'

'You don't need to worry.' He took her face in his hands. 'I don't normally do this.'

'I don't either,' she whispered.

He kissed her deeply and then, lifting her hair, let his mouth find her throat.

'So are you—? Do you still want to—?'

To answer him she reached down and took him in her hand, her fingers closing around his solid, straining length.

He pulled her closer, his breath jerking against her mouth, and then he kissed her hard, his hands pushing beneath the waistband of her trousers and panties, yanking them down.

She was lifting her hips, trying to help him. Her head bumped into the roof of the car but she didn't care. Nothing mattered except dousing this heat that was both necessary and merciless.

His eyes tangled with hers and she felt him push up and push through. And then he was inside her, hot and hard and sleek, and she was reaching for him blindly, moving with an urgency that robbed her of thought, leaving only a shapeless elemental craving.

The car was rocking from side to side. It was sex at its most basic. A frenzied assault on their senses, their mouths and hands frantic.

'Look at me, Nia.'

His voice was hoarse, his breathing staccato.

She squeezed her thighs together, chasing the heat, feeling Farlan grow even harder, and then she tensed, muscles clenching, nails digging into his jumper, body melting around his as he stiffened and shuddered inside her.

Heart pounding, she lay limply against Farlan's chest, her face buried in his jumper, breathing in the warm scent of his body.

The damp stickiness between her thighs was already growing cold, and her leg ached where it was wedged against the door, but she was too busy struggling with the reality of what they had just done to care.

What she had just done.

The consequences of her actions exploded inside her head in the same way that Farlan had just exploded inside her body.

She knew she should regret it. It had probably made everything a hundred times more awkward between them, and giving in to temptation had been weak and selfish and wrong. And yet how could anything that had felt so good, so right, be wrong?

It had been like skating together on a frozen lake. For those few miraculous moments they had been in harmony, their bodies perfectly synchronised, every touch, every breath flowing like water.

Farlan shifted against her—and just like that she heard the ice crack beneath them, and a cool, relentless thread of reality begin winding its way up through her body.

But this wasn't just about her and her feelings…

'Nia—'

His voice was hoarse, uncertain. Fearing his regret, or worse, she kept her head lowered. Just for a moment she wanted to linger here, in his arms, cocooned in this snow-covered vehicle, in the space between hope and fantasy, where their mutual hunger had distorted time and merged the past with the present.

'Nia.'

There was no escaping his hand, and as he tilted her face up to his there was no escaping his questioning eyes either.

But he didn't speak again, and she felt her heart begin beating faster once more.

She had been foolish and reckless, but not a day passed when she didn't feel some kind of regret for the way she had acted, for the way her life had turned out.

She was tired of living with regrets, and she didn't want to add these moments to the list. Whatever he said now—whatever happened next—she had wanted Farlan and he had wanted her.

Maybe she hadn't been in control of herself or her hunger, but acting on her desire had made her feel more powerful and alive than she had in years, and she wouldn't—*she couldn't*—wish that away.

She took a breath. 'I'm not expecting you to feel the same way…' The words spilled out of her mouth. 'But I just want you to know that I don't regret it.'

There—she had said it.

She couldn't go back in time.

She couldn't unpick the mess she had made or erase the memories.

But if this was the last moment they shared she was glad that she had told him the truth. Glad that in the future she could look back and know that this time, at least, they hadn't parted with mistrust and confusion.

'I don't regret it either.'

His hands tangled in her hair, bunching it in his fists as if to prevent her escape. He kissed her again, his mouth heating hers.

'How could I regret that? Did you think I would? That I could?'

He seemed confused, almost stunned. And, meeting his gaze, she saw that he looked as blindsided as she felt.

'I don't know.' She stopped. 'Maybe. It all happened so fast.'

Except it hadn't—not really.

Ever since Farlan had walked into the drawing room five days ago she had felt as though she was standing at the shore, watching a wave build out at sea, waiting for it to come crashing over her head.

Only the details—the time, the place—had been unscripted. As had the aftermath.

'I didn't plan it—'

'I know.'

The gentleness of his voice made her still inside. Made her remember and regret. Last time she hadn't said enough and she had made a mess of everything. This time she didn't want there to be any misunderstandings.

'You don't need to worry. This was a one-off. I'm not expecting anything from you. I know this kind of thing can happen.'

She knew she was speaking too quickly—babbling, in fact. But this was a different kind of truth. One that she didn't want to tell. And just saying it out loud hurt.

She didn't want to linger on it, or have to see the relief in his eyes, and so, shifting her weight, she leaned sideways and rooted around on the floor for their jackets.

'Apparently so,' he said.

As she handed him his jacket his green eyes locked onto hers, his expression impassive, impossible to read.

'And, just so we're clear, I'm not expecting anything from you either.' Reaching up he pushed her hair away from her face. 'So, no regrets, then?'

The past swelled up between them, but there was too much to say, too many words for this cramped space.

She shook her head.

'Good.' Leaning forward, he kissed her, gently at first, then harder. 'Then maybe we should get inside, otherwise we *will* have something to regret. Like catching hypothermia.'

* * *

Slamming the door against a flurry of windborne snow-flakes, Farlan felt shame heat his face.

Had he really just made a joke about hypothermia?

His jaw tightened. He was savagely, crushingly furious with himself.

He might not have been in Scotland for seven years, but he understood the dangers of a blizzard.

Having spent his teenage years on a farm, he knew that freezing temperatures and snowdrifts killed livestock. And they killed humans too.

If their phones had had any signal then they would probably have got away with nothing worse than a few scary hours sitting in a whiteout, waiting for a rescue party. But without a phone signal, in a car without a working heater, they were always going to be in trouble.

And yet, despite knowing what was at stake, he had ignored Nia—ignored her when she had first told him that there was more snow forecast, and then again when the sky had started to bleach out.

She had tried to persuade him to leave, but instead of listening, instead of letting her change his mind, he had overridden her natural and legitimate concerns about the weather and the distance they would need to travel to reach the road.

He had told himself that a couple more minutes wouldn't matter either way.

But it had mattered.

Only what had mattered more to him—what always mattered the most—was that he had stayed firm.

It was like a badge of honour never to let himself be

swayed, and because of that he had put his life, Nia's life, in jeopardy.

'We should probably light a fire.'

She had turned to face him, and in the brighter light of the bothy he saw that she was pale and shivering again.

Galvanised into action, he swore softly and, grabbing her hand, towed her across the room to one of the sofas that sat on either side of a cast-iron wood burner.

'I'll do that. You sit here.'

He glanced around. Next to the sofa there was a basket stacked high with colourful plaid woollen blankets and, tugging two from the pile, he wrapped them around Nia's shoulders.

It was the easiest fire he'd ever built. The kindling was already neatly arranged in the grate, and the logs were so well-seasoned the wood burner roared into life almost as soon as he lit the match.

She started to stand up. 'I'll make some tea—'

'Sit.' He pushed her firmly back down. 'I can make tea, Nia.'

In the kitchen, he found the tea easily, and there was long-life milk next to the tea caddy. He poured out two cups and then, catching sight of a bottle of Laphroaig, he put the milk down and took the whisky instead. Unscrewing the bottle, he tipped a measure into her cup, then his own.

The liquid burned his throat twice, heat and peat, but he was glad—grateful to have something to offset the panic building in his chest.

If the snow had got heavier more quickly…

If they had been headed in a slightly different direction…

The 'ifs' piled up like snowdrifts.

He watched her take a sip of tea, his head swimming with all the possible alternative outcomes they had so narrowly avoided.

'It could have been so much worse,' he said quietly. 'If we hadn't found this place when we did.'

He could see the car in his mind's eye a tiny speck on a white landscape, drifts of snow swallowing it whole. He felt the sharp quickening of terror. The thought was unbearable.

'I'm fine, Farlan.'

Looking up, he found her watching him, her brown eyes reddish gold in the firelight. His heart twisted with guilt. She was worried about him.

Worried. About *him*.

The fact that she could feel that way, given his utter recklessness, stunned him.

'Nia…' Taking her hand, he pulled her against him, guilt swamping his anger. 'This is my fault. This is all my fault,' he muttered.

'How is it your fault?'

She sounded almost cross, and when he looked down at her he saw that she was frowning.

'I'm not a simpleton or a child, Farlan. I've lived here all my life. I know the risks. I should have made it clearer. Insisted.'

His mouth twisted. 'You tried. I didn't listen.'

She bit her lip. 'Then I should have said it louder,' she said quietly. 'Stuck to my guns. But, as you know, I've never been very good at that.'

Remembering how the snow had blotted out the windscreen, he stared at her in silence. No, she wasn't any good at sticking to her guns. And he had crucified her for that fact—at the time and then for years afterwards.

Put simply, she had been wrong and he had been wronged. Only now he was beginning to see another side to her actions—and to his response.

Back then he had been angry with Nia for listening to her parents even though she'd been a teenager and he'd been asking her to give up everything she had ever known for him—a boy. And at twenty-two he had still been more a boy than a man.

Persuading her to spend another ten, fifteen, twenty minutes sledging was different. That's what he'd told himself.

But all that was different was he was the one doing the persuading.

And that was what mattered. It was what had always mattered.

But he couldn't explain to Nia why he needed to have that power. Not here, not now, and truthfully probably not ever.

To explain would mean talking about his past, revealing the pitiful details of a life he would rather forget—a life he'd worked hard to forget.

Maybe if he and Nia had worked out he might have told her some of it. But after what had happened he didn't trust her, and he doubted he ever would.

His eyes flicked to her face.

None of that was important right now.

Reaching out, he caught her hand in his. 'It's not your

fault, Nia. I should have listened, and I didn't, and I'm sorry. Sorry for putting you in danger.'

He tightened his fingers around hers, wanting, needing, to feel the warmth of her skin.

'It's just that once I make up my mind, I find it hard to change it. You might have noticed I have a bit of a thing about that...'

He'd been trying to lighten the mood, but as she looked up at him he felt his heart slow, and all at once he was conscious only of how badly he wanted to pull her closer.

And not just to comfort her.

He let the silence drift as their eyes met. Hers were soft with whisky and fatigue and something else— something that made his thoughts turn to slow flurries.

Unthinkingly, he leaned forward, his body tingling as her lips parted. Around them the air shivered, the heat from the stove pushed against them—

They both jerked apart as a familiar sound broke the silence.

A text alert.

Her phone, not his.

'I should—'

'Of course.'

He watched, his pulse jumping with a sudden and disproportionate agitation, as she checked the message.

'It's Allan,' she said, looking down at the screen. 'He just wants to know if we got back okay.'

They hadn't. And when Allan found that out, then what?

Those ATVs did exactly what their name suggested.

They went anywhere, on any terrain. It would take two maybe three hours tops for a rescue party to reach them.

He felt himself tense. *If Nia wanted to be rescued.*

She was edging away from him, texting back.

'What are you saying?'

Her eyes lifted to his and his hand moved from her waist to her hair, his fingers sliding among the strands.

'Just that we're safe, and that we'll be fine until morning.'

Until morning.

In other words they would be spending the night together.

He felt his groin turn to stone with a speed that was predictable and painful.

And pointless.

What had happened had been a one-off, right?

Loosening his grip, not wanting her to feel that he was hard again already, he nodded.

'Yes, we will.'

He forced his gaze away from her face, from the swell of the breasts that she had so recently bared to his mouth, to the far less arousing pile of logs that were stacked with aesthetic symmetry on either side of the wood burner.

'So, first I'm going to get that fire going properly, and then we should see if there's anything to eat.'

Nia looked down at their knees, almost touching, and frowned. 'We should probably get out of these damp clothes.'

He knew what she meant, but it didn't stop a tug of longing, sharp like hunger, from pulling at him inside. Or keep her eyes from jerking away from his.

'Good idea,' he said, letting her off. 'We can dry them by the fire.'

He unlaced his boots and yanked them off. Straightening up, he reached for his belt, his fingers suddenly clumsy as he realised it was still undone.

Their eyes met.

'Don't worry, I trust you not to take advantage of me,' he teased.

She smiled then, as he'd hoped she would, and began pulling off her trousers.

The kitchen was well-stocked.

'Well, we won't starve anyway,' he said, holding up a tin of caviar and a jar of Fortnum and Mason porcini and truffle tomato sauce.

'I'll put some pasta on,' she replied.

As she bent down to pull out a pan, his eyes were drawn irresistibly to the length of her legs—more specifically to where the hem of her jumper rode high on her thighs.

He felt the muscles in his arms twitch. If he was on set, he would be yelling *Action!* right now. Suddenly, the urge to reach over and pull her against him was almost overwhelming.

'There might even be some parmesan,' she said.

Dragging his gaze away, he opened the fridge.

There wasn't. But there was a bottle of Bollinger champagne.

'Nia—' he began.

Turning, she caught sight of the bottle, and then his face, and burst out laughing. 'I suppose we do have something to celebrate.'

Farlan felt his blood lighten. He liked hearing her laugh and watching her smile. It made him think about something other than making movies. It made him forget the past.

They had a picnic by the fire. Sitting cross-legged, they ate caviar with crackers, followed by pasta and then to finish, figs in port.

'That has to be one of the best meals I've ever eaten,' he said, bouncing a smile across the space between them.

He leaned back and let his gaze slowly track around the room. Bothies were supposed to be basic. Just four walls and a roof to give temporary shelter to a hiker or a hunter stranded by dangerous weather.

That had been his experience anyway, the one and only other time he'd stayed in one.

His shoulders tensed. He'd been with his brother Cam, camping. The tail-end of a hurricane had dumped a month's worth of rain in a matter of hours.

It had been the last summer before his brother had left to go on the oil rigs.

Before Farlan's life had imploded again.

Before Cam had become the latest in the ever-lengthening line of people who had made a choice that wasn't him.

Heading off the traces of fear and misery that always accompanied those memories, he glanced past Nia at the plum-coloured chenille sofas that sat on either side of the huge log burner, wondering why the sight of them made a beat of anger pulse down his spine.

'This is a nice place,' he said tightly. 'Maybe a bit spartan for my tastes—'

A flush of cochineal spread slowly over her cheeks. 'It was one of my mother's projects. She had a very specific vision.'

The fine hairs rose at the nape of his neck. He knew all about the Countess of Brechin's vision—insofar as he knew he hadn't ever been a part of it. But Nia's parents had intruded in his life anyway. They had taken away the girl he'd loved, deprived him of the future he'd planned, and he wasn't going to let them get inside his head again now.

'I'm just playing with you,' he said. Softening his expression, he reached over and picked up a faded copy of *Tatler*. 'I guess I was expecting something a little more rudimentary. The last bothy I stayed in had no electricity or running water.'

She nodded. 'They are mostly like that—the ones that anyone can use. But this part of the estate is private and—and it was just a bit of fun, really.'

He didn't like seeing that wariness in her eyes. Knowing he was the cause of it made him like it even less.

'She did a good job. It's beautiful,' he said.

Looking across into her pale, upturned face, he felt his heartbeat ricochet against his ribcage.

'But not as beautiful as you,' he added quietly.

They stared at one another in silence, and again he felt the shock of what they had just done.

What he wanted to do again.

It had felt so right, being inside her, holding her. He had known that holding her was unnecessary, and self-indulgent, that he'd needed to break the mood, only he'd been powerless to move.

Nia had done that.

He thought back to what she'd said in the car.

'I'm not expecting anything from you. I know this kind of thing can happen...'

Was that true?

For him? No. That would require some kind of pre-existing relationship, and there had been no one since Nia. Hooking up with someone you had slept with once hardly qualified.

But for her? Had there been others since him?

He felt a sting of anger. Was that why she was on the pill? Was there some ex in the mix? Someone more recent?

His hands clenched.

Even before he'd started making movies he'd always had an ability to play things out in his head scene by scene. He'd always seen it as a gift, but now, picturing Nia, her lips kissing some nameless man, their bodies entwined in a tangle of sheets, he felt jealousy burn through him.

Suddenly he wanted to ask her why she was on the pill—except that would sound completely mad.

But this whole week had been crazy...

Coming back to Scotland, to Lamington, seeing Nia. Then today, being out there in a blizzard and having sex with her in the car like a teenager. And now being in here, with the two of them half-naked...

No wonder he wasn't himself.

Watching her kneel in front of the stove, he felt his pulse stumble. The log looked huge and brutal in her hand and, remembering the moment when the snow had blotted out the light, he felt a flare of fear, worse than before.

Putting his hand on her arm, he pulled her against him, curling his arm around her body, needing to feel the slow, steady beat of her heart. She rested her head on his shoulder and together they watched the fire in silence.

'I'm sorry,' he said.

'I'm sorry too,' she said quietly.

'No.' Shifting her weight, he looked down into her face. 'I told you—you have no reason to be sorry.'

'I wasn't talking about now.'

He stilled.

'I'm talking about what happened before. With us. How it happened. What I did and what I didn't do.'

There was a long pause.

Nia felt her throat tighten. His expression didn't alter, but there was new tension in him, like the warning hum from the electric fences on the estate.

'Hey, let's not do this right now.'

He spoke easily, but again she sensed the tension, and could hear the unspoken plea. *Don't mess with the mood.*

She hesitated, but she couldn't sit there and leave other words unspoken.

Her mouth firmed. She should have said something earlier. Only with his green gaze resting on her face, and his warm body so close, she had got lost in the moment and in her memories.

It would be so easy just to lie here next to him and listen to the sound of his breathing. But soon he would get up and leave, and once again she would be left with only memories.

It had been seven years. She needed to live. To move on. To kiss again, to love again. She couldn't do that unless she put the past behind her. And to do that she had to face what she had done—admit the truth.

'I need to say this. There were so many things I got wrong b-before—' the word snagged on her tongue '—things I didn't say. I want to say them now. I want you to know all of it.'

Maybe not everything.

She couldn't betray her aunt and uncle like that.

But she could make him understand.

'When we went to Lamington that day I was nervous. I knew my parents wouldn't be happy for me, but I didn't think they would be so utterly opposed to the idea. When they were, I panicked.' Her eyes found his. 'I should have left with you, but I thought I could talk them round.'

'But they talked you round instead.'

The bitterness in his voice whipped against her skin.

'No.' She shook her head. 'No. Of course, I listened to them—'

'Why "of course"? It was *our* lives—not theirs.'

'I was nineteen, Farlan.' She only just found the words. 'And I know you don't like them, and what my father said was completely unacceptable—'

'*Unacceptable?*' He shifted backwards. His whole body was shaking. 'It was appalling. He said I was a nobody.'

Her body felt as if it was splitting in two. To hear her father say those words had been horrifying. Hearing Farlan repeat them now made her feel sick—actually physically sick.

'He was wrong. You were never a nobody. You were—*you are*—the most amazing man I've ever met.'

Her heart was pounding and the need for him to feel the truth of her words was overriding everything else, even the shuttered expression on his face.

'But this is my life, Farlan. I don't think you ever understood that. I don't think I really understood it either. Until that day when we came back to the estate.'

He let his hand drop down to his side. 'You were my life, Nia, and I was supposed to be yours.'

'And you were…' She faltered for a moment. 'But even if I had done what you asked of me—if I had left my family, my home, Scotland—it wouldn't have been for ever. I would have had to come back to Lamington in the end.'

He grimaced. 'Lamington. Always Lamington. It's just a house, Nia. A really big house, but still just a bunch of bricks and mortar. And you're a snob.'

She felt a fluttering anger rise up inside her. 'And *you're* an inverted snob. You know nothing about Lamington. Or me.'

'Oh, I know everything about you, Lady Antonia.'

'No, you don't,' she snapped. 'Lamington isn't just "a really big house", it's part of the village. We employ local people, train them, support them—'

'More like exploit them,' he said coldly.

'How dare you?' She felt her face dissolving in shock. 'They're like family to me.

'Paid family.' He shook his head slowly, the green of his eyes sharp like broken glass.

'Yes—paid. Like me.' Her voice was shaking. 'I have a role here too, Farlan. And responsibilities. And a vision that's every bit as important to me as your films are to you. Only you don't understand that, or like it, or value it, and that's why I broke up with you.'

It was suddenly difficult to speak past the lump in her throat.

'Nia—'

She put up a hand. 'I know my parents. They are snobs, and they're difficult, and sometimes I don't like them very much but I knew they would come round in the end. Only then I thought about what that would really mean. I knew that you loved me, and that you would give up everything for me, just like I was going to do for you, only I knew how unhappy that would make you, and I couldn't do that to you,' she whispered.

Lowering her head, she hugged her knees to her chest.

'Why didn't you tell me?' She heard his intake of breath, and then two strong arms curved beneath her. 'No, you don't need to answer that.'

She felt Farlan's lips brush against her hair.

'I know why. I didn't give you a chance.'

His arms tightened around her.

'I'm sorry. I should have let you talk on the phone that day, but I was so furious, and hurt…'

He sounded defensive.

Looking up, she saw that his mouth was set in a grim line. 'I know,' she said. 'I should never have told you on the phone. I was going to come to the station, but then, when I heard your voice, I couldn't bear it, so I told you, and you were so angry. I couldn't think of the words I needed to say, and then you just hung up—'

There was a long silence. A muscle was working in his cheek.

'I tried to call you back,' she said. 'I tried so many times. But your phone—'

'I threw it away.' He smiled humourlessly. 'Big mistake. My whole life was on that phone.'

Her eyes slid away from his. So many misunderstandings.

'I'm sorry.' She felt sick. 'I made a mess of everything.'

She felt his fingers touch her face, tilt up her chin.

'*We* made a mess of everything. Maybe if we'd been older, or if we'd waited a bit longer or gone travelling first—'

But it was more than that. It was easy to blame their break-up on tiny individual decisions, but none of that would have mattered if they'd been meant to be together.

Lovers who were at cross-purposes didn't stay lovers for long for one obvious reason. For a relationship to work, you needed to be able to communicate with each other, and she and Farlan had only ever communicated effectively on one level.

Her heart skipped a beat and, looking up, she found him watching her, his gaze steady and unblinking. A current of heat spiralled up inside her.

For a moment neither of them moved.

'Nia…'

He spoke her name softly and she felt her mouth turn dry.

'What happened in the car—'

'Shouldn't have happened,' she said quickly.

His hand slid among the strands of her hair. 'You said that about what happened in the library.'

'I know.' She bit her lip. 'We can't—'

'You don't want to?'

She stared at him mutely. It was a rhetorical question—they both knew that.

'We didn't plan it. It just happened. It had to happen. I don't know why.'

She knew he was right. It had felt like a compulsion—a desperate need that had overridden all rational thought. Only however frantic it had been, it had still been opportunistic. Like finding fallen apples in an orchard. But this—this would be like picking them off the tree.

She met his gaze, felt panic mingling with desire, and something in his eyes steadied her.

'It's not wrong, Nia, to want what we had.' Lowering his face, he let his lips graze hers. 'To want to make it right for just a few hours.'

They couldn't change the past. They couldn't go back to being those two young lovers. But would it be so very wrong to steal back a few hours of that time?

'One night…' She breathed it out against his mouth, and then, wrapping her arms around his neck, she shifted against him, slotting herself over the hard ridge of his erection.

'Yes, one night.' His voice was hoarse. 'If that's what you want, Nia?'

'Yes…' she whispered and, clasping his face in her hands, she kissed him.

CHAPTER SIX

SHE MADE A little sound as her lips touched his, her stomach swooping upwards like a fish on a hook. There was no need for caution. No need to balance her desire with quantifiable reality.

This wasn't about the past or the future.

There would be no tomorrow.

But she wanted this. She wanted him. And that was enough.

'Let's just have one last night, Farlan. Just you and me. And in the morning it'll be like a dream.' Leaning forward, she brushed her lips against his again, breathing in his scent. 'A beautiful dream.'

He closed his eyes, and she felt a chaos of hope and hunger beneath her skin, and then he kissed her again, and the flowering intensity of his desire made her whole body tremble.

'Wait—' With a groan, he broke the kiss and, scooping her into his arms, carried her to the sofa. 'You're probably already black and blue from earlier. This time we're going to take it slow.'

She stared up at him, her blood turning to air. And then he lowered his mouth to hers.

He tasted warm and smoky from the whisky, and she felt a fluttering heat rise up inside her as he parted her lips, kissing her fiercely, opening his mouth to her, deepening the kiss.

Only she wanted more.

'Take it off,' she whispered against his mouth. And, grabbing the hem of his sweater, he tugged it up and over his head.

Heart thudding, Nia did the same.

His eyes narrowed, and with deliberate slowness she reached behind her back and unhooked her bra, peeling the delicate straps away from her shoulders and breasts.

The air between them crackled like the wood in the fire.

Glancing up at his bare chest, she felt her breath catch.

It was the first time she had seen him naked, or nearly naked, in seven years, and her beautiful boy had filled out. To be so close, to have the freedom to touch him, stripped away all and any inhibition she might have felt.

She leaned forward and touched his skin. It was warm and a pale golden colour, like lightly toasted bread. Gently, she traced the contoured lines of his obliques, and then, with fingers that shook slightly, she stroked the fine hairs that ran down the middle of his stomach to where they disappeared beneath the waistband of his trunks.

He jerked backwards, his eyes narrowing, and then his hand caught hers. Glancing down, she felt her mouth dry. He was hard already, his erection tenting against the soft cotton…

* * *

Gazing down at Nia, Farlan felt his body turn to stone. He'd had no idea that her near nakedness could bring such a ferment of desire.

He had touched her in the car, but he hadn't been looking at her—really looking at her. Now that he was, he just wanted to gaze and gaze, to drink in the soft curve of her breasts and their taut, ruched tips.

But he couldn't not touch her.

Leaning forward, he kissed her shoulder, her collarbone, chasing the pulse in the insanely smooth skin of her throat to the hollow behind her ear.

His groin was aching, the pain almost at that peak where it was pleasurable. Lifting his head, he found her mouth again, maddened by its shape, and its softness, and by the flutter of her breath against his lips. Slowly, he teased the bow of her mouth, top and then bottom, his head starting to spin as she moaned softly.

Heat flared inside him.

He was so hard already, but he could wait. He had waited, he realised a moment later. Always he had been waiting—for this moment, with this woman.

His hand slid over her face and he pulled her closer, cupping her cheek. He kissed her again, parting her lips, tasting her, breathing her in.

Reaching out, he touched her breast, covering it with the palm of his hand, feeling the tiny shivers of anticipation dance over her skin as the nipple hardened.

'Nia,' he whispered. 'My beautiful Nia.'

Her brown eyes were drowsy with desire. She stroked his face, running her finger over his jaw, scraping the stubble, teasing his mouth with her thumb.

He dragged in a breath as her other hand began to caress the thick length of his erection. It would be all over quickly if he let her carry on doing that.

Capturing her hands, he raised them above her head and licked slowly down her body, his groin throbbing as she squirmed and arched beneath him.

When he reached the triangle of soft curls he parted her with his tongue, flattening it against her swollen clitoris, feeling her unfold, tamping down the decadent ache spreading out inside him.

He let go of her hands and her fingers found his head, pressing him closer, and then closer still, and then she was moving more urgently. 'I want you inside me.'

She was pulling him up and over her body, her hands skimming his ribs. Now he let her take him in her hand, her thumb smoothing over the hard, straining head as she fed him inside the slick heat between her thighs.

His body was starting to shake.

Sliding his hand under her bottom, he raised her hips, wanting more depth, and then she was reaching up, clasping his face in her hands, kissing him as he began to move rhythmically with her, their bodies blurring as she arched upwards and he surged inside her.

Inching backwards, Farlan gently lifted Nia's arm from his chest and waited, holding his breath as she murmured in her sleep.

But she didn't wake, and after a couple more seconds he felt around on the floor for his trunks, pulled them on and then made his way silently across the room, using the red glow of the fire to find his way in the darkness.

In the kitchen, he found a glass and filled it from

the tap, gulping the ice-cold water greedily, thinking that the hollowed-out feeling in his chest must be thirst.

Only the pang didn't fade. Not even when he'd drunk another glass.

Breathing out slowly, he put the glass in the sink.

His body felt great—replete and drained in a way that only happened after sex, as if all the tension had been ironed out of it.

His head, on the other hand was a knotted tangle of confusing and conflicting thoughts.

He felt his hands twitch and he pressed them against the counter, trying to steady himself.

He'd thought he had it all worked out, that he had Nia all worked out. He'd been so sure that she was in the wrong, that she had allowed herself to be persuaded into choosing her aristocratic lifestyle over him.

And she had.

Only not for the reasons he'd believed.

The ache in his chest crept outwards.

He had been so desperate for proof that he came first, that he was everything to her, and now—guttingly—it turned out that he had been. Thanks to his obsessive need to know that, he had failed to see the truth staring him in the face.

Instead—ironically—he had let himself be distracted by the very things he had accused her of preferring.

As far as he'd been concerned she had Lamington and the estate, so he'd framed her commitment to him in terms of what she was prepared to give up.

But he hadn't understood.

His mouth twisted. It hadn't even crossed his mind that, for Nia, Lamington wasn't just a big house filled with beautiful objects. That she cared about the on-going life of the estate and the people who lived and worked on it.

Remembering Allan's text message, he felt his chest tighten. They cared about her too.

And it wasn't just a matter of duty. She had a vision for Lamington—although, unlike his film career, they had never got around to discussing that.

No wonder she had broken up with him.

Except that hadn't been the reason either.

His fingers tightened against the worktop.

Nor had she simply given in to her parents' demands.

Instead she had thought about their relationship and their dreams, and about him and his dreams. And, knowing how much he loved her, knowing him better than he knew himself, she had correctly guessed that he would do anything to make her happy—including running the estate with her, even if it made him miserable.

And she hadn't been able even to think about that happening, much less make it happen.

His shoulders tensed.

Would it have changed anything if they had talked it through properly, like adults?

Maybe.

If Nia had been more forthright, and he hadn't been always pushing people to put him above everything and everyone else. In other words, only if they had both been different people.

Shivering, he glanced around the darkened kitchen, the chill and the darkness reminding him of another kitchen.

A lifetime ago.

Almost a third of his life had passed since he had last stepped foot in his grandparents' house. In that time so many other memories had faded, but that one remained crisp and unfiltered.

He could see the kitchen as if he was standing in it now. The faded, scrubbed table. His grandmother's enamel pans. The ashtrays piled high with the brown-stained stubs of his grandfather's cigarettes.

They hadn't been bad people. They had taken him in. Given him a bed and food and clothes, a place in their home.

But it had been a grudging place. They had taken him in because there had been nowhere else for him to go.

Only Nia—briefly—and then Tom and Diane had ever made him feel wanted and accepted for himself.

And now that was gone—ruined in a day.

'Farlan?'

He jerked round. Nia was standing in the doorway. She was naked.

He felt as though he'd been kicked in the solar plexus.

The disconnect between the desperation of his thoughts and her luminous beauty was so shocking that for a moment he couldn't speak.

'Are you okay?' she asked.

The concern in her voice made the ache in his chest spread out like an oil spill, and suddenly the need to confess was like a weight in his stomach.

But could he tell her? Could he tell Nia the truth about why he had backed her into a corner, forced her to choose between her family and an unknown, uncertain future with a man she had known for only a little over six months?

Thinking about the tangle of fresh starts and failures that had made up his childhood, he felt his spine tense.

He wouldn't even know where to begin.

And there wasn't time to unravel everything.

Not right now. Not when all he wanted to do was spin out these precious moments with her, with this beautiful woman he had loved and lost, before morning came and he had to lose her again.

'I'm fine. I was just getting a glass of water.'

Her eyes were fixed on his face, soft and questioning, and he knew she wanted to believe his words.

And yet this was not a normal night for either of them.

Should he tell her about his life? About the loneliness and the rejection? About how for most of his childhood he had felt like an unwanted birthday present that was always being regifted?

Watching her hover in the doorway, he tried out a few sentences in his head. But then his gaze dropped from her face to the pale curves of her breasts, then lower, to the tiny thistle tattoo, and a beat of pure dark need pulsed across his skin.

The time for talking was over.

Right now he wanted—*needed*—to blank out his mind to everything except the feel of her mouth on his and, walking swiftly across the room, he kissed her hungrily, nudging her backwards into the warm darkness.

Nia woke to the sound of someone humming.

No, not someone. *Farlan.*

Rolling over, she gazed blindly across the room as memories of the night before spilled into her head.

Farlan.

She felt her face grow warm. Her body felt almost weighed down with a kind of languid satisfaction and, shifting onto her side, she pressed her thighs together, feeling a pleasurable chafe of tenderness.

Last night had been like a febrile erotic dream, every movement, every touch rich and enticing.

They had kept on reaching for each other, their mouths and hands insistent, stirring, tormenting, pleasuring one another.

It had been as though they'd both understood that time was short.

Without saying so out loud they had known that this was one night of bliss they could steal back from time, suspended, separate somehow, from the onward progress of minutes and hours.

Had known that when it was morning they would wake, and the dream would fade away, and they would go back to their separate lives.

Across the room, the pale square of the window was clearly visible behind the curtains. She hugged the blanket closer. It was morning already.

Her heart contracted.

Last night it had been so simple. Reaching for one another had been all that was required. They hadn't thought further than that. Sex had been both the starting and the finishing line.

Remembering the feel of his mouth on hers, she shivered beneath the blanket.

And that would have been fine—only last night had been more than just sex: they had made love.

'You're awake.'

Glancing over at the doorway, she blinked. If she had been imagining that this morning they would naturally follow on from last night's intimacy, then she had clearly been alone in those thoughts.

Farlan was fully dressed, and watching her without any sign of yesterday's narrow-eyed hunger.

'It's a beautiful day. The blizzard must have blown itself out overnight. Would you like tea or coffee?'

She stared at him mutely, silenced by the cool, almost brisk tone of his voice and the unspoken message it contained.

'Tea, please,' she said quickly, trying to match his manner.

He turned and disappeared back into the kitchen and she sat up, wishing that she had paid more attention to where she had dropped her clothes.

And that she could shift the strange pang of disappointment beneath her ribs.

Kicking back from that thought, she picked up her phone.

Nine-fifteen.

She had slept so late.

'Here.'

Farlan was back. Still stunned by the time, she reached up unthinkingly and the blanket fell away from her body.

His face stilled. 'I'll put it here.' He backed away, his eyes locking on hers. 'I'll let you get dressed.'

Watching him retreat, she found her clothes and

dressed hurriedly. Picking up her tea, she frowned. 'This is real milk.'

'Yeah, when I went outside to check the car I noticed a farm.'

Her eyes jerked up. He was leaning against the doorframe again, rubbing the stubble on his face. Watching the flickering tendons in his hand, she felt something tug beneath her skin.

Wrenching her gaze away, she walked across the room and drew the curtains. When she looked outside it was hard to believe that last night's storm had even happened. Everything was so still. Beneath the clear blue sky the snow was smooth and deep and even in every direction as far as she could see.

'Classlochie Farm? That's quite a hike.'

He shrugged. 'About forty minutes. But I needed to clear my head so—'

She lifted her cup to hide the flush on her cheeks. He had thrown those words out without hesitation. Clearly he had meant what he'd said last night.

It shouldn't hurt as much as it did. It was what she'd expected and what she wanted too, she told herself.

'I told them we'd got stranded and they gave me some milk. They offered some eggs and bacon too, but I said I was already running late.' He hesitated. 'I suppose we should talk about last night…'

She felt his gaze on her face. 'Yes, I suppose we should,' she said slowly.

She smothered a gasp as he put his hands on her arms and pulled her closer.

'No regrets, right?'

For a moment she didn't answer. His hands felt

warm and firm against her skin—and good, unbelievably good. She felt her heart swell for a second. Then she shook her head.

'No. No regrets. I just want it to be okay between us.'

It was incredibly tempting to believe that seven years ago they had simply been knocked off course, that Tom and Diane renting Lamington was fate stepping in to bring them back together.

But his words floated back to her from that first night in the drawing room. And she didn't believe in fairy tales any more either.

She and Farlan 'worked' here, in this remote little bothy, for the same reason they had 'worked' in his flat in Edinburgh. Because it wasn't real life.

Only aged nineteen, and hopelessly in love, it had been hard for her to see the implications of that fact.

Her heart contracted. It was still hard to accept it aged twenty-six. And she hadn't—not really, not willingly.

But last night in the cramped cabin of the Land Rover, and then again by the glow of the fire, she had been forced to admit—to herself anyway—that what they'd shared didn't, and couldn't ever, work in a real-world situation.

It was better to know that now, before it was too late.

Her chest was suddenly a muddle of pity and panic. *Like Catherine and Richard, her aunt and uncle.*

When she was younger, they'd seemed like a fairy tale couple brought to life. Her aunt so beautiful and he an aspiring artist, with a sweet smile and a spaniel. And both so young.

Watching them together, she had been transfixed by

the intensity of their love. And the fact that everyone else had been appalled had only seemed to make it all so much more romantic.

Against all opposition, they had married and quickly produced two children. But with bills to pay, and a family to support, Richard had stopped painting and taken a job at an art gallery in Dubai.

Nia shivered inside.

To say that he hated it would be understatement. He loathed it. And Catherine loathed her life in her air-conditioned mansion. And a lot of the time it felt as if they loathed each other too.

She so hadn't wanted that to happen to her and Farlan, and that hadn't changed.

More importantly, he hadn't changed.

He might be a wealthy, successful film director, but he still didn't understand her connection to her home, to Lamington.

'And we are okay.'

His voice pulled her back and, looking up, she met his gaze. His eyes were clear and green.

'It hurt both of us, the way it ended, and we needed to put that right.' His thumb caressed her cheek. 'Now we can put it behind us and move on.'

Move on.

He meant find someone else.

Her pulse quickened.

Someone he could lie beside in bed and hold as she slept.

Someone who made his heart beat faster when he saw her in a crowded room.

Someone to share his dreams.

Someone to love.

Staring out of the window, she let her eyes track across the landscape to the distant hills that edged the Kilvean estate, belonging to Lord Airlie.

She wanted that too.

She wanted to be with a man and know that she was his and he was hers and nothing could ever come between them.

'Yes,' she said quietly. 'We can both move on.'

Neither of them spoke much on the drive back down to the main road.

There was nothing more to say.

Her heartbeat jumped as they bumped over the cattle grid.

The unstoppable, irresistible bare-bones hunger of last night had been intense and all-consuming, but now they were driving through the gates and past groups of sheep as if the smooth white fields had swallowed all that passion whole.

Was that what she wanted?

Back at the bothy she had thought so, only now—

'I'll drop you at the cottage and then walk back to Lamington.'

His voice cut across her thoughts and, glancing up, she realised it was too late for last-minute doubts. They were already here.

The gardener's cottage looked postcard-pretty.

'Thank you for driving.' She gave him a small, tight smile. 'I promise I'll get someone to look at the car.'

'I wouldn't worry about that,' he said softly.

'Really? But you said that there was something wrong with the brakes.'

'There probably is. But you don't need to worry about that. Not any more.'

She watched in confusion as he turned away, raising his hand in greeting as another car came round the corner and parked behind the Land Rover.

A young man in smooth leather brogues slipped across the snow towards them. 'Mr Wilder? Gordon Muir. We spoke this morning.'

'Of course.' Farlan held out his hand. 'Thanks for making this so easy.' He turned to Nia. 'This is Lady Antonia.'

Blushing, Gordon Muir held out his hand.

'Lady Antonia. Congratulations! You're about to take delivery of an incredible car.'

Take delivery? Nia frowned. 'I'm sorry, I think you must have the wrong person. I don't know—'

Farlan stepped forward casually. 'Gordon, could you just give us a moment? I need to have a quick word with Lady Antonia.'

Turning to Nia, he spread his hands.

'I wanted to surprise you, but now I can see I should probably have said something earlier.' His green eyes rested on her face. 'Look, I know you have more than enough money to buy a fleet of Land Rovers. But I also know you have zero interest in cars and that one is old and worn-out and, frankly, dangerous.'

He smiled at her then, that smile no one could resist.

'So I bought you a new one.'

Her head jerked up. 'You did what?' She felt like Gordon Muir, slip-sliding across the snow. 'When?'

'This morning. Really, it's not that big a deal.'

Glancing over his shoulder, she saw a brand-new Land Rover. She was no expert, but she had looked into replacing her old one often enough to know this sleek, black SUV came with a big price tag.

'I can't accept this.'

He was quiet for a minute, and then he took a step towards her. 'Please, Nia. Please let me do this for you.'

She wanted to be angry, but it was hard. Hard to be angry that he cared about her. And what made it harder still was that he knew her so well.

He had guessed correctly—although for the wrong reasons—that she would never get round to replacing the car and so he'd sorted it out himself.

He had done that for her, and the pleasure and pain of knowing that made her feel slightly shaky.

'I can't—' she began.

He caught her hand. 'Yes, you can.' His eyes on hers were the soft green of young beech leaves. 'If something happened to you... I just need to know you're safe.'

Her heart thudded. 'Thank you,' she said quietly.

Their eyes met and he stared down at her, and suddenly she was breathless at his closeness.

Terrified that he would guess, she tried to smile. 'I'd better go and take a look, then.'

Watching Nia pick her way delicately across the snow-covered road, Farlan could feel his body straining towards her like a Pointer reaching for a scent.

On waking, his guilt about the night before had returned, so that buying the car for her had seemed perfectly rational.

And then he'd told her that they could both move on.

But could something that felt so momentous happen and yet leave no trace?

His eyes flickered momentarily across the smooth white fields, but he knew he hadn't been thinking about last night's blizzard.

Reaching out, he touched the bonnet of the old Land Rover. Despite the chill in the air it was still warm and, staring through the mud-flecked windscreen, he could almost picture their frantic, jerky coupling.

He breathed in sharply against the headrush.

It would pass, he told himself quickly. He wouldn't forget it, or her, but he would make it all fit into his life and find a way to move forward.

'So, what do you think?'

Having enthusiastically explained every feature of the new car, Gordon had just been picked up by his colleague, and they were alone again.

'I think it's amazing.' Nia's eyes found his. 'Thank you again for sorting this out for me.'

'My pleasure. I know cars aren't your thing.' He grinned. 'However, they are mine.'

'Tom told me about your supercar.' She smiled.

'Yeah, it's a great ride. It's just on loan, but I've actually put in an order for one back in the States.'

It had been an enthralling drive. But for some reason the memory of it wasn't giving him the same rush of excitement as before.

'How long is it until you go back?' she asked quietly.

I can go back whenever I want.

The rogue thought popped into his head unasked-for.

He glanced down at her. 'Ten days.'

For a moment she looked somewhere over his shoulder, and then she met his gaze. 'And nights?' she said slowly.

Her words floated between them, pale and sparkling like snowflakes, and a beat of heat pulsed inside him.

Was she saying what he thought she was?

The desire to pull her close, to press his mouth against hers and taste her again, was irresistible, overwhelming...

He held her gaze. 'Nine, actually.'

She nodded, bit her lip, hesitated. 'I was wrong. Back at the bothy, I was wrong.' Her voice dried up for a second and she began again. 'I thought I wanted to have just one night with you, but I don't.'

His heart was jumping in his throat. The space between them seemed both hair-fine and the size of an ocean.

He knew what she was offering because it had already crossed his mind a thousand times since he'd woken that morning.

Only thinking something and saying it out loud were a world apart—especially now, when the aftershocks were still making the ground ripple beneath his feet.

They couldn't rewrite the script or change the ending. For him and Nia the credits had already rolled.

His hands clenched, and with something approaching relief he realised that he was still holding the keys to the old Land Rover.

'I think we both got what we wanted, Nia.' He took an unsteady step backwards. 'And now I should probably get back to Tom and Diane. I'll drive this over to

Lamington. It can stay there until you decide what you want to do with it.'

And without waiting for her reply he swung himself into the driver's seat, gunned the engine and drove away.

CHAPTER SEVEN

AN HOUR LATER, having showered, changed his clothes and given Tom and Diane a bowdlerised version of what had happened with Nia, Farlan sat down on the window seat in his bedroom.

He felt as if he was coming down with the flu: his limbs were leaden and he was aching all over. Probably he just needed to sleep…

Glancing over at his bed, he tightened his jaw.

It didn't seem possible that he had already got used to lying with his arms wrapped around Nia's soft body, and yet apparently he couldn't face the thought of sleeping alone.

Particularly with their last conversation buzzing around his head.

Leaning his head against the glass, he felt frustration blur his fatigue—both the sexual kind and exasperation at his and Nia's complete inability to communicate.

Although, to be fair, this time she had made her wishes quite clear.

Nine nights.

He ran a hand through his hair, unsure what was more disconcerting. The fact that Nia had come right out and said what she wanted or the fact that he had turned her down.

Outside, the wind had picked up again, and he watched enviously as a bird wheeled away across the sky, riding the uplift.

When he was directing he felt just like that bird. It was so effortless, so natural, and it had been the same with the upward trajectory of his career. Not once had he doubted himself or questioned his abilities.

But as for relationships...

The nervous skinny child he'd been had blossomed, and people were eager to know him, so it wasn't that he didn't have relationships. He did. What was hard— impossible, really—was letting his friendships develop and deepen.

He knew it was a hangover from his childhood. Basically he didn't trust anyone not to change their mind about him—except maybe Tom and Diane.

He sat for several moments, his eyes tracking the bird.

It was a big deal for him when people changed their minds. In his experience it always had consequences— rarely good, often bad. Life had been unsparing in drumming that lesson into him, and for that reason he was careful never to put his needs in someone else's hands.

Nia had been the only exception to that rule.

His jaw clenched. He hated having to admit that fear played a part in so many of his relationships with people.

But it did.

It had.

Seven years ago with Nia, and then again with her this morning, when she'd thrown that curve ball at him.

Her changing her mind had been enough to make him push her away. Even though he wanted exactly what she wanted.

He shuddered as the memory of his reply pushed its way into his head and, jerking his gaze away from the window, he ran his hand over his face.

There were a thousand ways he could have responded, and he'd had to pick that one.

Across the room, his neatly made bed mocked him.

He couldn't just sit here brooding and, standing up, he walked swiftly to the door. Maybe if he moved fast enough he might be able to put some distance between himself and all thoughts of Nia.

As he walked through the house he could hear Tom and Diane, talking to Molly in the kitchen. Of all the beautiful rooms at Lamington, he knew it was their favourite. It was warm, and bright, and they found something comforting in the hum of the refrigerator and the smell of baking bread.

He lingered in the hall, drawn to the laughter and the domesticity. But he wouldn't be much company, and the effort of pretending he felt fine was beyond him right now.

Spinning round, he made his way down to the garage.

The muscular contours of the supercar had drawn him there, but instead he found himself standing in front of Nia's old Land Rover.

He scowled.

Great, he'd managed not to think about her for roughly five minutes.

His gaze rested on the Land Rover. It looked like an old seaside donkey stabled next to a thoroughbred racehorse.

Why hadn't she replaced it before?

Then everything would have been fine.

Picturing her pale, unguarded face, he swore softly.

From somewhere nearby he heard the sharp, insistent trill of a mobile phone and, peering into the Land Rover, he saw Nia's phone juddering across the seat.

As he yanked open the door it rang out.

For a moment he stared at it in silence, remembering her words.

Nine nights.

It had caught him off guard—Nia saying out loud what he had been thinking and pretending not to think.

Only why pretend? One night *wasn't* enough. They both knew it.

But only Nia had been brave enough to say it.

Admitting it now served no purpose. It was too little, too late.

His chest tightened.

That was what his grandfather had used to say to him when he had forgotten to do a chore and then tried to make amends by offering to help the next time. It was too little, too late.

Gazing blankly out of the kitchen window, Nia felt numb. It was over three hours since Farlan had driven off and she had stumbled into the cottage, her skin hot and tight with the shame of his rejection.

She had spent almost every one of those one hundred and eighty minutes replaying their conversation and trying to work out what had possessed her to act like that.

It hadn't been planned—she knew that. On the drive back down to the cottage she had actually thought it was over, that one night of hot sex had finally done what time and absence had failed to do. She'd started to think that maybe she had a chance of finding happiness.

Then everything had slipped away from her.

Her heart thudded as she thought about the huge, glossy black car parked outside in the drive.

Back in the bothy, it had been easy to tell herself that, however wild and urgent and incredible it had been, it was still just sex.

But then she'd found out what Farlan had done.

And just like that the fact that he had been thinking about her in some way that didn't involve sex, that he cared not just about giving her pleasure but keeping her safe, had made the prospect of moving on dissolve like early-morning mist.

All she'd been able to think about was that he would be leaving soon, and the thought of that night being their last had felt like a hot knife pressed against her skin.

Gazing up into his eyes, she had thought he felt the same way.

Only he hadn't.

She had misread the signs.

Too many years spent managing her parents' whims had blunted her ability to read people. *To read men.* They had made her doubt herself, and sadly there was no one to fulfil their high expectations except her; nowhere to hide from their gaze.

And, despite neither of them ever having worked for a living, they had an antipathy to idleness in others, so Nia had never had much time for fun.

Except with Farlan.

And since him she had been too busy, too distracted by the day-to-day demands of running the estate and managing her parents, to do more than take the occasional day off.

Her cheeks burned.

And she had been celibate for so long.

No wonder everything had got snarled up inside her.

Like every human, she craved intimacy and touch, and with her body so recently reawakened, still aching from their lovemaking, she had wanted more.

She jumped.

The phone was ringing—the landline, not her mobile.

As usual, it wasn't where it was supposed to be, and after searching for some moments she found it on the windowsill by the front door.

'Darling, why do you never answer your mobile phone?'

It was her mother.

'I always answer, Mummy. I was just out in the garden and I left my phone there,' she lied.

Her phone must have slipped out of her pocket when Gordon had been talking to her, but to explain that would mean explaining about Gordon, and she didn't want to risk something slipping out about Farlan.

'Then you must have been out in the garden for a very long time,' her mother said waspishly. 'I've been calling for hours.'

'How is everything?' she asked quickly, hoping to distract her mother. 'How's Daddy and Aunt Catherine?'

'Catherine's exhausted. Run off her feet as usual. But Daddy's fine. We've been playing bridge most afternoons at the club, with Fergus and Margaret Cavendish.'

Her mother paused for just a shade too long to be natural.

'David is here too. He asked after you. I think he was rather hoping you might come out and join us.'

Nia stared out of the window.

David Cavendish was three years older than her and, thanks to his athletic good looks and his father's property empire, he was a favourite of her mother's.

Her shoulders tensed. She should be used to it by now. Her mother still hadn't forgiven her for turning down Andrew's proposal, but her furious lectures and cold-eyed disapproval had now given way to these conversational depth charges.

Mostly Nia let them explode at a safe distance. But today, in the aftermath of Farlan's rejection, she felt unusually vulnerable.

'How long is he staying?' she asked.

She could almost hear the snap of her mother's spine as she sat up straighter.

'Two weeks. He got injured playing polo. I told him you probably wouldn't be able to spare the time, but…'

The unspoken hope in her mother's voice made her wince with guilt. It might be a little old-fashioned, but was it so bad for a mother to want her daughter to find a husband?

And why shouldn't she take a few days off?

It would be fun to lounge by a pool…to have a conversation with a man that didn't feel as if every third word was boobytrapped.

Outside, she could just see the Land Rover's snow-flecked tyres.

Johnny and Allan could manage the estate perfectly well for a few days, and there was nothing else to stop her from going.

For a moment she let her imagination make pretty pictures inside her head.

Teak loungers clustered round a perfect oval of blue like an oasis in the desert. Ice bumping against a slice of lemon in a tall glass and a light breeze sending ripples across the mirror-smooth surface of the pool.

From somewhere upstairs a door slammed shut. She frowned. That wasn't a breeze.

A deafening noise filled the cottage. It sounded like the time when she and Farlan had knocked all those books off the shelves in the library, only sped up and a lot louder.

Still frowning, she walked towards the window that looked out onto the garden and the fields beyond.

Her mouth fell open.

A black helicopter, its rotors spinning at an impossible speed, was juddering downwards, whipping the snow upwards like confetti in reverse.

She cleared her throat. 'Mummy, I've got to go. Something's happening in the field.'

Ignoring her mother's squawk of protest, she hung up and, grabbing a jacket from the hooks by the back door, she stepped out into the garden and through the gate.

The blur of the rotors slowed, and then finally stopped.

Silence.

The door popped open and she watched in astonishment as Farlan jumped out into the snow.

Of course—it would have to be Farlan.

But she'd been so distracted it had taken her brain a few seconds to remember he had a helicopter.

She swallowed hard as he walked towards her. He looked pale and serious and very handsome, his black clothes stark against the white of the snow surrounding him.

'What do you want?'

She was surprised at the strength in her voice, but not by the jolt of heat as his green eyes met hers.

'You left this in the car.' He reached into his pocket and pulled out her phone. 'I thought I'd drop it round.'

'Thank you.' She took the phone, the mundaneness of their exchange hurting, if possible, more than his rejection had earlier.

Was this what they had been reduced to?

With an intensity that left her reeling, she wished suddenly that she had gone with her parents to Dubai, that he had stayed a memory. And suddenly, before she even knew what she going to do, she was turning and walking away.

'Nia—'

He caught up with her as she reached the gate, grabbing the top rail firmly, using his superior strength to keep her from opening it.

Abruptly, she let go, spinning round to face him. 'Why are you still here? You dropped by to give me my phone, right? Well, now you have—so you can go.'

His breath was white in the air. 'If it was just about

the phone, Nia, I would have got Diane to drop it round. I came to talk to you.'

'Don't bother,' she said flatly. 'We both got what we wanted, remember?'

His eyes locked with hers. 'I was wrong to say that.'

Reading their expression, she felt misery and anger and frustration flood through her. So that was why he was here: he felt sorry for her.

Every cell in her body was suddenly quivering, ready to split apart. It was all so futile. All of this. It was like trying to meet him in a maze, only with every turn they just ended up further apart.

'It doesn't matter. Really, truly. Why should it matter, Farlan?' She could hardly get her words out. 'You were wrong. I was wrong—'

'How were you wrong?' Now he seemed angry.

'For being stupid enough to want more than one night with you. And then for thinking it would be a good idea to tell you that was what I wanted.' She shook her head. 'Actually, I didn't even think about it, I just thought *This is how I feel and I need to tell him.* And so I did.' She met his gaze head-on. 'And now I get to relive my stupidity, so you can tell me how "wrong" you were to say what you were thinking.'

'I was wrong to say it.' He grabbed her shoulders. 'I was wrong to say it because it wasn't true.'

She felt as if it was only his hands that were holding her upright.

'One night isn't enough for me either. I knew that the moment I woke up this morning.'

For a moment, she wavered. She wanted it to be true

so badly. But with an almighty effort she pulled away from him, shaking her head. 'I don't believe you.'

His jaw tightened. 'You think I'm lying?'

Her chest was aching. Exhaustion was rolling over her in waves. 'Yes, I do. You always know your own mind. If that's what you'd been thinking then you would have said something, but you didn't.'

For a moment he seemed almost stunned, as though she had slapped his face.

'I did think it,' he said a moment later. 'But we'd said it would only be one night, so I wasn't sure.'

He exhaled heavily. There was a tension to him that hadn't been there before. Just as there had been in the car yesterday, she thought a moment later. When he had realised that there was too much snow and the threat had suddenly become real.

She stared at him, trying to read his expression.

What threat was there here?

He took a breath. 'I don't like not being sure.'

Something in his voice wrenched at her inside. A memory of that first time they'd met, of her thinking she had never met anyone so young and yet so old at the same time.

'I don't think anyone does,' she said quietly.

Her anger had faded. She didn't know why, but it just wasn't there any more.

'I messed up.'

His hand brushed against hers and she could hear the struggle to keep his voice steady.

'I know I upset you, and I'm sorry for that—so very sorry. That's why I came over…to tell you, to explain, to apologise.'

His clear green eyes were fixed on her face, as if he was scared to look away in case she vanished.

'I know it's probably too late, and I will completely understand if you never want to speak to me again—'

'You will?' she asked incredulously.

He screwed up his face. 'Not really. I'm just trying to think of anything and everything I can say that will make things go back to how they were before.'

'Do you mean before today? Or the "before" before that?' she said softly. 'I think we need to be clear. Just to be on the safe side. I mean, we do seem to make a habit of being at cross-purposes.'

'Are you?'

A pulse throbbed through her body as he took a step closer.

'Still cross with me, I mean?'

Should she be? He had hurt her, and yet it wasn't that simple. There were old hurts and, yes, they had talked about the past, but it was naive to think that one conversation would act as a balm to those wounds.

'I was cross, and upset—'

This time his hand took hers. 'I never wanted to upset you.' His fingers curled around hers. 'And I want to make it up to you if you'll let me. If you'll give me a second chance.'

She felt the world grow hazy. Whatever happened, he was going to leave in ten days. All she would be doing was postponing the inevitable, making him more necessary to her existence.

But he was so beautiful, and she wanted him.

'What do you have in mind?' she asked.

He pulled her closer. So close that she could feel his heartbeat slamming into her body.

'That depends. How much time can you spare me?'

She pretended to think. 'I have ten days free.'

A breeze stirred between them, loosening her hair. Reaching out, he tucked the stray strands behind her ear, his thumb caressing her cheek.

'And nights?'

'Only nine, I'm afraid.'

His eyes glittered in the weak sunlight. 'Could you pencil me in?'

Her heart felt as if it might burst. She felt almost weightless with happiness. But she needed to be sure... to make sure nothing came between them this time.

'If that's what you want. To be with me.'

Tilting her face up to his, he kissed her gently. 'I've never been more certain of anything. There's nowhere else I want to be. Unless you've changed your mind?'

'I haven't,' she said simply.

His hands surrounded her face and they kissed again. The lost look in his eyes had faded and he was back in control.

'Can I take you to lunch now? It's a hotel up near Loch Ashie. It's a bit of distance by car. But we won't be going by car...'

Now she understood why there was a helicopter sitting in the field.

'You must have been pretty confident I'd say yes,' she said slowly.

His eyes followed hers, and for a moment she expected his mouth to curve up into one of those impossible to resist smiles, but instead he shrugged.

'You know what they say. Hope for the best; plan for the worst. I was hoping—' he grimaced '—praying, really, that you would say yes.'

'And if I hadn't?'

Now he grinned. 'Kept flying till I reached Moray. There's a monastery there—Benedictine monks. I was going to turn my back on the world and join their order.'

She burst out laughing. 'Then you'd better take me to lunch right now, or I might be tempted to see if that's true.'

CHAPTER EIGHT

'So, TELL ME about your plans for Lamington.'

Stretching out his legs, Farlan looked over at Nia, satisfaction beating over his skin.

They had reached Brude House within twenty minutes, and they were lounging in the comfortable bar overlooking the battleship-grey waters of the loch.

'You want to talk about Lamington?' she said.

She looked pleased, and with a stab of guilt he wondered why he hadn't asked her that question before. But as she started speaking about her plans for a cookery school he realised that he knew why.

Lamington had always been his glittering, faceless rival. A threat even before everything else that had happened. A threat he would never be able to defeat because Nia *was* Lamington.

She didn't just live and work on the estate, she was its custodian. It was in her careful hands to preserve and pass on to her children so they could then pass it on to their children.

The idea of Nia having children with some unknown man made him want to turn the table over and roar like a stag.

Fortunately the waitress arrived, to tell them that their table was ready.

Lunch was delicious.

Brude House might not be as old or grand as Lamington, Farlan thought, but Lachlan and Holly had done a good job of turning it into a top-flight place to stay and eat.

The decor of the dining room was glamorous, yet casual, but it was the food that impressed.

A pea and curd cheese mousse the colour of young acorns was followed by lamb with broad beans and tiny wild garlic capers that exploded on your tongue like sherbet.

Watching Nia's eyes widen, he felt a sudden, wild thumping of his heart. There were so many places he wanted to take her. Things he wanted to show her and only her. And he could now.

This was all about having fun.

In bed, and out of it.

Forcing himself to stretch carelessly, he stared across the table, his eyes tracing the curve of her breasts against the smooth fabric.

'What do you think?' he asked.

'It's amazing.'

The excitement in her smile made something crack open inside him.

'Getting here was pretty amazing too.'

'We can do it again if you like. I can take you anywhere, Nia. Wherever you want to go.'

She bit into her lip. 'I'm still trying to work out how you found this place. I mean, how do you stroll back into the country after seven years away and find some-where so perfect?'

The flicker of curiosity in her soft brown eyes re-minded him of the dancing flames at the bothy, and he felt his body stiffen at the memory.

He shrugged. 'Goes with the territory. When you're rich and, more importantly, famous people want to know you.'

His stomach clenched. *Why didn't they want to know you when you were poor and young and powerless? You were still the same person.*

'So they send you stuff, invite you to stay in their hotels, eat at their restaurants. I get a free lunch—they get publicity. Everyone gets what they want,' he said, with no trace of the bitterness he was feeling.

But he could hear the echo of the words he'd spo-ken earlier—knew too that she'd heard it and that he'd hurt her. He badly wanted to undo his words—to say other words that would explain why the past wouldn't let go of him and why these ten days were all he could ever give her.

Instead he pulled her closer and kissed her soft mouth, letting the slow heating of his desire blank his mind.

'In this case, though, the owners are friends of mine.'

She frowned. 'They are? Why didn't you say?'

Her expression was suddenly intent—too intent—and he glanced away, nodding at the waitress. 'Could we have more water please?' Stretching his face into a careless smile, he went on. 'What was I saying? Oh, yes. I met Lachlan and Holly in LA, doing the catering at some VIP event. We got chatting, found out we were all Scottish and just hit it off.'

'So why did they come back to Scotland?'

She seemed genuinely interested. He liked that about her. It was one of the first things that had attracted him to her. His breathing hitched. That and her eyes, and her lips, and her laugh, and the soft curves of her body, and the fact that she was the smartest person he knew...

'Lachlan was homesick.' He grinned. 'He even missed the rain. He'd always planned on coming back, and Holly was sick of LA. Anyway, I texted him and told him I was over, and he said to drop in if I was in the area.'

She smiled. 'It was lucky for him that you didn't go and join those monks, then.'

'Lucky for me,' he said softly.

He held her gaze and then, reaching out, rested his hand on top of hers. He still couldn't believe that she was here—that she had given him a second chance. Standing in the garage, he had been so sure that he had messed it up for good. And the more he'd told himself that it didn't matter even if he had, the more certain he'd become that it did.

He glanced across the table. She had changed before they'd left into a fitted navy dress. It looked expensive, and was cut modestly, and yet it made him want to strip her bare.

But it hadn't been just sex that had made him do the unthinkable, the impossible, and go after her. Nor had it been about returning her phone.

Remembering her small, stunned face after he'd rejected her had made him feel sick with self-loathing.

Her knowing her own mind was what mattered. That was what he'd told himself. But when she had made it clear what she wanted he'd thrown it back in her face.

He'd been a hypocrite and a coward and a fool.

He was also the luckiest man in the world.

The waitress came to clear the table, and as he watched Nia smile and talk to her he felt a sense of contentment. He watched people all the time as part of his job. As a film director he was paid to do it. But he would watch Nia for free all day...every day.

And now he had ten days and nine glorious nights with her, stretching out ahead of him to a distant, shimmering horizon.

He glanced over at her and found her looking at him. Hidden beneath the tablecloth, he felt his body harden. *Was she thinking the same thing?*

She smiled. 'I've had a lovely time, so thank you for bringing me.' Her smile stilled and she began fiddling with her glass. 'I was wondering if you had any plans for the weekend... For us, I mean.'

Heat rose up over his chest, coiling around his neck so that it was difficult to breathe.

He did have plans.

And all of them involved Nia wearing very few clothes.

Sometimes none at all.

For obvious reasons, he'd given a lot less thought to what he would be wearing, but he'd made up for that by imagining various different settings and positions.

Now, though, might not be the best time to admit any of that.

'Nothing specific,' he said blandly.

'It's just that the Beaters' Ball is happening tomorrow.'

He saw her hesitate.

'At Castle Kilvean. It's Lord Airlie's home—just up the road from Lamington.'

She hesitated again.

'I usually go, and I was wondering if you might like to go with me.' Straightening her back, she glanced around the dining room. 'You brought me here, and I'd really like to take you somewhere special in return.'

Farlan leaned back in his seat and let the silence grow.

This was an affair.

Affairs were supposed to be about sex and fun.

Not getting dressed up to spend an evening with a bunch of strangers. Besides, balls weren't really his cup of tea...

He frowned. *Why did it have to be all about what he wanted?* Wasn't that part of the reason everything had fallen apart last time. Him needing to come first.

'It's okay, I know it's not your thing—'

Leaning forward, he cupped her face in his hand, his thumb caressing the curve of her cheekbone. 'It is now,' he murmured. He kissed her again, his mouth parting hers, his fingers tightening in her hair. 'I would love to go to the ball with you, Lady Antonia. On one condition.'

'What's that?' She was smiling now.

'Promise you won't run away from me at midnight.'

'I promise,' she agreed.

His throat tightened. She thought they were flirting, and if life had treated him differently she would have been right. But for him a promise was never enough. For him promises were always just waiting to be broken.

He gritted his teeth. Even now, after all this time, he still hadn't mastered his fear. Hating the feeling, he looked away, jerking his head at the waitress to break the mood.

'So, who is this Lord Airlie?' he asked.

'He's a neighbour and a friend.'

Something in her voice, or maybe the way she'd said 'friend', made his muscles tense.

'What kind of friend? Old? New? Best?'

Was he just imagining it, or did her face change minutely? Her eyes?

'A good one,' she said.

She met his gaze. 'Andrew's a good person and a good boss. It was actually his idea to ask all of his estate workers and household staff to join in with the ball— you know, to make it more inclusive. I think you'll like him,' she added.

That was unlikely, he thought, feeling a slow swell of jealousy rising as he watched her face soften. He wanted to ask her more about this other man, only he couldn't bear the thought of how it would sound.

Or of hearing what she might say.

'I'm sure I will.'

The waitress was back. 'Would you like to see the dessert menu, sir?'

Looking up, he gave her his lazy smile. 'No need. I already know what we want.'

'How did you know I wanted the pear?' asked Nia ten minutes later, scooping up the final mouthful of poached pear.

Watching her lick the spoon, he felt his groin tighten. *Who needed dessert when you were going home with a woman like Nia?*

He shrugged. 'You love pears. Apples too. But there wasn't anything with apples on the menu so...'

'I suppose everyone is too health-conscious for puddings in LA.' She glanced at his espresso. 'Does it make you miss Scotland ever—all that wheatgrass and kale?'

It was an innocent question, but he felt his shoulders tense. 'I miss the country,' he said slowly. 'The cities and the mountains, the history and the poetry.'

'What about your family?'

What family?

He put down his coffee cup, the bitterness of his thoughts blotting out the rush of caffeine, feeling something shifting inside him. A mass of memories, pushing forward like water in a dam.

His grandparents had been the closest he'd had to a family, in that they had been related to him by blood and had let him live under their roof. But they were dead.

He had no idea where his parents were, and he had lost contact with Cam.

Not that Nia knew any of that. They had never talked about their families except in the broadest of brushstrokes. It hadn't seemed relevant. It still wasn't.

'They had a farm, didn't they?' she asked.

He let her words fall into the comfortable hum of conversation coming from the other tables. He didn't want to talk about the farm now—or ever, in fact. And especially not with Nia.

'They sold it.'

She frowned. 'Oh, I'm sorry. Farming is such hard

work right now. Some of our tenants are really struggling. Are they still local?'

He shook his head. 'I don't have anyone here left to miss,' he said lightly.

The dam was holding.

She squeezed his hand and some of his tension eased, and then his heart began beating into the silence inside his chest. That had been true then, but what about now?

What about Nia?

'I thought you had family in England too?' she said.

Her voice broke into his thoughts just as from across the room there was a burst of laughter. He felt suddenly irrationally angry.

'What if I do? Why do you care?' He shifted back in his seat. 'This *arrangement*—' he tossed the word towards her carelessly '—is about sex. I'm not in it for the pillow talk. Or any kind of talk, for that matter.'

She flinched as if he'd slapped her.

There was a long pause.

'I see. Well, I'm sorry, Farlan, but I didn't agree to any "arrangement" where you get to talk to me like that,' she said stiffly. 'I'll let you finish your coffee in peace.'

Putting her napkin on the table, she reached for her bag.

'Nia—' He caught her wrist. 'Don't go. Please. I'm sorry. I don't know why I said that—'

Except he did.

It was always the same whenever he thought about his family. The same fear—the fear that wrapped itself around him and turned his words into sharp, jagged rocks in his throat so that speaking them was impossible.

Only if he didn't say something now Nia would leave, and more than anything he didn't want her to leave.

'Please. Don't go, Nia,' he repeated. 'It's just difficult talking about it…about them.'

She was looking at him warily, but she had stopped moving, and he felt a surge of relief. He hadn't pushed her too far.

'Why is it difficult?'

The dining room was awash with afternoon sun, and her face was illuminated in the soft golden light. He felt his stomach clench. She was still angry, but more than that she was worried about him.

'I haven't talked about them for a bit,' he said. *Make that ever*, he corrected silently. 'And when I do I get lost in it—I let it get out of control in my head.'

The need to talk to her, to tell the truth, was pressing down on him. But how could he explain the threadbare patchwork of his childhood?

The Elgins ticked every box. They were rich and titled and Nia could trace her ancestors back nearly four hundred years.

'My family is not like yours, Nia. It's messy and complicated—'

Her fingers tightened around his. 'All families are messy and complicated.'

He shook his head, his mouth twisting. She had no idea, and he didn't want her to know either.

Okay, her parents were difficult, snobbish people, but the only time she had experienced the random cruelty that life could throw at people had been thanks to him.

He wasn't about to make his pain part of her life.

He couldn't do that to her.

'Not yours. Your family is perfect.'

There was a longer pause.

'It's not. It's not perfect.' She took a breath. 'That's why I broke up with you. I panicked. I thought anything was better than—'

'Than what?'

For a moment she seemed to be fumbling with something inside her head, and he knew she was deciding what to say and what to conceal, balancing an equation. He knew because he did it himself, and the fact that he and Nia should have that in common wrenched at him.

'My aunt and uncle. They were exactly the ages we were when we first met when they got married. They were so in love.'

Her mouth curved up into a smile at the memory.

'I was thirteen—just at that age when you start to question things, to look at life with your own eyes, and they seemed perfect to me. Catherine was so pretty, and Richard was an artist. A really good one. But he wasn't making any money so he gave it up.'

She breathed out unsteadily.

'They used to argue all the time, but now they just lead separate lives. I think sometimes they hate each other...' Her voice stumbled. 'I didn't want that for us. Only I didn't know how to explain without betraying them.'

So it hadn't just been a generic fear about their mismatched backgrounds. She had already seen first-hand what happened when two people put their dreams on hold...when fantasy met reality head-on. She had witnessed her aunt and uncle's slow, tortuous falling out of love.

'Are they still together?' he asked.

She nodded. 'They live in Dubai.'

Something clicked inside his head. Nia had mentioned Dubai the other day. Her parents were staying out there.

He hated seeing the strain in her eyes. 'Couldn't your father help them? I know he's not well, but couldn't he maybe loan them some money?'

Something in her face shifted, and he knew that she was doing another of those mental calculations.

Finally, she shook her head. 'He can't help. He doesn't have any money.'

There was a small silence.

'I know that sounds stupid, and I know I told you they needed to go somewhere warm for his health, but I lied. He does have a weak chest, but that's not the reason we're renting out Lamington. We need the money.'

His head was spinning. *Nia's family needed money?*

'I don't understand—'

'I found out about eighteen months ago, when I met with the accountant.' She shrugged. 'I suspected something was wrong, but I didn't realise how wrong until then.'

'Did your parents know how bad things were?'

'Not really. I've tried talking to them since, but…' She smiled weakly. 'Their interest in money is limited to spending it. They think it will just get sorted out— and it has, always. In the past.'

He could picture her, trying to explain to them, just as she had tried to explain to them about him—could sense, too, the strain she had been under and undoubtedly still was.

His hand found hers and she met his gaze.

'There's always been something to sell. But now there's nothing left except the land. And Lamington.'

There was an ache in her voice, and an exhaustion that made his fingers tighten around hers. 'You won't lose Lamington.'

Once he had hated her home—now nothing seemed to matter more than reassuring her that it would stay her home forever.

'Sometimes I wish I would,' she whispered. 'That I could just be normal like everyone else. Like I was with you...before.'

He stared at her in confusion. Not once had it occurred to him that Nia might feel that way. 'Is that why you didn't tell me?' he asked.

She shook her head. 'It's not your problem, Farlan.'

I want it to be. The words rose in the back of his throat. *I want to help.*

But how could he help anyone—particularly Nia—when he couldn't tell her even the bare bones of his life? And yet how could he not when she had shared something with him—a truth that hurt?

Feeling his body tense, he took a moment to compose himself. 'You asked about my family's farm...'

Her eyes widened fractionally and then she nodded slowly.

'My grandfather fell over and broke his hip. My grandmother couldn't cope so they sold the farm. They moved to Elrick, but they're both dead now.'

No need to tell her that there had been no room for

him at their new house—that once the farm had gone he hadn't been needed. Or wanted.

But then he'd never been wanted—not by those who should have fought tooth and nail to keep him close and safe. To his family he had always been a burden and an inconvenience.

'I'm sorry,' she whispered.

Exhaling, he lifted her hand to his lips. 'No, I'm sorry for being a jerk and messing up lunch.' He held her gaze. 'Let's get out of here. We could have a look around the town,' he offered. 'I've heard it's very pretty. Romantic...'

She lifted her chin. 'And you don't have a problem with that? You know—fitting it in with our "arrangement"?'

Groaning, he screwed up his face. 'I deserve that.'

She nodded. 'Yes, you do. But I guess we could go take a look, if you're not in any rush to get back.'

'I'm not.'

Her eyes were soft and teasing now. 'Really? Maybe you should have joined those Benedictine brothers after all.'

He felt his whole body harden, like iron quenched in a forge. 'That's big talk, Lady Antonia. And later I am going to call you out on that.'

She slipped past his outstretched hand, laughing, but he caught her easily, pulling her against his body and kissing her fiercely.

Ten days. Nine nights.

It would be enough to satisfy this craving.

Then he would go back to the States and get on with his life.

CHAPTER NINE

Shifting against the warmth of her pillow, Nia opened her eyes and rolled onto her side towards Farlan, her fingers feeling for his warm skin.

There was no one lying beside her.

Frowning, she shuffled up the bed. Farlan was crouching naked in front of the fire, his eyes fixed on the darting flames as he slotted a log into the glowing orange stack.

Her mouth drying, her eyes fluttered over the curve of his back.

For a moment she just stared at him.

He looked as if he was posing for a sculptor, or about to take part in some Olympian game in Ancient Greece.

His body was a perfectly weighted balance of tension and geometry, the smooth, contoured muscles gleaming in the firelight like polished marble.

She held her breath. It still felt miraculous that he was here with her…that he wanted what she wanted.

Nine days, eight nights, and counting.

No more cross-purposes. No more confusion or hurt. They were of one mind.

She thought back to that moment in the restaurant

when she had told him the truth about Lamington and her parents' finances.

And then he had confided in her.

It was their gift to one another.

An honesty neither had managed in the past.

And this was their reward.

A honeymoon, almost, like the one they would have had if they had been meant to share their lives as they'd once hoped.

The thought made her chest burn, and for a moment she wanted to tell him that he was the only man she had ever loved, that not a day had passed without her thinking about him.

Instead, she reached over and pressed her hand against the sheet that still bore the imprint of his body.

It was already cooling.

Her heart shivered. Soon he would be gone for ever. There wasn't a moment to lose.

'Come back to bed,' she murmured.

He turned, his eyes narrowing as they took in her naked body, his body instantly all muscle and tension. His gaze was blind, hungry. His erection was heavy and proud. He wanted what she wanted.

And he wanted her.

Crossing the room, he pulled her against him, his mouth seeking hers, and her hands reached for his body.

Later, they lay on the twisted bedding, watching the fire, their damp skin blurring their bodies into one, her breasts pressing against the hard wall of his chest.

The room was blissfully warm. Outside, the sky was starting to turn clay-coloured.

What time was it? she wondered.

In answer to her unspoken question she heard the church bells chime three o'clock.

There'd been so many days like this when they had first got together. Days spent in bed, in Farlan's flat.

Whenever they'd been alone time had grown thick and amorphous, so that she would step out into the street expecting daylight only to find that day was already night.

Not that she had minded. She had loved those long, languid mornings in bed. Loved, too, those afternoons when he'd pulled her into the flat and she had unzipped him, both of them frantic, panting, still fully clothed, their orgasms so quick and sharp that they never even reached the bed.

Afterwards, it had always been her who'd broken the spell. Farlan had been happy to stay there, holding her in his arms. She had been the one needing to reinstate order and normality.

Now, though, as he caressed her hip and the curve of her bottom, she wanted to stop the church bells from chiming. To stop time itself and just stay in his arms in this cosy little room for ever. Only it was stupid and dangerous to think that way...

She felt his teeth nip her collarbone lightly.

'What are you thinking?' he asked.

'Nothing, really,' she lied.

There were rules, she was sure, for this kind of affair. Someone more experienced, more practised in the art of no-strings flings, would definitely know them, but even she could guess that talking about lying in his arms for ever would not be a good idea.

'I was just thinking about the ball,' she said quickly.

It was another lie.

The Beaters' Ball was tonight, and usually she would have been thinking about it for hours beforehand, but it had hardly crossed her mind. Farlan had made everything lose shape and colour.

He slid his hand through her hair, catching strands in his fingers and lifting them up to the light. 'What about the ball?' he asked.

He spoke casually, but she could feel the muscles in his arms tightening a little, as though her answer mattered to him.

'I was just thinking it's a shame Tom and Diane can't go.'

The Drummonds had flown to Dublin for a wedding, and were both very disappointed to be missing it.

Farlan didn't answer immediately, and then he shrugged. 'There'll be others.'

'I know.'

Shifting against the solidity of Farlan's chest, Nia looked away from the fire and tilted her head back. She felt her breath catch in her throat. He was as mesmerising as any fire. He drew the eye in the same way, and it was impossible to look away.

She knew that it wouldn't matter how many days and nights they spent together—she would never get used to his beauty. Nor find another man who would make her feel so complete and so completely desired.

So why waste time at a ball that he would probably hate?

'We don't have to go,' she said. 'Like you say, there'll be other balls.'

Not while Farlan was here, though.

Something flickered across his face, like sunlight washing over the moors, and he lowered his mouth and ran his tongue over her lips. 'I know we don't.'

He was kissing her now, following her pulse down her neck to the hollow at the base of her throat. Shivering, she squeezed her thighs together against the slow, decadent ache that was starting to build there.

There would be three hundred guests at the Beaters' Ball, and they would have to talk and eat and dance with some of them. They would be surrounded by people.

'We could just stay here—'

'We could, but we're not going to,' he muttered against her skin. 'I know I don't have a title, but just for one evening I want to be your Prince Charming, Lady Antonia.'

Her fingers moved down over his stomach, hovering over the thistle tattoo below his hipbone. She heard him suck in a breath, and then he was rolling over, taking her with him so that she was straddling his hips.

'You have a one-track mind,' he said. His eyes were dark in the half-light.

'Only with you,' she said.

He didn't smile. Instead, holding her gaze, he caressed her waist, his hands moving upwards to cover her breasts. She whimpered as he licked first one and then the other nipple, making them swell and throb.

'You're making it so much harder for me.' His voice was hoarse.

'To do what?' She was moving against him now, back and forth, so that the head of his erection pushed against the relentless ache between her legs.

'To leave.'

So don't leave, then, she thought. *Stay here with me.*

But they had tried that before and they both knew it wouldn't work.

This was all they had.

This bed.

This room.

And, leaning forward, she pulled his mouth back to her breast and lifted her hips to meet his thrusts, his hard body driving out the pain of that thought.

Smoothing his hand over his face, Farlan turned off the water. For a moment he stood in the shower, his hands pressed flat against the cold tiles, steam rising off his skin, and then he grabbed two towels, wrapped one around his waist and began rubbing his head with the other.

Depending on his mood, it usually either baffled or annoyed him how no amount of hot water and huge, feather-soft towels could erase the memory of years of shivering in unheated bathrooms.

Today he had other things on his mind.

His mouth twisted.

One thing—one woman.

Nia.

He had left her back at the gardener's cottage to get changed for the ball, and he had returned to Lamington to do the same.

Glancing down at his watch, he frowned. It had only been an hour since he had dragged himself away from her soft, pliant body, and yet already he was missing her.

He had told himself that it would be enough—that coming back here had started something between them that needed to be finished properly this time. And that if they allowed themselves these few days to let it run its course then he could finally get on with his life.

Except that wasn't proving nearly as easy as it sounded.

In the beginning they had agreed to have sex.

That was how it had started in the car.

Remembering their urgent, frantic coupling that day, he felt his body harden. It had been sex in its most basic form: to satisfy a craving. But then, in the bothy, it had shifted into something more sybaritic. Pleasure for the sake of pleasure. And it had been incredible.

His heartbeat accelerated.

If she had been anyone else he would have thought she was the one—that elusive woman who would share his life with him. She had tasted sweeter than honey, and when she'd melted into him he had found himself responding to her just as he had seven years ago.

It had felt so right.

They both knew they could never have a 'normal' relationship, but after that neither of them had been willing to walk away, so they had agreed to this affair.

He stared at his reflection in the mirror. It should be like directing himself in a movie he'd written. No surprises. No disappointments or unrealistic expectations. Just him and Nia. Simple.

Except now it didn't feel simple.

Instead it felt as if he'd pulled on a loose thread and now everything was unravelling in ways he didn't understand and couldn't control.

Like this ball.

His eyes narrowed.

Where did going with Nia to a ball at a neighbour's castle fit into this arrangement?

He felt his chest tighten as it did whenever he thought about Lord Airlie.

Since that lunch at Lachlan and Holly's place Nia hadn't said any more until just now, in bed, and he hadn't asked. But when he had mentioned the Beaters' Ball to Molly, she had gone into raptures about the Marquess.

Grabbing his toothbrush, he began brushing his teeth savagely.

Not only was the Marquess of Airlie wealthy and handsome, he also ran a philanthropic foundation and was the patron of several charities that specialised in supporting local people. He was a perfect gentleman too, according to Diane, who had been completely bowled over by his handwritten invitation to lunch at Castle Kilvean.

All that was missing from his perfect life was a wife.

Farlan spat into the sink.

He got the feeling that Airlie already had someone in mind to fill that vacancy.

Stalking into the dressing room, he stopped in front of the beautifully pressed Highland evening dress that Molly had delivered to his room earlier. He stared at it in silence, his stomach tightening.

Frankly, he couldn't think of anything he wanted to do less than spend an evening hanging out with a bunch of snobby Scottish aristocrats. Especially as he could have got out of it.

Nia had said as much.

So why hadn't he just told her he didn't want to go?

Reaching out, he touched the gleaming silver buttons on the black Prince Charlie jacket.

For the same reason he had agreed to go in the first place. He knew it would make her happy. And more than anything he wanted to make her happy, make her smile and laugh.

In other words, whatever it was that was supposedly going on between him and Nia, what was happening inside his head had nothing to do with sex at all.

Nia took a step back and turned slowly on the spot, staring at the unfamiliar version of herself in the cheval mirror. It was obviously her, but she never really wore anything but black in the evening, as her mother had a horror of anything showy.

Only this wasn't showy, she thought, turning slowly again, her gaze drifting over the old gold taffeta. It was beautiful.

She had bought it in London, after that terrible meeting when the true state of the family finances had been spelled out to her by Douglas.

Leaving the accountant's office, she had been so angry and upset. With her parents for their absurd and selfish extravagances. But more so with herself.

It had all been for nothing. That had been her first thought. She had given Farlan up and it had all been for nothing. All those long, lonely years she had spent embracing the pain had been worthless.

She was going to lose Lamington anyway.

She bit her lip. Even then he had never been far from her thoughts.

Nothing had changed, and yet everything had changed.

Over these last two days she had allowed herself to be a 'normal' woman, with feelings and needs. She had confronted the past and let go of it. For the first time in a long time, maybe ever, she liked herself.

And Farlan liked her too.

She thought back to that moment in the restaurant when he had finally told her about his grandparents. He clearly still missed them. Otherwise why would someone like him—someone so gifted at communicating, at telling stories—find talking about them so hard?

It hurt, knowing that he carried that pain, those bad memories. But tonight she was going to make sure they made some good ones.

Even though she was expecting him, the knock on the door startled her. Heart bumping, she picked up the hem of her skirt and made her way downstairs to the front door.

Farlan stood outside, his broad shoulders filling the porch. She had been expecting him to wear white tie and tails, but he was wearing a traditional Prince Charlie jacket, white shirt, ghillie shoes and a Drummond tartan kilt.

He looked devastatingly handsome and romantic.

'You look beautiful, Nia,' he said softly.

'Thank you.' She swallowed. 'I've never seen you in a kilt.' *Or anything remotely tartan.*

'Tom's chuffed to bits.' He grimaced. 'We're going to send them a photo or my life won't be worth living.'

Her eyes gleamed. She knew he was wearing it for her, and the fact that he would do that made a lightness spread through her whole body, so that she felt as if she might float away.

Taking her hand, he pulled her against him and kissed her softly on the mouth. 'Time to go to the ball, Cinderella.'

She felt the muscles in his face move as he smiled.

'I couldn't find any mice, so no coachmen, I'm afraid.'

She glanced past his shoulder at the sleek, dark sports car. 'Looks like we won't be needing any.'

The glare from the supercar's headlights skimmed the hedges, tunnelling swiftly through the darkness so that they reached Castle Kilvean in just under half an hour.

After a short time spent in the queue of cars moving slowly along the drive, they were walking upstairs towards the huge ballroom.

'Lady Antonia Elgin and Mr Farlan Wilder.'

As the announcer called out their names Nia felt a shiver run down her spine. How many times had she dreamed of this exact moment? Only of course in her dreams she had been Mrs Antonia Wilder.

Farlan's wife—not just his temporary lover.

It was what she still wanted to be.

Her heart felt so full she was suddenly afraid it would burst.

'Nia?'

Farlan was looking at her, his eyes narrowed on her face.

'Is everything okay?'

It wasn't. But taking his hand was easier than dealing with the emotions that were surging up inside her.

Later. She would deal with them later. But right now they could wait.

Turning to Farlan, she smiled. 'I'm fine. Shall we go down?'

Beneath a white and gold ceiling lit by a vast number of chandeliers, the huge ballroom was already half-full of guests. She felt her pulse accelerate. It was silly in some ways, but there was something about a Highland ball. The clashing tartans, the sound of the pipes, the women in their long dresses and sashes and the men looking so handsome in their kilts.

And Farlan was the most handsome of them all.

The pipers were playing a jig—'The Major Ian Stewart.'

'Do you want to dance?' she said suddenly.

Taking her hand, he smiled the smile that no one could resist. 'I thought you'd never ask.'

They danced until they were hot and breathless. And as the music started up again Farlan pulled her closer, his fingers brushing against her dress.

He had never seen her wear that colour before and he wondered why. It was perfect, the faded gold high-lighting the delicacy of her features and picking out the burnished strands in her hair.

'Let's get a drink,' he said, leaning into her.

It was incredibly noisy. Apart from the music there was a swell of voices, people shouting, talking, laughing.

He grabbed some drinks from a circling waiter and nudged her towards the edge of the ballroom, where it was quieter.

'Having fun?' he asked.

She smiled. 'Yes, are you?'

The eagerness in her voice made something pinch in his chest.

'It's a great party,' he said.

She nodded. 'Dancing always makes me feel so happy.'

Her soft brown eyes were sparkling and her cheeks were flushed pink. She looked young and carefree, and with a jolt he realised that she must have been so on edge before.

'Seeing you happy makes me happy,' he said gruffly.

His words fell away into the tune of 'The Duke of Atholl's Reel.'

Too happy.

'Nia, I—'

'Antonia! I was hoping to bump into you earlier. But there's just so many people—'

'Andrew—'

Nia turned towards a tall, handsome man in a busy red and blue tartan, her eyes lighting up with delight.

'I did see you earlier, but then you disappeared into the throng.'

They kissed on both cheeks and then Nia gestured to Farlan. 'Farlan, this is our host, the Marquess of Airlie—Andrew, this is Farlan Wilder. He's—' She stumbled.

'Staying with the Drummonds.' Stepping forward to finish Nia's sentence, Farlan held out his hand.

'The famous film director,' said the Marquess.

They shook hands.

'We quite often have guests from Holyrood, Mr Wilder, but never from Hollywood. So this is a rare treat.'

He had a voice like Nia's: smooth, English-sounding,

but with a tiny inflexion of Scots. And, much as Farlan wanted to hate this man, he seemed warm and genuine.

'This is a great party, Lord Airlie,' he said.

'Please, call me Andrew. And, yes, it's going rather well.' He caught Nia's eye. 'Much better than last year's effort.'

Nia laughed. She glanced at Farlan, making their private joke a shared one. 'The dance floor broke.'

Andrew nodded. 'During a particularly vigorous Eightsome Reel. We had to evacuate everyone while they replaced it.' He grinned. 'It was chaos. But I imagine compared to what you have to oversee on set our little gathering must seem like a piece of cake.'

'Not at all. Watch out—'

Catching Nia's wrist, somehow slipping his arms around her waist, Farlan pulled her out of the way as a group of giggling teenage girls stumbled off the dance floor.

'My actors would be drinking tinted water, not champagne, so on the whole I'd say you have the harder task—but maybe you should come over to LA and see for yourself.'

He could feel the heat of Nia's body, the press of her skin against his. The girls had gone now, but he was still her partner, and it was perfectly natural to let his hand rest on her hipbone, to let his fingers splay out possessively.

'I might just do that.' Andrew smiled. 'And in return perhaps I could invite you to come over for lunch. I have a date in the diary with your hosts at the end of the month. It would be wonderful if you could join us.'

For a moment, the invitation quivered in the air.

Farlan felt Nia's eyes on his profile.

It was a reason to stay. It would be just until the end of the month.

His heart beat faster.

But staying on longer would only confuse things, and he knew all too well the painful consequences of sending mixed messages.

'I would have loved to, but unfortunately I'll be back in the States by then.'

'What a shame.' Andrew glanced over at Nia, his blue eyes politely flirtatious. 'Don't worry. I'll be happy to step in and distract her. In fact, I was wondering if I might persuade you to part with her for "The Duke of Perth."'

'Oh, I don't—' Nia began.

The idea of Nia dancing with this confident, charming man, of her gazing into his eyes and laughing breathlessly during the turns, made jealousy burn through him. But Farlan forced himself to smile.

'I'm happy to sit one out. I've had quite enough Dukes for the moment.'

His jaw felt rigid with the effort of smiling as he watched Andrew steer Nia back to the dance floor, his hand resting lightly against her back. He watched as she moved among the crowd, feeling his pulse oscillating in time with her hips.

It was obvious even at a distance that she and Airlie knew the same people. Every few yards couples stopped to greet them and share a joke. And they looked like a couple too.

Nia looked relaxed and happy. Her eyes were shining. And, watching her smile, he felt his stomach clench.

Stupid, arrogant idiot that he was, he had actually thought that he was the reason for her happiness, that he made her happy.

And he did. In bed.

But here she was at home among friends.

She was safe. *Loved.*

He turned abruptly and walked away from the dance floor through the huge doors and outside to the gardens, following the torches along a path away from the castle. The cold air stung his eyes, but that was good. It helped blur the image that had just dropped into his head of Nia lying upstairs in Andrew Airlie's arms.

He wished it would freeze his heart too.

Why shouldn't that happen? Why shouldn't Nia have that?

Airlie was offering her more than sex. He was offering her a future. A future without the fear that it would all fall apart.

Farlan knew he could never have that for himself, but he wanted that for her. He wanted Nia to be able to love without fear. And he wanted someone to love her, to take care of her. To do what he had failed to do and put her first.

'There you are.'

He turned. Nia was standing behind him.

'I've been looking for you everywhere.'

She was alone. His relief was so overwhelming that he had to take a breath to steady himself before he spoke.

'I was just getting some air.'

She was shivering and, pulling off his jacket, he

slipped it over her shoulders. 'Come on, let's go back inside.'

But she didn't move. 'Actually, if you're okay with it, I thought we might go back to the cottage.'

He stared at her in silence, his heart pounding.

'Or we could go back to Lamington…'

Her words hung between them like the moths fluttering above the torchlight.

He knew what she was offering. It was the final step in resetting their past. The two of them together in the house where they had separated.

Leaning forward, he kissed her on the mouth. 'Your carriage awaits.'

The big house was quiet and still and dark. They left the lights off, and Farlan led her upstairs and into his guest bedroom.

It was so familiar—he was so familiar—and yet she could feel her heart racing as if she had fallen through a rabbit hole into a parallel world where they had never split up.

She stopped in front of the dressing table. Farlan was behind her, his unblinking gaze reflected in the mirror, watching her image. 'Could you undo me?'

She met his gaze, her mouth drying at the heat in his green eyes as he nodded.

Turning round, she felt her pulse begin to leap in her throat as his fingers brushed against her skin, and the zip slid down her back.

'Nia…'

He whispered her name, his breath warm against her cheek, and she turned towards him as the dress slipped to the floor, pooling at her feet. Now she was naked except for her stockings, her panties and her heels.

She heard his breath hitch, and her muscles clenched as his hands slid up over her waist, capturing her breasts, his fingers pulling at the already aching tips. Pulling her round, his lips found hers, and he kissed her with an urgency that made her head spin.

'Undress me...'

With fingers that felt thick and unwieldy she pulled at his shirt, her hands growing steadier as they touched the smooth, toned muscles of his chest.

They started to tremble again as she unbuckled his kilt.

He was naked underneath.

Naked and very aroused.

Reaching out, she ran her fingers over his smooth length, feeling her stomach tipping as his eyes narrowed.

'I want you,' he said hoarsely.

'So take me,' she whispered.

He lifted her up onto the dressing table and then dropped to his knees. Hooking his thumbs into her panties, he slid them down her legs and over the tops of her stockings, and she breathed out shakily as he ran his tongue between her thighs.

She gripped the dressing table, her nails scraping against the smooth wood. Her legs were trembling and his hands splayed over her skin, steadying her as she felt her body begin to lift free of its moorings.

Moaning softly, she began to move against his mouth, her pulse beating on his tongue. Soon he pulled away and flipped her round, his hand capturing her face, his mouth finding hers. And then he was pushing into her, his hand moving to her clitoris, the slow, measured sweep of his finger making her arch backwards.

His arm was around her waist and he was lifting her body against his as she let go, crying out as he thrust the blunt head of his erection up inside of her.

In the mirror, his darkened eyes locked with hers and her muscles clenched around him. And then he was crying out too, shuddering in pleasure, pressing his face against her shoulder, his heartbeat raging in time to hers.

He pulled away gently and scooped her into his arms, carried her over to the bed.

She lay there, her body quivering with the tiny aftershocks of her release. They were both breathing unsteadily, their skin warm and damp.

After a moment or two he pulled her closer and she nestled into him. She would never get tired of this. Of how it felt to have his arms around her. Of how his body felt inside her. The heat and the pressure and the rhythm.

Already she wanted him again—only at some point all this would have to stop and he would leave.

But she wasn't ready for that to happen. She wasn't sure she would ever be ready.

She thought back to what she'd told herself earlier. That tonight was about making good memories. But what if those memories weren't enough?

'What are you thinking?' he asked, and tipped her face up to his.

'I was just thinking it was lucky I didn't know you

weren't wearing anything under your kilt or we'd have had to have left earlier.'

'You'd have done that for me?

Her heart was still beating fast and, looking up into his soft, green gaze, she felt it beat even faster.

She dropped a kiss on his chest. 'Of course.'

His hand slid over the curve of her hip, his fingers grazing the top of her stockings. 'Lord Airlie must be disappointed we left. I think he was hoping to dance with you again.'

She felt a pang of guilt. She hadn't thought about Andrew once. Every thought, every breath, every glance had been centred on Farlan.

'Andrew is the host—he has lots of duty dances to perform.'

'And is that what that was? A duty dance?'

Farlan had been aiming to keep his voice casual, but clearly he'd failed.

She looked up at him, her eyes searching his face. 'What do you mean?'

He let his gaze float away to the window to where the hills met the Castle Kilvean estate.

'Just something Molly said to me when I told her about the ball. She said Lord Airlie had everything he wanted...' His eyes locked onto hers. 'Except a wife.'

She shifted backwards against the pillow, her hair like honey in the soft light of the table lamp. Outside, he thought he could hear the distant sound of bagpipes.

'He wants to marry you, Nia.'

She shook her head. 'I'm not going to marry Andrew,' she said slowly.

'He hasn't asked you yet?'

There was another long silence.

'Actually, he has.'

Her words bumped into each other inside his head like fairground dodgems. He stared at her, shock muting the pain in his chest. 'This evening?'

'No.' She shook her head. 'About a year ago.'

A year ago. So after she had found out that her family estate was in financial difficulties.

As if reading his mind, she gave him a small, tight smile. 'My parents were pretty upset that I turned him down. When Andrew proposed I think they thought it would be the perfect solution to our problems.'

Farlan could all too easily imagine her father's clipped, furious disbelief.

Glancing down at her pale face, he pushed a stray curl away from her face. 'You say he's a good man?'

She nodded. 'He is.'

'And yet you turned him down.' It was a struggle to keep his voice even. 'Why did you do that?'

Her eyelashes grazed her cheekbones as she looked down at his hand on her hip. 'I've known Andrew for ever. And I love him. But only as a friend.'

'Sometimes love can change.'

His spine tensed. Why had he said that? It made no sense. He didn't want Nia to marry Andrew-bloody-Marquess-of-Airlie. He didn't want her to marry anyone. The thought made him want to rage and smash things.

But he could feel the old familiar ache filling his chest—the swell of panic, the need to push and push and push…

'Sometimes love that starts as friendship develops into passion over time,' he said.

She was shaking her head. 'That's not going to happen.'

'I saw you tonight with him,' he persisted. 'He made you happy.'

He felt as if he was stabbing himself. But it was the right thing to do.

He edged away from her. 'I want you to be happy, Nia.'

'I *am* happy. Here. With you.'

He pushed off the bed. He couldn't do this. Couldn't say what he needed to say with her so close.

'This isn't real. And you deserve better. You deserve the best and Lord Airlie is the best. He's rich and kind and he loves you.' He went for the jugular. 'And when I've gone, he will still be here. You need to think about that—about your future.'

She was looking at him as if he was a stranger. 'And you think Andrew's my future?'

Her eyes were bright.

'I can't marry a man I don't love, and—' Her voice faltered and she cleared her throat. 'And I don't want to think about the future.'

There was a silence.

Then, lifting her face, she met his gaze. 'All I can think about is you and me and how I don't want it to end just yet.'

He could hardly believe what she was saying—or that she was saying it. For a moment he couldn't speak, so great was his fear that he had misheard or misunderstood. And then he felt relief surge through his body, driving out the tension and pain of moments earlier.

He reached for her blindly, his hands curving around

her arms. 'I don't want you to marry Airlie, and I don't want this to end just yet either.' His fingers tightened, anchoring her to him. 'There's no reason we can't carry on as we are for a month or two.'

Aside from his job, his home and countless meetings with producers and actors...

Heart thumping, he pushed the thought away. He would fly back to the States as and when it was necessary.

His eyes locked with hers. 'I can make that happen. If that's what you want. And after that—'

She put her mouth against his, her soft lips breathing warmth and hope. 'That's what I want.'

He felt his heart swell. There was no doubt in her voice or her face.

And so, not wanting anything to change the certainty of the moment, he pushed her back onto the bed and lowered his body to hers.

CHAPTER TEN

'OH, NIA, THANK GOODNESS you're here.' Darting across the drawing room, Diane kissed Nia on both cheeks and, hooking her arm, practically towed her towards a sofa. 'Come and sit down with me.' She patted the cushion and then turned to her husband. 'Tom, tell Molly we'll have coffee now.'

Grinning, Tom saluted. 'Yes, ma'am.' He winked at Nia and then pulled her into a squeezing embrace. 'She's champing at the bit to hear about the ball.'

Diane nodded. 'I want you to tell me everything. And I want to see some photos.'

Nia frowned. 'I thought Farlan sent you some?'

'He did.' A deep, familiar voice cut into the conversation. 'But apparently they didn't meet requirements.'

She felt her heartbeat accelerate, and her skin felt suddenly too hot and tight. Farlan had followed Tom into the room and, glancing over at him, she felt heat crackle down her spine.

Tom and Diane had arrived back from Dublin late last night.

Even though she and Farlan had both agreed to extend their 'arrangement', neither of them had wanted to say anything to Tom and Diane, so Farlan had waited until they'd gone to bed before making his way down the drive to the gardener's cottage.

A little bubble of happiness rose up and popped inside her chest. She had been looking out for him from her bedroom, and when he'd caught sight of her he had climbed up the front wall to her open window.

His lips had been cold from the outside air, but his kiss had been hotly passionate. And what had followed had been equally passionate—both an admission of their longing and an affirmation of what they had decided in the early hours of the morning in his guest room after the ball.

He had got up early this morning, grumbling about having to leave her, and after he had gone she had rolled over in bed, pressing herself into the heat left by his body, breathing in the intimate scent of him.

And now he was dropping into the armchair beside her sofa. Real. Warm. His green eyes gleaming as they met hers.

'Good morning, Lady Antonia. Did you sleep well?'

His leg brushed against hers and she felt fingers of heat slide over her skin. She didn't think she had ever wanted anyone or anything more than she wanted Farlan in this moment.

'Yes, I did, thank you. And you?'

'On and off,' he said softly. 'I had to keep changing position.'

As Diane looked up, Nia felt her face grow warm.

Fortunately Molly chose that moment to bring in the coffee, and a delectable array of shortbread and ginger biscuits.

'So what was wrong with Farlan's photos?' asked Nia, after Molly had left.

Diane rolled her eyes. 'I'll show you.' She pulled out her phone. 'This is why you don't ask a man to take photos at a ball.'

Nia bit into her lip, trying not to smile. In one, the plaid of Farlan's kilt filled the wing mirror of the supercar, and in several others Nia could see herself and Farlan reflected in the flank of the car.

Diane was frowning at Farlan. 'I wanted photos of the two of you, all dressed up and looking beautiful, and you took these.'

Farlan grinned. 'What can I say? I'm a creative—I went for the artistic shot.'

Leaning forward, he put his hand around Nia's and tilted the phone towards Tom. She felt her body tingle from the contact.

'This is a great one of the brake callipers.'

Catching sight of Diane's face, Nia burst out laughing. 'Oh, please don't worry, Diane. He *did* take some of us, I promise. And Andrew had a couple of photographers there, and they took absolutely masses of photos.'

Farlan was pulling out his own phone. 'Come on, Dee. You know I wouldn't let you down. Here. Take a look at these.'

Gazing down at the screen, Nia felt her heart twist. She could vaguely remember Farlan handing the phone to someone as they'd walked into the ball. But so much had happened the memory had gone adrift. Now, though, staring down at the screen, she could almost feel the weight of his arm around her waist as he pulled her against him.

It was a great photo.

A fortuitous, few seconds when everything had conspired to capture them both in a perfect moment in time.

She was almost as tall as him in her heels, so her head was only fractionally tilted back. In the background of the photo people were milling about, but even from the static one-dimensional image, anyone could tell that they were completely unaware of anyone but each other.

She heard Diane gasp.

'You both look so lovely!'

Nia felt the catch in the older woman's voice resonate through her body.

'Oh, Tom, I wish we'd stayed.' Diane was looking up at her husband, her eyes bright with tears.

Tom squeezed her shoulder. 'Now, Dee, don't you start, or you'll set me off.'

Sighing, Farlan pushed the tray of coffee out of the way and sat down on the table. He leaned forward and smoothed the tears from Diane's cheeks. 'There's going to be other balls. This is the Highlands, Dee. There's one kicking off round here practically every weekend.'

'But not while you're here.' Diane sniffed. 'You'll be back in LA next week.'

Nia felt her pulse twitch.

There was a short silence, and then Farlan smiled. 'Actually, I won't be. I've decided to stay on for a bit longer—'

He yelped as Tom yanked him to his feet.

'I knew once you got here you'd want to stay. A true Scotsman can't resist the pull of the pipes.'

Grinning, Farlan shook his head. 'The way you play them, he can.'

After Burns Night Tom had bought some bagpipes and practised enthusiastically.

'Oh, hush, you.' Diane smiled at him. 'So, are you really staying?'

'If that's all right with you, Dee?'

'I've never been happier about anything,' she said.

As Farlan pulled Diane into a hug his eyes found Nia's, and she felt her muscles tighten in a sharp involuntary spasm.

And in the confusion of tears and laughter that followed his announcement neither Tom nor Diane noticed the way their gazes locked, or the flicker of hunger that passed between them.

Later, as they lay in bed at the cottage, Nia knew that she too had never been happier about anything than Farlan staying on in Scotland.

She glanced down to where he lay sleeping, his head resting on her stomach, his profile cutting a clean line against her pale skin.

Not even when they had met all those years ago and she had fallen hopelessly in love with him.

That had been like a thunderclap.

When their eyes had first met she had felt it crackle down her spine and along her limbs like lightning.

Even then, with no actual physical experience of men, she had known that what she was feeling was special. Unique. Miraculous.

He was everything she had ever wanted.

But she had been too young and too sheltered, too

unsure of herself to let their love follow its own path. Too conscious of her role as heir to Lamington.

Her fingers trembled against the sheet.

It had been drummed into her since birth that duty always outweighed personal desires and dreams. Was it any wonder, then, that pitting her first love against four hundred years of history had torn her in two?

She had grown up surrounded by beautiful things in glass cases. Books that were never read. Paintings and tapestries that were never allowed to see daylight.

Faced with the possibility of an imperfect 'real' love she had ended everything.

But she wasn't that same fearful, uncertain girl any more.

She had grown up.

She had learned to 'manage' her parents, and she also managed the family finances and ran a twenty-eight-thousand-acre estate.

Most important of all, she had learned to trust her judgement. She knew her own mind now—and this relationship with Farlan wasn't based on some naïve ideal.

She knew her faults—and his—and she loved him anyway.

Her heartbeat stalled.

She tried the words out inside her head.

I love Farlan.

She felt dizzy with panic and shock.

But why?

Breathing out shakily, she pressed her fingers against her eyes, blocking out the sight of Farlan's naked sleeping form.

How could she not have seen it before?

It seemed so obvious to her now that she loved him and had never stopped loving him.

It had just been easier to tell everyone that she had stopped.

To tell herself that she had.

She had buried the truth deep and learned to live a quiet, colourless life.

When he wasn't there—when their relationship had been defined by impossibility—she had been able to do it. But he was here now. And what had once seemed so impossible, so out of reach, was already in her grasp.

Her hand trembled against the soft stubble on his head.

Outside there was a growl of thunder and the sudden drumming of rain like gravel against a windscreen. The sudden intrusion of reality made her flinch.

Farlan didn't want this to end. But all he had really offered was a couple of months, and then after that...

There were too many possible interpretations of 'after that' for her to contemplate, and only one she wanted to be true.

She stared down at him, her heart racing. She could wake him now, tell him that she didn't want just a couple more months, that she didn't want him to go anywhere without her.

But he might not be ready.

He might never be ready to hear that.

Remembering how his mood had shifted in the restaurant, she felt her breath catch in her throat. He had been angry and hostile, but there had been fear not fury in his eyes.

If that was how he reacted when she tried to find out

more about his family, how might he react if she told him she wanted to share her life with him?

She couldn't risk losing what she had right now for yet another impossible dream of love.

Shifting down a gear, Farlan turned the steering wheel, his mouth curving down as he threaded it through his hands.

'What is it?' Nia asked.

She was sitting beside him and, turning, he grimaced. 'Ignore me—I'm just being a spoiled brat.' Sensing her confusion, he grinned. 'It just feels a bit "agricultural."'

'You mean the car?'

He nodded. 'Don't get me wrong, it's a great car, but…'

As he let the sentence tail off, her eyes gleamed. 'Oh, I see. It's not edgy enough for Mr Hollywood Big Shot.'

They could be playful now, teasing one another without fear of everything imploding.

He burst out laughing. 'I wish! I'm just the new kid on the block right now. Compared to the Mr Big Shots in Hollywood I'm like a firecracker. Seriously.'

Outside the window, the countryside was starting to recede. In its place, houses and shops were starting to hug the road. He could feel something shifting inside him, like the pistons and the flywheel inside the car's engine.

'If you don't believe me then maybe you should come out with me to LA and see for yourself.'

There was a pause, and then he felt her hand on top of his. 'I'd love that,' she said quietly.

He felt a swooping happiness, pure and swift like a swallow curving through the sky. And, reaching over, he caught her fingers and lifted them to his lips.

'Then I'll make it happen.'

Was it really that easy? He felt his pulse accelerate. Apparently so. Only what had changed? Why was it so easy for them to communicate now when before everything had been so charged with misunderstanding?

He didn't understand it, but he couldn't deny how easy it was between them now. Or how happy it made him.

'After two hundred yards, turn right at Lennox Place.'

The glacial voice of the satnav broke into his thoughts and he smiled at Nia. 'We're nearly there.'

It was the only 'date' he had in his diary for the whole trip. Everything else he had been happy to leave to serendipity and Diane. But this was personal: it was the Gight Street Picture Palace.

The cinema had been small and shabby, but years ago it had been his hideout. His refuge. A place where he'd been able to watch heroes and heroines defeat the bad guys, fight alien hordes, go back in time and fall in love.

From that first visit when the lights had dimmed he'd been captivated, swept away not just by the dramas playing out on screen but by the thought of being behind the camera. Telling stories where he got to choose the ending.

Most times, he hadn't even cared what film was on. He'd sat through all of them. And later, every week wherever he was in the world, he would check the listings there, always thinking of the day when his film would play there.

Then it had shut down.

He had been gutted, and as soon as he'd had the money to do so he had bought the site with a view to restoring it. Now, after nearly two years and several million pounds, the restoration was complete. Today was the official opening, and he was the guest of honour.

Nia glanced over at him. 'Do you think there'll be many people there?'

He would have been happy to keep his presence private, but he understood why the trust who now managed the Picture Palace for him had been keen to alert the media. It was good publicity and he couldn't begrudge them that.

He shrugged. 'Maybe... I guess there would be more if I was some hot-looking actor.'

'If they're turning out on account of your hotness, there should be quite a crowd,' she teased.

They parked at the Imlah, a sleek boutique hotel with a red brick Victorian facade that was owned by some friends of Lachlan and Holly. There they were picked up in a near identical car and driven to the Picture Palace.

Nia caught his eye, and he smiled at her, a moment of recognition at a shared, private joke.

There was indeed a large crowd waiting at the cinema, including camera crews and lots of photographers, and he pulled her against him as the car drew up.

'Stay close to me, okay?'

He'd been to enough premieres for the crowd not to bother him, but he could still remember how intimidating it had been to step out into a barrage of questions and flashing cameras for the first time.

There was just time to wave at the crowd and pose

for a few photos, and then he was meeting and greeting the board of trustees, the architect and the design team.

Having given a speech thanking everyone involved, he cut the ribbon.

'It's not too crazy for you, is it?' He stared down at Nia, ignoring the photographers' shouts, feeling the shock of her beauty colliding with his ever-present hunger. 'We should be able to leave soon. All the formal stuff is done.'

'There's no rush.' She smiled at him. 'Let me be proud of what you've made happen here.' She nudged him towards the crowd. 'Go on.'

He signed autographs and smiled, but without Nia beside him he felt as though he had lost a limb. Glancing over his shoulder, he caught sight of her and felt his heart thump. Okay, he was done here.

'Farlan—'

He turned automatically as someone called his name—and froze.

His vision shimmered and his throat tightened, cutting off his breath.

'I heard you were coming here today. I thought I'd come down and say hello.'

The faces in the crowd thickened and blurred.

All except one.

Farlan stared at the man in front of him, his heart slamming in his chest. Panic was seeping through his body like frostbite. He tried to will it away, but he could feel himself shutting down. He was trapped in ice.

Green eyes met his own momentarily, and then he spun away and walked towards Nia.

'We're leaving,' he said hoarsely.

He had no idea how they got back to the Imlah. His conscious mind was blank. All he could think about was getting into the car and driving as fast and as far away as he could from the past.

And the pain.

He gripped the steering wheel as memories burrowed their way to the surface. Memories of driving fast to nowhere. Only he wasn't driving the car.

From some immense, impenetrable distance away he heard Nia's voice talking to him. He couldn't focus on what she was saying, but she was talking calmly, steadily, and he felt some of the tension leave his body.

Pulling off the road, he switched off the engine and gazed down the hillside at some unnamed loch. The sun was dazzlingly bright and a light wind was sending small, choppy ripples across the mercury gleam of the water. It looked so beautiful and serene. If only he could dive beneath the mirror-smooth surface and escape the turmoil in his head.

'What is it? What's the matter?' asked Nia.

The numbness had left his body, but his brain still felt frozen. Something shivered inside him, and then he felt her hand on his: warm, soft, firm…

'Please, Farlan. Please talk to me.'

'I don't know where to start,' he said after a moment.

He felt her hesitation. Then, 'Did something happen?'

'Not something. Someone. There was someone in the crowd I knew.'

He could taste metal in his mouth. The pain felt as though it would burst through his skin.

'His name's Cam. He's my brother.'

* * *

Nia stared at him. Outside the car, clouds were starting to tumble over the hills. Seconds later fat, globular raindrops began hitting the windscreen. Inside her head she was shuffling the assumptions she'd made, thumbing through them like a deck of cards.

'I didn't know you had a brother,' she said carefully.

The expression on his face made her stomach muscles tremble.

'I didn't know if I still had one. We lost touch...must be sixteen years ago. After he moved out.'

She hesitated, not wanting to press against the bruise in his voice, but even less able to just sit and watch his pain. 'From the farm?'

He stared at her blankly, then shook his head. 'No. I had to go to the farm because he left.'

Nia blinked. What did he mean by 'had to'? She took the easier question. 'So why did he leave?'

'He wasn't going to.' Farlan's mouth twisted. 'But then he met this bloke down the pub. He was a roustabout on one of the oil rigs, and he talked Cam into taking a job on one.'

Nia frowned. Usually the answers to questions left her understanding more, but with Farlan she seemed to understand less and less.

'Why did that mean you had to move to the farm?' she said slowly.

His face shuttered. 'I couldn't live on my own. I was only thirteen.'

'So you were living with Cam? It was just the two of you?'

Was that even legal?

'What about your parents?' She'd thought they were divorced and both had remarried, but if he'd been that young…

There was a long pause.

'My mum left when I was seven. I haven't seen her since.'

Nia was starting to feel sick. In the restaurant, she had wanted him to tell her about his family. Selfishly, greedily, she had wanted to share more than sex with him. Now, though, every word he spoke hurt her.

Worse, it hurt him.

'When she left it was okay for a couple of years…'

She felt his hand tense.

'And then my dad met Cathy.' He looked away, tracking the clouds that were racing across the sky. 'She didn't really like me and Cam, and she had three kids of her own, so…' His voice faltered. 'Anyway, she persuaded my dad that it would be better if we moved out, so he bought us this caravan and me and Cam moved in there. Only then Cam left.'

Her throat was so tight it hurt to swallow, to speak. 'Why didn't you move back in with your dad?'

His eyes met hers and he smiled stiffly. 'He said there wasn't room for me, so I just stayed living in the caravan. On my own.'

She couldn't look away. Her heart felt as though it would burst. How could anyone do that to their child?

'How long were you there?' she whispered.

'About four months, and then Cam called. When he found out I was on my own he got in touch with my grandparents.'

Surely that must have been the happy ending he'd deserved—except his shoulders were still tense.

'They weren't bad people,' he said, in answer to her unasked question. 'They fed me and clothed me. They did their duty right up until I was sixteen. But when they sold the farm it was clear they weren't expecting me to go with them.'

He'd been alone and homeless at sixteen.

Six years later they had met.

It had never occurred to her that his autonomy was a result of neglect and abandonment.

She had been so in awe of him. To her, he had seemed beautiful and untamed.

Now, though, she could see that he had been not wild, but lost.

A lost boy without a mother or father.

No wonder he found it so hard to talk about his family. It was a miracle he even understood the meaning of the word.

He was staring away from her, but she didn't need to see his face. She could feel everything.

Unbuckling her seatbelt, she slid over and wrapped her arms around him. Her cheeks were wet—with her tears and his.

'I don't know what I did wrong…' he said.

'You did nothing wrong.' Eyes stinging, she lifted her face to his, her love for him exploding inside her. 'You were a child.'

'Not a very easy one.' He shook his head. 'Whatever anyone said or did, I needed proof. I was always pushing back, pushing them away to see if they meant it.' His eyes found hers. 'I did it with Tom and Diane, just like I did it with you. When I first met them I thought they'd get sick of having me around, like everyone else had. I didn't want to believe they were different, so I made it as hard as I could for them.'

The pain in his voice knocked the air out of her body. 'I know. But you don't have to push back any more. Tom and Diane aren't going anywhere, and neither am I.'

He stared at her. 'You are an incredible woman, Nia, and I'm so sorry. For everything.'

Clasping his face, she stroked his cheeks gently. 'Everything?'

His mouth curved upwards—not quite a smile, but she hadn't lost him.

Outside the sky had split in two and a rainbow was arching across the water.

'No, definitely not for everything.' He kissed her softly on the mouth. 'Let's go home.' His face creased. 'But first I better give Rosie at the Picture Palace a call…apologise for leaving without saying goodbye properly.'

They didn't talk much on the way back to Lamington. Farlan never spoke much when he was driving, and she was lost in her thoughts.

His story had shocked her. But she understood now why he had been so unforgiving, so absolute, seven years ago. She could make sense of the anger that had always been there beneath the surface.

It was an anger that stemmed from a not unreasonable fear of rejection.

So why hadn't she told him that she loved him?

'Yours or mine?' he asked.

If only there was an 'ours.'

She managed to smile. 'Mine. Then I can change out of these clothes.'

Walking into the cottage, she could feel the need to tell him the truth like a weight pressing down on her. 'Farlan—'

'What's this?'

She frowned. He was holding an envelope with her name on it. 'I don't know…'

His eyes flickered round the room. 'It wasn't here when we left.'

She opened it. 'It's from Andrew. It's the photos from the ball.'

Glancing down at them, she felt a rush of warmth for her neighbour. He was a good man, but she didn't want him.

'How did he get in?'

Farlan was standing beside her, his green eyes narrowed.

'I keep a spare key under the flowerpot.'

'So he just lets himself in?'

'Yes, he does. Because he's a friend.'

The memory of what Farlan had told her in the car merged with the suffocating intensity of her need to tell him the truth.

'And that's all he can ever be.'

Dropping the photos onto the table, she took his hands in hers.

'The other day you asked me why I turned Andrew down, and I told you it was because I didn't love him. That was true a year ago and it's still true now.' Her hands were shaking. 'But that wasn't the only reason.' She took a breath. 'The main reason I can't marry Andrew, or any other man for that matter, is because I love you, Farlan. I've never stopped loving you.'

Her fingers curled around his.

'I know we broke up a long time ago, but in my heart I've always felt married to you—and I think you feel the same way.'

Farlan stared at her in shock.

Nia loved him.

And he loved her.

He felt a rush of relief.

It was that simple. All he had to do was tell her.

But it wasn't that simple.

His eyes flickered over the photos spilling across the table. Yes, she loved him. Andrew Airlie had seen it the moment he'd looked at the pictures of the two of them. That was why he'd dropped them round.

And Farlan loved her.

But less than an hour ago he had been crumpled up in a car, swamped by a past that still defined him.

He thought back to how he'd driven away from the cinema. He had been a slithering mass of panic. It had spread through him with a speed and a savagery that had been impossible to stop, and left him blind to anything but the need to flee.

Only he couldn't outrun the past and the pain.

It was a wound that wouldn't heal. He could never be whole.

All those times he had been handed on to the next person were like fault lines inside him—invisible, but irreparable.

Being on his own had been terrifying. Whenever he

felt it was going to happen again he panicked, and all the accumulated fear and powerlessness of his childhood broke through as unstoppably as lava.

Remembering how Nia had comforted him, he felt a wave of remorse. How could he inflict that on her? Not just now, but maybe for ever?

It wasn't fair. She deserved better.

A photo of Andrew Airlie and Nia snagged his gaze. She could have better. Airlie would wait for her and one day—

He slipped his hands free of hers. 'I'm sorry, Nia, but I don't feel the same way,' he lied. 'And I'm sorry if I gave you the impression I did.'

He stepped backwards.

She looked confused, as if maybe she had misheard him, and then her hesitant smile stilled. 'Farlan, I know why you don't trust me, but—'

'I do trust you, Nia.'

He knew she would slay dragons for him, spill every last drop of her blood to keep him safe. He just couldn't trust himself to be enough for her. Not to disappoint her as he had everyone else in his life. Because she alone would stand by him whatever it cost her.

'But I don't love you.'

The expression on her face was like a blade in his heart.

'I don't believe you,' she said hoarsely. 'I think you're just scared.'

'Then you're mistaken. I'm sorry, Nia. Truly. But this isn't what I signed up for.'

He took another step backwards.

'I think it's probably best if we call time on this—on

us—don't you? I've got an interview in London tomorrow, and then I'll fly back to LA.'

Misery hammered in his head so that it hurt just to stand there.

'I truly am sorry, Nia.' He turned, then stopped. 'You'll be needing this,' he said stiffly.

He held out the car key, but she didn't move. So he dropped it on top of the photos and then, ignoring her pale, frozen face, he walked across the room and out through the door.

That was what he'd decided to do, and he was a man who knew his own mind.

CHAPTER ELEVEN

SHIFTING BACK IN his seat, Farlan glanced round the cockpit of the helicopter, steadying his breathing. Methodically, he checked the instrument panel, grateful for the distraction and the comforting familiarity of the process.

There was nothing left to do. It was time to leave.

As the helicopter rose up into the pale blue sky and swung away from Lamington some of his composure began to fail. To the left he could see the gardener's cottage, and as he passed over it his whole body tensed. But he ignored it.

He ignored the ache in his chest too.

When he had come downstairs that morning, Molly had already been up, making bread, and he had stood and watched her push and knead the dough.

It was, he knew, harder than it looked. One of those complicated balancing acts between science and intuition.

But, frankly, it had to be easier than dealing with the memories of what had happened yesterday at Nia's cottage. And infinitely less painful than remembering the stunned, devastated expression on her face.

He shifted in his seat, guilt tightening his shoulders. It was his fault. All of it.

He'd come back to Scotland believing he could press the reset button and move on.

Walking into the drawing room at Lamington on Burns Night he'd been full of anger and resentment. He'd wanted to throw his success in Nia's face, to exorcise the ghost of the woman who had cast him aside but never left his thoughts.

Or his heart.

Only of course it had never once occurred to him during the last seven years that he still loved her.

And she loved him. *Unconditionally.*

He knew that for a fact.

The tension in his shoulders was spilling down his back now.

His heart was suddenly pounding so hard it was blocking out the sound of the rotors.

For so long he had held everything in. Directing his life as though it was a movie, treating his past like something that could be edited or touched up or just left on the cutting room floor.

Yesterday he had told Nia the ugly, shocking details of his life and afterwards she hadn't pushed him away.

She had only held him closer.

Grimacing, he stretched out his neck. His back felt as if it was on a rack. He needed to stop, move around, shift this tension.

Thankfully he'd checked out a couple of helipads enroute and called ahead. The nearest was only around ten minutes away, and twelve minutes later, he brought the helicopter down onto the landing pad with textbook smoothness.

Switching off the rotors, he unbuckled and climbed out of the cockpit. A light wind was blowing, and the sun felt warm on his face.

He had stopped to stretch his body, to release his mind, but inexorably his thoughts returned to that moment when he'd told Nia about his childhood.

Seven years ago he'd pushed her to prove her love, demanding that she leave everything and everyone behind for him. And then when, quite understandably, she had panicked, he hadn't bothered to listen or stay around long enough to talk about her reasons.

He had run away.

That had been understandable too, given how many people had made him feel he only had a walk-on part in his own life.

But yesterday Nia had offered her love unprompted. *And he was still running.*

Still running—only this time he was running from a rejection that hadn't happened. It had been a hypothetical rejection of their future.

That didn't just make no sense. It was crazy.

He swore softly. He was such an idiot.

There were multiple awards back at his house in LA. As an award-winning film director he was supposed to be all-seeing. And yet he had been so focused on outrunning his fears that he'd missed the obvious, glaring truth.

He didn't need to outrun them.

It was light that drove out the darkness—not more darkness.

Remembering Cam's face at the Picture Palace, he felt his eyes blur.

Love blotted out rage and resentment.

It was bigger than fear.

He loved Nia with every beat of his heart, and she loved him. But finding a way to persuade her of that was going to be a challenge after the way he'd acted and what he'd said.

He pulled out his phone.

It was time to make a few calls.

Turning onto her side, Nia stared out of her bedroom window. It had rained most of the night, and the snow of a few days earlier had all but vanished. In its place, the raw umber-coloured bare earth looked stark against the washed-out blue sky.

She had forgotten to draw the curtains last night, but it wasn't the daylight that had woken her.

It was the distant drone of a helicopter's rotor blades.

Her eyes ached from the crying bouts that had punctuated the hours since Farlan had left yesterday, and she felt her throat tighten around the lump that refused to shift.

Then he had just been leaving the cottage. There had still been hope in her heart that he would return.

But now he was leaving for good.

He hadn't said as much, but he didn't need to.

She knew he would never be coming back, and that today would just be the first of many endless days, stretching out to the horizon. An infinite, empty expanse of regrets and shattered dreams and loss. Hope followed by despair, just like the first time.

Her heart felt as if it was being squeezed by a fist.

No, she thought, *it won't be like last time. It will be worse.*

This time there were no misunderstandings—at least not on his side. Farlan couldn't have made it clearer. He had spelled it out as if he was making a public service announcement, not breaking her heart.

He hadn't been looking for a future with her or dreaming of something fixed and for ever.

What they had shared had been enough for him.

Her fingers bit into her duvet.

The sound of the rotors was growing louder.

She knew Farlan would have to fly over the cottage on his way to London, but it was agonising to hear the helicopter getting closer, to remember the time he had landed in the field and swept her off to lunch.

That had felt like a turning point in their relationship. It had been the first time he had opened up to her about himself, about his life before they'd met. She had really thought it meant something—not just to her, but to him too.

She couldn't have been more mistaken.

He hadn't wanted a second chance.

He'd just wanted sex and closure.

The helicopter was overhead now, and she gripped the duvet tighter. And then it was gone, the sound fading faster than she could have imagined.

She glanced round the room, tears weighting her eyelashes.

He was like the snow.

There was nothing to show he had ever been here.

It was as if she had dreamt all of it.

Staring through the window, her eyes followed the movement of the helicopter as it skimmed over the fields and then dissolved into the pale February sky.

With it went the last tiniest hope she had.

Rolling over, she started to cry, huge wrenching sobs that filled the little bedroom.

But nobody could cry for ever.

And an hour later, with puffy eyes and a blotchy face, she made it downstairs and curled up on the sofa beneath the duvet she'd brought down with her.

Her phone sat on the table beside her. She had texted Allan to say that she had a 'bug', and then switched it off. She'd also disconnected the landline.

Hugging the duvet tighter, she stared dully at the phone. She fumbled with the equation in her mind.

Leave it on in case Farlan called.

Or switch it off in case he didn't.

Realistically, the chances of Farlan calling were less than zero. Plus, her mother might ring and she couldn't face that.

She flinched, imagining the stream of questions. She shivered. Her mother must never know. Neither of her parents could ever know.

A fire: that was what she needed. And then a cup of tea.

Shrugging the duvet away from her shoulders, she knelt down beside the ash-filled grate of the wood burner and began clumsily making a small pyramid of kindling. Then her body stiffened, her fingers trembling against the wood.

Somebody was knocking on the door.

Suddenly she couldn't breathe. Heart thudding, she stared at it as if it was alive.

'Nia?'

Her heart dipped with disappointment. It was Diane.

'Allan dropped by earlier, honey. He said you had a bug. I tried calling, but—'

'I'm fine, Diane,' she managed. 'Really, I'm fine.'

'I just want to see you're okay, and then I'll go.'

Nia winced. There was a steely note beneath the softness. Diane was not going to leave without seeing her.

Getting to her feet, she walked across the room and opened the door.

She had thought she had no tears left to cry, but when she opened the door and saw Diane's face, she crumpled wordlessly into the older woman's arms.

'Oh, honey…'

Diane led her back into the cottage and they sat down side by side on the sofa.

'I'm sorry.' Nia drew a breath. 'It's nothing, really. I just need to get some sleep.' Swiping at her cheeks, she edged out of Diane's arms. 'Thank you for coming to check on me, but I'll be fine. And I don't want to give you whatever this is.'

'I don't think that's likely,' Diane said gently. 'You can't catch a broken heart.'

Nia lifted her head, shock replacing her misery.

'You know…?' she whispered.

'I guessed.' Diane sighed. 'When he showed me the photos from the ball.' There was no pity in her eyes, just understanding. 'I know he's hurt you, but please try not to hate him.'

'I don't.' Nia was crying again now. 'That's the problem.'

They talked some more, and in between talking Nia cried. Finally she ran out of tears again, and Diane handed her a tissue.

'Here—blow.'

She watched as Nia obediently blew, and then, reaching over, took her hand and squeezed it.

'Right. You get cleaned up, and then I'm taking you out.'

'Out?' Nia was startled. 'No, really, Diane. I can't go out.'

'Yes, you can,' Diane said firmly. 'You have to face the world at some point, and it might as well be now. Just look outside, Nia. It's a wonderful world.' She hugged her. 'Tom's coming to pick us up, and then he's going to take us over to Braemar. Now, go and get dressed.'

Upstairs, the window in the bathroom was ajar. Catching sight of the view across the fields, Nia pushed it open. The sky was calm and clear, and the yellow sun looked as if it had been drawn with a crayon.

She breathed in shakily. The air smelled of damp earth and something else. Something fresh and green. *Spring*.

Her eyes snagged on a clump of primroses by the back gate. Diane was right. The world was wonderful. And she was so lucky in so many ways.

Turning on the cold tap, she splashed her face with water and dried it on a towel. She had lost Farlan once and survived. This time she was going to do more than just survive. She was going to make her life better.

In the past, she had believed that making sacrifices meant losing some part of herself; she had thought that was her duty.

Now, though, she knew it was a choice.

She couldn't be everything to everyone and still be true to herself.

Being with Farlan had given her a glimpse of the life she wanted and the woman she could be, and she was ready now to make the changes she should have made years ago. So she was going to keep running the estate, but she would hire a manager. And stop baby-sitting her parents.

Diane was waiting by the door. 'Ready?'

Nia nodded. She wasn't whole or happy. Not yet. But today she would take the first step towards getting there.

'Ready,' she said quietly and, grabbing her coat, she followed Diane to where Tom sat waiting in the car.

They got back after a late lunch in a pub. There had been a few difficult moments, Nia thought as Tom reached the village. Vivid flashes of lunch with Farlan that had made her want to fold in on herself. But she was glad she had gone. Glad that Diane had knocked on her door.

She felt a rush of affection for the Drummonds. They were such good people. They had taken care of her, and they would take care of Farlan.

Her heart beat a little faster.

She could think about him now without crying—just about—and if she could get through the rest of today surely the hardest part would be over.

'Now, you're coming back to Lamington for a cup of tea. And I won't take no for an answer,' Diane said firmly. 'We'll sit in the kitchen. It's cosier there.'

Nia hesitated. But Diane had been right last time.

The kitchen was bright and warm, as usual. Unusually, the television was on, and Molly wasn't alone. Johnny and Allan were there too, and Stephen, and Carrie who helped Molly around the house.

Molly was smiling. 'Lady Antonia, come and watch. It's Mr Wilder.'

No, no, I can't.

The words formed soundlessly in her head, panic and pain sweeping over her like a riptide. Her legs felt like wooden batons, but somehow she found herself walking towards the screen.

She recognised the interviewer. Slim, dark-haired and pretty, she was the co-host of an afternoon chat show. She was describing Farlan's visit to the Picture Palace. There was footage from the opening, and then clips from some of his films and then suddenly they switched back to the studio.

Nia's heart twisted, the pain more savage than any physical wound. Farlan was sitting there on a sofa, wearing a sleek grey suit and that impossible to resist smile.

'So, Farlan—' the interviewer gave him a dazzling smile of her own '—your first film was a cult indie drama, and your last one was the action movie of the summer. What's next?'

On the television screen, Farlan tilted his face upwards in a way that made Nia swallow hard.

'Well, Chrissie, there's a couple of things in the pipeline. Probably the one I'm most excited about is a contemporary reworking of the story of Orpheus.'

Chrissie bit into her lip. 'That sounds like a challenging project…' She leaned forward in her chair. 'What was it that attracted you to that particular story?'

Nia felt her throat tighten as Farlan looked into the camera.

'It's timeless. Boy loves girl. Boy loses girl. Boy gets girl back. But there's a twist.' His smile faded. 'Boy loses girl again through his own wilful stupidity because he doesn't have faith that what he wants will actually happen. I guess it was that part that really spoke to me on a personal level. You see, I know how Orpheus felt.'

Nia's pulse accelerated. His eyes seemed to be looking directly at her—only of course he was talking to millions of unseen viewers.

'Seven years ago I fell in love with this beautiful girl. We were young, and I was pretty intense back then. I still am now. Anyway, we broke up.' He shifted in his seat. 'I never forgot her. She was always there in my head. Her face. Her voice. Then we met again a couple of weeks ago and I realised I would never be able to forget her because I still loved her.'

'And what happened?' Chrissie was leaning forward, her mascaraed eyes on stalks.

Farlan frowned. 'I messed up again. I could have led us both out of the Underworld but I messed up. And now I don't know how to live without her.'

There was a small silence, and then Chrissie turned to the camera. 'Sadly, we've run out of time, but thank you for talking with me today...'

The presenter carried on talking, but Nia couldn't focus on what she was saying. She was staring at the pattern on the sofa behind Farlan. It was the same as the sofa in the drawing room at Lamington. Her eyes searched the screen. And that painting—

He was here.

Farlan was here.

She covered her mouth with her hand, breathing raggedly.

'Nia—'

It was his voice. So familiar, and yet not familiar. He sounded like she felt. As if he was being torn apart inside.

She turned. The kitchen was empty. Everyone had left.

Everyone but Farlan.

'What are you doing back here?'

He took a step towards her. 'I can't leave. I tried, but how can I leave you? You're my soul, my heart, and I love you.'

His eyes were fixed on hers, clear and green and hopeful. It was what she had wanted to hear because she loved him so much. But then she thought about his face in the car, and then again at the cottage.

'And I love you. I've never stopped loving you. But we keep hurting each other so badly.'

'I know.' His face was pale. 'And I know that's on me. I have stuff going on in my head and I've tried to deal with it, but it's too big for me to handle on my own.'

His face, the look of pain and the shame on it, made her heart turn inside out. 'It's not your fault, Farlan.' She took a step forward, her words spilling out in a rush. 'You're not to think that.'

'Maybe not what happened in my childhood, but how I've handled this, us…that's on me.'

He took another step closer—close enough that they could touch.

'But I'm going to make changes. I've got myself a therapist. And I'm going to get in touch with Cam. I'm still angry with him, but he was just a kid too, and he did his best.' His face was strained. 'Please tell me it's not too late for us. I love you so much, Nia.'

He was struggling to speak.

'I've never loved anyone else. I couldn't. You've always had my heart. And you always will.'

Nia could feel the tears filling her eyes. She loved him, he loved her and they had fought their way back to one another. But, more importantly, they were going to keep fighting to stay together.

'You and I are poetry,' he said shakily.

Her heart tumbled inside her chest. 'And everyone else is prose,' she whispered.

With a groan, Farlan pulled her into his arms. 'I'm so sorry I left—'

'It doesn't matter.'

She could feel the tears in her eyes, but her voice rang with a love that matched his own.

For a moment they stared at one another, mute with relief and gratitude that after so much, after everything that had happened, they were finally in the right place at the right time.

'How did you do this?' she said wonderingly after a moment. 'Diane said you'd left. I heard the helicopter.'

'I did leave,' he admitted. 'But I didn't get very far. I called the studio, told them if they wanted the interview they'd have to come to Scotland.'

She bit her lip. 'Very masterful.'

He grinned. 'Well, as we both know, I am a Hollywood Big Shot. Anyway, then I called Dee and she sorted everything out. Got you out of the cottage so the camera crew could get set up. Everything just fell into place.'

'I guess it was meant to be,' she murmured.

Stepping back, he cupped her face. 'I know you said you've always felt like we were married, but I was wondering what you thought about maybe making that feeling legal?'

There was a silence.

Nia gazed up at him. Her mouth was dry and her eyes felt hot. 'Are you asking me to marry you?'

'Yes,' he said simply.

She wrapped her arms around his neck. 'Then I'd like that very much,' she whispered, her eyes closing as his mouth found hers.

'In that case...' He drew away. 'We need to start planning our big day. You and I have a date at the altar, or rather the anvil at the Blacksmiths in Gretna Green in twenty-nine days.'

Catching sight of her stunned expression, he pulled her closer.

'We've waited seven years, Nia, I don't want to wait any more.'

Her brown eyes softened. 'Neither do I.'

She was smiling, and lowering his mouth he kissed her, arms tightening around the woman he loved now and for ever.

* * * * *

#3893 THE SHEIKH'S MARRIAGE PROCLAMATION
by Annie West

When Tara Michaels arrives on Sheikh Raif's doorstep fleeing a forced betrothal, he knows protecting her will be risky—but entranced by her stubborn beauty, he knows one way to keep her safe... He must make her his bride!

#3894 CROWNING HIS INNOCENT ASSISTANT
The Kings of California
by Millie Adams

Countless women would be thrilled to marry King Matteo de la Cruz. Yet his brilliant personal assistant, Livia, flat out refuses his proposal...and then *quits*! Matteo is outraged, then intrigued... Can anything make his ideal queen reconsider?

#3895 PRIDE & THE ITALIAN'S PROPOSAL
by Kate Hewitt

Fiery Liza is the last woman Fausto should marry. But this proud Italian can't resist the way she challenges him. He's determined to fight fire with fire—by claiming Liza with a shocking proposal!

#3896 TERMS OF THEIR COSTA RICAN TEMPTATION
The Diamond Inheritance
by Pippa Roscoe

Skye Soames's search for her family's long-lost diamonds leads her to Benoit Chalendar's mansion in the Costa Rican rain forest. The billionaire offers to help her find the diamonds—*if* she agrees to a marriage pact to save his company!

YOU CAN FIND MORE INFORMATION ON UPCOMING HARLEQUIN TITLES, FREE EXCERPTS AND MORE AT HARLEQUIN.COM.

HPCNMRB0221

SPECIAL EXCERPT FROM

H HARLEQUIN

PRESENTS

Fiery Liza is the last woman Fausto should marry. But this proud Italian can't resist the way she challenges him. He's determined to fight fire with fire—by claiming Liza with a shocking proposal!

*Read on for a sneak preview of
Kate Hewitt's next story for Harlequin Presents*
Pride & the Italian's Proposal.

"I judge on what I see," Fausto said as he captured her queen easily. She looked unfazed by the move, as if she'd expected it, although to Fausto's eye, it had seemed a most inexpert choice. "Doesn't everyone do the same?"

"Some people are more accepting than others."

"Is that a criticism?"

"You seem cynical," Liza said.

"I consider myself a realist," Fausto returned, and she laughed, a crystal clear sound that seemed to reverberate through him like the ringing of a bell.

"Isn't that what every cynic says?"

"And what are you? An optimist?" He imbued the word with the necessary skepticism.

"I'm a realist. I've learned to be." For a second she looked bleak, and Fausto realized he was curious.

"And where did you learn that lesson?"

She gave him a pert look, although he still saw a shadow of that unsettling bleakness in her eyes. "From people such as yourself." She moved her knight—really, what was she thinking there? "Your move."

Fausto's gaze quickly swept the board and he moved a pawn. "I don't think you know me well enough to have learned such a lesson," he remarked.

"I've learned it before, and in any case, I'm a quick study." She looked up at him with glinting eyes, a coy smile flirting about her mouth. A mouth Fausto had a sudden, serious urge to kiss. The notion took him so forcefully and unexpectedly that he leaned forward a little over the game, and Liza's eyes widened in response, her breath hitching audibly as surprise flashed across her features.

For a second, no more, the very air between them felt tautened, vibrating with sexual tension and expectation. It would be so very easy to close the space between their mouths. So very easy to taste her sweetness, drink deep from that lovely, luscious well.

Of course, he was going to do no such thing. He could never consider a serious relationship with Liza Benton. She was not at all the sort of person he was expected to marry, and in any case, he'd been burned once before, when he'd been led by something so consuming and changeable as desire.

As for a cheap affair... The idea had its tempting merits, but he knew he had neither the time nor inclination to act on it. An affair would be complicated and distracting, a reminder he needed far too much in this moment.

Fausto leaned back, thankfully breaking the tension, and Liza's smile turned catlike, surprising him. She looked so knowing, as if she'd been party to every thought in his head, which thankfully she hadn't been, and was smugly informing him of that fact.

"Checkmate," she said softly.

Jolted, Fausto stared at her blankly before glancing down at the board. "That's impossible," he declared as his gaze moved over the pieces. And with another jolt, he realized it wasn't. She'd put him in checkmate and he hadn't even realized his king had been under threat. He'd indifferently moved a pawn while she'd neatly spun her web. Disbelief warred with a scorching shame as well as a reluctant admiration. While he'd assumed she'd been playing an amateurish, inexperienced game, she'd been neatly and slyly laying a trap.

"You snookered me."

Her eyes widened with laughing innocence. "I did no such thing. You just assumed I wasn't a worthy opponent." She cocked her head, her gaze turning flirtatious—unless he was imagining that? Feeling it? "But, of course, you judge on what you see."

The tension twanged back again, even more electric than before. Slowly, deliberately, Fausto knocked over his king to declare his defeat. The sound of the marble clattering against the board was loud in the stillness of the room, the only other sound their suddenly laboured breathing.

He had to kiss her. He would. Fausto leaned forward, his gaze turning sleepy and hooded as he fastened it on her lush mouth. Liza's eyes flared again and she drew an unsteady breath, as loud as a shout in the still, silent room. Then, slowly, deliberately, she leaned forward...

Don't miss
Pride & the Italian's Proposal.
Available March 2021 wherever
Harlequin Presents books and ebooks are sold.

Harlequin.com

HPEXP0221

Love Harlequin romance?

DISCOVER.

Be the first to find out about promotions,
news and exclusive content!

Facebook.com/HarlequinBooks

Twitter.com/HarlequinBooks

Instagram.com/HarlequinBooks

Pinterest.com/HarlequinBooks

YouTube.com/HarlequinBooks

ReaderService.com

EXPLORE.

Sign up for the Harlequin e-newsletter and
download a free book from any series at
TryHarlequin.com

CONNECT.

Join our Harlequin community to
share your thoughts and connect
with other romance readers!
Facebook.com/groups/HarlequinConnection

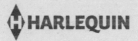

"Powerfully good."
—*Entertainment Weekly*

"The most memorable Western
heroes since Larry McMurtry's...
Lonesome Dove."
—The Associated Press

FROM *NEW YORK TIMES*
BESTSELLING AUTHOR

Robert B. Parker

Enter the richly imaged portrait of the Old
West, featuring guns-for-hire Virgil Cole
and Everett Hitch.

APPALOOSA
RESOLUTION
BRIMSTONE

DON'T MISS THE JESSE STONE NOVELS
from *New York Times* Bestselling Author

ROBERT B. PARKER

NIGHT AND DAY
A Jesse Stone Novel

When the sun sets in Paradise, the women get nervous. A Peeping Tom is on the loose. And according to the notes he sends Police Chief Jesse Stone, he's about to take his obsession one step further.

penguin.com

M695T0510

Robert B. Parker

ROUGH WEATHER

Hired as a bodyguard for an exclusive society wedding, Spenser witnesses an unexpected crime: the kidnapping of the young bride, which opens the door for murder, family secrets, and the reappearance of an old nemesis.

continued . . .

"DETECTIVEDOM'S MOST CHARMINGLY LITERATE LOUT." —*People*

"EVERYONE INTERESTED IN MYSTERY AND CONTEMPORARY WRITING IN GENERAL SHOULD READ AT LEAST ONE OF THE SPENSER NOVELS." —*Library Journal*

BAD BUSINESS

A suspicious wife and a cheating husband pose a few dangerous surprises for Spenser. "A kinky whodunit . . . snappy . . . sexy." —*Entertainment Weekly*

BACK STORY

Spenser teams with Jesse Stone to solve a murder three decades old—one that's still cold as death. "Good and scary. This [is] superior Parker." —*The Boston Globe*

WIDOW'S WALK

Spenser must defend an accused murderess who's so young, cold, rich, and beautiful, she *has* to be guilty. "Delicious fun. Bottom line: A merry *Widow*." —*People*

POTSHOT

Spenser is enlisted to clean up a small Arizona town. "Outrageously entertaining . . . a hero who can still stand up for himself—and us." —*The New York Times Book Review*

continued . . .

HUGGER MUGGER

Spenser hoofs it down South when someone makes death threats against a Thoroughbred racehorse. "Brisk . . . crackling . . . finishes strong, just like a Thoroughbred."

—*Entertainment Weekly*

HUSH MONEY

Spenser helps a stalking victim—only to find himself the one being stalked . . . "Spenser can still punch, sleuth, and wisecrack with the best of them." —*Publishers Weekly*

SUDDEN MISCHIEF

A charity fund-raiser, accused of sexual harassment by four women, is wanted for a bigger offense: murder . . . "Smooth as silk." —*Orlando Sentinel*

SMALL VICES

Spenser must solve the murder of a wealthy college student—before the wrong man pays the price . . . "His finest in years . . . one can't-put-it-down story."

—*San Francisco Chronicle*

CHANCE

Spenser heads to Vegas to find the missing husband of a mob princess—but he's not the only one looking . . . "As brisk and clever as always." —*Los Angeles Times Book Review*

THIN AIR

Spenser thought he could help a friend find his missing wife. Until he learned the nasty truth about Lisa St. Claire . . . "Full of action, suspense, and thrills." —*Playboy*

THE
PROFESSIONAL

Robert B. Parker

BERKLEY BOOKS

New York

THE BERKLEY PUBLISHING GROUP
Published by the Penguin Group
Penguin Group (USA) Inc.
375 Hudson Street, New York, New York 10014, USA
Penguin Group (Canada), 90 Eglinton Avenue East, Suite 700, Toronto, Ontario M4P 2Y3, Canada
(a division of Pearson Penguin Canada Inc.)
Penguin Books Ltd., 80 Strand, London WC2R 0RL, England
Penguin Group Ireland, 25 St. Stephen's Green, Dublin 2, Ireland (a division of Penguin Books Ltd.)
Penguin Group (Australia), 250 Camberwell Road, Camberwell, Victoria 3124, Australia
(a division of Pearson Australia Group Pty. Ltd.)
Penguin Books India Pvt. Ltd., 11 Community Centre, Panchsheel Park, New Delhi—110 017, India
Penguin Group (NZ), 67 Apollo Drive, Rosedale, North Shore 0632, New Zealand
(a division of Pearson New Zealand Ltd.)
Penguin Books (South Africa) (Pty.) Ltd., 24 Sturdee Avenue, Rosebank, Johannesburg 2196,
South Africa

Penguin Books Ltd., Registered Offices: 80 Strand, London WC2R 0RL, England

This is a work of fiction. Names, characters, places, and incidents either are the product of the author's imagination or are used fictitiously, and any resemblance to actual persons, living or dead, business establishments, events, or locales is entirely coincidental. The publisher does not have any control over and does not assume any responsibility for author or third-party websites or their content.

THE PROFESSIONAL

A Berkley Book / published by arrangement with the author

PRINTING HISTORY
G. P. Putnam's Sons hardcover edition / October 2009
Berkley premium edition / September 2010

Copyright © 2009 by Robert B. Parker.
Excerpt from *Painted Ladies* by Robert B. Parker copyright © by Robert B. Parker.
Interior map copyright © 2007 by Jeffrey L. Ward.
Cover design copyright © 2010 by Kevin Bailey/RBMM.
Interior text design by Amanda Dewey.

ISBN: 978-0-425-23630-7

BERKLEY®
Berkley Books are published by The Berkley Publishing Group,
a division of Penguin Group (USA) Inc.,
375 Hudson Street, New York, New York 10014.
BERKLEY® is a registered trademark of Penguin Group (USA) Inc.
The "B" design is a trademark of Penguin Group (USA) Inc.

PRINTED IN THE UNITED STATES OF AMERICA

10 9 8 7 6 5 4 3 2 1

For Emma, who arrived; and for Gracie, who left.

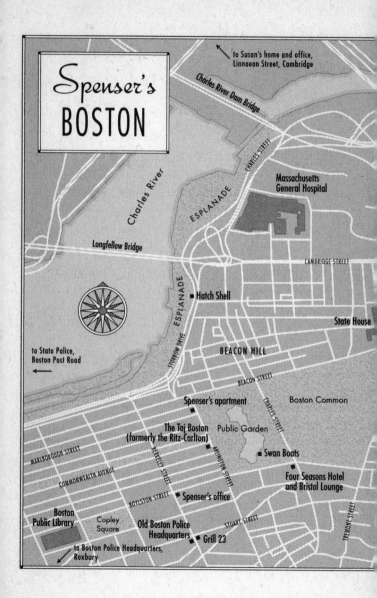

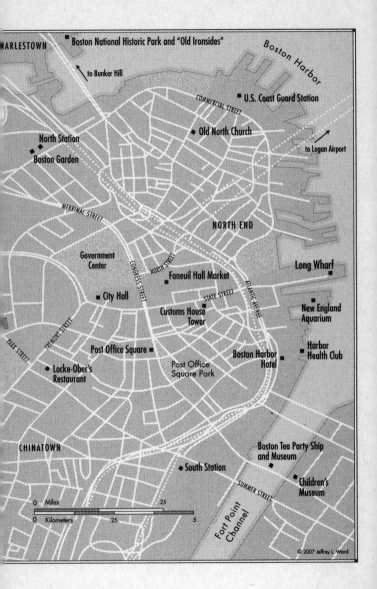

CHARLESTOWN

Boston National Historic Park and "Old Ironsides"

to Bunker Hill

Boston Harbor

U.S. Coast Guard Station

COMMERCIAL STREET

North Station

Boston Garden

Old North Church

to Logan Airport

MERRIMAC STREET

NORTH END

Government Center

CONGRESS STREET

NORTH STREET

Faneuil Hall Market

Long Wharf

City Hall

Customs House Tower

STATE STREET

ATLANTIC AVENUE

New England Aquarium

PARK STREET

TREMONT STREET

Post Office Square

Post Office Square Park

Boston Harbor Hotel

Harbor Health Club

Locke-Ober's Restaurant

CHINATOWN

Boston Tea Party Ship and Museum

South Station

SUMMER STREET

Children's Museum

0   Miles   25
0 Kilometers   25   5

Fort Point Channel

© 2007 Jeffrey L. Ward

THE PROFESSIONAL

Chapter

............................◆◆............................

1

I HAD JUST FINISHED a job for an interesting woman named Nan Sartin, and was happily making out my bill to her, when a woman came in who promised to be equally interesting.

It was a bright October morning when she walked into my office carrying a briefcase. She was a big woman, not fat, but strong-looking and very graceful. Her hair was silver, and her face was young enough to make me assume that the silver was premature. She was wearing a dark blue suit with a long jacket and a short skirt.

I said, "Hello."

She said, "My name is Elizabeth Shaw. Please call me Elizabeth. I'm an attorney, and I represent a group of women who need your help."

She took a business card from her briefcase and placed it on my desk. It said she was a partner in the law firm Shaw and Cartwright, and that they had offices on Milk Street.

I said, "Okay."

"You are Spenser," she said.

"I am he," I said.

"I specialize in wills and trusts," she said. "I know little about criminal law."

I nodded.

"But I went to law school with Rita Fiore," she said.

So the silver hair was premature.

"Ahh," I said.

She smiled.

"Ahh, indeed," she said. "So I told Rita my story, and she suggested I tell it to you."

"Please do," I said.

Elizabeth Shaw looked at the large picture of Susan that sat on my file drawer near the coffeemaker.

"Is that your wife?" she said.

"Sort of," I said.

"How can she be 'sort of'?" Elizabeth said.

"We're not married," I said.

"But?"

"But we've been together a considerable time," I said.

"And you love her," Elizabeth said.

"I do."

"And she loves you."

"She does."

"Then why don't you get married?" Elizabeth said.

"I don't know," I said.

She stared at me. I smiled pleasantly. She frowned a little.

"Was there anything else?" I said.

She smiled suddenly. It was a good look for her.

"I'm sorry," she said. "I guess I was trying to find out a little about your attitude toward women and marriage."

"I try to develop my attitudes on a case-by-case basis," I said.

She nodded, thinking about it.

"Rita says there's no one better if the going gets rough."

"Uh-huh."

"How about if the going isn't rough?" Elizabeth said.

"There's still no one better," I said.

"Rita mentioned that you didn't lack for confidence."

"Would you want someone who did?" I said.

I must have passed some kind of initial screening. She shifted in her chair slightly.

"Everything I tell you," she said, "must, of course, remain entirely confidential."

"Sure."

She looked at Susan's picture again.

"That's a very beautiful woman," she said.

"She is," I said.

She shifted again in her chair.

"I have a client, a woman, married, with a substantial trust fund, given to her by her husband as a wedding present. We manage the trust for her, and over the years she and I have become friendly."

"He gave her a trust fund for a present?"

Elizabeth smiled.

"The rich are very different," she said.

"Yes," I said. "They have more money."

"Well," she said. "A literate detective."

"But self-effacing."

She smiled again.

"My client's name is Abigail Larson," Elizabeth said. "She is considerably younger than her husband."

"How considerably?"

"He's sixty-eight. She's thirty-one."

"Aha," I said.

"'Aha'?"

"I'm jumping to a conclusion," I said.

"Sadly, the conclusion is correct. She had an affair."

"Lot of that going around," I said.

"You disapprove?" Elizabeth said.

"I guess it's probably better if people can be faithful to each other," I said.

"She's not a bad woman," Elizabeth said.

4

"Affairs aren't usually about good and bad," I said.

"What do you think they're about?"

"Need," I said.

Elizabeth sat back a little in her chair.

"You're not what I expected," she said.

"Hell," I said. "I'm not what I expected. What would you like me to do?"

"I'm sorry. I guess I'm still testing you."

"Maybe you could test my ability to listen to what you want," I said.

She smiled at me.

"Yes," she said. "In brief, the man she had the affair with took her for some money and ditched her."

"How much?" I said.

"Actually, just enough to hurt her feelings. Restaurants, hotels, car rentals, a small gift now and then."

"And?" I said.

"That was it," Elizabeth said, "for a while. Then one day she saw him, in a restaurant, with a woman whom she knew casually."

"Nest prospecting," I said.

"Apparently," Elizabeth said. "Anyway, she talked to the woman the next day to tell her a little about her experience with this guy. . . ."

"Whose name is?" I said.

"Gary Eisenhower," Elizabeth said.

"Gary Eisenhower?" I said.

Elizabeth shrugged.

"That's what he tells them," she said.

"Them?"

"The two women talked, and then they networked, and one thing led to another, and in ways too boring to detail here, they discovered that he had exploited four of them, often simultaneously, over the past ten years."

"Have you met this guy?"

"No."

"Well, if you do," I said, "be careful."

"I think I'll be all right," she said.

"So the seduced and abandoned have joined forces?" I said.

"Yes."

"And what do they want?"

"They'd like to see him castrated, I'm sure, but that's not why I'm here."

"Oh, good," I said.

"They came to me as a group because I was the only lawyer that any of them knew, and we agreed that pursuing him for the money would cause them embarrassment. Their husbands would find out. It might make a great tabloid story. So they agreed to move on, sadder but wiser, so to speak."

"But," I said.

"But he has returned. He has contacted each of them. He says he has proof positive of each adultery and will expose them to their husbands and the world if they don't pay him."

"What kind of evidence?" I said.

"They thought they were being discreet," Elizabeth said. "These women are not stupid, nor, I guess, inexperienced."

"No letters," I said. "No e-mails, no messages on answering machines."

"Yes."

"Hidden cameras, hidden tape recorders?"

Elizabeth nodded.

"Uh-huh," she said. "I guess he was planning on shaking them down all along."

"Maybe," I said. "Sometimes people like to keep a record. Allows them to revisit these special moments, when things are slow."

"So," Elizabeth said, "maybe shaking them down was an afterthought?"

"Maybe," I said. "They don't want to pay."

"Don't want to, and can't. Their husbands control all of the substantial money."

"So you want me to make him cease and desist, without causing a stir," I said.

"Can you?" she said.

"Sure," I said.

Chapter

❖

2

I MET THE FOUR WOMEN in a bigger conference room than we needed at Shaw and Cartwright. Elizabeth Shaw sat at one side of the table. The women sat two apiece on each side of her. I sat across from them.

Elizabeth introduced them.

"Abigail Larson, Beth Jackson, Regina Hartley, Nancy Sinclair."

They each had a small notepad in front of them. And a ballpoint pen. Doubtless provided by the firm. They all smiled at me. All of the smiles displayed white, even teeth. They were all extremely well dressed. They all had very good haircuts. They all looked in shape. None looked older than thirty-five. It is easier to be good-looking when you're thirty-five, and even easier if you're rich.

THE PROFESSIONAL

Though Elizabeth Shaw, who was probably neither, was holding her own. I smiled back at all of them.

No one said anything. They all looked at Elizabeth.

"Perhaps you could tell us a little about yourself," Elizabeth said to me.

"I used to be a cop, now I'm a private detective," I said.

"Do you have a gun?" Regina said.

"I do."

"Have you ever shot anyone?" she said.

"I have."

"Could you tell us about that?" she said.

"No."

"Well, for heaven's sake," Regina said.

She had very black hair, which she wore in bangs over her forehead. Her eyes were large and made to seem larger by her eye makeup. She had on a simple print dress that had probably cost more than Liechtenstein, and her skin was evenly tanned, which in October, in Boston, meant she had either traveled to warmer climes or used an excellent bronzer.

"If we're going to hire you, I think we should be able to ask you questions," Abigail said.

I think she was trying to sound stern, but her voice was too small for stern.

"You can ask anything you want," I said. "Doesn't mean I have to answer."

"Well, how are we supposed to decide," she said.

"Me telling you about shooting somebody won't help."

Abigail was a blonde, with a short haircut that had probably cost as much as Regina's little dress. Her eyes were blue. She looked tan.

"I just think it would be so interesting," she said. "I mean, I bet nobody here even knows anyone who has shot someone."

"I am hopeful that I won't have to shoot anyone on this job," I said.

Abigail said, "I wouldn't actually mind if you shot the bastard."

"No," Beth said. "I don't think any of us would mind."

Both Beth and Abigail were blondes. In fact, everyone at the table was a blonde except Regina, and me, and Elizabeth. Maybe they did have more fun.

"Tell me about him," I said.

All the women looked at Abigail. She shrugged.

"He's one slick item," she said. "He's handsome, charming, fun to be with, wears clothes beautifully, and he's very sexy, the sonovabitch."

"So far, except for sonovabitch," I said, "we could be talking about me."

The women all looked at me without response.

"So much for lighthearted," I said. "Can you give me anything more substantive? Like where he lives?"

"I . . ." Abigail paused. "I don't actually know."

"Who does," I said.

They all looked at one another and discovered that none of them knew. It startled them.

"Okay," I said. "Where did you get together?"

"We'd meet for cocktails," Abigail said. "Or drinks and dinner in, like, suburban restaurants. At least that's what he and I did."

All the other women nodded. That's what they did, too.

"And where did you, ah, consummate your relationship," I said.

Spenser, the soul of delicacy.

"I, for one, am not going to discuss that," Regina said.

"Oh, for crissake, Reggie," Abigail said. "How the hell did he get the goods on you?"

She looked at me.

"We were all bopping our brains out with him," she said. "With me it was usually in a motel along 128."

"Sometimes we'd go away for a weekend," Beth said. "Maine, the Cape, New York City."

Beth had a small, attractive overbite, and wore sunglasses that probably cost more than Abigail's haircut.

"Did you go often to the same motels?" I said.

"I did," Abigail said. "There was one near the Burlington Mall we went to four, five times."

"The one with the little fountain in the lobby?" Regina said.

All of them had been there. He had several favorites that all of them had been to. They showed no geographic pattern.

"And no one has an address for him," I said.

No one did.

"Or a phone number?"

They had phone numbers, but they weren't the same numbers.

"I'll make a prediction," I said. "These will all turn out to be prepaid disposable cell phones."

"Which means?" Elizabeth said.

"That we won't know who the owner was or where he lived."

"It sounds as if he didn't ever want us to be able to find him," Regina said.

"Be my guess," I said.

"Then . . . that means . . . that means he was never, ever sincere, even at the start," she said.

This guy was really good, I thought. Even after he started blackmailing them, there was still the hope for something.

"Probably not," I said.

"So how can you ever find him?" Abigail said.

"It's not as hopeless as it sounds," I said. "Each of you has been with him, quite often. We'll talk, each of you and me. One of you, maybe more than one, will remember something."

"Do you really think you can find him?" Abigail said.

"Yes."

"How?"

"I'm very resourceful," I said.

"Can you be more specific?" Abigail said.

"No," I said.

"If you do find him," Regina said, "what will you do?"

I grinned at her.

"Step at a time," I said.

"But how will you make him leave us alone?" she said. "You look like you could beat him up. Will you beat him up?"

"Soon as I find him," I said.

Reggie seemed satisfied.

Chapter

............................◆◆............................

3

SUSAN AND I were having drinks before dinner in the South End at a slick new restaurant called Rocca. Susan was sipping a Cosmopolitan. I was moving more quickly on a Dewar's and soda.

"It's sort of an elaborate scam," Susan said. "Isn't it?"

"Kind of," I said. "But he gets a double dip out of it."

"Sex *and* money?" Susan said.

"Yep. With an assortment of handsome women."

"All of whom," Susan said, "are married to older men."

"Rich older men," I said.

"Doesn't mean none of them love their husbands," Susan said.

"No, it doesn't," I said. "But none of the women love their husbands enough to stay faithful."

"Often it's not a matter of love," Susan said.

"I know."

"Still," Susan said, "he chose wisely."

"Which suggests it's not random," I said.

My scotch was gone. I looked around for a waiter, and found one, and asked for more. A handsome, well-dressed man walked past our table with a group of people. The handsome man stopped.

"Susan," he said. "Hello."

"Joe," Susan said. "What a treat."

She introduced us.

"Joseph Abboud?" I said. "The clothes guy."

"The clothes guy," he said.

"You got anything off the rack would fit me?" I said.

Abboud looked at me silently for a moment and smiled.

"God, I hope not," he said.

We laughed. Abboud moved on after his group. I drank my second scotch. We looked at the menu. The waitress took our order.

"Is that how you're going to find him?" Susan said. "That it's not random?"

"There must be some connection among the women and with him," I said.

"Do you have a thought?" Susan said. "On what it might be?"

"No," I said.

"But you will," she said.

"I will," I said.

"These women don't know each other?"

"They do now," I said. "But they didn't originally, except a couple of them."

"So what they have in common seems to be," Susan said, and smiled, "Gary Eisenhower."

"And rich older husbands," I said.

"And perhaps some evidence of promiscuity," Susan said. "I mean, every young wife doesn't cheat on her husband. Why did he think these women would?"

"Maybe they are the result of an exhaustive elimination process," I said.

"Despite what I've said, it may be optimistic to think it requires an exhaustive process," Susan said.

"So lovely, and yet so cynical," I said.

"My line of work," she said. "The success rate is not always startling."

"Hell," I said. "Neither is mine."

"I suppose, though," Susan said, "that we are both optimists in some sense. We believe that things can be made better."

"And sometimes we're right," I said.

"That's part of the payoff, isn't it," Susan said.

"Yes," I said. "Plus, of course, the fee."

Chapter

❖

4

ABIGAIL LARSON had seemed the most lively of my four clients. So I tried her first. She lived in Louisburg Square. But she wanted to meet at the bar at the Taj. Which was once the Ritz-Carlton. But the Ritz had opened a new location up on the other side of the Common, and the name moved up there.

Except for the unfortunate name, the Taj hadn't changed anything. So the bar was still good, and the view from a window table of the Public Garden across Arlington Street was still very good. It was ten to four in the afternoon, on a Thursday, and I had snared us a window table. Abigail was twenty minutes late, but I had been trained by Susan, who was always late except when it mattered. And I remained calm.

I stood when she came in. The bartender waved at her, and two waiters came to say hello as she came toward my table. She put out her hand. I shook it, one of the waiters held her chair, and she sat. She ordered a lemon-drop martini and smiled at me.

"You're drinking beer?"

"I am," I said.

"I get so full if I drink enough beer to get tipsy," she said. The smile continued. "A martini does the job on much less volume."

"I'm hoping not to get tipsy," I said.

"What fun is that?" she said.

Gary Eisenhower must have been delighted when he met her. She did everything but hand out business cards to let you know that she fooled around.

"Tell me about Gary," I said.

"I thought we already did that, in Shaw's office," she said.

Her lemon-drop martini arrived. She sampled it with pleasure.

"Smoothes out a day," she said.

I drank a little beer.

"I was hoping just sort of informally for some reminiscences," I said. "You know, how did you meet? Where did you go? What did you do?"

"What did we do?"

"Other than that," I said.

"You got something against 'that'?" she said.

"No," I said. "You can tell me about 'that,' too, if you like."

She smiled at me.

"Maybe I will," she said.

I waited.

"Actually," she said, and took in some more of her lemon drop, "I met him here."

She glanced around the room, looking for a waiter, spotted one, and nodded. He smiled and went to the bar.

"I come here quite often," she said.

"I suspected as much," I said.

"Often I go to my gym, in the late afternoon, and afterward I shower and change and meet my girlfriends for a cocktail."

"Replenish those electrolytes," I said.

"What?" she said.

I shook my head and smiled.

"Just musing out loud," I said.

"Anyway," she said. "I'd see him at the bar sometimes, and after two or three times, he'd smile and nod as I came in, and I'd do the same. One day I came in alone and sat at a table, and he was at the bar. I smiled at him and nodded, and he picked up his drink and walked over and asked if he could join me. . . . God, he was handsome."

She drank some more of her lemon drop. She took small, ladylike swallows. She didn't guzzle, but she was persistent.

"And he was very charming," I said.

"And sexy and fun," she said. "And we both had a couple of cocktails, and talked, and one thing led to another . . ."

"And," I said, "I'll bet he had a room in the hotel."

She looked at me for a moment as if I'd just performed necromancy.

"Yes," she said, "he did. And . . ." She shrugged.

"What's a girl to do," I said.

She nodded slowly, looking at the depleted surface of her lemon drop.

"I know now he was using me," she said. "But God, he was good."

She stopped staring into the martini and finished it.

"What gym do you go to?" I said.

"Pinnacle Fitness," she said.

"The big flossy thing on Tremont?" I said.

"You know it?" she said.

"I was there once with a client," I said.

Another lemon-drop martini arrived.

"Do you work out?"

"Some," I said.

"You look very fit," she said.

"You, too," I said.

Mistake.

She smiled again and her face flushed slightly.

"You should see me with my clothes off," she said.

"Probably should," I said.

She smiled again and her face flushed a little more.

"Do you have a room upstairs?" she said.

"Sadly, no," I said.

"I could probably get us one," she said.

"It's a kind offer," I said. "But no, thank you."

"Are you married?"

"No."

"But?"

"But I'm in love with Susan Silverman, and we've agreed on monogamy."

"My goodness," Abigail said.

"I know," I said. "Makes me kind of boring, but there it is."

"What a waste," she said.

"Everyone says that."

I drank another swallow of beer.

"When did the money stuff come up?" I said.

"Not right away. He paid for everything the first time we were together, here. I don't think he took any money from me for, oh, I'd say at least a year, year and a half. Then he said there was some waterfront property in Chatham, which was way underpriced, and he knew he could buy it, we could go there and spend time, and later when the market rose, he'd sell it for a nice profit."

"But all his money was tied up, and he didn't want to cash in a CD because of the penalties," I said. "So maybe you could lend him the down payment and you'd get it back with interest when the house was sold."

"That's almost exactly right," she said. "How did you know?"

"Amazing, isn't it?" I said. "You ever see the house?"

"Yes, we spent several weekends there."

"And your husband?"

"He thought I was with my girlfriends," Abigail said. "You know. He used to call it a sisterhood retreat."

"Your husband doesn't know," I said.

"God, no, that's the big reason we hired you."

"No suspicions? Then or now?"

"None. He's very busy and very important. Tell you the truth," she said, "I don't think it occurs to him that it could happen."

"You are intimate?"

"Sure. John's not in the very best shape, and he gets tired at night, and, you know, he's sixty-eight."

"So your intimacy is not as frequent as it might be," I said.

"Or as long-lasting, or as . . . ah, enthusiastic."

"So Gary Eisenhower was an appealing alternative."

"Very," she said. "I think I would have let him get away with the money."

"The ride was worth the money," I said.

"Yes. But the blackmail. I can't live that way, none of us can. My husband can't know."

"You have a picture of Gary?" I said.

"No, I threw them out as soon as I found out what he was," she said.

"Too bad."

"I didn't want my husband finding them, either."

"You love your husband?"

"Love?" She shrugged. "I care about him, certainly. Why do you ask?"

"Just a curious guy," I said.

Chapter

◆◆

5

IT WAS A LITTLE AFTER NINE in the morning on an overcast day with some thin fog in the air. I was drinking coffee and reading "Arlo & Janis" when Nancy Sinclair came carefully into my office, as if she was entering the confessional.

"Mr. Spenser?" she said. "I'm Nancy Sinclair, from the other day at Elizabeth Shaw's office?"

"Of course," I said.

As far as I could recall, she had not spoken when we had our meeting. She looked like a dressed-up cheerleader: a plaid skirt and a white shirt, dark stockings and boots. She was small. Her hair was short and thick. Her jewelry was gold and simple, and so was her wedding band. Her eyes were blue and very big, and she seemed

to have a look of permanent surprise, as if the world amazed her. She sat opposite me, in front of the desk, with her knees together and her hands folded in her lap. She didn't say anything.

"How 'bout them Sox?" I said.

She smiled brightly.

After a while I said, "How you doing?"

"Fine."

"Is there something you'd like to discuss?" I said.

She nodded.

"Is it about Gary Eisenhower?" I said.

She nodded again. I waited. She smiled at me hopefully. I nodded helpfully.

"I love my husband," she said.

"That's nice," I said.

"He loves me," she said.

"Also nice," I said.

"We love each other," she said.

"Good combo," I said.

"I don't . . ."

She seemed to be thinking of how to say whatever it was she wanted to say.

"I don't want you to get the wrong idea," she said.

"I'd be thrilled with any idea," I said.

She smiled brightly again. It was what she did when she didn't understand something. I was already pretty sure that understanding stuff wasn't a big part of her skill set.

"I did have an affair with Gary Eisenhower," she said. "I don't deny it. But it was not because Jim and I don't love each other."

"What was it because?" I said.

She blushed slowly but pervasively. It was kind of interesting watching the blush spread slowly over her face and down her neck, and onto the small expanse of chest that her white shirt collar exposed. She looked as if she might be blushing to her ankles.

"I'm oversexed," she said.

"Doesn't make you a bad person," I said.

"It does," she said. "I keep promising myself it will never happen again. But it does. I can't seem to stop myself."

"So Gary Eisenhower isn't the first," I said.

"God, no," she said. "I once had sex with a man who came to plow the driveway. I'm . . . This is so embarrassing. . . . I'm insatiable."

"And your husband's not enough," I said.

"We have a good sex life. I'm just . . . I've fought it since junior high school. I am some sort of nymphomaniac."

I nodded.

"I think 'nymphomania' is sort of an unfashionable term these days," I said.

"Whatever," she said, her face still bright red under her makeup. "I'm addicted to sex. It is a shameful thing, and it has made my life very difficult."

"Ever talk to anyone about it?" I said.

"I talked once with the minister at our church, before I got married."

"And?"

"We prayed together," she said.

"At least he didn't ask you out," I said.

"Excuse me?"

I shook my head.

"My mouth sometimes operates independent of my brain," I said.

She smiled brightly.

"For a little while after we prayed together, it seemed almost as if it had worked. . . ."

"But?" I said.

She shook her head.

"It didn't," she said.

Her blush had faded. She seemed now to be having an easy conversation with a casual acquaintance about a perfectly pleasant subject. No wonder the praying had worked for a while.

"But what I need you to understand," she said, "is that I love my husband. And he loves me. To find out about me would just kill him."

"I'll try to prevent that," I said.

"Have you made any progress?" she said.

"Not much. Do you ever work out at Pinnacle Fitness?"

She nodded.

"Yes," she said. "I have a membership. Why do you ask?"

"Just looking for a pattern," I said.

"Do you have a picture of him?" she said.

"No."

"I do," she said.

"May I see it?" I said.

"I took it when he was asleep," she said, "with the camera in my telephone."

"He doesn't know?" I said.

"No."

She took an envelope from her purse.

"It's a bit salacious," she said.

"Me, too," I said, and put my hand out.

She smiled brightly again and handed me the envelope. I opened it. In the envelope was a computer print-out of a digital photograph of a naked man lying on his back on a bed in what was probably a motel room. It was not my kind of salacious. And even if it had been, Nancy had edited out the groin area with a Magic Marker.

Decorum.

Chapter

······································◆◆◆◆······································

6

ALL OF MY CLIENTS were members of Pinnacle Fitness. Which was a pattern. Which gave me something to do. Of course they might also have gone to the same gynecologist, or belonged to the same square-dance club. But a pattern was a pattern. And it was better than having nothing to do. So I walked over to Tremont Street and took a look.

The club was on the top of a newish building across Tremont Street from the Common. Until I was a grown man, I had never even been in any place as glossy as Pinnacle Fitness. It was a monument to the fitness illusion that somehow working out was fun and glamorous. I thought about the gyms where I'd trained as a kid, when I was a fighter. I had started in Boston at Henry Cimoli's

decrepit dump on the waterfront, when the waterfront was decrepit. Henry used to say the location was perfect for screening out the frauds, because only a legitimate tough guy would dare to go down there. Then the waterfront yuppified and so did Henry, and when I went there now I felt sort of misanthropic for not wearing spandex. But there are things that can't be compromised. I refused to dress up to work out.

The lobby of Pinnacle Fitness had sofas and coffee tables and a snack bar where you could get juices and smoothies and tofu sandwiches on seven-grain bread. It was probably not a good place to get a linguica sandwich. I went to the front desk.

"Gary Eisenhower here?" I said.

The young woman at the front desk had a blond ponytail and very white teeth. She was wearing a white polo shirt with the club logo on it and black satin workout pants.

"Excuse me?" she said.

"Gary Eisenhower," I said. "Is he here?"

"Does he work here?"

"I don't know," I said.

She frowned cutely.

"I don't believe we have anyone by that name working here," she said.

"Oh," I said. "Good. So he's a member, then?"

"I, ah, I don't recognize the name," she said.

"Could you look him up for me?" I said.

"I . . . I'm sure the client-services manager can help you," the young woman said. "That's her office right there."

The client-services manager had an open-door policy. I knocked on the open door and she turned in her swivel chair and smiled at me radiantly and stood. She, too, had a blond ponytail and very white teeth. But she was wearing a white top and a black skirt. The skirt was short, and there was a lot of in-shape leg showing between the hem and the top of her black boots.

"Hi, I'm Margi," she said. "How can I help you?"

"I'm looking for Gary Eisenhower," I said.

"Is he a member here?" Margi said.

"That's what I was going to ask you," I said.

"Why do you wish to know?" Margi said.

"I'd like to get in touch with him," I said.

"It is club policy, sir, not to give out member information."

"Something illicit going on here?" I said.

"Of course not," Margi said. "It is simply that we respect our members' privacy."

"Me, too," I said. "So he is a member?"

Margi was getting brisker by the minute; no wonder she made client-services manager.

"I didn't say that, sir."

"Of course not," I said. "But if he's not a member, then there's no privacy issue, is there."

"Of course not," Margi said. "May I ask why you are interested?"

"So what you can do is check your membership records, and if he is not a member, you can tell me."

She frowned. The reasoning had become too convoluted for her. I thought her frown was even perkier than the one I'd seen at the front desk. But I feared that she would never advance beyond client services.

"Are you some kind of policeman or something?" she said.

"I am," I said.

I used to be a policeman, and "or something" covers a lot.

"I don't mean to give you grief, Margi. Just check. If he's not a member, tell me and I'll move on," I said.

I was interested as well as to what she'd do if he was a member.

She looked at me, still frowning, giving it as much thought as she was able. Then she heaved a big sigh and turned to her computer.

"Eisenhower," she said. "Does that start with an I?"

"E," I said, and spelled it for her.

She clicked at her computer for a little while, and then I could see her face relax.

"We have no one by that name as a member," she said.

She could have been lying to get rid of me. But I

didn't think she was smart enough to fake the look of relief when she didn't find him. I thanked her.

"Could I buy you a linguica sandwich?" I said.

She looked horrified.

"On Portuguese sweet bread?" I said.

"No," she said, and smiled at me brightly. "But thanks for asking."

Chapter

❖

7

IT WAS NEARLY NOVEMBER. Baseball season was over. And the wind off the Charles River was beginning to have an edge. I was at my desk, with my feet up, thinking about pattern, when two men came in without knocking and closed the door behind them. I opened the right-hand drawer on my desk. The bigger of the two was bald, with biceps that strained against the sleeves of a shiny leather jacket. The other guy was slim and dark, with deep-set eyes and graceful hands.

"Lemme guess," I said. "You're George, and you're Lenny."

The muscular guy looked at the slim guy.

"He's being a wiseass," the dark, slim guy said.

"Maybe he should stop," the muscle guy said.

There was scar tissue around his eyes, and his nose was flat and thick.

"You used to be a fighter?" I said to him.

"Yeah."

"You any good?"

"I look like I was any good?" he said.

"No," I said.

"Do a lot better outside the ring," he said.

The slim, dark guy said, "Shut up, Boo."

" 'Boo'?" I said.

The dark, slim guy looked at me.

"He's Boo," the dark, slim guy said. "I'm Zel. Why you interested in Gary Eisenhower?"

"Why do you ask?" I said.

"Guy I work for wants to know," Zel said.

"Who is he?" I said.

Zel nodded quietly to himself, as if confirming a suspicion.

"Yeah," he said. "That's how it nearly always goes."

"How's that?" I said.

"Everybody's a wiseguy," Zel said. "Everybody's a tough guy."

"Must be disappointing for you," I said.

"That's what Boo's for," he said.

"Glad he's for something," I said.

Zel nodded again in the same sad way.

"So what's your interest in Gary Eisenhower?"

"Who wants to know?"

Zel shrugged.

"Okay," he said. "Boo?"

Boo smiled happily and started around my desk. I took a gun out of my open desk drawer and pointed it at both of them. Boo stopped. He looked disappointed.

"I got one of those, too," Zel said.

"But yours is under your coat," I said.

"True," Zel said. "Back off, Boo."

Boo looked more disappointed, but he stepped back in front of the desk.

"Hard on Boo," Zel said. "He gets all juiced to smack somebody around and then he can't."

"Loving your work is a good thing," I said. "Maybe another time."

"You think you can handle Boo?" Zel said.

"Sure," I said.

"Without the piece?" Zel said.

"Yeah," I said.

"I heard you were good," Zel said.

Boo stared at me. Apparently, he hadn't heard that. Or it hadn't impressed him.

"Kind of like to watch," Zel said. "You decide to try it."

"Been a while," I said, "since I had a fight to prove I could."

"Yeah, I know," Zel said. "Seems kind of pointless, don't it."

"Tiring, too," I said.

"Boo ain't to that point yet," Zel said.

"Probably won't get there soon," I said.

"'Less he starts losing a few," Zel said.

"You want to know my interest in Eisenhower. I want to know who wants to know," I said.

"You show me yours, I show you mine?" Zel said.

"Might work," I said.

"And if it don't?" Zel said.

"I could shoot you," I said.

"But you won't," Zel said.

"Probably not," I said. "Unless Boo becomes a distraction."

Zel nodded. He looked at me for a while. Then he nodded to himself slowly.

"I work for a guy name of Chester Jackson," Zel said.

"What's his interest?" I said.

"Don't know," Zel said. "Show me yours."

"Guy is blackmailing a group of women he had affairs with," I said. "They want me to make him stop."

"Who are the women?"

"Nope," I said.

Zel nodded.

After a while he said, "I think Mr. Jackson will want to talk with you."

"Sure," I said.

Zel took a business card out of his shirt pocket and put it on my desk. Chester Jackson had offices at

International Place. I picked up the card and put it in my shirt pocket.

"Chester married?" I said.

Zel shrugged.

"Maybe to a younger woman?" I said.

Zel smiled faintly and shrugged again.

"I'll stop by," I said.

Zel nodded.

"Adiós," he said. "Come on, Boo."

They walked out. At the door Boo turned and looked at me hard.

"I ain't forgetting you," he said.

"Few people do," I said.

Chapter

❖❖

8

THE SECRETARY HAD a British accent. She ushered me in to see Mr. Jackson as though it was an audience. We were high up. There was the usual spectacular view of the harbor. And in front of the view, on a credenza, was a big photograph of Beth. Chet stood up and came around his desk when I came in.

"Chet Jackson," he said, and put out his hand.

He had a big chin and short black hair with a lot of gray showing. The hair was receding from his forehead. His face was unlined. He smelled of very good cologne. His grip was strong. He had on a blue suit with a blue-and-white striped tie against a gleaming white shirt. There was a white handkerchief in his breast pocket.

I sat. He sat.

"Coffee?" he said. "Tea? water? Something stronger?"

"No, thanks."

Chet nodded decisively.

"Okay," he said. "What can you tell me about Gary Eisenhower?"

"He's blackmailing a number of women," I said. "They asked me to find him and make him stop."

"Have you found him?"

"No."

"But you've been looking for him at Pinnacle Fitness," Chet said.

"Yes."

"Why?"

"Thought I might find him there," I said.

"What made you think that?"

"Probably," I said, "same thing that made you go there."

"What makes you think I went there?"

"I'm a trained investigator," I said. "One day I ask about Eisenhower there, next day Zel and Boo come around."

"Who are these women who employed you?"

I shook my head.

"I am a man of considerable leverage," Chet said.

"How nice for you," I said.

"And I don't like flippant," Chet said.

"What a shame," I said.

Chet swiveled in his chair and with his back to me looked out his window at his view. After a suitable pause he swiveled back and looked hard at me.

"I want to know who you represent," he said. "And I want to know what led you to Pinnacle."

"I'll be damned," I said. "That's pretty much what I want to learn from you."

We sat silently then, looking at each other. Then Chet smiled at me.

"You're not scared of me, are you?" he said.

"I'm trying to be," I said.

Chet leaned back in his chair a little and laughed.

"Goddamn it," he said. "I like your style."

"That's grand," I said.

We sat again.

I looked around the office.

"What do you do for a living?" I said.

"I make money," Chet said.

"How?" I said.

"Little of this," Chet said. "Little of that."

"Folks that employ people like Zel and Boo," I said, "and make their money by doing a little of this, a little of that, most of those folks have offices in the back of billiard parlors."

"I played football at Harvard," Chet said.

"Wow," I said.

Chet was rubbing his chin with the palm of his left hand.

"Okay," he said. "I'm going to take a chance on you."

He nodded at the picture of Beth on the credenza.

"That's my wife," he said. "Beth. I think she's been involved with Eisenhower."

"Uh-huh," I said.

"Can you confirm or deny that?" Chet said.

"Nope."

"Is she one of your clients?"

I shook my head.

"You wouldn't tell me if she was," Chet said. "Would you?"

I shook my head.

"Can you tell me anything?"

"I figured Gary had a plan ahead of time," I said. "All the women I represent have a common pattern. Young, older husbands of significant wealth. And all of them belonged to Pinnacle Fitness."

Chet nodded.

"Beth belongs," he said.

I nodded. He stopped rubbing his chin and massaged his forehead with both hands for a minute. Then he put his hands flat on his desktop and leaned a little toward me.

"I'm a tough guy," he said. "I make a lot of money in a lot of different ways, and none of the ways is easy."

I nodded.

"I don't mind that," he said. "I don't care too much

about too many things. People get in my way, I don't mind moving them out of the way."

I nodded.

"But this is hard," he said.

I was sick of nodding, so I just waited.

"And the reason it's hard is that I made a mistake."

He paused and looked at the back of his hands on the desktop, and breathed a couple of times.

"I let myself love Beth," he said.

"Opens you up a little," I said. "Doesn't it."

"Chink in the armor," he said. "But there it is. I'm fifty-eight. She's thirty. I'm in good shape and all. But I'm almost twice her age."

I went back to nodding.

"We were fine until I began to get a sense that she might be seeing somebody else. No real evidence, little stuff, mostly sort of a feeling. I guess if your wife is cheating on you, at some level, you know."

"If you let yourself," I said.

"After a while I let myself," he said. "I put Zel on her, see what he could find out."

"She doesn't know Zel?" I said.

"No. She doesn't know anything to do with my business."

"Makes it easier," I said.

"Zel's good at things," Chet said. "He tailed her and found out that she was seeing somebody and what

his name was." Chet shook his head. "If that's his real name."

"And you started looking into places she might have met him," I said.

"Zel did, yeah. Health club, country club, restaurants, couple of stores on Newbury Street."

"And he didn't find Eisenhower," I said. "But he established an, ah, relationship with various people to report if anything about Eisenhower surfaced. So when I showed up at Pinnacle Fitness, asking about him . . ."

"We heard about it," Chet said. "And I asked Zel to check it out with you."

"What's your plan if you find Gary Eisenhower."

"I'll have him in for a talk," Chet said.

"How far will you go?" I said.

"Do you mean will I kill him?" Chet said. "I don't think that would get me where I want to get."

"Which is?"

"With Beth, and nobody else."

"And if you aced him, she'd suspect."

"Wouldn't you?" Chet said.

"You're not the only aggrieved husband," I said.

"But you'd be suspicious, wouldn't you?"

"Yeah," I said. "Have you spoken to your wife about any of this?"

"No."

"Might be a good thing," I said.

"Might be," he said.

"But?"

"But I can't," he said. "I simply goddamn can't."

I nodded.

"The best moments in my life," I said, "have come because I loved somebody."

"Yeah," he said.

"And the worst," I said.

"Yeah," he said.

Chapter

❖

9

I SAT IN THE client-membership offices with a young woman named Courtney and signed up for a six-month membership at Pinnacle Fitness. I didn't see Margi from the client-services office. Though Courtney could have been Margi with a change of makeup. Then the client-training director took me to the client-training office to assess me physically. He took my blood pressure and pulse. He weighed me. And pronounced me fit. He turned me over to a personal trainer, an in-shape young man named Luke, who offered to help me learn the various pieces of equipment. I declined.

"I've worked out a lot," I said. "I'll be okay on my own."

Luke nodded.

"I kind of figured that," he said. "You need anything, give me a shout."

I got a locker and a padlock. I didn't really need one, except for the gun. I hated wearing a gun while working out. So I changed into some sweats and left the gun in the locker. If Margi spotted me from the client-services office and rushed me, I might be able to run for it.

I was limited in my workouts by the fact that I could use only equipment near the front window, where I could watch for Gary Eisenhower entering the lobby. Who kept not showing up every day.

Susan came with me for a guest workout one day. Everything she wore to work out in fit her exactly and matched perfectly. Her thick, dark hair was held in place by what must have been a designer headband. And her makeup was impeccable. She'd been doing a lot of power yoga lately, which made her even stronger and more supple than she already was. A lot of people looked at her.

"My," Susan said, as she looked around Pinnacle Fitness. "You fit in here like a rhinoceros at a petting zoo."

"I'm undercover," I said, "disguised as a thug."

"It's very convincing," Susan said. "You're waiting for Gary Whosis to show up?"

"Yes."

"How long do you plan to wait?"

"I have a six-month membership," I said.

"You are a stubborn boy," she said.

"I am."

"Maybe I can help," she said. "Show me the picture again."

"It's still censored," I said.

"How too bad," Susan said.

We worked out as long as we could stand to and then went to change. When I came dressed from the shower, through the front window of the gym I saw Zel and Boo come into the club lobby. I went out.

"Looking for somebody?" I said.

"Same as you," Zel said.

Behind him, Boo was giving me the deadeye stare that was supposed to freeze my blood in my veins.

I said, "How ya doin', Boo?"

"Fuck you," he said.

I nodded.

"You looking for Gary Eisenhower?" I said to Zel.

"Yep."

"But you don't know what he looks like," I said. "So actually you swung by to see if I'd made any progress."

"Yep," Zel said.

"I haven't," I said.

"You know what he looks like?" Zel said.

"No," I said.

"The hell you don't," Zel said. "You wouldn't be here if you didn't know."

I shrugged.

"How about it, Zel," Boo said. "Lemme go with him a little."

Zel ignored him.

"We're after the same thing," Zel said. "Don't see why we can't cooperate."

"What's Boo after?" I said.

"Boo wants what I want," Zel said.

"And you want?"

"What Chet tells me," Zel said.

"Too many levels of command for me," I said. "I think I'll mosey along on this by myself."

"Don't mind if we mosey on along behind you," Zel said.

"Nope."

"What if you did mind?" Boo said. "What you gonna do?"

"Let's wait until I mind," I said.

Boo wanted so badly to prove he was tougher than I was that I felt almost bad for him.

"Two things, Boo," Zel said. "One, it ain't time for you to do your thing. And two, I ain't so sure you can do it with him."

"Like hell," Boo said.

"Listen to Zel," I said to Boo.

"See you around," Zel said.

He jerked his head toward the elevator. Boo was still giving me the stare.

"Boo," Zel said quietly. "We're leaving."

He walked to the elevator and pushed the button. Boo stared at me. The elevator arrived and the door slid open.

"Boo," Zel said. "Now!"

Boo turned and went to the elevator. Zel followed him in. The door slid shut. I looked back toward the health club. Susan, showered, made up, coiffed, and in street clothes, was standing inside the big window holding a two-and-a-half-pound dumbbell. I went back inside the club.

"What was your plan?" I said.

"The ugly guy you were having a stare-off with," Susan said. "If things unraveled, I was going to run out and hit him with the dumbbell."

"Appropriate choice of weapon," I said.

"For either one of you," Susan said.

I crooked my arm for her to take.

"Buy you a drink, Wonder Woman?" I said.

She took my arm.

"Maybe two," she said.

Chapter

❖

10

I **WENT EVERY DAY** to Pinnacle Fitness. I had to be careful. If I improved my body further, the paparazzi would begin following me. So I worked out sparingly and spent a lot of time watching the snugly dressed young women, looking for exercise tips. I was in my second week at Pinnacle when one of the female trainers walked up to me and put her hand out.

"Hi," she said. "I'm Estelle. Can I help you with your training?"

We shook hands. She had shiny black hair, worn long and straight. There was something faintly Asian-Pacific about her appearance, though it was too faint to tell me what.

"No, thanks," I said. "I don't think anyone can."

She smiled warmly.

"I don't believe that," she said. "If you need anything, please let me know."

I said, "Okay, Estelle."

Since I'd joined no one had spoken to me like that. Why now? I glanced through the front window at the lobby. Across the lobby at the snack bar, a man wearing an ankle-length black overcoat was sipping a smoothie, the healthy devil. He had a short beard and aviator-style sunglasses, and a bright blue silk scarf hanging open around his neck. He didn't seem to be paying attention. Estelle paid me no more attention, either. When he finished his smoothie, the guy in the overcoat left. Sleuthing makes you suspicious. The guy hadn't been in the club. Had he really come up to the top floor of the building to drink a smoothie?

When I was through for the day, I took the elevator down and went out onto Tremont Street. The guy in the overcoat was sitting on a bench across the street at the edge of the Common, reading a newspaper, digesting his smoothie. He fit the physical description of Gary Eisenhower, as best I could tell. But the beard and the sunglasses made it a little hard to judge the face from this distance. If only his loins were blacked out with Magic Marker.

I crossed with the light and headed on down across the Common. Overcoat fell in behind me, at a distance. Even if I hadn't started thinking about him in the health

club lobby, I would have made him when he started tailing me. His elaborate lack of interest in me was classic overacting. We crossed Charles Street to the Public Garden. It was late afternoon and already dark in the Back Bay. The Public Garden was full of people walking away from work. I angled left through the Public Garden, crossed at Arlington, and went up Boylston Street toward my office. The guy in the overcoat trailed along. I went in the Boylston Street entrance of my building and walked up a flight to my office. Overcoat lingered outside.

In my office I took off my leather jacket, put on my baseball hat and a black raincoat, and went down the back stairs, into the alley, and out onto Berkeley to the corner of Boylston. Overcoat was where I thought he'd be, in the lobby of my building, looking at the tenant directory.

I crossed Boylston Street and stood looking in the window of a Starbucks coffee shop. In the reflection I saw him come out of the building. He headed across Boylston on Berkeley Street toward the river. I tailed him down Berkeley, across Newbury, across Commonwealth Ave, to Beacon Street. He turned right, crossed Arlington, and turned into a low apartment building on the river side of Beacon Street, where it was still flat before Beacon Hill began to rise toward the State House. I stood across the street behind the black iron fence where it turned the corner at Arlington Street. In another minute or so, the lights went on in the second-floor front.

It was raining lightly; there was a mild wind. I felt like a real private eye, standing in the dark, in the city, with my collar pulled up and my hat pulled down. After a while, I walked across to the doorway of the apartment building and read the names under the doorbells. The second floor was E. Herzog.

I lived only a couple of blocks from E. Herzog, so I turned back into the light rain and walked home.

Gee whiz, I thought, *who can you trust.*

Chapter

❖❖

11

I TAILED HIM for the next couple of days. I thought it might make some sense to see if I could learn anything. And in truth, I was probably showing off a little. When he'd try to tail me, I spotted him at once. I was behind him for the rest of the week and he never knew it. I couldn't wait to tell Susan.

The next day, Wednesday, I called Martin Quirk and asked him if he could run the names Gary Eisenhower and E. Herzog for me.

"You want me to come by and iron yours shirts, too?"

"I know you," I said. "You'd use too much starch."

"I find anything," Quirk said, "I'll let you know."

I spent the rest of Wednesday hanging around Newbury Street, where Gary shopped with a woman I didn't know in a series of shops that didn't have my size. Thursday was spent mostly in the lobby of The Langham Hotel, where Gary spent the afternoon in a room with one woman, and much of the evening in the same room with a different woman. Neither was a client.

Friday I spent the morning outside a boutique hotel near the State House, while Gary spent it in the hotel with a date, not one of my clients. Gary didn't let a lot of grass grow, I had to give him that.

Friday afternoon he did some shopping in Copley Place. I didn't like Copley Place. It was a large mall in the middle of the city, with a lot of marble and high-end shops, anchored at either end by a large hotel. One could come to the hotel and shop in the mall, and never go outside. The drawback was that inside the mall you had no way to know if you were in Chicago, or Houston, or East Lansing, Michigan.

Gary seemed to like it okay. He bought a cashmere topcoat and a twelve-thousand-dollar suit, and a pair of imported shoes, the price of which I didn't catch. Then he went to one of the hotel bars and had drinks with Estelle, the friendly trainer. They spoke at length and quite intensely, and laughed quite often, and when he left her he kissed her good-bye. Then, carrying his

purchases, he headed out of Copley Place and on down Boylston Street.

I drifted along behind him as he walked down Boylston from Copley Place. There was a lot of foot traffic in the late afternoon, and I closed it up a little. He turned at Arlington Street, as I had expected, but then he crossed into the Public Garden and walked toward the little bridge that arched over the Swan Boats. Halfway across the bridge he stopped and leaned on the railing and looked down at the still water. The romantic devil just liked to be on the bridge. I understood that. I did, too. The Swan Boats were in dry dock for the winter. But the pond hadn't been drained yet. When I reached him I stopped and leaned on the bridge railing, too. He kept staring at the water.

I said, "Gary Eisenhower, I presume?"

He looked up as if he was startled. Then he began to smile.

"Goddamn," he said. "You're pretty good."

"Everyone says so."

"How'd you know it was me?" he said.

"Got a picture," I said.

"How the hell . . . ?"

"A woman took it while you were sleeping."

"Damn," he said. "Probably used one of those phone cameras."

"Yep."

He grinned wider.

"Fucking technology," he said. "Want to go some-place and have a drink and talk about things?"

"We'd be fools not to," I said.

Chapter

❖

12

WE WALKED OVER to the Four Seasons and got a table in The Bristol Lounge. Gary ordered a "Maker's Mark, rocks, water back." I had a beer. Gary put his shopping bags on the floor beside him and unbuttoned his overcoat but didn't take it off. Under the coat he had on a coffee-colored coarse-weave turtleneck sweater. He took a long swallow of his bourbon when it arrived, and sipped a little water.

"Oh, Momma," he said. "Nothing like it when you need it."

"Or even when you don't," I said.

"You got that right," he said.

He looked around.

"Nice room," he said.

"Yes, it is."

"One of the places I bring them," he said.

"Nothing but the best," I said. "You ever pay?"

He grinned at me and sipped more bourbon.

"Not often," he said.

He stirred the remaining bourbon and ice with his forefinger for a moment.

"Nice gig," he said. "I hope we can work something out. I'd hate to give it up."

"Tell me about the gig," I said.

"You probably got most of it figured out," he said.

"Tell me anyway," I said. "I'm much dumber than I seem."

Gary leaned back in his chair and laughed hard.

"Aren't we all," he said.

He drank the rest of his bourbon, spotted the waitress, pointed to the glass. She nodded and looked at me. I shook my head.

"Okay," Gary said. "I'm good with women, you know? They like me. For a while I used that to get a lot of tail."

"Good to have a hobby," I said.

He grinned.

"That's what it was at first, a hobby," he said. "But I like a lot of action."

"And you believe in diversity," I said.

"I do," he said. "And that makes the hobby get kind of expensive."

"Lot of wining and dining before you even get to the hobby part," I said.

"Pretty much at first," Gary said. "After you sort of get established it gets cheaper, you know? You cut out the wining and dining, get right to the hobby."

I nodded. The waitress came with Gary's drink. It made him happy. He drank some of it.

"But one day," I said, "it occurred to you that you might be able to turn the hobby into a living."

He pointed to me.

"Exactly," he said. "You sure you're not smart?"

"Pretty sure," I said.

"I think you're too modest," Gary said.

"That, too," I said. "So how did you do the black-mail?"

"Hey, dude, what a terrible word," he said.

"Okay," I said. "How did you go about professional-izing your hobby?"

"First time I tried it," Gary said, "I rented a motel room for a couple days. I got some software in my computer that allows pictures to be taken through the screen. I set it up focused on the bed, so it looked like it was just on the table, where I'd been typing or something. And I set it to go off every few seconds. As backup, I put a tape recorder under the bed. So when the action started I made sure the positions were right for pictures and sound. It worked. And as time went along, I refined

it. Got a tiny video camera, set it up in the corner of the room. In a shadow. Taped sight and sound."

Gary sipped some bourbon. As he swallowed, he held the glass up in front of him and gave it a little kiss.

"In some ways, the sound is better than the pictures," he said.

"But harder to identify," I said.

"Yeah. That's why you need the pictures. But the stuff they said . . ." He shook his head. "You know how a lot of women say stuff during sex?"

"I recall something about that," I said.

"You married?" Gary said.

"No, but I'm with the girl of my dreams," I said.

"Girl of your dreams?" Gary said.

"Uh-huh."

"She say stuff?"

I didn't say anything.

Gary shrugged.

"*À chacun son goût,*" he said.

"*Oui,*" I said.

He grinned.

"Anyway, I got some excellent action," he said. "Some of it pretty kinky."

I nodded.

"You want to hear about it?" Gary said.

"Another time," I said.

"You got a problem with kinky, Spense?"

"Not among consenting adults," I said. "And don't call me Spense."

"Oh, sure, apologize," he said. "Anyway, it was duck soup. So I started doing it regular. I made sure the women were married and had money, preferably married to older rich men, so they might be looking for action but would never want to give up the husband and his money."

"Estelle help you with that?" I said.

"Boy, you don't miss much," Gary said. "How'd you know that?"

"She fingered me for you," I said.

"Oh," he said. "Yeah."

"She'd have access to the membership records," I said.

"She does," Gary said. "She knows what we're looking for."

"Many failures?" I said.

"Now and then," Gary said. "Not as often as you'd think."

He was a very handsome man. Six feet tall, maybe a little more, wide shoulders, narrow hips, good color, dressed like a male model.

"She doesn't mind you having sex with all these women?" I said.

"I think she likes it," he said.

I nodded.

"So how often do you practice your, ah, profession," I said.

"It's still a hobby, too," Gary said. "I do it every day."

"Why?" I said.

"Why?"

"Yeah," I said. "Why?"

"'Cause I can, for crissake."

"Well," I said, "it's nice to like your work."

Chapter

······◆◆······

13

GARY WAS ON HIS THIRD bourbon. But it was going in much more slowly, and he showed little effect from the first two. I had my second beer.

"So where do we stand?" Gary said.

"What's the E stand for," I said.

"E?"

"As in E. Herzog."

Gary looked at me for a long moment.

"Oh, shit," he said.

I waited.

After a while, Gary grinned at me.

"Okay," he said. "You're smart. That dumb stuff is just a ploy."

"Maybe," I said. "But what I've done so far doesn't prove anything."

"You think?" he said.

"Your big mistake was trying to tail me. If you hadn't made it, I would have had a much harder time finding you."

"You spotted me following you the other day and turned it around and followed me."

"Yep."

Gary shook his head.

"Amateurs and professionals, huh?"

"What's the E stand for?" I said.

"Elliot," he said.

"Is Elliot Herzog your real name?" I said.

Again, Gary grinned at me.

"One of them," he said.

I nodded.

"So what are your plans," I said, "for the ladies who employed me?"

He smiled.

"Abigail, Beth, Nancy, Regina," he said. "The gang of four."

"Are they the only ones with whom you are at the moment practicing your profession?"

"Not hardly," Gary said.

"Maybe you should plan to stick with them," I said. "And leave my gang alone."

He picked up a butter knife and tapped a little beat on the table with it while he looked at me.

"I got no reason to change my plans," he said.

"I'm supposed to give you a reason," I said.

He shrugged.

"What are you gonna do?" he said. "These ladies are willing to pay because they don't want their husbands to know. That hasn't changed. None of them will press charges. If you tell the cops or whatever, every one of them will deny that they ever had anything to do with me."

"I could keep punching your lights out," I said, "until we reach an agreement."

"Yeah, maybe," he said. "I have a sense that it might not be your style. But say it was. If you did it once, okay, I'm sore for a few days. I might be tougher than you think I am. And when I felt better, I'd get hold of your employers and they'd call you off, for fear I'd expose them."

"And if they didn't?" I said.

"I'd expose them," he said. "They're not the only fish in my creel, you know?"

"I don't seem to terrify you," I said.

"I been living this life for a long time," he said. "I'm pretty light on my feet."

"And the cops don't terrify you," I said.

"Nothing much does," he said. "You got the tab on this?"

"Sure," I said. "Expense account."

"Sort of like me," he said, and stood up.

"See you around," he said.

"Yep," I said.

He picked up his shopping bags and strolled out of the lounge. I watched him go and smiled. I kind of liked him. I picked up his butter knife by the blade and slipped it into my coat pocket. Then I paid the bill, tipped handsomely, and strolled out of the lounge, too.

Chapter

14

G OT SIX E. HERZOGS," Quirk said to me. "None of them named Elliot. Got no Gary Eisenhowers."

"There's a surprise," I said.

We were having lunch at Locke-Ober.

"How come you know everybody?" I said.

"Been coming here a long time, most of them are politicians or lawyers."

"That you met in your work," I said.

"Yep," Quirk said.

He grinned.

"Arrested some of them," he said.

"Not enough," I said.

"Everybody got arrested that should get arrested," Quirk said, "we wouldn't have no place to put them."

"How about the butter knife?" I said.

Quirk nodded.

"There were prints on the butter knife," he said. "Yours were on the blade, and there were two others."

"One would be whoever set the table," I said.

"Young woman named Lucille Malinkowski," Quirk said.

"Why have you got her prints on file?"

"Don't know, nothing criminal. Maybe she was in the army, maybe she has a gun license, maybe she used to work someplace where she had to have clearance. I didn't know you'd care."

"And the other one?

"Belongs to a guy named Goran Pappas," Quirk said.

" 'Goran'?"

"Aka Gary Pappas," Quirk said.

"Why is Gary in the system," I said.

"He did three in MCI-Shirley for swindling," Quirk said.

"From a woman?" I said.

"Yes."

"What'd Gary look like?" I said.

"Six feet one inch, one hundred seventy pounds, dark hair, brown eyes, even features, age thirty-eight at the time of his arrest."

"Which was?"

"In 2002," Quirk said.

He produced a computer printout of Gary Pappas's mug shot. It was Gary Eisenhower.

"Anybody want him now for anything?" I said.

"He's not in the system," Quirk said. "Course, the system's imperfect."

"It is?" I said. "How did that happen?"

Quirk didn't bother to answer.

"You want to discuss Gary with me?" he said.

"He's blackmailing a bunch of women," I said.

"Tell me about it," Quirk said.

I told him most of it, leaving out the names.

"Not a bad gig," Quirk said. "Banging good-looking women every day, getting money for it."

"It might get boring," I said.

Quirk looked at me.

"Or not," I said.

Quirk nodded.

"So they hired you to make him stop," Quirk said.

"Yes."

"You got any evidence?" Quirk said.

"Got no evidence we can use."

"Women won't testify?"

"No."

"So what are you supposed to do?" Quirk said. "Scare him?"

"I tried that," I said.

"How'd that work for you?" Quirk said.

"It didn't," I said.

"Disappointing," Quirk said.

"Makes me feel old," I said.

"Want me to stop by and have a talk with him?" Quirk said. "Unofficially?"

I shook my head.

"Don't think he'd care," I said.

"About the homicide commander?" Quirk said.

"I don't think cops worry him," I said.

"Now I feel old," Quirk said.

"This is a pretty cool guy," I said. "He knows what he's doing, and he doesn't seem to scare."

"Like you and me," Quirk said.

"Yeah, but he's better-looking," I said.

"Than you and me?" Quirk said. "How is that possible?"

Chapter

❖❖❖

15

SUSAN AND I made love on Sunday morning at her place with the bedroom door closed and Pearl grumbling unhappily outside it. When we were through, Susan whisked the covers up over us, as she always did, and we lay quietly on the bed for a while.

"You know, don't you," Susan said, "that I was a cheerleader at Swampscott High School?"

"I do know that," I said.

Susan flipped the covers back and rolled out of bed, and stood naked beside it.

"Sis-boom-bah," she said, and jumped into the air and kicked her heels back.

"Is that in honor of my performance?" I said.

"Ours," she said. "And us."

I nodded.

"Sis-boom-bah," I said.

Susan opened the bedroom door and Pearl bounded in, jumped on the bed, turned around maybe fifteen times, and flopped down where Susan had been. I looked at her. Then I looked at Susan.

"There's a definite difference," I said.

"Pearl was never a cheerleader," Susan said.

We showered and dressed, which took me considerably less time than it took Susan. She was just snapping her bra when I headed for the kitchen to start breakfast. Pearl stayed where she was.

By the time I had made my whole-wheat blackberry pancakes and put them on the plates, she came out with her face on and her clothes in place. It was weekend informal, a scoop-neck black T-shirt, jeans, and loafers. But everything fit her so perfectly and she was so beautiful that I felt the same rush of amazement and triumph I always felt in moments like these.

She sat at the table and sipped her orange juice. I put the pot of coffee on the table and sat across from her and looked at her. She looked back at me, and finished her orange juice, and said something that sounded like "hum," which I knew to be positive. I drank some orange juice and poured us some coffee. Pearl sat attentively beside the table. I would have been quite willing to discuss the particulars of what Susan and I had just done together, but I knew it violated some inward standard of

privacy that she maintained. Sex is good; talking about it afterward is not good. So I shut up. Shutting up rarely leads to anything bad.

"I was thinking about your person," she said.

"You're my person," I said.

"No, no, I mean the Gary Eisenhower person. Did you tell me he has sex every day?"

"Seems to," I said.

"With people he doesn't love," she said.

"That's my impression," I said.

"What do you think of that?" she said.

"Sounds great," I said. "But, present company excluded, of course, it is really an adolescent fantasy, which, humor aside, most adult men would get bored with."

"Would you?"

"Yes," I said.

"With me?" she said.

"Never been tested."

"Do you think we make love enough?" Susan said.

"Yes," I said. "And very high quality."

She nodded and took a small bite of pancake.

"Yum," she said. "Blackberries."

"Did I pass?" I said.

"Pass?"

"The little quiz you just gave me," I said. "Did I pass?"

She smiled.

"Yes," she said. "But I was actually thinking about Gary Whosis."

"You think he wouldn't pass?"

"I think if he does in fact have sex with as many women as often as he does, that there's something more than simple pleasure."

"That would be true of us," I said.

"That our sex life is about more than simple pleasure?"

"Yes."

"True, and what is it?"

I grinned at her.

"Love?"

"That would be my guess," Susan said.

I grinned at her.

"Sis-boom-bah!" I said.

Chapter

❖❖❖

16

WE WERE ALL in the conference room again, me, Elizabeth Shaw, and the gang of four, as Gary had named them.

"His real name is Goran Pappas," I said. "He also uses the name Elliot Herzog. He lives on Beacon Street, just before it climbs the hill. He's done time for swindling. He appears to have preselected you, using information provided him by a woman at the health club. There appear to be other women in his life beyond you four."

"His name is Goran?" Regina said.

"He uses the nickname Gary," I said.

"Gary Pappas?" she said.

"How'd you find all this out?" Abigail Larson said.

"Amazing, isn't it?"

"No, really, how do you know?" Abigail said.

I looked inscrutable.

"Vee haf our vays," I said.

"It seems to me our next question," Elizabeth said, "is now that we have him located, what steps can we take to contain him?"

The women looked at one another. Then they all looked at me.

"What should we do?" Nancy said.

"He's a blackmailer," I said. "We could arrest him."

"Would we have to testify?" Nancy said.

"Yes."

Abigail looked at Elizabeth.

"Is that true?"

"You're the victims," Elizabeth said. "You'd have to make the complaint. You'd have to testify in court, if the case went there. We could probably keep it fairly low-key, with luck."

"But my husband would have to know," Nancy said.

"Very likely," Elizabeth said.

"Then I won't do it," Nancy said.

I looked around the room. All of the women were shaking their heads.

"Couldn't you just make him stop?" Regina said. "You know, beat him up or something?"

"Several things against that," I said. "One, I don't like doing it. Two, it's illegal. Three, I believe that if I did, he'd blow the whistle on you."

"Blow the whistle?" Abigail said.

"Send evidence of your infidelity to your husbands," I said.

Everybody sat. No one said anything. Everybody looked at one another.

Finally Regina said in a very soft voice, "Could you kill him?"

"No," I said.

"Do you know someone who would?" she said.

"Yes."

"Could you get him to do it?"

"No," I said.

"But why?" Regina said.

"That's enough," Elizabeth said. "There will be no more talk of that nature from any of you, if you wish me to continue as your attorney."

Everyone was quiet, as if they'd been chastised by the teacher.

"I could try to arrange some kind of payoff," I said.

"He wants so much," Beth said.

"How much?"

"Twenty-five thousand dollars a month," Beth said.

"From each of you?"

The other women nodded.

"I have access to some money of my own. Chet is very generous," Beth said. "But I can't keep paying out that kind of money without eventually having to turn to him."

The other women nodded in agreement.

"Can you come up with one big payoff?" I said. "I might be able to persuade him to take it and move on, rather than have me on his case all the time."

"I can't without Chet knowing," Beth said.

"Me, either," Abigail said.

The two others shook their heads. I looked at Elizabeth.

"Counselor?" I said.

"I'm a trust lawyer," she said. "I don't know what we should do."

I stood up.

"Good luck," I said.

Nobody said anything, but they all looked at me mournfully as I moved toward the door. I shrugged.

"Can't win 'em all," I said.

Chapter

◆◆◆

17

HAWK AND I were having a "Thank God it's late Thursday afternoon" drink at the far end of the bar in Grill 23.

"What's the book?" I said to Hawk.

He looked at the hardcover on the bar beside him. The flap was keeping his place about one hundred pages in.

"New one by Janet Evanovich," he said.

"Good?"

"Course it's good. Would I be reading it, it's not good?"

"You reading it, it wouldn't dare," I said.

Hawk smiled.

"Don't suppose you want me to pop Gary Eisenhower for you," Hawk said.

"There's nothing going on here," I said, "that anyone should die for."

"Just an offer," Hawk said.

"Thanks," I said.

Hawk sipped some champagne.

"What are friends be for," he said, "they can't scrag somebody for you now and then?"

"I'll take a raincheck," I said.

Hawk looked as he always did, as if he'd just been washed and polished. His clothes were immaculate. His shirt seemed to glow with whiteness. His shaved head gleamed in the bar's light.

"Maybe I should shave my head," I said.

"White guys don't look good with their heads shaved," Hawk said.

"Why is that?" I said.

"Don't know," Hawk said. "Don't look as good with hair, either."

"Are you making invidious racial comparisons?" I said.

"Uh-huh," Hawk said.

The bartender came down the bar and replaced our drinks.

"You say he knew the names of the women hired you," Hawk said.

"Yes."

"How many women he working, you think?"

"More than four," I said.

"So somebody tole him," Hawk said.

"Be my guess," I said.

"One of them don't believe she ain't special to him," Hawk said.

"You know this how?" I said.

"Simplest explanation," he said.

"True," I said.

"People believe what they need to believe," Hawk said.

"Also true," I said.

Hawk sipped his champagne. I had a little scotch.

"I got nowhere to go," I said. "No one will testify, no one will bargain with him. They all want something they can't have."

"And there's a lot you don't know," Hawk said.

"Susan says there's something wrong with Gary," I said. "That he has as much sex as he does, with various women about whom he doesn't care very much."

"Strange tail," Hawk said.

"I know," I said. "I'm not sure Susan gets that, exactly."

"She gets most things," Hawk said.

"She does," I said.

"I been thinking 'bout cutting back myself," Hawk said.

"Official male attitudes aside, is there such a thing as too much sex?"

"Sure," Hawk said.

"Even at your tolerance level?" I said.

"Even then," Hawk said.

"So what does that do for me?" I said.

"You the sleuth," Hawk said. "I just a simple negro man."

"Simple," I said.

Hawk was looking down the bar at a woman in a dark blue suit.

"Attractive to women, though," he said.

"I thought she was looking at me," I said.

"She not," Hawk said.

I sipped some scotch.

"I suppose I could go back a little, get a little history on Gary," I said.

"He done a triple at Shirley?" Hawk said.

I nodded.

"For swindling some woman?"

I nodded.

"Might make sense to talk to the woman," Hawk said.

"I'm a man of great intellectual curiosity," I said.

We finished our second round. The bartender delivered a third.

"You sure that woman isn't looking at me?" I said.

"What you care?" Hawk said. "You don't fool around no more."

I grinned at him.

"I was never fooling," I said.

Chapter

❖

18

I WAS IN MY OFFICE, at my desk, looking at Gary Pappas's full folder that Quirk had gotten for me. Susan was at a conference in Portland, Maine, and wouldn't be back until tomorrow. So Pearl was on the couch in my office, which had been purchased for her use. Though now and then, when she wasn't around, Susan and I used it for our own purposes. My office door opened softly. Pearl barked. My visitors hesitated.

"It's all right, she won't bite you," I said.

The door opened wider and in came Regina Hartley with a man. Pearl barked again, and they looked at me. Pearl had not bothered to get off the couch and remained prone while she barked.

"It's Bring Your Dog to Work Day," I said. "Have a seat."

They walked cautiously past her and sat in front of my desk. Pearl rested her head on her paws and murmured threateningly. I looked at her. She stopped.

"This is my husband, Clifford," Regina said.

"How do you do?" I said, master of the *bon mot*.

"We need your help," Regina said.

"Haven't done much for you so far," I said.

"This isn't about the other girls," Regina said. "This is just about us."

I nodded. She looked at her husband. He looked at me. I waited.

"This is awkward," he said.

"I often hear awkward things," I said. "I don't mind."

He was a slim man, very erect, very well dressed in a blue suit with a blue-striped pin-collar shirt. His hair was white and close-cut. His color was good. He looked at his wife again.

"I can't," she said.

He nodded and took a deep breath, and went off the high board.

"I'm gay," he said.

"Lot of that going around," I said.

"Regina knows. Has always known," he said. "We care about each other very much, but our lives sometimes run in, ah, separate, though I think parallel, directions."

"And that works for you?"

"Yes," he said. "It does."

Regina nodded.

"Are you out?" I said.

He was silent for a long moment. Then he shook his head.

"No," he said.

"Would being outed do you harm?"

"I fear so," he said. "I am being considered as a candidate for the United States Senate."

"And you fear your gayness would rule you out?"

"Not simply that I am gay," he said, "but that Regina and I have lived separate sexual lives . . . rather, I fear, vigorously."

"Nothing wrong with vigor," I said.

"You see my problem," he said. "If I am nominated, this Gary Eisenhower is like a loose cannon out there rolling around."

"Does he know?" I said.

"About me?" Clifford said. "No, but he knows about Regina, and when I run, he'll see his big chance, and I'm afraid it will all come out."

"Massachusetts has a pretty good history with gay issues," I said.

"I know," he said. "But it's not just gay issues. My wife has slept with an assortment of men." He smiled faintly. "And so have I."

I nodded.

"Not a matter of one boyfriend," I said.

"No," Clifford said.

I looked at Regina. She shrugged.

"No," she said.

I nodded.

"Why did you join with the other women?" I said to Regina.

"I thought maybe it would work," she said. "That we could find someone to make him go away."

"Can you keep paying him?" I said.

"For a while," Clifford said. "But it is intolerable."

I nodded.

"You like your life?"

"Yes," he said. "We both do."

Regina nodded.

"I adore her," he said. "We share everything, except sex. I hope to be with her all my life."

"Regina?" I said.

"I feel the same way," she said.

I leaned back in my chair. Pearl snored gently on the couch.

"Then fess up," I said.

"You mean tell everyone?" Regina said. "No! No, no, no!"

"Tell the truth," I said. "And you've taken away his every weapon."

"It would destroy my candidacy," Clifford said.

"Maybe," I said. "Say it did. You'd still have your life."

"No, Clifford," Regina said. "I won't let you do this to us."

"Would you lose your income?" I said.

"I inherited a considerable estate from my father," he said. "Essentially, I manage it."

"So your job is safe."

He smiled faintly again.

"Yes," he said.

I spread my hands and turned both palms up.

"The truth will set you free," I said.

"No," Regina said. "I won't have you do this. We've wanted this for all of our marriage. You cannot give it up now that it's so close."

I looked at him.

"She's right," he said. "I can't give it up. Not now. For both our sakes."

I didn't say anything.

"Can't you think of anything to do?" Regina said.

I looked at Pearl. She was asleep upside down with her feet draped over the back of the couch and her head hanging off. She appeared not to have thought of anything, either.

"Not yet," I said.

Chapter

.... ◆◆ ....

19

"I SEE IT ALL THE TIME in my patients," Susan said. "There is a way to save themselves and they won't take it. Can't take it."

We had a table by the window at Sorellina. Susan was sipping a martini, up with olives. I had a Dewar's and soda. I was sipping, too. It was just that my sips were much bigger than Susan's.

"Hell," I said. "If their fears are realized, he'll lose the nomination anyway."

"It's too bad," Susan said. "They seem to have achieved a life many people wish they could have. They have, apparently, a stable, loving relationship and sex lives that fulfill them."

"So they say."

"You don't believe them?" Susan said.

"I don't believe them or not believe them," I said. "We'll see."

"Well, say they are telling the truth," Susan said. "They're together. They have enough money."

"Yep."

"The American dream," Susan said. "Or one version of it."

"Yep."

"But because it's a variation on the traditional dream," Susan said, "this man has the power to destroy them."

"It's a power they've given him," I said.

"What would you do?" Susan said.

"I'd call a press conference. Tell everybody everything, and if they didn't like it they could vote for my opponent."

"But you wouldn't run for political office anyway," Susan said.

"'If nominated I will not run. If elected I will not serve,'" I said.

"Yes," she said.

"How about you?"

"Would I confess to save the life we have?"

"Um-hmm."

"Absolutely."

"And should we live separate sexual lives?" I said.

"Do you want to?" Susan said.

"No."

"Me, either," Susan said.

"So let's not," I said.

"Okay."

She picked up her menu. I had a large sip of my scotch, which emptied the glass. I asked our waiter for more.

"I been reading Gary Eisenhower's folder," I said. "I got it from Quirk. He was blackmailing a woman named Clarice Richardson. They'd had an affair, same MO, pictures, audiotapes."

"Married with a rich husband?" Susan said.

"Married," I said. "But not to a rich man. She was the president of a small liberal-arts college in Hartland. I think it's all women."

"Outside of Springfield?" Susan said.

"Yeah. She was afraid she'd lose her husband, for whom she cared. And her job, for which she cared."

"I think I'll have the raw tuna," Susan said.

"But she didn't have enough money to keep making her payments."

"So she went to the police?" Susan said.

"And Gary did three in Shirley."

Susan had put her menu down.

"So what happened to her?" Susan said.

"I thought you and I could go out to Hartland and find out."

"You and I?"

"Yeah."

"Will we visit the Basketball Hall of Fame?" Susan said.

"Sure."

"How about the Springfield Armory?" Susan said.

"Absolutely."

"Anything else?"

"When we weren't investigating, and sightseeing," I said, "we could frolic naked in our motel room."

Susan stared at me for a while.

"I am a nice Jewish girl from Swampscott," she said. "I have a Ph.D. from Harvard. Do you seriously think I would wish to frolic naked in a motel room outside of Springfield?"

"How about Chicopee?" I said.

Susan looked at me in silence for a moment while she took another sip of her martini. The she nodded her head slowly and smiled.

"Springfield it is," she said.

Her smile was like sunrise.

Chapter

······· ◆◆◆ ·······

20

S PRINGFIELD IS A CITY of about 150,000 on the
Connecticut River in Western Mass, near the Con-
necticut line. Hartland is a small town about fifteen
miles upriver. We checked in to the William Pynchon
Motel on Route 5, outside of Hartland, which made
Susan look a little grim.

"I'm not sure about the naked frolicking," she said. "I
agreed to Springfield."

"No need to decide now," I said. "Hartland is nice."

We drove into the town to look for Clarice Richardson, the woman who had put Gary Eisenhower in jail.

"Trees," Susan said.

She had the same look of gladiatorial grimness that

she'd had looking at the motel. We who are about to die salute you.

"Later we can have lunch," I said. "I spotted a dandy little tearoom."

"Oh, God," Susan said.

Parking in Hartland was not an issue. We left the car right across from the wrought-iron archway that led to the college campus.

"Should we start at the college?" Susan said.

"Don't know where else to start," I said.

"It's breathtaking sometimes," Susan said, "to watch you work."

"It's one of the reasons I brought you," I said. "Give you a chance to watch me in the field."

"The excitement never stops," she said.

We got directions to the president's office and spoke to the secretary in the outer room.

"I'm trying to locate Clarice Richardson," I said.

"Do you have an appointment?" the secretary said.

"With Clarice Richardson?" I said.

"Yes, sir," the secretary said. "Do you have an appointment with President Richardson?"

I took out one of my cards, the plain, elegant one with only my name and address, no crossed pistols, and handed it to her.

"Please tell President Richardson it's about Goran Pappas," I said.

She took my card.

"Please have a seat," she said, and went off down a short corridor.

"Brilliant," Susan said, "how you ran her to ground."

"Who knew," I said.

"Makes me think well of the school," Susan said.

"Yes," I said.

The secretary returned.

"President Richardson will see you shortly," she said, and went back to her desk.

Susan and I sat. The outer office was paneled in oak, with a big working pendulum clock on the wall and a wine-colored Persian rug on the floor.

"You think it's politically correct," I said to Susan, "to call that a Persian rug?"

"Iranian rug doesn't sound right," she said.

"I know."

"How about Oriental?" Susan said. "More general."

"I think Oriental may be incorrect, too," I said.

"How about a big rug from somewhere east of Suez?"

The door opened to the outer office and a strapping woman came in carrying a gun and wearing a uniform with a Hartland College police emblem on the sleeve. She glanced at us and went on down to the president's office, knocked, opened the door, went in, and closed the door.

"She's kind of scary," Susan said.

"Yeah, she's big," I said. "But for simple ferocity, I like your chances."

The secretary stood and said, "President Richardson will see you now."

Chapter

❖

21

CLARICE RICHARDSON stood when we came in. I had no real idea what a standard-issue college president looked like, but I was pretty sure Clarice Richardson wasn't it. She had to be in her early fifties, but she looked ten years younger. She had the kind of patrician face that you see around Harvard Square and Beacon Hill, and sandy hair cut short. She was wearing a cropped black leather jacket over a pencil skirt, black hose, and black boots with two-and-a-half-inch heels. She wore very little jewelry, except for a wedding ring, and her makeup was understated but expert. Especially expert around the eyes. She had big eyes, like Susan, and she crackled with a warm, intelligent sexuality that would call to you across a crowded cocktail party. She

wasn't quite Susan, but together in a relatively small room, Susan didn't overpower her.

The big female cop stood against the wall behind and to my right of Clarice's big modern desk. There was a modern credenza in the bay behind the desk, in front of the big picture window. On it were pictures of a gray-haired man with a beard, two young women, and a white bull terrier.

"Mr. Spenser?" Clarice said.

"Yes, ma'am, and this is my associate, Dr. Silverman."

If you have it, you may as well flaunt it.

"Susan," Susan said.

"Really," Clarice said. "Doctor of what, Susan?"

"I have a Ph.D. in psychology," Susan said. "I'm a therapist."

"Where did you do your doctorate?"

"Harvard," Susan said.

"Really? I did, too," Clarice said. "In history. When were you there?"

Susan told her. Clarice shook her head.

"I was there before you," she said.

"But we're both really smart," Susan said.

Clarice smiled.

"We must be," she said, and looked at me. "Because you said you wished to discuss a very charged subject, I have taken the liberty of asking Officer Wysocki to join us."

Officer Wysocki nodded. I nodded back. I had the strong impression she didn't like me.

"May I speak freely?" I said. "President Richardson."

"You may," said Clarice. "And please, call me Clarice."

"I'm a private detective," I said. "In Boston. I was employed recently by a group of women to locate a man who is blackmailing them. He was using the name Gary Eisenhower, but his real name as far as I can tell is Goran Pappas."

"Susan works with you?"

"Susan is with me," I said. "I thought she might be helpful in our conversation. And in truth, when she's not around, I miss her."

Clarice nodded. I looked at the photographs on the credenza.

"Your husband?" I said.

"Yes."

"Your daughters?"

"Yes, and our dog, Cannon. The girls used to call him Cannon Ball, but we shortened it to Cannon."

"And you're all together?" I said.

"Yes," she said.

"And you are still the president of this college," I said.

"Yes."

"So standing up to Pappas may have cost you a lot, but it didn't cost you everything," I said.

"In fact," she said. "It saved everything."

"Good," I said. "Can you tell me about it?"

Clarice looked at Susan.

"He seems an unusual private detective," she said. "Something of a romantic. Should I trust him?"

"Not if you have something you don't want him to know," Susan said.

"Did he bring you along, and tell me he'd miss you if he didn't, to impress me? So I would, so to speak, lower my guard. Or was he sincere?"

"Both," Susan said. "He is romantic. He understands things. And we love one another. But he is also the hardest man I have ever met, when he thinks it's necessary, and I guess you should know that, too."

"Suze," I said. "I didn't bring you along to blow my cover."

Clarice smiled.

"I'm sorry to discuss you like this, as if you were a wall sconce," she said.

"It's okay," I said. "I understand. Harvard girls."

"Exactly," Clarice said.

"Pappas has a hold on a number of people, such as he had on you," I said. "I'm trying to figure how to get them loose."

"Tell the truth," Clarice said.

"They won't."

Clarice nodded.

"It is idle to tell them they should," she said, and looked at Susan. "Is it not, Dr. Silverman?"

"It is," Susan said.

"So if you can tell me what you can about your experience with Pappas," I said, "maybe it'll help."

She nodded.

"Trudy," she said to the big cop. "It's okay, you can go. I'll be fine."

"I can wait outside, Clarice," Trudy said.

"No, thank you, Trudy. Go ahead."

Trudy nodded and looked at me hard and left. Clarice watched her go and then turned in her chair toward me and crossed her legs.

"How shall we begin," she said.

I fought off the urge to say "Start at the beginning."

Instead I said, "Tell it any way that makes sense to you."

She leaned back a little in her chair and looked for a moment at the pictures on her credenza, and took in a long breath and let it out, and said, "Okay."

Chapter

————————◆◆————————

22

"My husband's name is Eric," she said. "Eric Richardson. I met him in graduate school. We've been married for twenty-five years. He is a professor of history at this college."

As she talked I could look past the family pictures and out onto the campus. The day was overcast. No students were in sight. The maple trees had shed their leaves for the season and looked sort of spectral.

"About seven years ago," Clarice said, "for reasons not relevant to this discussion, Eric and I became estranged. We didn't actually separate. But we separated emotionally. I know we loved one another through the whole time, but we also hated each other."

She looked at Susan. Susan nodded.

"The girls were away at school, and we were"—she paused and glanced out the window—"here."

"Not a lot of options here," I said. "If it isn't working at home."

"No," Clarice said. "Though we both sought them."

"And Goran Pappas was one?"

"Yes," she said. "He was calling himself Gary Astor at the time."

"Gary Astor," I said.

She smiled without much pleasure.

"I know," she said. "Pathetic, isn't it?"

"In retrospect," I said.

She held her smile for a moment.

"I was at an alumnae function in Albany," she said, "when I met him in the hotel bar. He was, of course, charming."

She paused again and looked out at the gray campus.

"And I, of course, was starved for charm," she said. "He was relaxed, he was funny, he obviously thought I was wonderful, and sexy, and amazing. We talked all evening and went our separate ways. But we agreed to have drinks the next night, and we did, and then we went to my room."

We were silent for a time. Until Susan spoke.

"And so it began," she said.

Clarice nodded.

"We began to meet regularly at a hotel in Springfield,"

she said. "Near the Civic Center. It was quite lovely for several months . . . except for the guilt."

Susan nodded.

"And your husband?" Susan said.

"Eric is," Clarice said, "or he was at that time, the kind of man who tends to hunch his shoulders, and lower his head, and wait for the storm to pass."

"So no solace there," Susan said.

Clarice nodded.

"No," she said. "I imagine I would have felt better if he had been unfaithful, too."

Susan nodded slowly.

"I'm sorry, but I need to ask. Is there anything in particular you remember about your relationship?"

"For a while it was a joy."

"How about the, ah, sexual part."

"What I remember most was that he seemed very," she said, "very . . . forceful."

"Cruel?" Susan said.

"No, merely strong and forceful."

"And did things change?" I said.

"Sexually it didn't, until it stopped," she said. "Three months after we met, he showed me his pictures. He played his audiotapes."

She stopped and sat silently for a moment, looking at nothing. I opened my mouth. Susan shook her head. I closed my mouth.

"After a time," Clarice said, "he wanted money or he said he would ruin me. He was pleasant about it, just a simple business transaction, didn't mean we couldn't be friends, or"—she shook her head—"lovers."

"Did you have money?" I said.

"Not enough," she said. "He wanted me to embezzle from the college."

"And you wouldn't," I said.

She shook her head.

"I had cheated enough," she said. "I went to the police."

"In Hartland?"

She smiled.

"No," she said. "State police. They asked me to wear a listening device. I did, and they arrested him. There was some sort of justice, I think, in that. Like hoisting him upon his own petard."

"Then what?" I said.

"Then I told my husband," Clarice said. "And the college, and finally, at an open meeting, the students."

"My God," Susan said.

"I had bared pretty much everything else to a con man. I guessed I could bare my soul to the people I loved," Clarice said.

"And they forgave you," Susan said.

"My husband said it was time to get help . . . for both of us. I agreed. I offered to resign from the college. They

suggested instead that I take a leave of absence while my husband and I worked on things."

"And the students?" Susan said.

Clarice smiled with some warmth.

"I have found that girls of that age are both more and less judgmental than others," she said. "Some were astounded that a woman over forty could have an explicitly sexual affair. Some were titillated by it. A large number, I think, sort of shrugged and said, 'Yeah, yeah, you slept around. Doesn't everybody?' No one required me to wear a scarlet letter."

"How did Gary Astor take it?" I said.

"He was really very nice about it. When the detectives were taking him away, he grinned at me and said, 'For a good-looking broad, you got a lot of spine, Richie.' That's what he called me. He said Clarice was too European."

"And he did three in Shirley."

"Yes."

"Did you ever hear from him?" I said.

She flushed a little.

"His first year in prison he sent me flowers on my birthday," she said. "I never acknowledged them."

"Nothing since?"

"He wrote me a letter saying good-bye, that it had been fun while it lasted, that he'd always remember, ah, certain moments we'd had, and he wished me well."

"Anything else?" I said.

"No," she said. "He's a very pleasant man, I think. But he seems to have absolutely no moral or ethical sense. It's like someone with no sense of humor. There's nothing really to say about it, except that it isn't there."

"You ever miss him?" Susan said.

"I never want to see him again," Clarice said.

"And your marriage is stable?" Susan said.

"Eric and I spent two years in psychotherapy. Each with our own therapist. You remember Mr. Hemingway's remark?" she said.

"It heals stronger at the break," I said.

"You're a reader, Mr. Spenser?" she said.

"Susan helps me with the big words," I said.

Clarice smiled, with even more warmth in it.

"In retrospect, the entire incident was salvation for Eric and me. Each of us has come to terms with our demons. And we both had demons."

"A troubled marriage," Susan said, "nearly always has at least two."

"Has any of this been useful, Mr. Spenser?"

"It's been worth hearing," I said.

"But useful?"

"Gotta think about it," I said. "If any of my victims were willing, would you talk with them?"

She smiled again. This time with not only warmth but humor.

"The sisterhood is strong," she said.

"I'll take that," I said, "for a yes."

She nodded.

"You may," she said.

Chapter

❖

23

IT WAS MORNING, and we were in the car, drinking coffee, driving south on Route 91 heading for the Mass Pike. I was enjoying a donut.

"Sure you don't want one?" I said. "Cinnamon, my fave."

"Ick," Susan said.

"The naked frolic in a motel outside of Springfield seemed to go better than you thought it would," I said.

"A moment of weakness," Susan said.

"You think there's anything in the fact that what Clarice remembers best about her and Gary's sex life is how strong and forceful he was?"

"You think he might be a little vengeful?" Susan said.

"Something like that," I said. "I mean, even Hawk agrees that there's a limit to the number of women you can have sex with."

"And Hawk has tested the limits," Susan said.

"He has," I said. "You said once that there might be something more than sex and money in this deal."

"What could be more than sex and money?" Susan said.

"Pathology?" I said.

"Hey, I do the shrink stuff here," Susan said.

"And?"

"Might be," Susan said. "Worth looking into, I suppose."

"And how would I look into that?" I said.

"Talk to some of his other partners."

"Oh," I said.

I finished my donut and got another one out of the bag. Susan ate some grapes she'd brought with her from home.

"You think things really do heal stronger at the break?" I said.

"It's a nice metaphor," Susan said. "When a broken bone heals, there is often additional bone mass."

"So bones may in fact heal stronger at the break," I said.

"Maybe," Susan said.

"Think that holds in other things?" I said.

"Some things," she said. "Sometimes."

"There are very few absolutes in the therapist's canon," I said.

"Very few," Susan said. "Although, I guess, understanding the truth about yourself is important."

"You think they got there?"

"Clarice and her husband? Probably," Susan said. "No one gets there all the way. But they seem close. If she's accurate. I assume they addressed the causes of the break, understood them, and were tough enough to change."

"She was tough enough," I said, "not to knuckle under to Gary Eisenhower."

Susan smiled.

"You like that name, don't you?" Susan said.

"I do. If I adopt an alias, I may use it."

"Gee," Susan said. "You look just like a Gary Eisenhower, too."

"And from there it's an easy leap to Cary Grant," I said.

"Easy," Susan said. "Of course, guilt helped."

"Clarice?"

"Uh-huh."

"As in she was tough enough to confess publicly because she felt she deserved the public humiliation?" I said.

"As in exactly that," Susan said. "You're smarter than you look."

"Lucky thing," I said. "If I weren't, I probably wouldn't be able to feed myself."

"I'd feed you," Susan said.

"I know you would," I said. "But, guilt or whatever, it all worked for her. She kept her husband, her job, her children's regard."

"And her self," Susan said.

Occasionally as we drove we could see the Connecticut River flowing south beside us, heading for Long Island Sound. The year had gone too far into November for there to be much leaf color left. Here and there a yellow leaf, or none, or few, but mostly spare grayness, hinting of cold rain.

"So are you saying," I said, "that Gary's current victims in the gang of four haven't got enough guilt?"

"A little guilt is not always a bad thing," Susan said.

"And you a psychotherapist," I said.

"I'm also Jewish," she said.

"I think that's a tautology," I said.

"Oy," Susan said.

"You think I should start berating them," I said. "Make them feel more guilty?"

"I don't know if it would work," Susan said. "But I suspect it's not your style."

We came to the pike and headed east. I had one of those toll transponders that allow you to zip through the fast lane unhesitatingly. It made me feel special.

"It is interesting, though, that none of them feels guilty enough for your scenario to work."

"It would suggest something about their marriages," Susan said.

"And about them," I said. "Some of them feel they'd be ruined if this all came out. One couple, the husband is gay, for instance, and in line for a big job. He and his wife are close. She knows, of course, and they remain friends, with a, necessarily, open marriage."

"You don't think that such fears beset Clarice Richardson?" Susan said.

"And they are not illegitimate fears," I said. "She was lucky to be in a situation where decency could prevail."

"That, too, would probably influence her," Susan said.

"The recognition of those circumstances, and the hope that decency would prevail," I said.

"Yes."

"Maybe I could get them to see you professionally, and you could berate them."

"Until they felt guilty enough to cure themselves?"

"Exactly," I said. "How would that fly at the Psychoanalytic Institute?"

"Banishment, I think," she said. "It is, however, not a position I'm prepared to take."

"Is there a position you are prepared to take?" I said.

Susan smiled her fallen-angel smile. One of my favorites.

"How about prone, big boy?" she said.
"Shall I stop on the roadside?" I said.
Susan smiled.
"No," she said.

Chapter

❖

24

WHEN GARY EISENHOWER came into my office on a rainy Monday morning, he had a purple bruise on his right cheekbone and a swollen upper lip. He moved stiffly to one of my chairs and eased himself into it. When he spoke he sounded like his teeth were clenched.

"I need a gun," he said.

"I would guess that you do," I said.

"I'm a convicted felon," he said. "I can't just buy one."

"Also true."

"Can you give me one?"

"Probably not," I said. "Who beat you up?"

He made a slight movement with his lips, which, if it hadn't hurt, might have turned into a smile.

"How'd you know?" he said.

"I'm a trained detective," I said.

"Couple guys came around, tole me to stay away from Beth Jackson."

"You're still seeing her?" I said.

"Yeah."

"Even though she hired me to put you out of business?" I said.

"Yeah," Gary said.

"She your mole in the gang of four?" I said.

"How'd you know there was a mole?"

"You knew who hired me," I said.

He shook his head and winced.

"And—" I said.

"You're a trained detective," Gary said.

"You tell them to take a hike?" I said.

"The two guys?" he said. "No, I said, 'Sure thing.'"

"But?"

He started to shrug and remembered that everything hurt and stopped in mid-shrug.

"But she kept coming around and"—again the try at a smile—"what's a boy to do?"

"So they caught you again and decided to get your attention," I said.

"Yeah."

"One of the guys slim and dark, sort of quiet?" I said.

"Yeah, Zel, he said his name was. The one poured it

on me was some kind of ex-pug. He had a funny name, too, but I'm a little hazy about some of the details."

"Boo," I said.

"Yeah," Gary said. "Boo. He liked his work."

"So now what?" I said.

"I took my beating, but I'm not going away."

"So you'll see Beth again?"

"Absolutely."

"You care that much about her?"

"I like to fuck her," Gary said.

"She's not your only option," I said.

"I told you before, I'm tougher than I seem," Gary said. "I been punched around before. But I'll fuck who I want to fuck, and no one tells me who that can be."

"My God," I said, "a principled position."

"So I need a gun."

I shook my head.

"Can't give you a gun," I said. "But maybe I can take Zel and Boo off your back."

"You?"

"Yep."

"How you going to do that?" Gary said.

"Sweet reason," I said.

" 'Sweet reason'?" Gary said. "You being funny?"

"I hope so," I said.

"How quick can you do this?"

"Pretty soon. In the meantime ask Beth to, ah, lay off, at least for a few days," I said.

"What are you going to do," Gary said.

"Talk to some people, arrange a few things, call in some favors," I said.

"Who you gonna talk to?" he said.

"I have friends in low places," I said. "Can you keep it in your pants for a few days while I save your life?"

Gary nodded.

"Why you doing this for me?" he said.

"Damned if I know," I said.

Chapter

······················· ❖❖ ·······················

25

"Beth is still seeing Eisenhower," I said to Chet Jackson.

He sat across his desk from me, looking as hard-polished and expensive as he had last time.

"You think?" he said.

"It's why you sent Zel and Boo to see him," I said.

"They went to see him?" Chet said.

The view through the picture window behind him was still marvelous, but I'd seen it before. It was what I'd always thought about paying for a view. After a day or two you don't even notice it.

"Boo beat him up," I said.

"What a shame," Chet said.

"I don't want it to happen again," I said.

"And you think I've got something to do with it?"

I said, "Let's not screw around with this, Chet. I want you to call them off."

"And let that sonovabitch continue to bang my wife?" Chet said.

"That's a question to take up with the bangee," I said. "Not the banger."

The lines around Chet's mouth deepened. I could hear Susan's voice in my brain: *"Banger" and "bangee" are sexist distinctions,* the voice said, *implying aggression on the one side and passivity on the other.*

I know. I know. I can't think of everything. Then I heard her laugh.

"That's probably true," he said.

"But?"

"But I can't," he said.

I nodded.

"Because you love her," I said.

"Yes."

"Chet," I said. "This is not between you and Gary Eisenhower. This is between you and your wife. The problem won't be resolved by beating up Gary Eisenhower. It won't be resolved if you kill him."

"There'd be someone else," Chet said.

"Uh-huh."

"I know that," Chet said. "You think I don't know that? Hell, I even had some counseling about that."

"Uh-huh."

We were quiet. I could feel his resistance slide into place like a shield between us.

"I can't let the sonovabitch get away with it," Chet said.

"Even though you might do the same thing," I said.

"In his shoes? Sure," Chet said. "Might not get into blackmail, but the rest? Yeah, of course."

"So maybe you should back off with Boo," I said.

Chet shook his head.

"I gotta do something," he said.

"Will it help you with Beth?" I said.

He looked at me steadily for probably thirty seconds without speaking. Then he shook his head.

"I gotta do something," he said.

"Even if it doesn't take you where you want to go," I said.

"I'm a tough guy," he said. "But not that tough. I can't take it."

"Too bad," I said.

"You gonna do something?" Chet said.

"Yeah," I said.

"I may have to send Boo and Zel to see you."

"You may," I said.

We looked at each other. I felt sort of bad for him. But the shield was in place. The conversation was over. I stood and walked out.

Chapter

❖

26

I CALLED HAWK on his cell phone.

"You with Eisenhower?" I said.

"I in the lobby of a motel in Waltham," Hawk said. "Gary upstairs, with a woman."

"First of the day?" I said.

"Uh-huh," Hawk said.

"Well, it's early still," I said.

"Uh-huh."

"He had anything to say since you been tagging along with him?"

"He want to know do I think I can handle Boo, if he shows up," Hawk said.

"And you said you could."

"But modestly."

"If it comes to that," I said. "Zel is the real issue."

"Shooter?"

"Yep."

"I never heard of him," Hawk said.

"Me, either, but if you meet him, you'll know."

"Like Vinnie," Hawk said.

"Or Chollo," I said.

"They do have the look," Hawk said.

"So does Zel."

"I keep it in mind," Hawk said.

"Anything else?"

"Eisenhower say he don't mind me tagging after him," Hawk said. "Long as I don't cramp his style."

"Are you cramping it?"

"Not so's I can tell," Hawk said. "Mostly I trying to learn from it."

"It's good to make the most of a learning opportunity," I said.

"He a pretty cool dude," Hawk said. "As you honkies go."

"He is," I said. "Maybe he's got some sort of natural rhythm."

"He ain't that cool," Hawk said. "But he don't seem scared. He seem like he can handle getting beat up, ain't gonna change him."

"He claims he's tougher than he seems," I said.

"Might be," Hawk said.

"He ask you for a gun?" I said.

"Uh-huh," Hawk said.

"And?"

"I say why you need a gun, you got me."

"And he said?"

"I may not always have you."

"Which is true," I said.

"It is," Hawk said. "So I tell him you could retire your dick for a while, or at least use it someplace else."

"He didn't buy that," I said.

"Nope," Hawk answered. "Say he fuck who he wants when he wants and he ain't gonna change."

"Man of principle," I said.

"Sure," Hawk said. "People live by worse codes."

"And we know a lot of them," I said.

"Where you calling from?" Hawk said. "You sound kind of echo-y."

"Rowes Wharf," I said. "I'm looking at the water."

"You on you cell phone?" Hawk said.

"I am," I said.

"You dialed it by yo'self?" Hawk said.

"I did," I said.

"Man, you makin' progress," Hawk said.

"Susan's been helping me," I said.

Hawk's chuckle was very deep as he broke the connection.

Chapter

❖

27

S USAN AND I were in her booth in Rialto, where she always sat, because it was quiet and you could watch people come and go. We had just taken our first sip of our first drink when Hawk showed up with Gary Eisenhower.

"That's the best you could do for a date?" I said to Hawk.

"I just the babysitter," Hawk said. "You tole me to bring him."

Gary put out a hand to Susan and said, "Hi, I'm Gary."

Susan shook his hand.

"I'm Susan," she said.

Gary slid into the banquette next to Susan. Hawk took a chair on the outside next to me.

"So," Gary said. "This is the main squeeze?"

"Only," I said.

"Well," Gary said. "You going to limit yourself to one, this is a good one."

The waiter took their drink orders and went to get them.

"You are not yourself monogamous, Gary?" Susan said.

"You know I'm not," Gary said.

"I'd heard that," Susan said.

"Gets me in trouble sometimes," Gary said.

"I'd heard that, too," Susan said.

She looked at Hawk and at me.

She said, "I think you're pretty safe tonight, however."

"Yeah, are these guys the best? I mean the best."

"Yes," Susan said. "They are."

The waiter came to announce the specials. We listened and looked at the menu and ordered. We had a second round of drinks, except Susan. After that flurry of activity, Susan turned and smiled at Gary.

"I know it's none of my business," she said. "But I'll try not to let that inhibit me. Why are you so, ah, unmonogamous?"

"Unmonogamous," Gary said. "You got a way with words, huh?"

Susan waited.

"Unmonogamous." He laughed. "Well, I guess I'd answer why would I be unmonogamous. I mean, if you got a whole orchard full of peaches, why would you eat just one?"

Susan smiled and nodded.

"So," Gary said, "lemme turn it around? Why would I be monogamous?"

"I'm not necessarily arguing for monogamy," Susan said. "Just why in your case that nonmonogamy is so all-consuming."

"No, no," Gary said. "You didn't answer my question, you did one of those shrink tricks, turn it back to me. First you need to answer my question."

"Very astute of you," Susan said. "Did you know I was a shrink?"

"No."

"But you've had experience with shrinks."

"Enough to know bullshit when I hear it," he said. "No offense."

"None," Susan said.

"So. Why are you monogamous?" Gary said.

"Because unlike peaches, whose consumption is all there is—they taste good and that's the end of it—persons have a variety of meanings and dimensions, and surprises, and feelings. I like those things, too."

"And not sex?" Gary said. "You don't look like somebody who would not like sex."

Susan smiled.

"Notice the *too*," she said.

"Oh, yeah," Gary said. "That's good, I was thinking, *What a waste*."

"Nothing is wasted," Susan said.

"Love to find out someday," Gary said.

Hawk glanced at me. I shook my head.

"Why?" Susan said.

"Why?" Gary said. "For crissake, look at you."

"Thanks, but that's it, I look good?"

"Of course."

"No other reason?" Susan said.

Gary looked at me and winked.

"Be fun to see the look on his face," he said, and tipped his head toward me.

"Not for me," Susan said.

"You love him," Gary said.

"I do," she said.

"*À chacun son goût,*" he said.

Chapter

❖❖

28

H AWK TOOK GARY home after dinner. Susan and I lingered in our booth while Susan had a cup of coffee and I didn't. A cup of coffee at night would keep me awake until after the summer solstice.

"I know you brought me to meet Gary and see what I thought," she said.

"And what do you think?" I said.

"Wow," Susan said.

"Wow what?" I said.

"A clinical wow," she said. "He's absolutely fascinating."

"In a clinical way," I said.

"Absolutely," she said. "He flirted with me the entire evening."

"I know."

"And he was very aware of you all the time," Susan said.

"I noticed that," I said.

"Sometimes you've been known to intervene," Susan said.

"Not this time," I said. "I'm kind of clinical myself."

"Well," Susan said. "He's no simple matter."

"You mean he's not just a womanizer?" I said. "Who's turned a hobby into a business?"

"Maybe he is," Susan said. "People aren't usually just one thing, though."

"So a new theory wouldn't necessarily replace the old one," I said.

Susan nodded and gave me a big smile.

"So you've been paying attention all these years," she said.

"I'm more than one thing, myself," I said.

"You certainly are," Susan said. "But think about Gary Eisenhower for a minute. What is his pattern?"

"Good-looking women with rich husbands," I said.

"And where did Clarice Richardson fit into that pattern?"

"She's good-looking," I said.

"And she had a husband," Susan said. "But not a rich one."

"Maybe he was still perfecting his craft," I said.

"Probably," Susan said. "But we've been looking at *rich*, when perhaps we should be looking at *husband*."

"You mean it matters to him that they're married?'

"And maybe it matters to him that he can cuckold the husbands."

"Which would explain why he flirted with you in front of me," I said.

"You're not exactly a husband, but you'd fill the role."

"And if that's what he's doing," I said, "how much more fun if he can extract money."

"Exactly," Susan said. "Particularly in these circumstances, when the money comes out of the husband's pocket. Whether the husband knows it or not."

"I'm not clear quite where Clarice fits in to this," I said.

"No," Susan said, "I'm not, either. There are, of course, many men whose sexual fantasies are directed at successful women, or women in authority."

"Schoolteachers, doctors, lawyers." I grinned at her. "Shrinks."

"Yes."

"Take them down a peg," I said.

"Men like Gary often use sex to humiliate."

"Into which need the blackmail would also pay," I said.

"Yes. Plus, of course, the money is good as money."

"Sometimes a cigar is just a cigar?"

"Or sometimes it's a cigar as well as several other things," Susan said.

"You think the women are humiliated?" I said.

"Not necessarily," Susan said. "It may only be in his fantasy."

"You think all this is true of Gary?" I said.

"I don't know," Susan said. "It's a theory of the case."

"Or several," I said. "But they're worth testing, I think."

"There's no reason to avoid the scientific method," Susan said.

I pretended to take notes on the palm of my hand.

"Whoops," Susan said. "I'm slipping into a lecture."

"But gracefully," I said.

Susan smiled.

"Anyway, it might pay off to go back over Gary's, ah, career, and see what patterns you can find, and see if they support our theory," she said.

"Your theory," I said.

"Okay. What is your theory?"

"That you may be right," I said.

"I will also make a small bet with you," Susan said.

"Which is?"

"He'll call me for a date," Susan said.

"No bet on that," I said. "But I'll bet you don't accept."

"I only date you, snookums," Susan said. "But if I were to go out with someone else, it wouldn't be Gary Eisenhower."

"Because?"

"I'm pretty sure it wouldn't be about me," Susan said.

"Is that an informed guess?" I said.

"It's a woman's-intuition guess," she said.

"Good as any," I said

She finished her coffee. I paid the check. Susan got her coat. And we left. On the stairs I put an arm around her shoulder. She looked up at me and smiled.

"'Snookums'?" I said.

"I'm the only one who knows," she said.

Chapter

❖

29

I MET BETH JACKSON for lunch in a restaurant in the Chestnut Hill Mall. She had a salad. In the spirit of the season I had a turkey sandwich.

"You're still seeing Gary Eisenhower," I said.

Beth was wearing a fur hat like a Russian Cossack, and she looked cuter than a body has a right to. She speared a cherry tomato from her salad and popped it into her mouth and chewed and swallowed.

"So?" she said.

"Didn't you hire me to get him out of your life?"

"That was then," she said. "This is now."

"What caused the change?" I said.

She ate a piece of lettuce and pushed her plate away. She blotted her lips with her napkin. Then she folded

the napkin and put it down on the table. She took some lip gloss out of her purse and touched up her lips using a small makeup mirror. Then she put that away, put her purse on the floor beside her chair, and smiled at me.

"A girl's got a right to change her mind," she said.

"So now you don't want me to get him out of your life?" I said.

Her smile widened without becoming warmer. She put her hands together and touched the center of her upper lip with her steepled forefingers.

"I wanted you to get him out of everyone else's life," she said.

"So he could be all yours?" I said.

"Exactly," she said.

"He's blackmailing you," I said.

She shrugged.

"We need the money," she said.

"You and Gary?" I said.

"Yes," she said. "So we can be together. Chet can spare it."

"But why join the effort to get rid of him?" I said. "Why not just stay out of it, stay with him, and collect the money that the others are paying him."

"You think I'm the only one slipping back to him?"

"I've stopped trying to think," I said. "I'm just chasing information."

"I didn't want anyone to suspect that I was still with him," she said. "So I agreed to the deal with the lawyer

and you. I figured I could help him, even, by being on the inside, you know?"

She was as perky as a chickadee but dumber.

"You keep seeing him," I said, "and you may get him killed."

"Killed? Who's going to kill him?"

I didn't answer. I wasn't sure why, but I wasn't ready to quite give Chet up yet.

She smiled.

"You think Chet would kill him? For me?"

I didn't answer that, either.

"That's kind of exciting," Beth said. "Isn't that kind of fun? Like an old-fashioned movie. You know? Men killing each other over me?"

"It's probably less fun than it looks," I said.

"Oh, poo," she said. "I can handle Chet."

"Maybe," I said. "But maybe Gary can't."

"So it is Chet?"

"Might be," I said.

Christmas carols were playing. Many people were carrying packages with Christmas wrapping. It was like being in a commercial. I looked at Beth. I could see the tip of her tongue as she ran it back and forth over her lower lip.

"Well, I'm not backing off," she said.

"Of course not," I said. "What's the most interesting thing about him?"

"Interesting?"

"Unusual, maybe," I said. "What's different about him?"

"That's easy. He is into it all the way."

"Is he more intense than other men?" I said.

"He is all over you. He gets hold of you, and you better like it, because if you don't, you're going to have to do it anyway, you know?"

"Forceful," I said.

She nodded.

"And you like forceful?" I said.

"Yeahhhh," she said.

She was breathing fast, now, as if she had just run up stairs. And the tip of her tongue was running fast back and forth across her lower lip. When she spoke her voice sounded a little hoarse.

"You get off on this?" Beth said. "Talking about it?"

"Which do you like best?" I said. "Being with Gary or thinking that someone might try to kill him because of it?"

She put her steepled fingers to her mouth again and pressed and turned her head a little so that she was looking at me from the corners of her eyes.

"Both are nice," she said.

Chapter

❖

30

MY FURTHER RESEARCH into Susan's theories of the case began the next morning. I called Abigail Larson and asked her if she could stop by my office. She seemed happy to be asked.

She arrived about four in the afternoon dressed to the nines and smelling of martini. She arranged herself in one of my client chairs and crossed her legs. Her skirt was short.

"I thought you were off the case," she said.

"Mostly because I have no case," I said. "But I'm a nosy guy, and in my free time I still poke around at it."

"Well," she said.

"Can we talk about you and Gary a little?"

"Sure," she said. "But first, can a girl get a martini around here?"

"Absolutely," I said. "I'm a full-service gumshoe."

"Up," she said. "With olives."

I went to the little alcove where I had a refrigerator and a small cabinet, and made her a martini. I served it to her in a lowball glass.

"Sorry about the glass," I said. "I haven't gotten around yet to specialty glassware."

"Just so it contains alcohol," Abigail said.

I went back around my desk and sat. She drank some martini.

"God, that's good," she said. "I like a man that can make a good martini."

"Me, too," I said.

She didn't need a drink. She was drunk when she arrived. On the other hand, drunks are often talkative. The martini I gave her was big.

"Could I ask you some stuff about your sex life with Gary?"

"Well, aren't you quite the voyeur," she said.

She pronounced "quite" like "quit."

"It's an incidental benefit," I said. "Is there anything about Gary's behavior during sex that stands out in your memory."

"Hoo," she said. "You go right to it, don't you?"

"I do," I said.

"Turn you on to talk about it?" she said.

"I don't know," I said. "Let's talk about it and see."

"Men are weird," she said.

"You bet," I said. "What was there about him during sex that made him different, unusual, whatever?"

"Like was he big or not?" she said.

"Anything that seemed different from other men," I said.

"I had a lot other men, ya know," she said.

"I'm not surprised," I said. "How was Gary different."

She uncrossed her legs and slumped a little in the chair while she thought, or tried to. Her legs were straight out in front of her. The short skirt crept up her thighs a little higher.

"John . . . husband . . . just lays there, makes me do all the work, you know?"

"Sure," I said.

"Gary, he grabs hold of you . . ."

"And does the work?"

"Yes . . . no . . . holds me down, like . . ."

She stopped and looked at me blankly for a moment, then closed her eyes and began to slide slowly out of the chair. I got out around the desk in time to keep her off the floor, although her skirt was up around her waist. I got my arms around her under the arms, and got her up and sort of waltzed her slowly across my office toward the couch. She tried to kiss me as we went, and got the side of my mouth. I got her there and down onto the

couch and straightened her legs, and pulled down her skirt.

Then I went back to my desk and got out a yellow pad and made a couple of notes. So far I had learned several things. Abigail Larson was a boozer. Her husband was not a sexual athlete. She bought lingerie at La Perla. None of which seemed very useful. But it was all I was going to get today. I couldn't think of anything else to do but sit with her until she woke up. Which eventually she did. But she didn't feel chatty. And I sent her home in a cab.

Chapter

········· ◆◆◆ ·········

31

IN THE NEXT couple of days I talked with the rest of the gang of four and learned more than I ever wanted to know about having sex with Gary Eisenhower.

"It was like a rape fantasy sometimes," Nancy said.

"And you didn't mind?" I said.

"No," she said. "I've told you what I'm like."

"So you enjoyed the fantasy," I said.

She was silent a moment. Then, in a small voice, she said, "Yes."

Later I talked with Susan about it.

"None of that seems very enlightening," she said.

"Not to me. I was hoping it would to you."

Susan shook her head.

"About the rape fantasy thing?" I said.

"That was Nancy Sinclair?"

"Yeah."

"I suspect that tells us more about Nancy than it does about Gary," Susan said.

"Maybe he is just what he seems to be," I said.

"A happy-go-lucky cockhound?" Susan said.

"Yeah," I said. "Don't you ever come across some-body like that in your business?"

"People who are what they seem to be," Susan said, "generally don't seek psychotherapy."

"Good point," I said. "But as far as I can see, this is one of those instances when the cigar is just a cigar."

"Maybe you should talk to Clarice Richardson again," Susan said.

"Because she's smart enough to understand what she may have experienced," I said.

"Yes."

Susan was between patients. I was sitting in her office, across the desk from her. I was silent for a little while. I eyed the couch against the wall to my right.

"Anybody actually lie down on that thing?" I said.

"I believe you and I have," Susan said.

"I mean for therapy."

"You and I have," Susan said.

"Not that kind of therapy," I said.

"Yes," Susan said. "It is kind of a cliché, but some people find it very helpful."

I nodded. Neither of us spoke for a little while.

Then I said, "I can't do it by phone."

"No need," Susan said. "I'm sure she'll see you."

"Care for another trip to Hartland?" I said.

"No," Susan said.

"Two hours out, two hours back," I said.

"An easy day trip," Susan said.

"What about the naked frolic in the Hartland motel?"

"Nothing to stop you," Susan said.

"By myself?"

"Whatever floats your boat . . . snookums."

Chapter

❖

32

CLARICE RICHARDSON CAME around her desk and shook my hand when I entered her office.

"Come in," she said. "Sit down. I'm glad to see you."

I looked around.

"No campus cop this time," I said.

"You've charmed me into submission," she said.

"Happens all the time," I said.

"I assume you are still chasing Goran," she said.

"I'm trying to figure him out," I said.

Clarice smiled.

"You, too," she said.

"You mentioned when we talked last that when you were intimate, he seemed very strong."

"Yes," she said.

She smiled and looked away from me out at the now wintry landscape of her college.

"I attributed it to passion," she said.

"Susan suggested that it hints of sadism," I said.

"And she thought you should ask me about that?"

"She thinks you're the only one intelligent enough to understand your experience."

Clarice nodded.

"But not intelligent enough to have avoided it."

"Nobody gets out of here alive," I said.

She nodded.

"I didn't think of it at the time, but perhaps there was something . . . I'm not sure sadistic is exactly right . . . but vengeful, perhaps."

I nodded.

"Can you give me an example?" I said.

She blushed.

"I'm sorry," I said.

"I made this bed, so to speak. If I have to lie in it, I have to lie in it."

I might not have chosen that metaphor. But maybe if I felt guilty . . .

"He would say things," she said. "When he was . . . in me, he would say things like 'Got you now, don't I?' "

"Say it often?" I said.

"Things like that," she said.

"You think he had some animosity toward women?" I said.

"I never felt it," she said. "But in the circumstance, I was not at my most analytic, I fear."

"None of us is," I said. "Why do you suppose he had an affair with you?"

Clarice smiled.

"He found me attractive?" she said.

"Almost certainly," I said.

"And available," Clarice said.

"Were you wearing your wedding ring?" I said.

"I was," Clarice said.

"Even though you were, ah, trolling?"

"Maybe I was ambivalent," she said. "Maybe I didn't want to admit to myself I was trolling. Maybe I didn't want to look like an old maid."

"Fat chance," I said.

She smiled faintly.

"Thank you," she said.

"So he knew you were married," I said.

"But not to wealth," she said.

"Maybe the wealth was an afterthought."

She nodded.

"The thing is," Clarice said, "in an odd way, Eric and I owe this man a great deal. If I had not been with him, and if he had not tried to blackmail me, I don't think

either Eric or I would have found the strength to get help with our problems . . . nor to solve them."

"But you did," I said.

"Yes."

I stood.

"I won't bother you again," I said.

And I left.

Chapter

33

I TALKED WITH SUSAN on the phone for nearly an hour before we hung up. It was dark outside. My apartment was nearly still. There was a fire going, and the hiss of the logs supplied the only sound. I sat at my kitchen counter with a scotch and soda in a tall glass, with a lot of ice.

Was I involved in this thing because it resonated with me and Susan a long time ago? It had happened to me before. I didn't think I was, but I had learned enough to know that motivation, including my own, was often murky.

I sipped my scotch and looked at the fire.

One of my problems was trying to figure out which side I was on. I wasn't even sure how I wanted things

to turn out. I had some sympathy for the women in the case, more for some than for others. I kind of liked Gary. The cuckolded husbands deserved some sympathy, but maybe some blame, or at least some of them.

I drank the rest of my scotch and made another drink.

I wasn't exactly sure what real crime had been committed. I didn't want Regina and Clifford Hartley's complicated but functioning marriage to be destroyed. I thought it would be a shame if Nancy went on through life thinking her sexuality was a sickness. Abigail was a drunk. Beth was . . . I didn't know what Beth was, but it wasn't good.

But there was something wrong with the whole setup. Everything kept turning out not to be quite what it started out seeming to be. There was a lot of bottled-up stuff lying around, and Boo and Zel were rattling around like loose ball bearings. So why did I care? One reason was that no one else had hired me to do anything, and I like to work. It might have had to do with me being stubborn.

I drank some scotch. It was clarifying. People always claimed it was a bad sign if you started drinking alone. I always thought to sit quietly and alone and drink a little now and then was valuable. Especially if you have a fire to look at. What was it Churchill said? "I have taken more from alcohol than alcohol has ever taken from me." Something like that. Good enough for Winnie, I thought, good enough for me.

I took my glass to my front window and looked down at Marlborough Street. The lights in the brick and brownstone buildings seemed very homey. Outside it was dark and cold. Inside was light and warmth. There were people living there together, some of them happily, some not.

Sometimes I thought that Susan was the only thing in life that I cared about. But I knew that if it were actually so, it would destroy us. We both needed to work. We had to do things. Making moon eyes at Susan was not a sufficient career. It was cases like the one I was on that reminded me now and then that I could care about other things.

There was more sex in this case than I'd seen in a while, but none of it seemed connected to love. I realized as I looked out my window at the still city street that one of the things I was looking for in this mess was something grounded in love. Maybe the Hartleys, in their odd and bearded marriage, might be driven by love. Maybe not. Clarice Richardson's reformation and triumph might have been grounded in love. But it could have been grounded in guilt, and survival . . . and courage.

"Good for you, Clarice," I said. "Either way."

As I drank my final scotch, I decided that I had two things to do next. One, I had to defuse Chet Jackson, and second, I had to find out a little more about Gary Eisenhower, aka Goran Pappas. Having a plan made me feel decisive, or maybe it was the three scotches.

I washed my empty glass and put it away. I put a steak on the kitchen grill. In a sauté pan, I cooked onions, peppers, mushrooms, and a handful of frozen corn with olive oil, rosemary, and a splash of sherry. I had some herbed biscuits left from Sunday when Susan and I had breakfast. I warmed them in the oven and when everything was ready, I ate.

And drank some beer.

Chapter

······················· ❖ ·······················

34

THE FIRST TWO PEOPLE I saw when I went into Buddy Fox's were Ty-Bop and Junior. Ty-Bop was a skinny kid, strung out on something. He did the gun work. Junior was the size of Des Moines but meaner. He did the muscle work.

"Junior," I said. "How's it going with Weight Watchers?"

"You looking to see Tony?" Junior said.

Ty-Bop stared at me as he jittered against the back wall of the restaurant, listening to his iPod. He showed no sign of recognition, although he'd seen me probably a hundred times. His eyes were empty. His face was empty. He shot at what Tony told him to shoot at and, as best as I could tell, had no other interests except controlled

substances and whatever music he was listening to. I don't think I'd ever heard him speak. But he could shoot. He might have been as good as Vinnie, maybe even Chollo, who was the best I'd ever seen.

"Wait here," Junior said.

He went past the bar and down a hall. Ty-Bop looked at me blankly. I grinned at him.

"How are things, Ty-Bop?" I said.

He jived a little and his head might have moved, but it was probably to the music.

"Listening to a different drummer?" I said.

Ty-Bop's expression didn't change.

"Good," I said. "I like an upbeat approach."

The room showed little sign that the South End had undergone considerable social change in the last twenty years. I was still the only white face in the room. Junior returned and jerked his head at me. I gave Ty-Bop a friendly thumbs-up and followed Junior past the bar. He was so big he could barely fit into the hallway, and both of us were too much. He stepped aside and gestured for me to walk past him.

"You know the door," he said.

"Like my own," I said, and walked on down the hall.

Tony's office was small and without much in the way of ostentation. Tony was in there with Arnold, who was his driver. Arnold didn't shoot as well as Ty-Bop or muscle as well as Junior. But he was a nice combination of

both skills, and he had a little class. He was handsome as hell. And dressed great.

"Arnold," I said.

"Spenser."

Arnold was sitting on a straight chair, turned around so he could rest his forearms on the chair back. Tony was behind his desk. A little soft around the neck and jawline. But very dignified-looking, with a scatter of gray in his short hair, and none in his carefully trimmed mustache. As always, he was dressed up. Dark suit, white shirt, maroon silk tie and pocket hankie. He was smoking a long, thin cigar.

"Tony," I said. "Do you color your mustache?"

Tony Marcus smiled.

"Actually, motherfucker," he said, "I color my whole body. In real life, I'm a honkie."

"Nope," I said. "No white guy can say 'motherfucker' like you do."

Tony nodded.

"Whaddya want?" he said.

"Need a favor," I said.

"Oh, good," Tony said. "Been hoping some wiseass snow cone would come in and ask for a favor."

"You want me to pat him down?" Arnold said to Tony.

"No need," Tony said.

"He's got a gun," Arnold said. "I can tell the way his coat hangs."

Tony looked at Arnold.

"You done work with him, you think we need to worry 'bout the gun?"

"No."

"Okay," Tony said, and turned to me, and raised his eyebrows.

"Know a guy named Chet Jackson?" I said.

"Who wants to know?" Tony said.

"That would be me," I said. "I look like some kind of bicycle messenger?"

"Why do you want to know?"

"He's a danger to someone I sort of represent," I said.

"And you can't stop him?"

"Not without killing somebody," I said.

"So?" Tony said.

"Not my style," I said.

"So have Hawk do it for you," Tony said.

"Also not my style."

"But it your style to come ask me," Tony said. "A simple African-American trying to get along in a flounder-belly world?"

"Exactly," I said.

Tony smiled.

"I know Chet Jackson," he said.

"You have any clout with him?"

"I might," Tony said. "Pretty much got clout wherever I need it."

"So much for the simple African-American," I said.

Tony smiled again.

"You knew that was bullshit when you heard it," he said. "I don't know if I owe you anything or not. But you done me some favors."

"Cast your bread upon the waters," I said.

"Sure," Tony said. "Tell me a story."

I told him as much as he needed to know. Tony listened without interrupting while he smoked his cigar. When I was done, he put the cigar out in a big glass ashtray on his desk and leaned back in his chair.

"What the fuck," he said, "are you doing mixed up in crap like that?"

"I ask myself that from time to time," I said. "But I'm a romantic, Tony. You know that."

"Whatever that means," he said.

We sat. Tony got out a new cigar and trimmed it and lit it, and got it going evenly, turning the cigar barrel slowly in the flame of Arnold's lighter.

"So how you want to do this?" he said.

Chapter

35

According to his police folder, Goran Pappas had graduated in the top quarter of his Richdale High School class and gone on to Wickton College on a basketball scholarship.

Wickton was a small liberal-arts college just across the New Hampshire line, south of Jaffrey. I spent the next day there and worked my way slowly through a host of reticent academics to arrive late in the day in the office of the director of counseling services. According to the plaque on her desk, her name was Mary Brown, Ph.D.

"Dr. Brown," I said. "My name is Spenser. I'm a detective. I've been wandering your campus all day and am in desperate need of counseling."

She was a sturdy woman with gray hair and rimless glasses.

"I can see why you would," she said. "Please sit down."

I did.

"I'm trying to learn about a man who attended this college. Everyone who would know agrees he did. But no one will tell me much about him."

"Because they don't know much?" she said.

"Because they don't know, or think it's confidential, or don't like detectives."

"Surely that couldn't be it," she said.

"I was being self-effacing," I said.

"I have been here for more than thirty years," she said. "Perhaps I can help. What is the man's name?"

"Goran Pappas," I said.

She was quiet for a moment. The rimless glasses were strong, and they seemed to enlarge her eyes as she looked at me through them.

"I remember him," she said.

"What can you tell me?" I said.

She smiled.

"What can you tell *me*?" she said.

"About anything you want to know," I said.

"Then do so," she said.

I told her everything I thought she'd want to hear, omitting only the names, except for Goran. When I was through she sat for a time, frowning.

"My goodness," she said. "And what is it you are trying to accomplish?"

"To right the unrightable wrong, I suppose," I said.

"I understand the allusion," she said. "But specifically, what do you hope to accomplish?"

"I feel a little silly saying it. But . . . right now everything is coming out badly for pretty much everyone involved, except maybe the college president. . . . I'd like to make everything come out okay."

She looked at me silently through the distorting rimless lenses for a time and then reached up and tilted them lower on her nose and looked over them at me.

"My God," she said.

I shrugged and gave her my sheepish smile. She seemed stable enough to risk the sheepish smile. Less stable women were known to undress when I did the sheepish smile. I was right. She remained calm.

"How can I check on you?" she said.

"If I could borrow a sheet of paper," I said.

She gave me one. And I wrote down the names and phone numbers and recited them as I wrote.

"Captain Healy, homicide commander, Mass state cops," I said. "Martin Quirk, homicide commander, Boston police. FBI man named Epstein, AIC in Boston."

"AIC?"

"Agent-in-charge," I said. "And Susan Silverman, Ph.D., who's a psychotherapist in Cambridge."

I handed her the paper.

"In the interest of full disclosure," I said. "Dr. Silverman is my honey bun."

" 'Honey bun,' " Mary said.

"Girl of my dreams," I said.

"I'll get back to you, Mr. Spenser," Mary said.

Chapter

36

I WASN'T SURE WHO HAD TOLD what lies to accomplish it. But we were all assembled when Hawk brought Gary Eisenhower into Chet Jackson's office. Chet was at his desk. Tony was in a chair across from Chet, with Junior and Ty-Bop leaning against the wall in the back of the room; Beth sat on the couch near him. Zel and Boo leaned on the wall near Chet, looking at Junior and Ty-Bop. I stood near the door.

When he got inside the room, Gary paused and looked around.

"Hot damn," he said, and walked across the room and sat beside Beth on the couch.

"'S happening, Beth?" he said, and patted her on the thigh.

She smiled brightly.

"Okay," Chet said. "You put this together, Tony. Talk to us."

Tony looked around the office.

"Lotta firepower in here," he said.

Chet nodded.

"Hawk," Tony said. "Spenser. My friends, your goons. Lotta force."

I could tell that Boo felt dissed by being called a goon. But he didn't speak. Zel seemed uninterested.

"So?" Chet said.

"I hope there's no need for force," Tony said.

"To do what?" Chet said.

"To resolve our problem."

"Our problem? What problem do you and me have?" Chet said.

Tony looked around the room. He took out a cigar, trimmed it, lit it, got it going, took in some smoke, and exhaled.

"We don't have to get too explicit here," he said. "But you and I do business in the same territory, and we got an agreement in place that allows us to do that without, you know, rubbing up against each other."

Chet nodded without saying anything.

"That gonna end," Tony said, "'less you straighten out your love life."

"My love life," Chet said.

Tony took an inhale on his cigar and took it from his

mouth, held it up in front of him, and exhaled so that he looked at the glowing end of the cigar through the smoke.

"Specifically, Mr., ah, Eisenhower," Tony said. "I want him left alone."

"What the hell do you care?" Chet said.

"Don't matter why," Tony said. "Only matter that I do."

"And if I tell you to go to hell?" Chet said.

"You're out of business," Tony said.

Everyone was quiet. Beth looked bright-eyed and excited as she watched the back-and-forth between her husband and Tony Marcus. Gary Eisenhower looked sort of amused, but he nearly always looked amused. Maybe because he was always amused. The damned cigar kept being a cigar.

"You think you can put me out of business?" Chet said.

"I know I can," Tony said. "And so do you."

Chet nodded slowly.

"You and Spenser rig this deal?" Chet said.

"Don't matter who rigged it," Tony said. "It rigged. Take it or leave it."

"He a friend of yours?" Chet said.

I knew he was stalling while he tried to think it through.

"He sent me up once," Tony said. "So no, we ain't friends. But he done me some favors, too."

Everyone was quiet.

Then Boo said, "Mr. Jackson, you want me to take one of these clowns apart, you just say so."

Tony turned and looked at him with mild amusement. Zel shook his head sadly and stepped away from Boo, his gaze fixed on Ty-Bop, who was still nodding to whatever music he was hearing in the spheres, but he was as focused on Zel, and Zel was on him.

"Boo took too many to the head," Zel said, "when he was fighting."

"Screw you, Zel," Boo said. "We ain't hired to let people push our boss around."

Beth's eyes seemed even brighter, and I noticed her tongue moving along her lower lip again. Tony was incredulous.

"You think you gonna take Junior apart?" Tony said, tilting his head in Junior's direction. It was an easy tilt, because Junior occupied most of the room.

"Anybody in the room," Boo said.

His eyes still steady on Ty-Bop, Zel shook his head sadly.

"Boo," he said softly.

"You heard me," Boo said.

Behind his desk, Chet looked blankly at the scene. He very likely had no idea what he was supposed to do.

Boo was staring at Junior.

"How 'bout you, boy? You want to try me?"

Junior looked at Tony. Tony nodded. Junior smiled.

I said, "How 'bout me, Boo?"

And he turned toward me.

"You, wiseass?" he said. "Be a pleasure."

I slipped out of my jacket. Boo came at me in his fighter's stance. He threw a left hook to start, and I saw right away why his face was so marked up. He dropped his hands when he punched. I blocked his hook with my right and put a hard jab onto his nose. It didn't faze him. He kept coming. He faked a left and tried an overhand right. I took it on my forearm and nailed him with a right cross, and he went down. He got right back up, but his eyes were a little unfocused, and his hands were at his waist. I hit him with my right forearm and then torqued back and hit him with the side of my right fist. He went down again. He tried to get up and made it to his knees, and wobbled there on all fours. Zel squatted beside him.

"Nine, ten, and out," he said to Boo. "Fight's over."

Boo stayed where he was, his head hanging. Some stubborn vestige of pride that he wouldn't let go and be flat on the floor. Zel stayed with him.

"Come on, big guy," Zel said. "Let's get out of here."

Boo made a faint gesture with his head that was probably an affirmative, and Zel got an arm around him and helped him up. Boo was more out than in, but his feet moved.

As they passed, Zel said to me, "Thanks."

I nodded.

And they went out.

"So much for your muscle," Tony said.

Chet nodded.

"I thought he was tougher than that," Chet said.

"He was," I said.

"Probably been beating up loan-shark deadbeats too much," Gary said, and grinned. "Or guys like me."

Beth was staring at me silently. Her face was a little flushed. Her tongue was still on her lower lip, but it wasn't moving.

"What about it, Chet?" Tony said.

Chet looked at me and back at Tony. Then he looked at Beth.

"Okay," he said. "I lay off Gary Boy."

"Right choice," Tony said.

"But"—Chet turned to Beth—"it stops here. I am not going to be your patsy."

"Meaning?" Beth said.

"You drop Gary Boy here, or I'll throw you out without a dime."

"You'd divorce me?"

"I would."

She looked at Gary.

"You got no case," Gary said. "He wouldn't have to give you anything."

"And if I give him up?" she said to Chet.

"And keep your knees together," Chet said. "We walk into the sunset together."

"That's my choice?"

Chet looked at her as if they were alone in the room.

"I love you," Chet said. "But I can't be out of business. If I was, you'd leave me anyway, soon as the money ran out."

"You think that of me?" Beth said.

"I know it of you," Chet said. "But it's okay. I knew it when I married you. I made the deal. I'll live with it. But I'm not giving up both you and the money."

Beth looked at Tony Marcus.

"This man can actually put you out of business?" she said.

"Yes," he said. "He can."

Beth looked at Gary.

"What should I do?"

"I was you," Gary said, "I'd dump me and go for the dough."

Beth nodded.

"Okay," she said.

Tony grinned and stood up.

"Our work here is done," he said.

Chapter

❖

37

Now that he didn't have to babysit Gary Eisenhower anymore, Hawk was at leisure, so he rode up to Wickton College with me.

"So how come you didn't let Boo have a go at Junior?" he said.

"Junior would have killed him," I said.

"So?"

"No need for it," I said.

Hawk shrugged.

"And how come we going up to talk to these people 'bout Gary Eisenhower? Ain't that all wrapped up?"

"Told her I would," I said.

"Who?"

"Director of counseling at the college," I said.

We were on Route 2, west of Fitchburg. Mostly bare winter trees to look at.

"You a bear for cleaning up loose ends," Hawk said.

"I'm a curious guy," I said.

"You sho' nuff are," Hawk said.

We turned off Route 2 and headed north on 202 toward Winchendon. We stopped for coffee, and in another half-hour we were at Wickton College.

"Don't see a lot of African-Americans 'round here," Hawk said.

"You may be the first," I said.

"At least I the perfect specimen."

"You want to come in with me, Specimen?" I said.

"Naw," Hawk said. "I think I sit here and see if I attract the attention of some college girls."

"I don't want to discourage you," I said. "But no one paid any attention to me when I was here last time."

Hawk looked at me silently for a while.

Then he said, "What that got to do with me?"

I left him and went in to see Mary Brown.

"Your recommendations support you," she said when I was seated. "Particularly your honey bun."

"Good to know," I said.

"I obviously cannot break confidence with Mr. Pappas," she said. "But I can tell you things that are on the public record."

I waited.

"Our campus security officers do not have full police

powers, so if there's an incident we ask the local police to step in," she said.

I waited some more.

"Mr. Pappas had a penchant for women who were with other men," she said. "This precipitated several fights. Often with alcohol involved. On one occasion our security officers had to call local authorities to stabilize the situation."

"And Mr. Pappas got busted?" I said.

"Yes."

"And booked?" I said.

"Yes."

"So if I were to speak to the local cops, I might learn something."

"Yes."

"Do you know what I might learn?" I said.

"I believe so," she said.

"I don't wish to compromise your ethics," I said. "But if I'm going to know it anyway, why not save me a trip to the fuzz."

She thought about that for a time.

"He was released without penalty under the condition that he seek counseling from a psychotherapist."

"There's one around here?"

"One," she said. "He has offices in the medical center."

"Name?" I said.

She hesitated.

"His name is Paul Doucette," she said. "I've alerted him that you might visit."

"Hot damn," I said. "So you were going to tell me this before I even arrived."

"I thought I might," she said.

"So it wasn't my clever questioning," I said.

"No."

"How about charm," I said.

"Well," she said, and smiled. "That was certainly part of it."

"Oh, good," I said. "Is it enough to get me directions, too?"

"We have them preprinted," she said, and took a card out of a file on her desk and handed it to me.

"Thank you," I said.

"Your honey bun was very persuasive," Mary said.

When I came out of the administration building, Hawk was leaning on the fender, talking with two college girls.

"This is Janice, and Loretta," Hawk said. "We been discussing African tribal practices."

"Any particular tribe?" I said.

"Mine," Hawk said.

The girls said, "How do you do."

"Have to excuse us," I said. "Gotta go down to the medical center."

"He scared to go alone," Hawk said.

The girls said good-bye, we got in, and the girls waved after us as we drove away.

"What tribe was that again?" I said.

"I forgot," Hawk said.

Chapter

❖❖

38

THE MEDICAL CENTER was a two-story brick building with a lot of glass windows, and a parking lot beside it. When I parked, Hawk got out with me.

"You going to hang around out here?" I said to Hawk. "And further integrate the region?"

"Must be nurses here," Hawk said, and resumed residence on my front fender.

I went in to talk to Dr. Doucette. It took a while, but he squeezed me in between patients. He was a lean, fiftyish man with silvery hair combed straight back. He looked like he might play racquetball.

I gave him my card.

"Mary Brown called me, so I know who you are," he

said. "I'm Paul Doucette. I haven't much time, and there are obviously issues of confidentiality. That given, how can I help you?"

"Tell me what you can about Goran Pappas," I said.

"I interviewed him and found him a reasonably coherent young man with a passion for women, particularly women already with another man."

"Any reason for that?"

"The interest in other men's women?" Dr. Doucette said. "Probably, but it didn't seem to consume him. He seemed perfectly able to control it if he chose to. His life didn't make him unhappy, and he appeared to present no particular threat to society."

"So you had nothing much to treat him for," I said.

"Correct. I told the police and the college that in my opinion, he was well within the normal range of appropriate behavior."

"Did you explore the other-men's-women business with him?"

"I did."

"Can you tell me about it?"

"No."

"Would I be revealing my ignorance," I said, "if I suggested that if I were looking into it, I'd start with his mother and father."

"In my business," Doucette said, "as perhaps in yours,

it is sensible to start with the most obvious and see where it leads."

"Can you tell me where it led you?"

"No," he said. "I can't. But perhaps you can tell me why you want to know."

I smiled.

"Just because I don't know, I guess."

"Has Pappas committed a crime?"

"Well, sort of."

" 'Sort of'?" Doucette said.

I told him a brief outline of the Gary Eisenhower story.

Doucette nodded.

"So," he said. "I gather that from your perspective, though he won't be punished for the blackmail, the case is resolved."

"Yes."

He looked at his watch.

"And you'll settle for that," he said.

"Yes."

"For what it's worth," he said. "I agree with you."

"It's not perfect," I said.

"It never is," Doucette said.

"But I'll take it," I said.

"I do not believe Pappas is a bad man," Doucette said. "He is, by and large, what he appears to be."

"So you'll take it, too," I said.

"I did," Doucette said.

He looked at his watch again. I nodded and stood. We shook hands. And I headed out to the parking lot to see how many nurses Hawk had wrangled.

Chapter

❖❖

39

I HAD A DRINK with Gary Eisenhower at the bar in a new steakhouse called Mooo, up near the State House.

"I got this one," he said when I sat down beside him. "I guess I owe you that much."

"Probably more than that," I said.

"You think?"

He had a Maker's Mark on the rocks. I ordered beer.

"I took Jackson and his people off your back," I said.

"Pretty clever how you did that," Gary said. "You know some scary dudes."

"I do," I said.

"You're pretty scary yourself," Gary said.

With his forefinger he stirred the ice in his bourbon.

"I know," I said.

"How come you fought Boo?" Gary said.

"Junior would have killed him," I said.

"The huge black dude is named Junior?" Gary said.

"Yep."

"Man," Gary said. "I'd hate to see Senior."

I nodded.

"Why do you care if Junior kills Boo?" Gary said.

"No need for it," I said.

"Boo's not much," Gary said. "Except mean."

"I know."

"Why would he go with the biggest guy in the room?"

"It's all he's got," I said. "He's a tough guy. He doesn't have that, he has nothing. He isn't anybody."

"And you took that away from him," Gary said.

"I did," I said. "But he's alive. And in a few days he'll beat up some car salesman who's fallen behind on the vig, and his sense of self will be restored."

"That easy?" Gary said.

"Boo's not very smart," I said.

"I'll say."

Gary ordered another bourbon. I ordered another beer.

"Zel was, like, looking out for him," Gary said.

"Yeah."

"I don't know this game like you do," Gary said. "But I saw Zel move a little away from Boo when the trouble started, and focus in on the skinny black kid."

"Ty-Bop," I said.

"And I figure if things went bad for Boo," Gary said, "Zel would start shooting."

"Unless Ty-Bop beat him," I said.

"Either way," Gary said. "We weren't far from a shoot-out right there."

"True."

"In which several people might have got killed," he said.

"True."

"Including Beth," he said.

"Including Beth."

"You thinking about that," Gary said, "when you stepped up?"

"Sure," I said.

"Christ," Gary said. "A fucking hero."

"But you knew that anyway," I said.

Gary laughed and sipped some bourbon.

"So," I said. "I think you owe me more than two beers."

"How many?" Gary said.

"I think you need to stop blackmailing these women," I said.

"Ones that hired you?"

"Yep."

"You get some kind of bonus?" he said.

"Nope."

"You got a bonus, maybe we could split it."

"Stop blackmailing these women," I said.

"What if I fuck them for free?" Gary said.

"That's between you and them," I said. "But no blackmail."

"And I pick up this tab?" Gary said.

"Nope," I said. "I'll get the tab.

Gary grinned and put out his hand.

"Deal," he said.

And we shook on it.

Chapter

❖◆❖

40

IT WAS DECEMBER NOW. Gray, cold, low clouds, snow expected in the afternoon. I was in my office, drinking coffee and writing out my report on a missing child I'd located. My door opened without a knock, and Chet Jackson came in wearing a double-breasted camel-hair overcoat.

"The mountain comes to Mohammed," I said.

"Whatever," Chet said. "Mind if I sit down?"

I said I didn't, and he unbuttoned his overcoat and sat without taking it off.

"I want you to keep an eye on my wife," he said.

"To what purpose?"

"You know to what purpose," Chet said. "I want to make sure she's faithful."

"Eisenhower?" I said.

"That's one worry," he said.

"Hard to tail someone who knows you," I said.

"That's fine," he said. "If she spots you, she won't do it."

"Because she knows I'll report it to you," I said.

"Yes."

"And you'll divorce her and cut her off without a penny."

"Yes," he said. "I will."

"So I provide both information and a certain degree of prevention," I said.

"Exactly," he said.

"How long would you plan to keep track of her like this?" I said.

Chet looked startled.

"I . . . there's no timetable," he said. "We'll play it by ear."

I tilted my chair back and put a foot up on my desk.

"You want her to be faithful, but you don't trust her, and you're trying to compel her," I said.

"I love her," he said.

"And she loves you?"

"She's been with me for ten years," he said. "The sex is still good."

"You ever read Machiavelli?" I said.

"I imagine somebody mentioned him to me at Harvard."

"He argued that it is better to be feared than loved," I said. "Because you can make someone fear you, but you can't make them love you."

"I'll settle for what I can get," Chet said.

"I understand that," I said. "But I'm not your man."

I thought I saw a glitter of panic in Chet's eyes.

"Why not?"

"Couple of things," I said. "One, I'm sick of all of you. All the women and their husbands and the whole cheating rigmarole. Two, it's emotional suicide. And I'm not going to help you commit it."

"What are you, some kind of fucking shrink?"

"Doesn't matter what I am," I said. "I'm not going to work for you."

"What if I pay you more than you're worth?" Chet said.

"There is no such amount," I said. "But it's not about money. I won't dance."

Chet was rich. He had clout. People didn't turn him down. He was breathing as if he had just run a race. His wife didn't love him, and he didn't think he could live without her.

"I need some help here," he said.

His voice was hoarse.

"You do," I said. "But not the kind I can give you."

"You talking about a shrink?" he said.

"I can get you some names," I said.

"Fuck that," he said.

I didn't say anything.

"Fuck that," he said again, and got up and walked out.

Outside my office window, a couple of solitary snowflakes spiraled down. I watched them as they passed.

"Après vous," I said, *"le déluge."*

Chapter

◆◆

41

Normally when we ate together at my place, Susan and I sat at the kitchen counter. But it was Christmas, so Susan set the table at one end of the living room: tablecloth, crystal, good china, good silver, candles, and napkins in gold napkin rings.

"What do you think?" Susan said.

"Zowie," I said.

"Zowie?"

"You heard me," I said.

"Would Martha Stewart say 'zowie'?"

"If she wouldn't, she should," I said.

I had a fire going, and Pearl the Wonder Dog was in front of it on the couch, resting up after the rigors of the ride from Cambridge.

"What's for eats?" Susan said.

"I was thinking pizza," I said. "How 'bout you?"

Susan looked at me without expression.

"Or Chinese?" I said. "I bet PF Chang's is open. Pork fried rice?"

Susan's expression didn't change.

"I suppose subs wouldn't do it, either," I said.

"The baby and I are going home," Susan said.

"Boy, are you picky," I said. "Okay, how about we start with bay scallops seviche, then we have slow-roasted duck, snow peas, corn pudding, and brown rice cooked with cranberries?"

"And dessert?" Susan said.

"Blackberry pie."

"With ice cream?" Susan said.

"Ice cream or cheddar cheese that I bought at Formaggio."

"Or both?"

"Or both," I said.

"Oh, all right," Susan said. "We'll stay."

"Good girls," I said. "Would either of you care for some pink champagne?"

"Pearl's underage," Susan said.

"In dog years she's middle-aged," I said.

"She is still a baby," Susan said.

"Okay," I said. "I'll drink hers. How about you, little lady?"

Susan smiled, which was worth traveling great distances to see, and said, "It would be foolish not to."

I poured us each a glass of Krug rosé, put the ice bucket on the coffee table, and Susan and I squeezed onto the couch beside Pearl. Pearl looked a little annoyed, which was hardly in the spirit of the season, but she readjusted her position and went back to sleep with her head on Susan's lap. Which was what I had been planning on.

"So," I said. "Do Jews go to hell for celebrating Christmas?"

"Jews don't go to hell," Susan said.

"None?"

"And in particular," Susan said, "none who were cheerleaders at Swampscott High."

"And still retain their skills," I said.

"Several skills," Susan said.

"I know."

We drank our champagne. The fire enriched itself as the logs settled in on one another. Pearl sighed in her sleep.

"Do we love each other?" Susan said.

"We do," I said.

"And were you thinking of celebrating that love with some sort of holiday rendezvous?"

"I was," I said.

"If I have a heavy meal, as I expect to," Susan said, "my libido will be dysfunctional for hours."

"I've noticed that about you," I said.

"However, if we were to drink a bit more champagne and retire to your bedroom before dinner, we could cel-

ebrate Christmas in our own ecumenical way," Susan said. "And then eat the big meal."

"Brilliant," I said. "You're amazing."

"Hot, too," she said.

I nodded.

"Hotter than a pepper sprout," I said.

"So shall we do that?"

"You bet," I said.

"Okay, pour me another glass of champagne," Susan said. "And we'll proceed."

"Zowie," I said.

Chapter

❖

42

IT WAS THE WEEK before Valentine's Day, and I was in my office working on the first draft of my Valentine's poem to Susan, when Gary Eisenhower arrived with Estelle, the trainer and putative girlfriend. I put the draft in my middle drawer.

"Gary," I said.

"Spenser," Gary said. "You remember Estelle?"

"I do," I said. "How are you, Estelle."

"Feeling good," she said, and gave me a big smile.

Gary gave her a hug.

"Main squeeze," he said, and kissed her on top of head.

"Amazing that you find the time," I said.

"We manage," Estelle said.

I gestured toward the chairs and they sat down.

"We need to consult you," Gary said.

"Go," I said.

"It's about Beth Jackson," Estelle said.

"She seeing you again?" I said to Eisenhower.

"Not really," he said. "Her husband's all over her on that one. But she does see Estelle."

"I'm her trainer," Estelle said. "And we've become good friends."

"Still at Pinnacle?" I said.

"Yes, four days a week," Estelle said. "We do weights twice a week and Pilates twice a week."

"Estelle has been able to sneak me in a couple of times, and I've been able to spend a little time with Beth in one of the massage rooms."

"How modern of you," I said to Estelle.

She smiled brightly.

"Gary and I have our priorities straight," she said. "We know what we want."

"Which includes money," I said.

"Of course," Estelle said. "No point writing anyone off too soon."

"How's business?" I said to Gary.

Gary waffled his hand.

"Mezzo mezz," he said. "I'm just doing Beth to be polite. No income there at the moment. Meanwhile, I'm developing a new client list, but it's a little lean right now."

"Did you come to borrow money?" I said.

"No," Estelle said. "It's about Beth. I'm not only her trainer, I'm her friend."

"Friends are good," I said.

"There's someone threatening her life," Estelle said.

"Who?"

"She doesn't know. It's someone Chet does business with. He has threatened to kill Chet and Beth."

"Cops?" I said.

"Chet refuses to go to the police. Says it's nothing. Says he'll take care of it."

I nodded.

"Will you talk with her?" Estelle said.

I looked at Gary.

"You think it's serious?" I said.

"You know me, buddy," Gary said. "I don't think anything is serious."

"She's terrified," Estelle said. "She wants you to help her. But she's afraid to ask you."

I took in a long, slow breath.

"She thinks you're terrific," Estelle said. "You're the only one she thinks she can trust."

"She's probably right on both counts," I said. "When can she come in?"

"I'll bring her in tomorrow," Estelle said. "At five."

"Swell," I said.

Chapter

❖

43

Beth put a note on my desk when she came in. "Read this," she said.

Your husband had betrayed me.
For this you both shall die.

"Your husband has seen this?"

"Yes. He said it was a hoax and not to worry."

"But you are worried."

"I'm terrified. For both of us. Who would send such a thing?"

"I'll talk with him," I said.

"I promised my husband I would say nothing to any-one," Beth said.

"Except Estelle," I said. "And Gary. And me."

Estelle sat beside Beth across the desk from me and said nothing. The loyal, self-effacing friend.

"I'm frightened," Beth said. "I have to confide in someone. Estelle and Gary both urged me to see you."

I nodded.

"Why does your husband not want you to tell anyone?"

"I don't know. Since that time in his office, when you were there with those black men, he's changed. He's very curt with me."

"So I cannot discuss this with him," I said.

"No," she said. "I promised him."

"Promised him not to let him know you told anyone?"

"What's the difference," Beth said. "Will you help me?"

"Why not just leave him," I said. "Get out of town."

"And do what?" Beth said. "I'm thirty-four years old, and my only skill is undressing and lying on my back. Besides, that wouldn't protect him."

"Does he give you much money?" I said.

"He monitors every dime."

"So what about my fee?"

"Fee?"

"Yeah, I do this for a living," I said.

"I . . . But my life, our life, is in danger," Beth said.

"Can't you help her?" Estelle said. "Maybe we can find a way to pay you."

"Tell me more about the danger," I said.

"I don't know more," she said. "I know Chet does a lot of business with people he's never introduced me to. I know many of them are dangerous. And I know Chet is very . . . his word is *cute* . . . in his business practices."

"Boo and Zel still around?"

"They're taking care of Chet."

"Why not stay with Chet?"

"I can't stand to be with him like that all the time."

"And he's provided you no security?" I said.

"No. He doesn't seem to love me anymore."

"Hard to imagine," I said. "So you stay with him for the money. Why's he stay with you?"

"Sex."

"Well, as long as there's a bond," I said. "What would you want me to do?"

"Can't you provide security?"

"For no fee?" I said. "Twenty-four hours a day, seven days a week? For how long?"

"I . . . I don't know," she said.

I sat. The two women sat. I didn't like the story. Didn't mean it wasn't true. But I didn't like it.

"I need to think about this," I said.

"And what do I do while you're thinking?" Beth said.

"We'll go to a hotel," I said. "I'll register, and you'll stay there. I'll see that you're safe in the room. Room service, whatever. Estelle can stay with you if she wants

to. When I go, you lock the door. And you don't open it for anybody until I come by for you in the morning . . . and we'll go from there."

"Will you stay with me?" Beth said.

"No."

"We could have an awfully good time if you did," Beth said.

"No," I said. "We couldn't."

Beth stood up suddenly.

"Oh, go to hell," she said.

She turned and stalked out of my office. Estelle looked at me and shrugged and went after Beth.

I continued to sit at my desk. It was not clear to me what had just happened. On the other hand, it often wasn't, and I'd gotten used to it.

Chapter

.... ◆◆ ....

44

I WAS IN FRANK BELSON'S CUBICLE at Boston police headquarters at Tremont and Ruggles.

"Found your name in a guy's Rolodex," Frank said.

"A dead guy?" I said.

"Wow," Belson said. "You figured that out because I'm a homicide cop?"

"Want to tell me who it is?" I said.

"Guy named Chester Jackson," Belson said.

I leaned back a little.

"I know him," I said.

"Tell me about him," Belson said.

"I gather he didn't die of natural causes," I said.

"Somebody put a forty-caliber slug into his head from

about eight feet away, and a second one, from about three inches."

"To make sure," I said.

"Uh-huh."

"When did he get it?" I said.

"Secretary says he left his office at five p.m. Nine-one-one got an anonymous call at five-ten. Saying someone had been shot in the garage. There was a car in the area. It arrived at five-thirty, and there he was."

"What garage?" I said.

"Under International Place," Belson said. "'Bout two light years down."

"Was he parked there?"

"Yep. He was facedown on the floor with his car door open."

"So somebody was waiting for him," I said.

"This sounds more like me telling you than you telling me," Belson said.

"We'll get to me," I said.

Belson nodded.

"Yeah," he said. "We will."

"There's security in that garage, isn't there?"

"Yep. If you work there, you got a pass. If not, you have to be on a list."

"You got the list," I said.

"Amazingly, we thought of that," Belson said.

"Anything?"

"Not yet," Belson said. "Thought you might take a look."

"I will," I said. "If you walk into the lobby from the street and take the elevator down to the garage . . ."

"And aren't carrying something that looks like an infernal device," Belson said. "You're in."

"You'd be an idiot," I said, "to drive into the garage."

"Car was parked almost next to an elevator," Belson said.

"Assigned parking?"

"Yep. Sign says 'Reserved for C. Jackson.'"

"So," I said. "If you knew Jackson, you'd know he was a big deal and would be likely to have an assigned spot."

"So you could wander around the garage until you found it," Belson said.

"Probably be near an elevator, so maybe you could cut down on the wandering," I said.

"And you wait there until he shows up," Belson said.

"Maybe," I said.

"Or you know him, you know where he parks, you know when he's going to come for his car, and you get there a few minutes early," Belson said. "And pop him."

"No witnesses," I said.

"Nope."

"No suspicious-looking people hanging around," I said.

"None reported."

"How come nobody ever sees a shooting?" I said.

"Shooter might try to arrange it that way," Belson said. "And it's a godsend for us. Give us something to do so that we're not in the bars drinking Jameson with a beer chaser by two in the afternoon."

"God is kind," I said.

"Tell me about Jackson," Belson said.

He had a notebook on the desk in front of him, and as I talked, every once in a while he wrote things in it.

"I don't know quite what he does, but I know he makes a lot of dough, and I know all of it isn't clean."

"He wired?" Belson said.

"I would say so."

"Got any names?" Belson said.

"I know a name, but it's a guy just did me a favor, and unless I think he did Jackson, which I don't, I won't name him."

"We could insist," Belson said.

"You could," I said.

"We can be insistent as a sonovabitch," Belson said.

"I know."

"But you won't tell us anyway," Belson said.

"No."

"Known you a long time," Belson said.

"And yet here we are," I said. "Still in the bloom of youth."

Belson nodded.

"You get a suspicion," he said, "you let me know."

"At once," I said.

"Sure," Belson said. "I'll check with the organized-crime guys."

"I would," I said.

"What's your connection to him?"

I told him everything, as it was, except that I didn't name the other women. And I didn't mention Tony Marcus.

"And how did you resolve the problem?"

"Tireless negotiation," I said.

"Wife buy into it?" Belson said.

"She said she did."

"Think she might have not meant it."

"Probably," I said.

"Think she might have aced him?"

"She might have," I said. "But at the time Jackson was killed she was talking to me in my office with a woman named Estelle."

"What a coincidence," Belson said.

"It is," I said.

"Estelle who?"

"Don't know her last name. She's a trainer at Pinnacle Fitness."

"Want to tell me why they were there?"

"Beth said her life had been threatened and wanted me to protect her. Said her husband had been threatened, too. Estelle was there for moral support, I guess."

Belson wrote in the notebook.

"Were you planning on mentioning this?" he said.

"Sure," I said. "But I thought it would be good training for you to learn of it through sound investigative procedure."

"Geez," Belson said. "With your help maybe I'll make lieutenant."

"I think you have to take the lieutenant's exam first," I said.

"I'll get to it," Belson said. "You want to tell me about the wife, what's her name"—he glanced at his notes—"Beth."

I told him about her visit the previous evening.

"You remember what the note said?"

" 'Your husband had betrayed me,' " I said. " 'For this you both shall die.' "

Belson wrote it down.

"Didn't seem to work out that way," he said.

"Shit happens," I said.

Belson nodded.

"You believe all of this?"

"I don't think so," I said.

"Think she might have been setting up an alibi?"

"Maybe," I said. "But if she was, was Estelle in it, too?"

"And Gary Cockhound?" Belson said.

"It was a fairly elaborate fake, if it was a fake," I said.

"The kind amateurs use," Belson said.

"True," I said.

"On the other hand, since she didn't actually do it," Belson said, "who did? Eisenhower?"

"I don't think so," I said.

"What's your gut tell you?" Belson said.

"My gut says there's something wrong with this," I said. "It also says that Gary Eisenhower isn't part of it."

Belson wrote in his notebook.

"On the other hand," he said, "your gut isn't too bright."

"True," I said. "Mostly it just knows when I'm hungry."

Chapter

❖

45

I SAT WITH BETH in her expensive off-white living room, which looked like it had been decorated by the pound. Beth was in a black dress that proclaimed her mourning and showed off her body.

"I'm sorry for your loss," I said.

"You told the police about me," she said.

"I did."

"That was mean," she said.

"No, it wasn't," I said. "I'm your alibi. You would have told them you were with me, and I would have confirmed it, and the cops would have said, 'How come you didn't tell us about her?'"

"Why do I need an alibi?" she said.

"You're the spouse of a murder victim."

"And that automatically makes me a suspect?" she said.

"They have to eliminate you," I said.

"I suppose," she said.

"Any thoughts on who might have done it?"

"I should think the warning note I showed you would be a clue," she said.

"Not much hard information," I said. "Do you still have the envelope?"

"Envelope?"

"That it came in."

"Oh, no," Beth said. "I threw it away. There was no return address or anything."

"Was it addressed in hand or typed or one of those little computer address stickers?"

"Hand," she said.

"Remember where it was postmarked?"

"Boston, maybe," she said. "I don't know. I'm not used to threatening letters. I'm not a detective. I just threw the envelope away."

"Sure," I said. "Nice outfit you're wearing."

"Oh, this, well, it's . . . I'm kind of in mourning. You think it's okay?"

"Swell," I said. "Are you his only heir?"

"There's a couple of ex-wives," she said. "No children. I'm the only one in the will."

"Well," I said. "There's a plus."

"It is a plus," she said. "But there's no need for you

to be so snarky about it. My husband has just been murdered."

"True," I said.

"I mean, we had our problems, sure. . . ."

"And now you don't," I said.

She was sitting on the ivory-colored couch. I was sitting on a straight-backed armchair across from her. She squared her shoulders and sat more upright.

"Do you suspect me?" she said.

"I remain open-minded," I said.

"What a terrible thing to say. It's disgusting that you could even think that."

"Disgusting," I said.

"Why do you even care?" she said. "Has someone hired you to work on this case?"

"No," I said.

"Then why don't you go off somewhere and be disgusting on someone else's business."

"I've been involved with this for a while," I said. "It's my line of work. I feel some obligation to see what I can do."

"Well, don't think you have any obligation to me," Beth said. "I'd like it if I never saw you again."

"You, too?" I said.

Chapter

❖

46

I SPENT THE WEEKEND at Susan's place, where, after some early morning excitement, we usually sat in her kitchen and had a lingering Sunday brunch prepared mostly by me. This morning was a little different; we were having scrambled eggs prepared by Susan. It was one of her two specialties, the other being boiled water. I added a ragout of peppers, onions, and mushrooms to grace the plate, and we ate it with oatmeal toast. Pearl came from her spot on the living-room couch and joined us, alert for any spillage.

"I talked with Beth Jackson on Friday," I said.

"Are you still suspicious of her?"

"Let me recount our discussion," I said.

"I'm all ears," Susan said.

"Actually," I said. "Not all."

She smiled, and I gave her, almost verbatim, my conversation with Beth.

"You like to show off that you can do that," Susan said. "Don't you."

"Yes," I said. "Is there anything bothersome about what you heard."

"Your voice was sexually exciting?" Susan said.

"Besides that," I said.

"In relation to the murder," Susan said.

"Yes."

Susan was silent, her mind running over the conversation.

"Remember why she came to me the night of the murder," I said.

"She wanted you to protect her," Susan said. "And, at least peripherally, her husband."

"Correct," I said.

"And now"—Susan began to speak faster, trying to keep up with her mind—"when half the threat has been executed, she should be more desperate for protection."

"Bingo," I said.

"And she isn't," Susan said. "She doesn't want to ever see you again."

"Or words to that effect," I said.

"Which would lead a trained observer," Susan said, "to conclude that she no longer thought there was a threat."

"It might," I said. "Or she might have found me so disgusting that she preferred to look elsewhere for protection."

"No," Susan said. "Not if she's in fear of her life. However disgusting she may have found you, you are also safety. She would have embraced you."

"Who wouldn't," I said.

"I was speaking metaphorically," Susan said.

"Oh," I said.

"But we know she didn't do it herself," Susan said.

"I can vouch for that," I said. "In fact, it seems too carefully done. She comes to me at five. At five-ten an anonymous caller reports a shooting, cops are there by five-thirty. Beth doesn't leave my office until about six."

"A lot of people could have made an anonymous call," Susan said. "They saw it happen but didn't want to be involved."

"Nine-one-one records all call numbers. This one was from a disposable phone."

"They can't trace it?"

"Correct," I said.

"So it could have been someone who just happened to use a disposable phone, or it could have been a deliberate way to avoid identification."

"How many people you know that carry disposable phones?" I said.

"Nobody."

"Guy also tried to disguise his voice. Belson said it's a man speaking in a falsetto."

"So it could have been the murderer," Susan said.

"Could have been," I said.

"But why would he call the police? Wouldn't it be in his better interest not to?"

"One would think," I said.

"Unless he wanted to establish that the murder took place while Beth was with you," Susan said.

"Which means she was involved," I said.

"Or Estelle," Susan said.

"Or both," I said.

"Why would Estelle be involved?"

"Why do people usually kill other people?" I said.

"Mostly over love or money," Susan said.

"If Estelle's involved," I said, "it wouldn't be about love."

"You can't be sure," Susan said. "Human emotion is sometimes very convolute."

"I've heard that," I said.

Susan smiled and drank some coffee.

"How about Gary Eisenhower?" she said.

"You think he might do that?" I said.

"No," Susan said.

"Shrink insight or woman's intuition?" I said.

"Sometimes there's not much difference," Susan said.

"I don't think he did it, either," I said.

"Gumshoe insight?" Susan said. "Or male intuition?"

I grinned at her.

"Sometimes," I said, "there's not much difference."

"Does he have an alibi?" Susan said.

"Don't know," I said. "Belson was supposed to interview him today."

"So," Susan said, "pending what you get from Belson, if it wasn't Gary, who did the actual shooting?"

"Damn," I said. "You don't know that, either?"

"Sorry," Susan said.

"And you a Harvard Ph.D."

"I know," Susan said. "Puzzling, isn't it."

Chapter

❖

47

GARY EISENHOWER CAME to my office on Monday morning, while I was reading the paper.

"You know," I said, as he sat down. "I don't think I've ever disagreed with anything in Doonesbury."

"Doonesbury?"

"Guy's always on the money," I said.

"Yeah, right," Gary said. "Beth Jackson's husband got killed."

"I know that," I said.

"You know anything more?" Gary said.

"He was shot twice in the head in the parking garage at International Place," I said.

"They know who did it?"

"No."

"They got any suspects?" Gary said.

"No."

"What about Beth?"

"She's got an ironclad alibi," I said.

"No, I mean, is she safe?"

"Don't know," I said.

"You're not giving her security?"

"Nope."

"But," Gary said, "the letter said both of them, and obviously they meant it."

"She told me to get lost," I said.

"Don't you hate when that happens," Gary said.

"You get used to it," I said.

Gary grinned.

"Wouldn't know," he said. "I see Boo around, maybe he's looking out for her."

"Boo?"

"Yeah."

"Without Zel?" I said.

"Haven't seen Zel," Gary said. "Maybe they broke up."

I nodded.

"Cops talk to you yet?" I said.

"Yeah," he said. "Detective named Belson."

"How'd that go," I said.

"I'm clear," he said. "I was cultivating a new client. Belson talked with her. Told her he saw no need to involve her husband."

"New client a member at Pinnacle Fitness?"

He smiled.

"Sure," he said. "Thing keeps working, you don't go to something else."

"You seen Beth," I said. "Since the murder?"

"Yeah. She's not devastated."

"She got the money," I said.

"Yep, and she's talking about her and me picking up again."

"So you're not exactly devastated," I said.

"Money's good," he said. "But I kind of like it when they ain't free as a bird, you know? They got a husband and don't want to leave him, makes everything work better for me."

"How's Estelle feel about Beth?" I said.

"She likes her," Gary said.

"She doesn't mind your client list?" I said.

"Naw," Gary said. "Estelle's pretty cool. The whole blackmail scheme was more hers than mine, tell you the truth."

"Really?"

"Yeah," Gary said. "She used to do some videotape work, training clients, you know?"

"So the hidden cameras were her doing," I said.

"Yeah," Gary said. "Behind every successful man . . ."

"And she doesn't mind sharing you with other women," I said.

"No," Gary said. "She . . ." He paused. "The first time

we started using the hidden cameras and the voice record-ers, it was for her."

"You mean so she could watch and listen?"

"Yeah," Gary said. "It turns her on."

I nodded.

"How'd you feel about it?" I said.

"Well, you know, it was a little creepy at first."

He looked at the back of his hands for a moment. Then he looked up and smiled.

"But I'm a laid-back guy."

"And your partners in bed?" I said.

"What they don't know won't hurt them was the way we looked at it."

"Until you started the blackmail."

"It was a good parlay for us," Gary said.

"You and Estelle."

"Yeah," Gary said. "In most deals there's winners and losers, you know?"

"And your clients were the losers."

"I suppose," Gary said. "But nobody got hurt very bad. They liked the sex. I liked the sex. They were mar-ried to money. I only wanted some of it. Estelle and me were living pretty high up on the hog. Hell, Beth still wants to be with me, and, by the way, so does Abigail Larson."

I nodded.

"Abigail's a drinker," Gary said.

"Yep."

"Estelle says it makes her unreliable, and we shouldn't waste time with her."

"She still giving you money?"

"Naw, I . . ." He paused. "I'm a little embarrassed, but I sort of gave you my word on the blackmail."

"So you won't take her money?"

"Nope. Beth's, either. I mean, before her husband got killed."

"But you're still having sex," I said.

"Yeah," he said. "I figured that wasn't part of the promise."

"I like a man with standards," I said.

Chapter

◆◆

48

I FOUND ZEL AND BOO sharing a two-bedroom apartment in Jamaica Plain. There was linoleum on all the floors and a soapstone sink in the kitchen. Zel answered the door.

"Come in," Zel said. And nodded toward one of the empty chairs at the kitchen table. "Have a seat."

Boo was seated at the kitchen table, in his undershirt, reading *The Herald*. He stood when Zel let me in and left the room. Zel watched him go and put his hand out to stop me and stood between me and the door that Boo had left through. In a moment Boo returned with a gun.

"Put it away, Boo," Zel said.

Boo pointed the gun at us.

"Get out of the way," he said to Zel.

"Put it away," Zel said, and walked slowly toward Boo, keeping himself between us.

I focused on the gun in Boo's hand. It was a semi-automatic, maybe a .40-caliber. The hammer was back. His finger was on the trigger. If I saw any sign of finger movement I would go down and roll. I adjusted slightly to keep Zel between us.

"Get out of the way, Zel," Boo said again.

Zel took another step and reached out and took hold of the gun. Boo stared at him, his face squeezed tight, then let Zel take it. Zel eased the hammer down and put the gun in his hip pocket.

"I do the gun work, Boo," Zel said. "You know that."

Boo nodded slowly, then turned and left the room again.

"He got another gun?" I said.

"No," Zel said. "He's going in there to sulk."

"How bad is he?" I said.

"In the head?" Zel said, and shrugged. "You saw him, he drops his hands when he fights. He always has."

"So he's had his brain rattled."

"A lot," Zel said.

"Can he take care of himself?"

"Not against a guy like you," Zel said. "Amateurs, he does fine. He can still punch."

"I meant can he take care of himself in general," I

said. "You know, buy food, balance his checkbook, go to the dentist?"

"I take care of him," Zel said.

"Been doing that long?"

"Yeah."

We sat for a minute. Zel sat across the table from me, where he could watch the door to the room that Boo had gone to.

"You got any work now that Jackson got aced?" I said.

"Not right now, but I'm making some calls. People know me."

"Seen Mrs. Jackson at all?"

"Not since her old man got whacked," Zel said.

"Know why Jackson got whacked?" I said.

"No."

"Know who did it?"

"No."

"Any suggestions?" I said.

"How'd he get it," Zel said. "I know he got shot, but cops wouldn't tell me anything else."

"Two in the head," I said. "One from about eight feet. One from about three inches."

"Proves it ain't me. The one from eight feet woulda been enough."

"That a forty-caliber you took away from Boo?" I said.

"Never noticed," Zel said. "Jackson capped with a forty."

"Yep."

"Boo ain't much of a shooter," Zel said.

"From eight feet you don't have to be much of a shooter," I said.

"You any good?" Zel said.

"Yes," I said.

"Know anybody better?"

"Two guys," I said. "Vinnie Morris, guy from L.A. named Chollo . . . maybe Hawk."

"That's three," Zel said.

"So maybe three," I said.

"I hearda Vinnie Morris," Zel said.

"You as good as Vinnie," I said.

"Ain't been determined," Zel said.

"How come you weren't with Jackson when he got shot," I said. "I sorta thought that was your job."

"Told us to take the day off," Zel said. "Said he didn't need us."

"Was Boo with you when Jackson was shot?" I said.

"Boo's always with me," Zel said.

"I'd swear that gun you took from Boo was a forty," I said.

Zel took it out and looked at it.

"Nice call," he said. "S-and-W forty-caliber."

"Yours?" I said.

"They're all mine," Zel said. "I don't want Boo carrying no gun."

"How many you got?" I said.

"Six," Zel said.

"All of them clean as this one?" I said.

"I keep them clean," Zel said.

"Tools of the trade," I said.

"Sure," he said.

I looked at the door to the room where Boo was sulking.

"Too bad Boo never learned to keep his hands up," I said.

"Everybody tried," Zel said. "But when the fight started, he could never remember. Even before he got hit, Boo wasn't the brightest guy you'd meet."

I nodded. We sat again.

"I hear anything useful," Zel said, "I'll give you a shout."

"Please do," I said.

Chapter

........................◆◆........................

49

I SAT WITH ESTELLE at the café counter in Pinnacle Fitness. I had coffee, and Estelle drank green tea. I didn't care. I was still bigger and stronger than she was. The hell with green tea.

"Are you working on the murder case?" she said.

"I am."

Estelle was wearing the tight black sweats and the tight white tank top that was apparently the Pinnacle trainer's uniform.

"Who hired you?"

"I'm working on spec," I said.

She looked at me as if I might be odd.

"Do the police have a suspect?" she said.

"No."

"Have they had any success tracking the note?" she said. "You know, fingerprints? What machine it was written on? Kind of paper?"

"You've been watching those crime-scene shows," I said. "Haven't you."

She smiled.

"Especially the one with David Caruso." She glanced at me sideways. "He's hot."

"Hotter than myself?" I said.

"Oh, yes," she said. "Of course."

She must have had a thing for slim, handsome guys. How shallow.

"It was written on a computer," I said. "Printed out on paper you can buy at any Staples. No fingerprints that mean anything."

"'Mean anything'?"

"Well, yours are on it, and Gary's and Beth's, and mine," I said. "That's because we handled it. There are no unaccounted-for prints."

"Oh."

She thought about it for a while.

Then she said, "So how do you solve a crime like this?"

"You don't always," I said.

"But, I mean, how would you even go about it?" she said. "There's, like, no clues."

"You talk to people," I said. "You ask them questions. You listen to their answers. You compare what they said

to what other people have said. You try to assess body language. You try to listen for tone."

"Is that what you're doing now?" Estelle said.

"Yes."

"How am I doing?" she said.

"You're not telling me anything, but it is sort of enjoyable to study your body language."

"Enjoyable?"

"It's a dandy body," I said.

"Oh," she said. "Thank you."

"You don't really think I did it?" she said.

"I don't think," I said. "I just ask questions and listen to answers and study bodies."

"I'll bet you think," Estelle said.

"Mostly about sex and baseball," I said. "How's Beth?"

"I am not interested in baseball," she said, and looked at me sideways again.

"Good to know," I said. "How's Beth?"

Estelle's face became serious.

"Poor thing," Estelle said. "She's devastated."

I nodded.

"Devastated," I said.

"Yes, to have your husband murdered?" Estelle said. "You don't think that's devastating?"

"Never had a husband," I said.

"She's staying with us for a while," Estelle said.

"'Us'?"

"Me and Gary," Estelle said.

"You and Gary and Beth," I said.

"You have a problem with that?"

I shook my head.

"Not my problem," I said.

She frowned, though it seemed to me that she was careful that it be a pretty frown.

"It's nobody's problem," she said. "Unless you're some kind of mossback puritan."

"Goddamn," I said. "You've seen through my disguise."

Chapter

❖

50

BETH AND GARY and Estelle?" Susan said.

We were having coffee in her kitchen on a Monday morning, before she went to work.

"So it seems," I said.

Susan was in her understated tailored suit, working attire that did its best to conceal the fact that she was gorgeous. Her makeup was quiet; her hair was neat. She wore very little jewelry. And she remained gorgeous.

"If I weren't a sophisticated psychotherapist with advanced degrees from Harvard, I might be faintly shocked," she said.

"They didn't do three-ways in Swampscott?" I said.

"When I was in high school," Susan said, "I doubt that anyone in town knew what a three-way was."

"We're not in high school anymore, Toto," I said.

"Did they know in Laramie?" Susan said. "When you were a kid?"

"Of course," I said.

"Truly?" Susan said.

"Two heifers and a seed bull," I said.

"I sometimes forget you're a man of the West," Susan said.

"Howdy."

Susan smiled. She was eating half of a whole-wheat bagel. I settled for several cinnamon donuts.

"Could you perform in a three-way?" Susan said.

"Two women and me?"

"For instance," Susan said.

"Maybe," I said. "You?"

"No," Susan said. "How about two men and a woman?"

"No," I said.

"Me, either," Susan said.

"So," I said. "Lucky we found each other."

She smiled.

"It has been my experience that at least one member of a threesome is uncomfortable with the deal," Susan said.

"So why do it?" I said.

"To please one, or both, of the other partners," Susan said. "To convince oneself of one's liberation and openness, fear of being a prude."

"Vive la prudery," I said.

Susan nodded.

"You think it can sometimes work?" I said.

"Yes," Susan said. "I think people can often successfully be in a functioning relationship with two other people. You know, that sort of traditional European thing. Husband, wife, and husband's mistress . . . or wife's lover . . . or all of the above."

"Ménage à trois?" I said.

Susan shrugged.

"That seems to be Gary and the girls," I said.

Susan nodded.

"What do you think?" I said.

"I would have more hope for it if there was some separation," she said.

"Gary lives with one and visits the other?" I said.

"Or all three live separately," Susan said. "Despite what people say, and even believe, if they are genuinely invested in someone, it is more difficult to share that person with another than they expect."

"So it works better if you don't have to have your nose rubbed in it, so to speak," I said.

"Yes."

"Do you think it's healthy?" I said.

"Healthy is harder to pin down than it seems," Susan said.

She had slid into her professional mode—probably the suit.

"I know a number of people who maintain a happy and productive life with two partners, not under the same roof."

"Think it'll work for Gary and friends?" I said.

"There's something exploitive going on there, I think," Susan said.

"I think so, too," I said. "So?"

"No," Susan said.

"Think we should try it?"

"Who would the other guy be?" Susan said.

"Woman," I said.

"We can't even decide who'd have the extra lover," Susan said.

I nodded.

"How about neither?" I said.

Susan sipped her coffee, and put down her cup, and carefully blotted her lips with her napkin. Then she looked at me and smiled widely. I put my right hand up, and she high-fived me.

"There you go," she said.

Chapter

❖❖

51

BELSON AND I sat in Belson's car outside a Dunkin' Donuts on Gallivan Boulevard, drinking coffee and browsing a box of assorted donuts. I preferred the plain ones. Belson liked the ones with strawberry frosting and sprinkles.

"What kind of sissy eats strawberry-frosted donuts?" I said.

"With jimmies," Belson said.

"I had too much respect for you," I said, "even to mention the jimmies."

"Thanks," Belson said. "My poetic side."

"Um," I said.

"You know that Jackson's widow has moved in with your boy Goran?"

"And his girlfriend," I said.

"What the fuck is that about?" Belson said.

"Love?" I said.

Belson looked at me as if I had just spit up.

"They did the will," Belson said. "She is now worth eighty million, seven hundred, and twenty-three bucks."

"More or less," I said.

"That's the number they gave me," Belson said. "I assume it's rounded to the nearest dollar."

"Might explain why Estelle and Gary have welcomed her into their home," I said.

"But why does she want to go?" Belson said.

"Why do most people do anything?" I said.

"Love or money, or variations on either," Belson said.

"She don't seem to need money," I said.

"So we're back to love," Belson said.

"But you don't like it," I said.

"I don't see that broad doing anything for love," Belson said.

"You don't like Beth?" I said.

"I think she killed her husband," Belson said.

"Not herself," I said.

"No, but there's people who'll do anything you need if you have money."

"She didn't have it until her husband died," I said.

"So maybe she got a trusting hit guy," Belson said.

"Like who?" I said.

Belson shrugged.

"Don't know any trusting hit guys," he said.

We were quiet. Belson ate the last strawberry-frosted.

"Love and money," he said.

"Or sex and money," I said.

"Same thing," Belson said.

"You think they took it out in trade?" I said.

"It's what she's got," Belson said.

"And it's gotten her this far," I said.

"So it's a theory," Belson said.

He found a chocolate-cream donut under a cinnamon one, and took it out from under and dusted off the accidental cinnamon and took a careful bite. The donut had a squishy filling, and Belson was very neat.

"She know anybody would kill somebody?" Belson said.

"Her husband did," I said. "She probably met some. She knew Boo and Zel."

"I'll keep it in mind," Belson said.

"Doesn't explain why she's living with Gary and Estelle," I said.

"Nope," Belson said.

I located the cinnamon donut that Belson had put aside in favor of chocolate cream. We ate silently for a moment.

"We don't have any idea what we're doing," I said.

"No," Belson said. "We don't seem to."

Chapter

52

I OPENED THE BPD FOLDER on Beth. She had been born Elizabeth Boudreau in a shabby little town on the Merrimack River, east of Proctor. She was thirty-six. In the month she graduated from Tarbridge High School, she married a guy name Boley LaBonte, and divorced him a year later.

Nobody was paying me to do anything. On the other hand, no one was paying me to do nothing, either. Business was slow. I was nosy. And I had kind of a bad feeling about this long-running mess I'd wandered into and hadn't done a hell of a lot to improve. So I got my car from the alley where I had a deal with the meter maids, and headed north from Boston on a very nice February day with the temperature above freezing and stuff melting gently.

You enter Tarbridge on a two-lane highway from the south. The town is basically three unpainted cinder-block buildings and a red light. A few clapboard houses, some with paint, dwindle away from the cinder block. Up a hill past the red light, maybe a half-mile away, stood a regal-looking redbrick high school. The fact that Tarbridge had a municipal identity was stretching it a bit. That it had a high school was jaw-dropping. It had to be a regional school. But why they had located a regional high school in Tarbridge could only have to do with available land, or, of course, graft.

The town clerk was a fat woman with a red face and a tight perm. She had her offices in a trailer attached to one of the cinder-block buildings. The plastic nameplate on her desk said she was Mrs. Estevia Root.

I handed her my card, and she studied it through some pink-rimmed glasses with rhinestones on them, which hung around her neck on what appeared to be a cut-down shoelace.

"What do ya wanna see Mrs. Boudreau for?" the clerk said.

"I'm investigating a case," I said. "In Boston."

"Boston?"

"Uh-huh."

"What the hell are you doing up here?"

"Just background stuff," I said. "Where would I find Mrs. Boudreau."

"Probably in her kitchen, where she usually is."

"And where is the kitchen located?"

"Back of the house," Estevia said.

I nodded happily.

"And the house?" I said.

"Passed it on the way in, if you come from Boston," Estevia said. "'Bout a hundred yards back, be on your right heading out. Kinda run-down, looks empty, but she'll be in there."

I felt a chill. If Estevia thought it looked run-down . . .

"Did you happen to know her daughter?" I said. "Beth?"

"She run off long time ago, and no loss," Estevia said.

"No loss?"

"Best she was gone, 'fore she dragged half the kids in town down with her."

"Bad girl?" I said.

Estevia's mouth became a thin, hard line. Her round face seemed to plane into angles.

"Yes," she said.

"Bad how?" I said.

"Just bad," Estevia said.

It was all I was going to get from Estevia.

"Thank you for your time," I said.

Chapter

❖❖

53

I T WAS A very small house. It not only looked empty, it looked like it should be empty. There wasn't enough paint left on the front to indicate what color it might once have been. The roofline was bowed. The windows were closed and dirty. Something that might once have been curtains hung in tattered disarray in the windows.

I parked and went to the front door. There was no path shoveled. The uncut weeds of summer, now long dead, stuck up through the diminishing snow. There was no doorknob, and the hole where there had been one was plugged with a rag. I knocked. No one answered. I pushed on the door. It didn't move. I'm not sure it was locked; it was more likely just warped shut.

I went around to the side of the house and found

what might be a kitchen door. There was a screen door and an inner door. The screening had torn loose and was curled up along one side. The inner door had a glass window that was so grimy, I couldn't see through it. I knocked.

From inside somebody croaked, "Go 'way."

It didn't sound welcoming, but I figured the somebody didn't really mean it, so I opened the inside door and stepped in. She looked like a huge sack of soiled laundry, slouched inertly at the kitchen table, drinking Pastene port wine from a small jelly glass with cartoon pictures on it. The table was covered with linoleum whose color and design were long since lost. There were pots and dishes in the soapstone sink, piles of newspapers and magazines in various corners. A small television with rabbit ears was playing jaggedly. The scripted conviviality and canned laughter was eerie in the desperate room. A black iron stove stood against the far wall, and the room reeked of kerosene and heat.

"Mrs. Boudreau?" I said.

"Go 'way," she croaked again.

She was very fat, wearing some sort of robe or housedress. It was hard to tell, and in truth, I didn't look very closely.

"My name is Spenser," I said, and handed her a card. She didn't take it, so I put it on the table.

"You're Elizabeth Boudreau's mother," I said.

Her glass was empty. She picked up the bottle of port

with both hands and carefully poured it into the jelly glass. She put the bottle down carefully, and picked up the glass carefully with both hands and sipped the port. Then she looked at me as if I hadn't spoken.

"Could you tell me a little about Elizabeth?" I said.

"Elizabeth."

"Your daughter."

"Gone," the woman said.

"Elizabeth's gone?"

Mrs. Boudreau nodded.

"Long time," she said.

"What can you tell me about her?" I said.

"Bitch," her mother said.

I nodded. If Beth was thirty-six, this woman was probably sixty, maybe younger. She looked older than Angkor Wat.

"Why bitch?" I said.

"Whore."

This wasn't going terribly well.

"How about Mr. Boudreau?" I said.

She drank port and stared at me.

"He around?" I said.

"No."

"Dead?"

"Don't know."

"Can you tell me anything about him?" I said.

"Bastard," she said.

"Could you tell me where to find him?"

"No."

I had hung around in this reeking trash bin as long as I could stand it. There was nothing I could find out that would be worth staying any longer.

"Thank you," I said, and turned and went out.

I took in some big breaths as I walked to my car. The air felt clean.

Chapter

❖❖

54

BOLEY LABONTE OWNED a bowling alley and lounge called Kingpin Lanes, which sat in the middle of a big parking lot on South Tarbridge Road. There were two pickups and an old Buick sedan parked outside. Inside, four guys were bowling together. In the lounge three other guys were sitting at the bar, drinking beer and watching a woman with few clothes on dancing at a brass pole to music I neither recognized nor liked. It was two o'clock in the afternoon.

I sat at the bar and ordered a beer. The bartender was a red-haired woman with an angular face and skin you could strike a match on.

"Boley around?" I said.

"Who wants to know?" the bartender said.

I gave her my card, the understated one, where my name was not spelled out in bullet holes. She looked at it.

"A freaking private eye?" she said.

"Exactly," I said.

"Why you want to talk with Boley?"

"None of your business," I said.

"Yeah, I guess not," she said, and took the card and walked down to the end of the bar and ducked under, which was not easy given how tight her jeans were. She opened a door marked *Office* and went in; a moment later she came out and ducked back behind the bar.

"Boley says he'll be right out," she said.

I nodded and sipped my beer. The girl on the pole was a kid, maybe eighteen, nineteen, looking deadly serious, starting her long climb to stardom. A man came out of the office and walked down the bar and sat on the stool next to me.

"How ya doin'," he said. "I'm Boley LaBonte."

We shook hands.

"I'm looking into a case involving Elizabeth Boudreau," I said. "I understand you were married to her."

He had dark, curly hair, worn sort of long and brushed back. He had a thin mustache. His flowered shirt was unbuttoned to his sternum, showing a hairy chest and a gold chain. The material of the shirt stretched a little tight over his biceps.

"That was a trip," he said.

"What can you tell me about her?" I said.

"Jesus," he said, and looked at the bartender. "Mavis, gimme a Coke."

She put it in front of him, and he drank some and looked at my beer bottle.

"You okay?" he said.

I said I was.

"Beth Boudreau," he said. "I heard she's doing good."

"Married money," I said.

"Good for her," Boley said. "You know anything about where she come from?"

"I talked with her mother this morning," I said.

"Alberta?" Boley said. "She still alive?"

"Sort of," I said. "Is there a Mr. Boudreau?"

"Nope," Boley said. "Never was. Alberta got knocked up."

"Jesus," I said.

"Yeah," Boley said. "Hard to think about."

I nodded.

"Anyway," Boley said. "Alberta Boudreau was always fat and homely, and my old man says never had a date. Then one day she comes up pregnant. It was a joke in town, Alberta was one for one, you know?"

"Who was the father?"

"Don't know. Nobody seems to," he said.

He drank some more Coke.

"This ain't Boston," he said. "Or Cambridge. Every-

body's like shocked back, what? Thirty-six years ago, something like that. But goddamn, Alberta has the kid. Everybody thought she had it to prove she'd gotten laid."

"Could be other reasons," I said.

"Could be," Boley said.

He finished his Coke, and the bartender delivered a second one without being asked.

"How they get along?" I said.

"Beth and her mother?" Boley said. "Don't know. Don't know anybody was ever in the house."

"I was," I said.

Boley made a face.

"I don't want to know," he said.

"No," I said. "You don't. How about school. Beth catch any grief about all this in school?"

"I dunno. I'm ten years older than her. But . . ." He drank some Coke. "You know how school is."

"I do," I said. "How'd you meet her?"

"She was working the pole here," Boley said. "At the time, I'm the bouncer. Used to box a little—Golden Gloves and stuff." He shrugged. "Good enough for here."

"And now you own it," I said.

"Yeah," Boley said. "Guy owned it was a lush, he was going under. My old man died, left me a little insurance dough. I got it cheap."

"Great country," I said.

Boley was looking at me.

"You used to fight," he said. "Am I right?"

"Yep."

"It's the nose, mostly," Boley said. "And around the eyes. Ever fight pro?"

"Yep."

"Heavy?"

"Uh-huh."

"You good?" Boley said.

"I was good," I said. "Not great."

"So you was never gonna be champ," Boley said.

"No."

"But I bet you ain't lost many on the street," Boley said.

"Not many," I said.

"Thing about boxing," Boley said, "you know. You may not win, but you got a plan."

I nodded.

"And," Boley said, "when you box, you learn that getting hit ain't the end of the fucking world."

I nodded again.

"Just another day at the office," I said.

He grinned. We were quiet for a time, watching the girl making love to the brass pole.

"Beth was like that kid," Boley said. "She come here thinking she was a performer, you know? Thinking this was her ticket out of Palookaville."

"But it wasn't," I said.

"Not from dancing," he said.

"You sleep with her?" I said.

"Course," Boley said. The bartender brought him another Coke. "Sleep with them all, part of the deal. I hire 'em to strip for the customers and fuck the owner." He grinned. "Which is me."

"You sleeping with this kid?" I said.

"Sure."

"How old is she?"

"She's eighteen," Boley said. "Gotta be eighteen to do this, and I'm careful about that."

"Any of the dancers freelance with the clients?"

"On their own time," he said. "Not on mine. Don't look like much now, but most nights we're jumping. It's a nice business for me. I'm not gonna hire anybody underage. I'm not gonna serve anybody underage. I'm not gonna allow no soliciting on my premises."

I nodded.

"You still bouncing?" I said.

He shook his head.

"I hire it done now," he said.

"How was the marriage?"

He shrugged.

"She was hot enough," he said. "And she tried to be nice to me. I mean, I was not only her husband, I was her income, you know?"

"She still, ah, dance?"

"No, I wouldn't tolerate that when she was married to me."

"Propriety," I said.

"Whatever. But the thing I always knew was she didn't like me. It was . . . she liked to fuck me, but she resented the rest of it. And man, did she have a temper. Come a point it would blow and she couldn't control it."

"That why you divorced?" I said.

"Nope."

"Why'd you divorce?" I said.

"She was fucking other people," he said. "I cut her loose."

I nodded.

"You know where she went next?" I said.

"Nope."

"You get married again?"

"Yep. Nice woman. I didn't meet her here. Two daughters. Nice house in Andover," he said.

"Your wife understand the arrangement with the strippers?" I said.

Boley grinned at me.

"Don't ask," he said. "Don't tell."

The music stopped. The kid on the pole stopped dancing and, wearing only a G-string, walked unself-consciously off the stage.

"At night the G-string goes," Boley said. "But I ain't

wasting it in the middle of the afternoon on a couple shitkickers in down vests."

"It's a hard life," I said.

"It is, and most of them are too stupid to do anything else," he said.

"Hard for Beth," I said.

"Hard for everybody," Boley said. "You need to be tough if you're gonna get anywhere."

"And smart," I said.

"Yeah," Boley said. "That helps."

"You think Beth was smart?" I said.

"She was tough, okay," he said. "But she didn't know much."

"You can be smart and not know much," I said.

He nodded and drank some Coke.

"Smartest broad I ever fucked," he said.

And that in itself must be some kind of fame.

Chapter

❖❖

55

THIS ONE GOT Quirk's interest. He stood with Belson and me, looking down at the body of Estelle, face-down near the edge of the Frog Pond in the Common.

"According to the contents of her purse," Belson said, "her name is Estelle Gallagher. And she works at Pinnacle, where she is a certified physical trainer."

"Appears to be the same Estelle," I said.

She had been shot by someone who had apparently put the gun right up against the back of her head. She'd been shot twice. The second time probably as she lay face-down on the ground. One of the bullets had exited her face somewhere in the area of her nose, and it rendered a visual ID problematic. The three of us looked down at her in the harsh light of the crime-scene lamps. It made

everything bright enough so that the crime-scene people could scoot about with cameras and tape measures and brushes and powders, and various kits containing nothing I understood. Several Boston cops, of lesser rank than Quirk, were going over the area foot by foot.

"Estelle Gallagher," I said. "Never knew her last name."

"Don't look Irish," Quirk said.

"No disgrace to it," I said.

"Not now," Quirk said.

He turned and walked to where a uniformed guy was standing with Gary and Beth. I followed him. Beth was holding on to Gary's arm with both of hers. She was crying.

"I'm sorry for your loss," Quirk said.

"It's terrible," Beth said.

Gary looked dazed.

"Do you have any thoughts on who or why?" Quirk said.

"No," Beth said, and cried some more.

"You, sir?" Quirk said to Gary.

He shook his head slowly.

"No one had any reason to do this to Estelle," he said.

His voice was flat and not very loud. He looked as if Beth's clutch on his arm was weighing him down.

"She lived with you two," Quirk said pleasantly.

"Yes," Beth said. "She was a friend."

"She was my girlfriend," Gary said in the same affect-less voice. "Been my girlfriend a long time."

Quirk didn't say anything.

"When's the last time you saw her?" he said. "Either of you?"

They looked at each other as if to compare notes.

"This morning," Gary said. Beth nodded. "Before she went to the club. I was having some breakfast with her. Beth was still in, weren't you?"

"Yes," she said, still sniffling. "But I heard you talking. I actually last *saw* her last night before I went to bed."

Quirk nodded and looked at Belson.

"Frank," he said. "We got a time of death yet?"

"Nope."

"Okay, get a statement from these folks, and when the time of death is established, see if they got an alibi."

"Alibi?" Beth said. "You think one of us would do this?"

"Course not," Quirk said. "But it would be comforting to know you couldn't have."

He jerked his head at me and walked away.

When we were far enough away to talk, he said, "What's this fucking threesome?"

"You may have nailed it," I said.

"A fucking threesome?"

"Yeah."

"And they all knew about each other?"

"I think so," I said.

"I'm not sure any of the nuns at Saint Anthony's told me about this," he said.

"Probably not," I said.

"First her husband, now her, ah, roommate. I was this Eisenhower guy, I'd be a little careful walking around with old Beth."

"Or she with him," I said.

"Or she with him," Quirk said. "Tell me what you know."

Which I did.

Chapter

56

"WE IN A MARRIOT HOTEL," Hawk said. "In Burlington fucking Massachusetts."

We were in a new restaurant called Summer Winter.

"Susan says it's great," I said.

Susan smiled at him and nodded. Hawk looked around the room.

"Don't see no brothers," Hawk said.

"I know," Susan said.

They grinned at each other. Sometimes they communicated on levels even I didn't quite get. Hawk looked at me.

"What you know from the po-lice," he said.

"Gun killed Estelle was the same as the gun that killed Jackson," I said.

"Thing keeps getting more incestuous," Hawk said. "Don't it."

"It do," I said.

The waitress brought our drink order. She was pleasant to all of us. Though she was, perhaps, a little extra-pleasant to Hawk.

Hawk sipped from his margarita.

"Beth and Eisenhower got an alibi?" he said.

I nodded.

"They were together at some sort of fund-raiser cocktail party at The Langham Hotel," I said. "Twenty people saw them."

"Too bad," Hawk said.

"You think they're involved?" Susan said.

"Ah is just a poor simple bad guy," Hawk said, "trying to get along. Ask the dee-tective."

"Who else is there?" I said.

"Couldn't it be a party or parties unknown?" Susan said.

"Sure," I said. "But on the assumption of same gun, same shooter, they would need to be connected to both Estelle and Jackson."

"They have alibis for both," Susan said.

"Rock-solid," I said. "For both."

Susan guzzled nearly a full gram of her martini.

"Suppose," I said, "that someone you knew was murdered yesterday evening, and the cops asked you for an alibi."

"I washed my hair," Susan said. "Took a bath, put on some night cream, and got in bed with Pearl and watched a movie on HBO."

"And if they asked what movie, and could you remember the plot?"

"I could tell them that, but the movie has been running all month on my cable system," Susan said.

"So Pearl is basically your alibi," I said.

"Hawk?" I said.

"There be a young woman . . ." Hawk said.

"Of course there was," I said.

I drank some of my short scotch and soda.

"Last night I had a couple of cocktails," I said. "Made supper, ate it, and watched the first half of the Celtics game before I fell asleep."

"So you don't even have Pearl," Susan said.

"I don't," I said.

"So you're saying that people often don't have any way to prove where they were of an evening, and these people have two ironclad alibis."

"That's what I'm saying."

"Most people," Susan said. She looked at Hawk. "Except maybe for the man with the golden lance, here . . ."

"Black opal," Hawk said.

Susan nodded.

"Except for the man with the black-opal lance," she said. "Most people could go days at a time with no alibi except for whomever they live with."

"And," Hawk said. "If they both under suspicion . . ."

"The alibi is suspect," Susan said.

"Sorta," I said.

"You think they hired a third party?" Susan said.

"Yes."

"Both of them?" Susan said.

"I don't know," I said.

"Beth surely could not have escaped such a childhood unscathed," Susan said.

"Nobody do," Hawk said.

"She had somebody do Jackson," I said. "She'd get his money."

"She have somebody do Estelle," Susan said. "Beth would get Eisenhower."

"She don't get Jackson's money until somebody kills him," Hawk said. "How'd she pay."

I looked at him for a moment.

"Oh," Hawk said. "Yeah."

"What?" Susan said.

"She started out broke," I said. "How'd she pay her way this far?"

Susan was silent for a moment.

Then she said, "Oh. The, ah, barter system."

Our food came, and we ate some. Susan looked at Hawk.

"Well," she said.

Hawk nodded.

"Okay," he said. "You're right."

"Thank you," Susan said.

She looked at me.

"So if it were Beth, and if she were hiring somebody to kill her husband, and Estelle, and taking it out in trade, who would she hire? Who does she know that she could hire?"

"Eisenhower's been in jail," I said. "Husband was on both sides of legitimate. She might know a lot of people, or she might know one who could broker the deal."

"She know Zel and Boo," Hawk said. "She know Tony Marcus."

"Ty-Bop?" I said.

"He don't freelance," Hawk said.

"Not even for love?" Susan said.

Hawk smiled at her.

"Ty-Bop don't know nothing 'bout love."

"Junior?" I said.

"Ain't a shooter," Hawk said.

"Probably knows how," I said.

"Maybe. You looking in that direction, I think you got to look at Tony. He tell Ty-Bop to shoot you. Ty-Bop will shoot you. He tell Junior to break your back. Junior will break your back. But gun work is Ty-Bop. And strong-arm is Junior. He don't ask one to do the other man specialty. And they don't do anything unless Tony tells them to. It's a matter of respect."

"You understand that?" Susan said to me.

"Yes," I said.

"But if Tony wanted Ty-Bop to shoot someone for love?"

"Ty-Bop do it," Hawk said.

"Does Tony know about love?" Susan said.

"Loves his daughter," Hawk said.

"So he's a possibility," Susan said.

"Yep," I said.

"But if you rule him out, you also rule out Ty-Bop and Junior," Susan said.

"Yep."

"How about this man Zel?" Susan said.

"Maybe," I said.

"Boo?"

"Hard to imagine Beth seducing any of these people," I said.

"Remember how far she's come, and how she got here," Susan said.

"You're saying she could?"

"If she needed to," Susan said.

"Could you?" I said.

"If I needed to," Susan said.

"Egad," I said.

Chapter

❖

57

Tony Marcus came into my office wearing a double-breasted camel-hair coat and a Borsalino hat. Ty-Bop jangled in beside him and stood not quite motionless near the door.

"Arnold say you wanted to see me," Tony said.

He unbuttoned his coat, took his hat off, and put it on my desk, and sat down in front of me.

"I didn't know you still made house calls," I said.

"In the neighborhood," Tony said. "Going to have lunch with my daughter."

"Give her my best," I said.

"Sure," Tony said. "What you want?"

"You know Chet Jackson got whacked," I said.

Tony nodded.

"Couple days ago a woman named Estelle Gallagher got clipped with the same gun killed Jackson," I said.

Tony nodded.

"You keep track," I said.

"I do," Tony said.

"They're both connected with Gary Eisenhower," I said.

"Uh-huh."

Ty-Bop was studying the picture of Pearl that stood on top of a file cabinet just to the left of Susan's. I would have studied Susan had I been he, but Ty-Bop was mysterious.

"And Beth Jackson," I said.

"Uh-huh."

"You had any dealings with them since Jackson's office?" I said.

"You think one of them done the killings?" Tony said.

"They both have solid alibis," I said. "For both killings."

Tony smoothed his mustache with his left hand and nodded.

"Remarkable," he said.

"That's what I thought," I said.

"So you figured one or both contracted it out," Tony said.

"Maybe," I said.

"And you figure who they know might do it?"

"Yep."

"And you thought of me," Tony said.

"One possibility," I said.

Tony sat back in his chair and smoothed his mustache again. After a while he smiled.

"Yeah," he said. "We talked."

"How'd she get hold of you?"

"She called," Tony said. "Talk with Arnold."

"How'd she know where to call?" I said.

"Her husband had a number," he said.

"So the cops must have stopped by," I said.

"They did," Tony said. "I'm used to cops. Didn't tell them nothing. They didn't know nothing. They went away."

"What did Beth want?"

"She say she saw me in her husband's office that day and she thought I was very 'interesting.'" Tony grinned. "Say she want to see me."

"And?"

"And I say sure," Tony said.

"So you did," I said.

"Yep. Fucked her about sixteen times."

"Nice for you," I said.

Tony grinned.

"She enthusiastic," he said.

"But you didn't elope," I said.

"Nope, after we been fucking for a week or so, she say she need a favor."

"I'm shocked," I said.

"Yeah, I was surprised it took a week," Tony said. "Said she wanted somebody to ace her old man and could I help."

"And you said?"

"No."

"How'd she take that?"

"Not well. She say after all we meant to each other. And I say, 'I got nothing against your old man.' And she said, 'But don't you love me?' And I say no. And we go on like that. And finally I have Arnold take her out and drive her home."

"Give her a referral?"

"Hell, no," Tony said. "I put some people down, will again. But I did it 'cause it needed to be done. Not 'cause some broad bops me for a week."

"She have any other candidates?" I said.

"To pull the trigger for her?" Tony said. "There must have been one."

"But you have no idea?" I said.

"None."

"You have any sense that Eisenhower was involved?"

"Nope."

"Or that he wasn't?" I said.

"Nope."

I nodded. We were quiet. Ty-Bop had stopped looking at the picture of Pearl and was now, as best I could determine, looking at nothing I could identify. Tony

picked up his hat, put it on, stood, and buttoned up his coat.

"You owe me," he said.

"But who keeps track," I said.

"Me," Tony said.

He nodded at Ty-Bop, who went out of the office first. Tony followed. They didn't close the door behind them. But that was okay. It created sort of a welcoming image. I was a friendly guy. Might be good for business.

Chapter

.... ❖❖ ....

58

VINNIE MORRIS WAS a middle-sized ordinary-looking guy who could shoot the tail off a buffalo nickel from fifty yards. We weren't exactly friends, but I'd known him since he walked behind Joe Broz, and while he wasn't all that much fun, he was good at what he did. He kept his word. And he didn't say much.

We were in my car, parked at a hydrant on Beacon Street beside the Public Garden, across the street from where Beth lived with Gary Eisenhower.

"Her name's Beth Jackson," I said. "We'll sit here and watch. If she comes out and gets in a car, we'll tail her. If she comes out and starts walking, you'll tail her."

"'Cause she knows you," Vinnie said.

"Yes."

Vinnie nodded.

"And that's it?" he said. "You want me to follow this broad around, tell you what I see?"

"Yep."

"I don't have to clip her?"

"No," I said.

"I don't like to clip no broad, I don't have to," Vinnie said.

"You won't have to," I said.

He looked at her picture.

"Nice head," he said.

"Yep."

"How long we gonna do this?" Vinnie said.

"Don't know."

"She takes a car and I just ride around with you," Vinnie said.

"Correct," I said.

"Okay," he said.

"You care why we're tailing her?" I said.

"Nope."

One of Vinnie's great charms was that he had no interest in any information he didn't need. We sat with Beth for several days. Mostly she walked. So mostly I stayed in the car and Vinnie hoofed it.

"She goes to Newbury Street," Vinnie said. "Meets different broads. They shop. They have lunch. Today it was in the café at Louis."

"Must be an adventure for you," I said.

"Yeah. I thought Louis was a men's store."

"All genders," I said.

"You buy stuff there?"

"Don't have my size," I said.

"Got my size," Vinnie said.

"See anything you like?" I said.

"Most of it looks kinda funny," Vinnie said.

"That's called stylish," I said.

"Not by me," Vinnie said.

"She spot you?"

Vinnie stared at me.

"Nobody spots me, I don't want to be spotted," Vinnie said.

"I don't know what I was thinking," I said.

We did that for most of a week, with Vinnie doing all the legwork and me twaddling in the car. On a white, dripping, above-freezing Friday in late February, I called it quits.

"You stick with her till I call you off," I said to Vinnie. "Or you can't stand it anymore. You don't need me. She's obviously a walking girl."

"I won't get sick of it," Vinnie said. "I like looking at her ass."

"Motivation is good," I said.

Vinnie got out of the car, and I drove home.

Chapter

················· ◆◆ ·················

59

G ARY EISENHOWER came to see me. I was in my
office with my feet up, listening to some Anita
O'Day songs on my office computer and thinking
lightly.

"Who's the broad singing," Gary said when he came
in.

"Anita O'Day," I said.

"I need to talk," he said.

I turned Anita off and swiveled my full attention to
him.

"Go," I said.

He sat in one of my client chairs.

"I . . ."

He shifted a little and crossed one leg over the other.

"I . . . I feel really bad," he said. "About Estelle."

I nodded.

"And I . . . I . . . I got no one else to talk to about it," he said.

"Happy to be the one," I said.

"I mean, I been with Estelle for, like, ten years," Gary said.

"Long time," I said.

"I . . . I cared about her."

"Through all the philandering" I said.

"Sure, I told you. She liked it, too. We were in that together."

I nodded.

"For crissake, who would want to kill Estelle," Gary said.

I shook my head. I wanted to go where he wanted to. I suspected he was circling it. He shifted in his chair and crossed his legs in the other direction. He tapped out a little drumbeat on his thighs for a moment.

"The thing is," he said. "The thing that kills me is . . . did I do something to cause this?"

I looked interested.

"I mean," he said, "did I, like . . . did I bring her into contact with someone who would kill her?"

I waited. He didn't say anything else. I waited some more. He interlocked his fingers and worked his hands back and forth. Clarice Richardson had been wrong, I thought. Gary was not devoid of something like a moral

269

or ethical sense. Whatever it quite was, it was nagging at him now. He looked at me. The sense had apparently taken him as far as it was going to. Probably wasn't a very robust sense to begin with.

"I mean, why would someone kill her?" he said again.

"Money," I said. "Love and the stuff that goes with it."

"What stuff?" he said.

"Passion, jealousy, and hate," I said.

"Estelle didn't like Beth living with us," Gary said.

I nodded.

"I mean, she did at first," he said. "You know, she liked the money, and the truth of it is, she liked the three-way for a while."

"And you said you liked it okay," I said.

He smiled briefly, and for a moment the old Gary shone through.

"Hell," he said. "I like everything."

"Beth like the three-way?" I said.

He looked startled.

"Beth?" he said.

"Uh-huh."

"She never said she didn't," he said.

"So why didn't Estelle like Beth living there?" I said.

"I don't know," Gary said. "I mean, women are a pretty weird species."

"One of the two weirdest," I said.

Gary looked blank. Then he kind of shook it off.

"Anyway, Estelle started saying stuff like Beth was getting too bossy, and how we couldn't get any privacy."

"She say that to Beth?"

"I don't think so," Gary said. "She said it to me quite a bit toward the end. But I never heard her talk to Beth about it."

"You say anything to Beth?" I said.

"Me? No. I learned a long time ago to stay out of a catfight."

"You think Beth might have killed Estelle so she could have you to herself?" I said.

"We was at the big Community Servings event, at the Langham," Gary said. "Cops told us when she died. Beth couldn'ta done it."

He said it too fast. Like he'd rehearsed it.

"The Hotel Langham affair your idea?" I said.

"Me? No. Beth wanted to go. Said she knew a lotta people went to it. Said she wanted them to see her boyfriend."

"You say anything about being Estelle's boyfriend?"

"Hell," Gary said. And there was no bravado in his voice. "I'm everybody's boyfriend."

"And Estelle's dead," I said.

Gary didn't speak. He nodded his head slowly, and as he did, tears began to well in his eyes.

Chapter

60

Hawk came to my place to babysit Pearl, and Susan went with me to New York for fun. We stopped for a tongue sandwich at Rein's deli on the way down. I made several amusing tongue remarks while we ate, which Susan said were disgusting. That night we stayed uptown at The Carlyle, had dinner at Café Boulud, and went to bed before midnight.

I was prepared for several hours of wild abandon when I got into bed. But by the time Susan got through with her nocturnal ablutions, I had nodded off. I woke up in the morning with Susan's head on my chest. I shifted a little so I could look at her. She opened her eyes and we looked at each other. She moved a little so we were facing.

"You've always been an early riser," Susan said.

"Is that a double entendre?" I said.

"I think so," Susan said.

"Shall we take advantage of it?" I said.

"Right after we shower and brush our teeth," Susan said.

"By then it may be too late," I said.

She smiled. And got out of bed.

"Not you and me, big boy," she said. "For us it's never too late."

"How come you sleep in sweatpants and a T-shirt?" I said.

She smiled again.

"So that when I take them off," she said, "the contrast makes me look really good."

"It works," I said.

"Yes," she said, and went into the bathroom and turned on the shower.

A half-hour later we were both back in bed, clean of body and mouth. When Susan made love she went deep inside someplace. She didn't withdraw. It was just the intensity of her focus that rendered everything except the lovemaking irrelevant. I liked to look at her then, her eyes closed, her face perfectly still, calm in contrast to what we both were feeling and doing. The event was busy enough so I couldn't look for very long, but when we were done and I was looking down at her, after a time she opened her eyes and looked at me and I could

see her slowly refocusing, swimming back to the surface from wherever she had been. It was always a moment like no other.

"You lookin' at me," Susan said in a surprisingly good De Niro impression.

"Sex is a complicated thing," I said.

Susan widened her eyes.

"Wow," she said.

"It enhances love," I said. "But not as much as love enhances it."

"You've noticed that," Susan said.

"I have."

"And you may be particularly aware of that interplay these days," Susan said. "Because of this business with Gary Eisenhower and the women."

"I would guess," I said.

Susan and I stayed in eye lock, another moment, then. She smiled.

"Perhaps," she said, "if you would get your two-hundred-something pounds off of my body, I could breathe and we could discuss it over breakfast."

"You were breathing good a little while ago," I said.

"Gasping," Susan said.

"In awe?" I said.

"For breath," she said.

I eased off her and lay on my back beside her, and she put her head on my shoulder.

"I mean, the old jokes are all true. The worst sex I

ever had was very good. But I have never had a sexual experience to compare to making love with you."

"Jewesses are hot," Susan said.

"You are beautiful, and in shape, and skillful, and enthusiastic. But I have been with many other women who fit that description close enough. But nothing to compare with you."

Susan turned her head so that she could look at me.

"There's a saying I read someplace, that appetite is the best sauce," she said.

"Meaning it's not just what you are, it's what I feel you are," I said.

"I would guess," she said, "in truth, that it is finally about what and who we are."

I nodded.

"It's what Gary Eisenhower and his women don't understand, and probably never will," I said.

"It is probably life's essence," Susan said.

I nodded.

"Maybe children, too," I said.

"Maybe," Susan said. "But we're not going to have any."

"This'll have to do," I said.

"It does very well," she said.

She kissed me. I kissed her back.

"I'm thinking pancakes for breakfast," she said.

Chapter

·························◆◆·························

61

WE HAD PANCAKES for breakfast and walked down through Central Park to Bergdorf and Barneys, where Susan shopped and I trailed along to watch her hold stuff up, and admire her and, occasionally, some of the other female shoppers. In the next couple of days, we strolled through the little zoo in Central Park. We had dinner at the Four Seasons and walked through Rockefeller Center and Grand Central Station, which I always liked to do in New York. We experienced life's essence several times before we went home.

Life's essence never disappoints.

It was a Wednesday morning when I got back to my office. There was a call on my answering machine from Vinnie.

"Call me," he said. "I might have something."

I called him on his cell phone.

"Where are you?" I said.

"In the Public Garden," he said, "watching her house."

"What's up?" I said.

"Nothing at the moment, but Monday she had a, like, a incident with a guy."

"Tell me," I said.

"Guy's waiting outside her house when she comes back from her health club. I'm trailing along behind, looking at her ass, and he, like, stops her as she starts up her steps. Puts his hand on her arm. She slaps it away. He says something. She says something. He puts his hand on her arm again. She shoves him away and runs up the steps into her house. He stands down at the foot of the stairs for a long time and looks at her front door. I'm up the street thinking if he tries to go in after her do I shoot him. But he didn't. After a while he walked away."

"It wasn't a friendly exchange," I said.

"No."

"You recognize the guy?"

"No, but he wasn't her type, that's for sure."

"What'd he look like?" I said.

"Big guy, 'bout your size, but, you know, he was walking on his heels."

"Like punch-drunk?" I said. "Like a punch-drunk ex-fighter?"

"Be my guess," Vinnie said. "Looked like a pug, nose was flat, and, you know, thick around the eyes."

"Anybody with him?" I said.

"Nope."

"Where'd he go after she went in and he stared at the door?"

"Walked down Arlington Street. I figured he was heading for the subway."

"You didn't follow him?"

"Nope. You just tole me to watch the broad."

"I did," I said. "Anything else happen?"

"Nope. She stayed in all the rest of the day."

"No sign that she called the cops?" I said.

"None showed up," he said. "This guy shows up again, you want me to shoot him or anything?"

"Only if you have to," I said.

"Okay," Vinnie said.

"I may stop around later and visit Beth," I said.

"Okay," Vinnie said.

"Don't shoot me."

"Okay," Vinnie said.

He sounded disappointed.

Chapter

❖

62

When Beth Jackson came out of Pinnacle Fitness and into the lobby, I was waiting for her.

"Buy you coffee," I said.

She looked at me as if I was something she stepped in.

"I don't want coffee," she said.

"I'll buy you whatever you want," I said.

"I don't want anything," she said.

"Well, here's the thing," I said. "I'm going to keep annoying you until you talk with me for a little while, so why not get it over with now."

"If you continue to annoy me," she said, "I shall call the police."

"Sure," I said. "In the meantime, lemme buy you some coffee and talk with you about Boo."

She stared at me for a moment, then sighed.

"Very well," she said, and stalked ahead of me to the snack bar.

I knew Boo would get her, and if it didn't, it would mean whoever Vinnie saw wasn't Boo. If it was Boo, she would have to talk to me enough to find out what I knew. We ordered coffee.

"What about this Boo person, or whatever Boo is?" she said.

"Boo is the slugger used to work for your husband," I said. "He and a guy named Zel."

The coffee arrived. I added some sugar and took a swallow.

"Oh," she said, "Boo. I hadn't thought of Boo since Chet died."

"Until Monday," I said.

"Monday?"

"Boo stopped you in front of your house. You and he argued. You shoved him and went in. He stayed outside for a while and looked at your door."

She didn't say anything. She looked at me silently for a long time. I let her look. I was interested in what she'd come up with.

Finally she said, "Are you spying on me?"

"Yuh," I said.

"Why?"

"What did Boo want?" I said.

"Boo," she said. "So that's who that was."

"You didn't recognize him," I said.

"No. I mean, I thought he looked familiar, but . . . no."

"And what did he want?" I said.

"Oh, God," she said. "I have no idea. I thought he was some kind of stumblebum, you know? I just wanted him to leave me alone."

I nodded.

"And I object to you lurking around spying."

"Noted," I said.

"Why are you doing that?"

"Got nothing else to do," I said.

"Do you think I'm doing something bad?"

"Are you?" I said.

"Gary and I are just trying to live our lives," she said, "in the midst of terrible tragedy."

"Boo want money?" I said.

"No . . . I don't know. . . . I just wanted to get away from him," she said.

"What's the first thing he said to you?"

Her face got sort of squeezed up. Her cheeks reddened a little.

"I won't talk about this anymore," she said. "I've done nothing wrong, and I won't let you question me as if I have."

She stood up abruptly and walked to the elevator. I watched her go.

Spenser, the grand inquisitor.

Chapter

◆◆

63

ONE OF SPENSER'S RULES for criminal investigation is that most things have two ends. I'd gotten nothing much from Beth's end, so I decided to try the other end, and went out to JP to visit Boo.

Zel was cooking sausage and peppers when I got there, and I sat at the kitchen table and drank a beer he gave me while he cooked.

"Boo ain't here," Zel said.

"Where is he?" I said.

"Out," Zel said.

"What's he doing while he's out?" I said.

"Got me," Zel said.

He moved the peppers and sausage around with a spatula.

"Low heat," Zel said. "Cook it slow. That's the secret."

"He go out much alone?"

Zel looked at me.

"Boo's forty-two years old," he said. "Course he goes out alone."

I nodded.

"You and he doing any business with Beth Jackson?" I said.

"Beth? Chet's wife? No, thank you," Zel said.

"Trouble?" I said.

"With a capital T," Zel said. "And that rhymes with B, and that stands for bitch."

"You don't like Beth," I said.

"Good call," Zel said.

"I'm a trained detective," I said.

"No," Zel said. "I don't like her."

"Because?"

"Because I kind of liked Chet."

"And she cheated on him," I said.

"She didn't give him no respect," Zel said.

I nodded.

"Boo like her?" I said.

Zel looked at me sharply.

"Why?"

"He had a confrontation with her Monday," I said. "Outside her house."

"Shit!" Zel said.

He poured some sherry wine over the sausage and peppers and watched it boil up briefly and then start to cook away. He lowered the heat to simmer, then turned from the stove and went to the refrigerator and got a bottle of beer for himself and another one for me. He put mine on the table in front of me and went and leaned on the counter near the stove. He drank some of his beer and looked at me.

"Boo ain't right," he said. "We both know that."

I nodded.

"But like I said, he's forty-two years old. I try to look out for him, but . . . I can't treat him like a little kid."

"He'd know it?" I said.

"It would be disrespectful," Zel said.

I nodded.

"But . . ."

Zel drank some more beer and checked his cooking.

"But Boo can't do time," Zel said. "He's okay if I'm with him, but if I ain't, he can't stand close places."

"Claustrophobic?" I said.

"Yeah, that's what he is, claustrophobic. 'Less I'm with him, he can't ride an elevator. Can't go in the subway if it's crowded. Has to leave the window open in his room a crack, no matter how cold it is."

"But he's all right if he's with you?"

"Yeah."

"Why are you worried about him doing time?" I said.

Zel checked his cooking again and shut off the heat under his pan.

"You ain't here to sell him magazine subscriptions," Zel said.

"You know why he would be having an argument with Beth Jackson?" I said.

Zel got another beer from the refrigerator. He held one toward me. I shook my head.

"Another thing," Zel said, "about Boo. He gotta be a tough guy. It's all he ever had, being a tough guy."

"And he's not so good at that," I said.

"Not against somebody like you," Zel said. "But for Boo, it almost don't matter if he wins. He gotta fight, you know? He wins, or he shows he can take it. Either way, he gotta be a tough guy."

Zel drank some beer.

"All he got," Zel said. "He does time, he'll be scared, and he can't stand to be scared, so he'll be a tough guy and he'll get hurt bad. Don't matter how tough you are. Inside, they can break you."

"You've been inside," I said.

"Uh-huh."

"And Boo," I said.

"What's made him so . . . odd," Zel said. "I mean, he started out with a lot of problems, and he was always kinda slow. But time in made all of it much worse."

"You know what he's doing with Beth Jackson?" I said.

"No."

"You know who killed Chet Jackson and Estelle Gallagher?"

"No."

"You think Boo was involved?" I said.

"Boo's mostly a slugger," Zel said.

"He had a gun when I was here last," I said.

Zel nodded.

"So you think he was involved?" I said.

"No."

"If he was, I'm gonna find it out," I said.

"He wasn't," Zel said. "I'd know."

"I think he was," I said.

Zel nodded.

"He can't do no time," Zel said.

Chapter

64

VINNIE CALLED ME at home from his cell phone. It was nine-eleven at night. I was watching the Celtics game.

"You might want to know this," he said.

"I might," I said.

I muted the sound on the television.

"Been watching Beth's ass all day. Followed her home from the club, 'bout five-fifteen, watched her go in. 'Bout six o'clock the boyfriend comes home. I watch him go in. By seven I figure they're in for the night, so I call it a day. I walk down Arlington to the Ritz, Taj, whatever the fuck it is now, and go in to take a leak. Then I'm in there, I figure I'll go in the bar, have a couple pops, think about Beth's ass, which I would now recognize at three

miles in the dark. So I'm in there for maybe an hour or so, and I have a few, and then I go out and head down Arlington to get my car. I know a guy works the door at The Park Plaza, and he's holding my car for me."

"Uh-huh," I said.

The Celtics were up four on the Wizards late in the first half.

"And I see the pug," Vinnie said.

I shut off the television.

"Boo?" I said.

"Same guy had the argument with Beth a while back," Vinnie said. "He's walking along Arlington same direction I am, like he could have been down at Beth's place. He's on the other side of the street. So I slow down and sort of let him get ahead of me and I see what he does. He crosses over in front of me at Boylston and goes into the subway. So I chuck along after him and go down, too."

"Was it crowded?" I said.

"Naw," Vinnie said. "Place was empty. So he goes through the turnstile and waits on the outbound platform, and I don't see any reason to waste two bucks, so I go back upstairs and get my car. On my way home I swung by Beth's building, but everything looked, you know, copacetic, so I kept going."

"Thank you, Vinnie," I said.

We hung up.

I dialed Gary Eisenhower's number. After four rings the answering machine picked up.

"Hi, it's Beth. Neither Gary nor I can come to the phone right now, but your call is important to us, so please do leave a message, and we'll get back to you as quick as we can."

When the beep sounded I yelled a couple of times that it was Spenser and pick up the phone. But nothing happened, so I hung up and got dressed and took a gun and hoofed it down to the apartment that Beth now shared with Gary, which was only a couple of blocks from my place.

The front door was locked. I rang Gary's bell; nothing happened. I rang a few other bells. One of the tenants answered. It was a woman.

"Hi," I said. "It's Gary from the first floor. I seem to have the wrong front-door key. Could you buzz me in."

"Call the super," she said, and broke the connection.

Neighborly.

I found the superintendent's number and rang the bell. After two rings he answered, sounding foggy.

"Yeah?"

"Police," I said. "I need you to come open a couple doors for me."

"Police?" he said.

"You heard me, now run your ass up here."

"Yeah, yeah, sure, officer, gimme a minute."

It took more than a minute, but it was only two or three before he appeared in the entryway and opened the door.

"You ain't wearing a uniform," he said.

"No shit," I said.

"You got a badge or something?"

I looked at him hard.

I said, "Ain't I seen a mug shot of you, pal?"

"Me? I never done nothing."

"That's your story. Open up apartment one-A pretty goddamned hubba hubba, or I'll run your ass down to the station for a look-see."

"One-A, yeah, sure," he said, and took out his key ring. "No need to get all worked up."

"Move it," I said. "Or I'll work you up, you unnerstand that?"

"Yes, sir, sure thing."

He went to Gary's door and unlocked it. I went in. The super came in behind me a step.

"Jesus," he said. "Jesus Christ."

"Call nine-one-one," I said. "Cops and an ambulance."

"But you're a . . ."

"Call it," I said.

Chapter

·····❖·····

65

BETH WAS DEAD, I knew that the minute I saw her. Her face was bruised, there was dried blood, and her neck was turned at an odd angle. Gary was unconscious but not dead. He had a big purple bruise on the side of his face at the hairline. But he was breathing pretty steadily, and his pulse wasn't bad.

The super, having called 911, stood in the doorway, as if he didn't dare enter and he didn't dare leave. It was maybe three minutes before two uniforms came into the room.

"He says he's a cop," he told one of the cops.

"That right?" the cop said to me.

He was a thick-necked guy with a red face, and he was showing signs of sitting down too much. His partner

was a younger guy, black, with sort of economical movements. The black cop squatted on the floor beside me and felt the pulse in Gary's neck. He nodded to himself and moved over to Beth.

"Right," I said.

"Show me something," the cop said.

"I'm private," I said.

"Impersonating an officer?" the red-faced cop said.

"Exactly," I said.

Squatting by Beth, the cop felt for her pulse and didn't find it. He stood.

"Charlie," he said. "We seem to have a murder here. Maybe you could postpone the impersonating-an-officer investigation till we solve this."

The red-faced cop looked at him a moment, and at me.

"They dead?" he said.

"She is. The guy seems like he'll make it," the black cop said.

The red-faced cop walked past me and looked at Beth.

"Shame," he said.

Two paramedics came in.

"Broad's dead," the white cop said. "Work on the other guy?"

One of the paramedics was a stocky blond woman.

"Lemme check," she said, and crouched beside Beth. The male paramedic started on Gary.

Charlie walked out into the foyer and began to talk on his radio. The black cop came to me.

"My name's Harper," he said. "What's yours?"

I told him.

"ID?"

I took out my license and my carry permit. The black cop looked at it.

"You carrying a weapon now?" he said.

"Yes," I said.

"I'll hold on to it for a while," he said.

I opened my coat so he could see the gun.

"You can take it out," Harper said. "Just go easy."

I took the gun off my hip and handed it to him. It was a short-barreled .38 revolver. Reliable. Easy to carry.

"You hit anything with this?" Harper said.

"Ten, fifteen feet," I said.

"All you need," Harper said, and put the gun in a pocket of his uniform jacket.

Belson came into the apartment with some crime-scene people and two homicide detectives.

"This guy," Charlie said, and looked at his notebook, "Spenser. He was impersonating a police officer."

Belson glanced at him.

"We all thought that," Belson said, "when he *was* a cop."

"Was carrying," Harper said. "With a permit. I got the piece."

"Give it back to him," Belson said.

Harper shrugged and handed me my gun.

Belson looked at the super.

"Who's this?" he said.

"I'm the superintendent. He told me he was a cop."

Belson nodded.

"Fucking crime wave in here," he said.

He nodded at one of the detectives.

"Get a statement from the super," he said.

Then he looked at the paramedics.

"Woman dead?"

"Yes, Sergeant," the woman said. "Appears to be blunt-instrument trauma."

"Guy?"

"He's way out," she said. "But vital signs are steady. He should come around."

"When?"

The woman shrugged.

"When he does," she said.

"You taking him to City?"

"We call that Boston Medical Center now," she said.

"You taking him there?" Belson said.

"Yes."

Belson turned to Harper and his partner.

"You two go with him. Make sure nobody tries to finish the job. When he wakes up, call me."

"What about her?" the paramedic said.

"Coroner will take her away. Right now she's evidence."

The medics put Gary on a stretcher, stabilized him, and took him to the ambulance. Charlie and Harper went with them. Belson turned to me.

"Impersonating a police officer," Belson said.

He was looking at the room as he talked to me. He always did that at a crime scene, and when he left, I knew he would have seen everything in the room, and he'd remember it.

"Mea culpa," I said.

"How many times you done that now," Belson said, "since I knew you?"

"Sixty-three times, I think."

Belson nodded, still slowly absorbing the room.

"Tell me what you know," he said.

Chapter

❖

66

I DON'T KNOW QUITE why I left Boo out of it, but I
did.

When Gary woke up he'd tell them what happened,
and they'd come for Boo. I wanted a little time to get
there first. I didn't quite know why I wanted to get there
first. I left Vinnie out, too—professional courtesy. I
said that I'd been watching her place and seen somebody suspicious-looking come out of the building. So
I'd called on my cell and got no answer. The rest of it I
told as it happened.

I don't think Frank bought it all, he came at it from a
few different directions, but my story didn't change and
Frank let it go. He knew I hadn't done it. And he knew

that sooner or later, he and I were working the same side of the street.

Mostly.

I got to JP a little before midnight. There was a light on in the window of the second-floor apartment that Boo shared with Zel. I rang the bell. After a minute Zel came to the door, and looked out and saw it was me, and opened the door.

"Trouble?" he said.

"Where's Boo?" I said.

"He ain't here, ain't been home all day."

"We need to talk," I said.

Zel nodded and stepped aside. He closed the door behind me and preceded me up the dim stairway. He had a gun in his right hip pocket.

In the kitchen, we sat on opposite sides of the table, under a single naked bulb.

"What?" Zel said.

I looked around the apartment. It wasn't much. Two bedrooms, a bath, and a kitchen. The doors to all the other rooms were open to the kitchen. There was no sign of Boo.

"Boo killed Beth Jackson tonight," I said. "Beat her to death."

Zel didn't move. He didn't change his expression.

"Cops know she's dead, but they don't know yet that it was Boo."

Zel nodded slightly.

"But you do," he said.

"Yeah," I said. "But they'll know soon enough. Boo left an eyewitness alive."

Zel shook his head sadly.

"Poor dumb bastard," Zel said.

"Gary Eisenhower," I said. "He was unconscious when we found him, but when he wakes up, he'll pretty sure be mentioning Boo's name."

Zel nodded.

"So why are you here," Zel said.

I paused. The room wasn't much, but it was neat. No dirty dishes, no crumbs on the table. The refrigerator was old and made a lot of noise. Otherwise, there was no sound anywhere, and no sense that there was anyone alive in the building but me and Zel under the one-hundred-watt bulb.

"I don't know," I said. "I just figured I oughta talk with you before the cops came to get him."

"Boo won't want to go," Zel said.

"They'll come in large numbers," I said.

"Yeah," Zel said. "They do that."

He got up and got two bottles of beer from the refrigerator and gave me one and sat down again.

"You know why he killed her?" I said.

"I got an idea," Zel said.

I nodded.

"Here's my theory," I said. "See what you think."

Zel nodded.

"I figure she came on to him," I said.

Zel turned the beer bottle on the tabletop and didn't say anything.

"I figure she came on to him so she could get him to kill her husband," I said.

"Why'd she want him dead?" Zel said, watching the bottle as he turned it slowly, as if turning it just right was as important as anything he was going to do this day.

"So she'd get his money," I said. "And be with Gary Eisenhower."

"And why Boo?" Zel said.

"She didn't know anybody else," I said. "She tried Tony Marcus, didn't work."

"She thought it would?" Zel said.

"She had a lot of faith in sex," I said.

Zel nodded and stopped twirling his bottle long enough to drink some beer.

"So Boo goes for it and pops Jackson," I said. "And she gets his dough and moves in with Gary and Estelle."

"Three of them," Zel said.

"Yep. I guess Estelle kind of liked the idea."

Zel shrugged.

"But it didn't work," I said. "Pretty soon Beth wants all of Gary, and Estelle don't like it."

Zel was twirling his bottle again. He hadn't drunk much of his beer. I hadn't drunk any of mine.

"So," I said. "Beth calls in Boo, and with the same gun he used on Jackson, he pops Estelle for her."

"Dumb," Zel said, and shook his head sadly. "Dumb."

"So there's Beth, thanks to Boo, right where she wants to be. Money, Gary"—I raised my hands—"what could be better."

Zel drank some beer.

"But . . ."

Zel nodded.

"But Boo thinks that he's done her these two huge favors," I said. "So she's supposed to love him."

"Boo never been with any women but whores, I think," Zel said.

"And Beth thinks that since she bopped him several times, she's done him several huge favors," I said, "and wants no more to do with him."

Zel nodded. His beer was gone. He got up and got another one from the refrigerator, looked at my bottle, saw that it was full, and sat down.

"They had a confrontation a week or so ago," I said. "He tries to talk with her, she shoves him and runs inside. Middle of the day, Boo stands for a while and walks away."

"You was following him?" Zel said.

I shook my head.

"Had a guy on her," I said.

"So you been thinking about her for a while," Zel said.

"Yes."

"Was the guy watching tonight?" Zel said.

"Was through for the night," I said. "And having a drink in the Taj bar. When he comes out, he sees Boo heading away from Gary's apartment and calls me."

"And you figure Boo went over there, kicked in the door, decked her boyfriend, and beat her to death?"

"Something like that," I said.

"Why tonight?" Zel said.

I shrugged.

"Love unrequited," I said. "The pressure built. He drink?"

"Some," Zel said. "I tried to keep him from drinking much, but he's hard to control."

"Bad when he's drunk?"

"Yes."

"Will he come back here?" I said.

"Sooner or later," Zel said. "Except I can shoot, I ain't much, and Boo's less. But we been together a long time."

"He's killed three people," I said.

"He can't do no time," Zel said. "I tole you that."

"I can't let him walk around loose," I said.

Zel looked at his beer bottle for a moment.

"I know," he said.

We sat for a moment. Then I stood.

"Thanks for the beer," I said.

And I left.

Chapter

❖

67

"Boo came home about two-thirty this afternoon," I said to Susan.

"You have someone watching?" she said.

"Vinnie," I said. "And Hawk. Vinnie's there now."

We were in Susan's living room, upstairs from her office. Susan usually had a glass of wine after her last patient, and when I could, I liked to join her. In honor of that, Susan had stocked some Sam Adams Winter Ale, which I was especially fond of, and I was having some while she sipped her wine.

"Did Gary wake up yet?" Susan said.

"He's coming around, Belson says. But he's still foggy."

"What are you going to do about Boo?" Susan said.

"I don't know," I said.

"You don't want to turn him in," Susan said.

"He's not right in the head," I said.

"And Beth exploited him," Susan said.

"Yes."

"You can't let him go," Susan said.

"I know."

"So," Susan said. "Basically you're stalling."

"I am," I said.

"What do you hope will happen?" Susan said.

"Mostly I'm hoping you'll stop asking me about it," I said.

Susan looked at me silently for a moment.

Then she said, "Wow. This is really bothering you."

"Yes."

"And you don't want to talk about it," she said.

"No," I said.

Susan stood and went to the kitchen. She got a second bottle of Winter Ale from the refrigerator, popped the cap, brought the bottle back, and set it on the coffee table in front of me. Then she kissed me on the top of the head and went back and sat down on the couch. Pearl, who was sleeping at the other end of the couch with her head hanging over the arm, raised her head up for a minute and looked at Susan, saw that there was no food forthcoming, and put her head back down.

"We won't talk about Boo," Susan said.

"Good," I said.

"But we could talk about Beth and Estelle and Gary," Susan said. "And their circle."

"Sure," I said.

"In one way or another, they all earned what happened to them," Susan said.

"None of them earned getting murdered," I said.

"Does anyone?" Susan said.

"Sometimes, maybe," I said. "I don't want to generalize."

"No," Susan said. "You almost never do. But at the heart of all this is their own behavior."

"Especially Gary," I said.

"Yes."

"Boys just want to have fun," I said.

"This boy exploited the pathologies of women," Susan said.

"And it caught up with him," I said.

"Pathologies are pathologies," Susan said. "They don't go away when you're through using them."

I nodded.

"Thing is," I said. "He probably had no intention that any of this would happen."

"No," Susan said. "Probably not. He's just careless. And he went around spreading his careless good times."

"And making money at it."

"Yes, that makes it a little worse," Susan said. "But I suspect that was just a nice side effect."

"Like a guy likes to go to the track," I said. "He likes to hang around the paddock when the horses come out. He likes to look at them. Likes to handicap. Likes to watch them run. And if he happens to win some money, even better."

"But if he doesn't win, he still goes to the track," Susan said.

"Yes."

"Fun-loving Gary," Susan said.

"And three people are dead," I said.

Susan smiled sadly.

"And what do you think of your blue-eyed boy now?" she said.

Chapter

·············· ◆◆◆ ·············

68

I SPENT THE NIGHT with Susan, which improved my
frame of mind, as it always did. She had early clients,
so I was in my office at eight thirty-five the next morning. Neither Hawk nor Vinnie had seen any sign of Boo
since he'd arrived home yesterday.

I was pouring my second cup of coffee when Quirk
came into my office and shut the door behind him.

"Coffee?" I said.

"Yeah," Quirk said.

He took off his overcoat and folded it carefully over
the arm of Pearl's sofa, then came and sat in a chair
opposite my desk. I gave him a cup of coffee and went
around my desk and sat down.

"Gary Eisenhower's awake," Quirk said.

"Uh-huh."

"He don't remember a thing," Quirk said.

"Who hit him?" I said. "Nothing?"

"He remembers the front doorbell," Quirk said, "and opening the door."

"That's it?"

"So far," Quirk said. "Doctors tell me it may come, may not. I guess he took a couple good shots to the head and probably hit the back of his head when he fell."

"Repeated blunt-force trauma," I said.

"You been watching those doctor shows," Quirk said.

"How else I gonna learn?" I said.

"Best any of us can figure," Quirk said. "It was a fist."

"Big fist," I said.

"And somebody who knew how to punch," Quirk said.

"How about Beth?" I said, just to be saying something.

"Same with the broad," Quirk said. "Apparently, she was punched to death."

"So you're looking for a guy knows how to punch," I said.

"You know how to punch," Quirk said.

"I do," I said. "On the other hand, so do you."

Quirk smiled slightly.

"And it wasn't either of us," Quirk said.

"No," I said.

"I figure," Quirk said, "guy didn't set out to kill anyone. Even guys who can fight don't normally set out to kill somebody with their hands."

"You figure he'd have brought a weapon," I said.

"I do."

I nodded.

"Confident guy," Quirk said. "Kicks in the door on some broad's apartment where she lives with her boyfriend, and apparently doesn't even bring a weapon."

"Or too mad to think," I said.

"What would he be so mad about?"

"What are they usually so mad about?" I said.

"Crime of passion?" Quirk said.

"Lot of that going around," I said.

Quirk nodded. He finished his coffee and got up and poured himself some more. He added sugar and condensed milk and took it back to his chair.

"Frank thinks you're not giving us everything," Quirk said.

"How unkind of Frank," I said.

"Yeah, sure," Quirk said. "You giving us everything?"

I drank some coffee and leaned back a little in my chair.

"You and me?" I said.

"You see anybody else here?" Quirk said.

"No," I said. "I'm not giving you everything."

"You know who killed her, don't you," Quirk said.

"Yes," I said.

"And you're holding that back why?" Quirk said.

"I'm not quite sure. But I won't tell you yet."

"I'm not sure the law lets you decide that," Quirk said.

"Sure," I said. "I know. You can bust me for interfering with an investigation, or some such, and take me downtown, and Rita Fiore will be along in an hour or so to get me out."

"You might be a little worse for wear," Quirk said.

"I might," I said.

"But we wouldn't have learned anything," Quirk said.

"True."

"When you gonna tell me?" Quirk said.

"Soon," I said.

Quirk nodded slowly.

"I known you a long time," Quirk said. "You are what you are."

I shrugged.

"Killer gets away," Quirk said, "because you stalled me, I'll come down on you as hard as I can."

"Which is quite hard," I said.

Quirk nodded.

"It is," he said, and stood and left my office.

I swiveled my chair around and looked out my window. It was bright and cold. Baseball was little more than a month away. The windows in the high-rises across the

street were blank today, reflecting the morning light so that I couldn't see through any of them.

It seemed simple enough. Boo had killed three people. I knew it. I tell Quirk. Quirk busts him. Case closed.

So why not?

I don't know.

I sat and looked up at the blue sky and across at the blank windows for a long time. A woman I'd once cared about had worked in an advertising agency over there. Sometimes, when the sun came at them from a different angle, I could see through the windows across the street and watch her moving about her office. Agency was gone now. Maybe the whole building was gone, replaced by a new one. It was hard to remember.

Chapter

❖

69

I WAS STILL LOOKING at the blank windows and the hard, blue sky an hour later when the door opened behind me. I turned my chair. It was Zel. He closed the door behind him and came to my desk and stood. He didn't take his coat off.

"I'm leaving town," he said.

I nodded.

"Where you going?" I said.

"Away," Zel said.

"Happening place," I said.

He stood. I sat. Neither of us spoke.

Finally he said, "Boo's dead."

I nodded.

"You do it?" I said.

"Yeah," Zel said.

"Means he won't have to do time," I said.

"He come home in the afternoon, sort of all jeeped up, you know. Talking real fast, not sitting down, and I told him you'd been there, and what you said about him and Beth. And he's listening, but he's sort of walking around like before a fight, you know? He's moving his shoulders, bouncing a little on his toes. Moving his fists like he's warming up."

I nodded.

"So I ask him, did he do it?" Zel said.

"And he stops everything, stands there like a statue, and looks at me. 'Yeah,' he tells me. 'I done her.'"

I took in some air.

"And I ask him, 'Why?'" Zel said. "And he tells me she's a lying bitch and didn't mean nothing she told him, and she just said what she said and done what she done so he'd do stuff for her."

"Like kill her husband and Estelle," I said.

Zel nodded.

"He was right," I said.

"Yeah," Zel said. "So I say to him he's been up all night and he needs some rest, and why don't he go to bed for a while. Boo don't sleep well, and I give him sleeping pills sometimes when he needs them. So I gave him a couple and say go lie on your bed."

"So he goes," I said.

"Yeah, but it takes a little while. He's going on about

he's glad he done it, and he's gonna kill anybody comes for him. And I tell him go to sleep, and when he wakes up we'll figure everything out."

Zel's voice was flat. For all the affect in it, he could have been reading a laundry list.

"And Boo's getting sleepy now, from the pills, so he goes in and lies on his bed. I go in with him, and he says to me, 'You're with me on this, Zel.' And I say, 'All the way, Boo, like always.' And he nods and closes his eyes. I go out, and in about a half-hour I go back in. He's asleep . . . lying on his side . . . and I shot him in the back of the head . . . and wiped down the gun and left it on the bed. . . . Same gun killed Jackson and Estelle."

"Yours?"

"Yeah, I never let Boo own a gun."

"You know he took it to do the shooting?"

"Yeah," Zel said. "I showed him how to shoot it."

"Can it be traced to you?" I said.

"No."

"So," I said. "Why you telling me this."

"Boo's pretty hard to like," Zel said. "You treated him as good as you could."

I nodded.

"You gonna tell the cops about me?" Zel said.

"No," I said.

Zel stood silently. He looked past me out the window. Then he turned and walked to my door, and opened it, and stopped and looked back at me.

"Now you know," Zel said, and went out.

I looked at the empty doorway for a while, then I took a big breath, and picked up the phone, and called Quirk.

Following is a special excerpt
from the next exciting Spenser novel

PAINTED LADIES

by Robert B. Parker

Available October 2010 in hardcover from
G. P. Putnam's Sons!

Chapter

························· ◆◆ ·························

1

MY FIRST CLIENT of the day (and of the week, truth be known) came into my office on the Tuesday after Thanksgiving and sat in one of my client chairs. He was medium height and slim, wearing a brown tweed suit, a blue paisley bow tie, and a look of satisfaction.

"You're Spenser," he said.

"Yes, I am," I said.

"I am Dr. Ashton Prince," he said.

He handed me a card, which I put on my desk.

"How nice," I said.

"Excuse me?"

"What can I do for you, Dr. Prince."

"I am confronted with a matter of extreme sensitivity," he said.

I nodded.

"May I count on your discretion?" he said.

"Sure," I said.

"I'm serious," he said.

"I can tell," I said.

He frowned slightly. Less in disapproval than in uncertainty.

"Well," he said, "may I?"

"Count on my discretion?"

"Yes!"

"At the moment I don't have anything to be discreet about," I said. "But I would be if I did."

He stared at me for a moment, then he smiled.

"I see," he said. "You're attempting to be funny."

"Attempting?" I said.

"No matter," Prince said. "But I need to know you are capable of taking my issues seriously."

"I'd be in a better position to assess that," I said, "if you told me what your issues were."

He nodded slowly to himself.

"I was warned that you were given to self amusement," he said. "I guess there's no help for it. I am a professor of art history at Walford University. And I am a forensic art consultant in matters of theft and forgery."

And pleased about it.

"Is there such a matter before us?" I said.

He took in some air and let it out audibly.

"There is," he said.

"And it requires discretion," I said.

"Very much."

"You'll get all I can give you," I said.

"All you can give me?"

"Anything," I said, "that your best interest, and my self-regard, will allow."

"Your self-regard?"

"I try not to do things that make me think ill of myself."

"My God," Prince said. "I mean, that's a laudable goal, I suppose. But you are a private detective."

"All the more reason for vigilance," I said.

He took another deep breath. He nodded his head slowly.

"There is a painting," he said, "by a seventeenth-century Dutch artist named Frans Hermenszoon."

"*Lady with a Finch*," I said.

"How on earth did you know that?" Prince said.

"Only Hermenszoon painting I've ever heard of."

"He painted very few," Prince said. "Hermenszoon died at age twenty-six."

"Young," I said.

"Rather," Prince said. "But *Lady with a Finch* was a masterpiece. Is a masterpiece. It belongs to the Hammond Museum. And last week it was stolen."

"Heard from the thieves?" I said.

"Yes."

"Ransom?" I said.

"Yes."

"And if you bring any cops in they'll destroy the painting," I said.

"Yes."

"So what do you want from me?" I said.

"The Hammond wants the whole matter entirely, ah, *sotto voce*. They have asked me to handle the exchange."

"The money for the painting," I said.

"Yes, and I am, frankly, uneasy. I want protection."

"Me," I said.

"The chief of the Walford Campus Police asked a friend at the Boston Police Department on my behalf, and you were recommended."

"I'm very popular there," I said.

"Will you do it?"

"Okay," I said.

"Like that?" Prince said.

"Sure," I said.

"What do you charge?"

I told him. He raised his eyebrows.

"Well," he said, "I'm sure they will cover it."

"The museum."

"Yes," he said. "And if they won't cover it all, I'll make up the difference out of pocket."

"Generous," I said.

"You're being ironic," he said.

"It is you I'm protecting," I said.

"I know," he said. "The painting, too. It is not merely

a brilliant piece of art, though that would be enough. It is also the expression of a distant life, cut sadly short."

"I'll do my best," I said.

"Which, I'm told," Prince said, "is considerable."

I nodded.

"'Tis," I said.

Chapter

···············◆◆···············

2

S USAN AND PEARL were spending the weekend with me. It was Saturday morning and the three of us were out for a mid-morning stroll in the Public Garden. Pearl was off leash, so she could dash about and annoy the pigeons. Which she was doing, while Susan and I watched proudly.

"So you are going to make this exchange Monday morning?" Susan said.

"Yep."

"How do you feel about it?" she said.

"I am, as you know, fearless."

"Mostly," Susan said.

"Mostly?"

Susan smiled and shook her head.

"What's bothering you about it?" she said.

"An exchange like this," I said, "they gotta be sure they get the money before they give you the painting. You gotta be sure you get the painting before you give them the money. They gotta be sure that once they give up the painting the cops don't swoop in and bust them."

"Difficult," Susan said.

"And their side gets to call the shots," I said.

"Which you don't like," Susan said.

"Which I don't like," I said.

"Ducks," Susan said, "you don't like anyone else calling the shots on what tie to wear."

"Except you," I said.

Susan smiled.

"Of course," she said. "Always except me."

A group of pigeons was pecking at some popcorn that had been thrown on the ground for them. Pearl chased them off and ate the popcorn. A mature woman in a leopard-skin coat stood up from the bench where the pigeons had gathered and walked toward us.

"Madam," she said, "control your dog. That popcorn is intended for the pigeons."

Susan smiled.

"Survival of the fittest," she said.

The woman frowned.

She said, "Don't be flippant, young woman."

"Yikes," I murmured.

Susan turned slowly toward the woman.

"Oh, kiss my ass," Susan said.

The woman took a half step back. Her face reddened. She opened her mouth, and closed it, and turned and marched away.

"They teach you *kiss my ass* at Harvard?" I said.

"No," Susan said. "I learned that from you. . . . Pearl likes popcorn."

"At least she called you *young woman*," I said.

Susan was glaring after the woman.

"By her standards," Susan said.

Suddenly Pearl stopped scavenging the popcorn and stood motionless, her ears pricked, as if she were pointing. Which she wasn't. She was staring.

Coming toward us was a yellow Lab with a massive head and a broad chest. He was wagging his tail majestically as he trotted toward us, as if he was one hell of a dog and proud of it. He stopped about a foot in front of Pearl and they looked at each other. They sniffed each other. They circled each other, sniffing as they went. Pearl didn't suffer fools gladly, so I stayed close. In case. Then Pearl stretched her front paws out and dropped her chest and raised her hind end. The Lab did the same. Then Pearl rose up and tore around in a circle. The Lab went after her. The circle widened and pretty soon the

two dogs were racing around the whole of the Public Garden. Occasionally they would stop to put their heads down and tails up. Then they would race around some more. An attractive blond woman was standing near us, watching.

"Your dog?" Susan said.

"Yes," she said. "Otto."

"Mine is Pearl," Susan said. "They seem to be getting along."

The woman smiled.

"Or would if they slowed down," she said.

We watched as the flirtation continued. The two dogs began to roll on the ground, mouthing each other in make-believe bites, unsuccessfully trying to pin each other down with a front paw.

"Do you bring Pearl here regularly?" Otto's mom said.

"Quite often," Susan said.

"We're in from New York, staying across the park."

Otto's mom nodded toward the Four Seasons.

"They seem so taken with each other," she said. "Do you have a card or something? I could call you. Maybe they could meet again, while we're here?"

"Please," Susan said. "Pearl will be thrilled."

Susan gave her a card.

"Otto doesn't mind that Pearl is spayed?" I said.

"Otto's been neutered," his mom said.

"Men!" Susan said to me. "This is love, not sex."

"Both are nice," I said.

The two dogs stood, panting, tails wagging, looking at each other.

"You should know," Susan said.

Chapter

❖

3

TODAY, PRINCE HAD on a gray tweed suit and a polka-dot bow tie.

"We're supposed to go west on Route 2," he said when I got in his car. "They'll call me on my cell phone and tell me where to go next."

The car was an entry-level Volvo sedan, which was a little tight for me.

"Do they know I'm along?" I said.

"I told them I was bringing a friend because I was afraid to come alone," he said.

"And?"

"They said you'd have to stay in the car and not get in the way."

I nodded.

"Do you have a gun?" he said.

"Of course," I said.

"Have you ever used it?" he said.

"Yes."

"To shoot somebody?"

"Mostly I use the front sight to pick my teeth," I said.

He smiled a little.

We drove west on Storrow along the river. It was bright today, and pretty chilly. But the boat crews were hard at it, as they would be until the river froze. To our left, we passed the former Braves Field, now a BU athletic field. The old stucco entrance was still there on Gaffney Street, and maybe vestiges of the right field Jury Box. An elevated section of the Mass Pike ran above the railroad tracks outside of left field.

"When the Braves played there," I said, "an outfielder named Danny Litwhiler is alleged to have hit a ball that cleared the left field wall and landed in a freight car headed to Buffalo, thus hitting the longest measurable home run in baseball history."

"I'm sorry, I don't believe I understand what you're saying," Prince said.

"Never mind," I said.

No one was tailing us as we went west on Route 2. Or if they were, they were better than I was. Which seemed to me unlikely. Probably had somebody set up to spot

us when we got to a certain point and then they'd call. I looked for a spotter. But I didn't see one.

We were approaching Route 128, which in this section was also known to be Interstate Route 95. The phone rang. Prince answered and listened.

After a minute of listening he said, "Okay."

He looked at me.

"Cross the overpass on 128 and turn around on the other side and start back, driving slowly," he said. "Stay on the phone."

I glanced back. The spotter was probably standing on one of the cross street overpasses. We crossed above 128 and drove on into Lincoln until we found a place to turn around, and drove back toward where we'd been. Prince had the cell phone to his ear. He nodded.

"Stop under the first overpass we come to," he said. "Okay. I get out with the money. Okay. And climb up with it and stand in the middle of the bridge."

Prince looked at me.

"You're to stay in the car or there's no deal."

I nodded.

We pulled over to the side under the first overpass. He swallowed audibly and got out of the car. I reached in back and got the suitcase full of money, and handed it out to Prince.

"Break a leg," I said.

He nodded and turned and lugged the big suitcase

slowly up the ramp behind us. That much money is heavy.

From where I sat, directly beneath the overpass, I couldn't even see the swap. I put the windows down, and shut off the engine, and listened intently. Cars went by on Route 2. Above me I thought I heard one. Maybe it stopped in the middle. Maybe its door opened. About thirty seconds later, maybe it shut. And maybe the car drove off. I waited. Silence. I looked back at the slope that supported the down ramp. In a moment I saw Prince scrambling down, carrying a surprisingly small paper-wrapped square. Maybe this was going to work out.

It didn't. Just as he came into sight, the package exploded and blew him and itself into a mess.

Robert B. Parker is the author of more than fifty books. He lived in Boston. Visit the author's website at www .robertbparker.net.